BAD GIRLFRIEND

BILLIONAIRES CLUB #13

Bad Billionaires 5

Billionaire's Club 13-15

Elise Faber

BAD BILLIONIRES 5
BY ELISE FABER
Newsletter sign-up

This is a work of fiction. Names, places, characters, and events are fictitious in every regard. Any similarities to actual events and persons, living or dead, are purely coincidental. Any trademarks, service marks, product names, or named features are assumed to be the property of their respective owners, and are used only for reference. There is no implied endorsement if any of these terms are used. Except for review purposes, the reproduction of this book in whole or part, electronically or mechanically, constitutes a copyright violation.

ONE

Tammy

Are you really breaking up with me via text?

Tammy winced as she read the text message and started to set down her cell.

But it vibrated again.

While I'm in your bathroom?

She winced. Okay, so her timing wasn't ideal.

Sighing, she tugged the covers back and pulled on her robe. Her frumpy, holey, old flannel robe that absolutely dwarfed her and was so unappealing that it had run off more than her fair share of men.

Which was why she only pulled it out for very special occasions.

Her period when she felt horrible and crampy and exhausted

and just wanted to veg on the couch and pretend that her uterus wasn't shredding itself to pieces.

The other very special occasion?

This.

The inevitable breakup.

The bathroom door cracked open as she was belting her robe, and a very pretty—probably too pretty for her—man walked out. Naked. She picked up his clothes, turned them right side out, and handed them to him.

"This is me breaking up with you," Tammy said. "Not in the bathroom," she added when he opened his mouth to say something she didn't want him to say, didn't want to *hear* him say. "Not that we were together in the first place."

"We've been sleeping together for three months."

She lifted a brow. "We've been *fucking* together. That's it. That's what I made clear from the moment I brought you home from Bobby's."

"That's not—" His face crumpled and she allowed herself to feel like shit for a moment.

Just a moment.

Because she'd been clear with him.

But also like shit because clearly she'd fucked up, and he was hurting and that was on her. She wasn't a monster. She didn't like people feeling crappy, especially because of something she did.

Liking it or not, she still had to end this.

The longer it went on, the more he would expect her to give, and the more she would feel like she was kicking a puppy.

Good times.

Which was why she pulled her shroud of bitch around her.

"It's not?" she asked archly, yanking it tight, buttoning it up for good measure. They'd discussed this that first night, and again after, when it had been so good neither of them wanted just one time together. They'd talked about it many times over the last twelve weeks—that this was for mutual pleasure and not building a connection—never building a connection—and they'd usually done it when her instincts had prickled and told her that he might be feeling more than her.

She should have listened to her gut.

But he'd said all the right things, given her all the right reassurances.

And he was seriously talented at giving her orgasms.

But tonight had been different.

He'd made it clear they weren't just fuck buddies—or he didn't see *her* as a fuck buddy, while nothing about him had changed for her.

She wanted pleasure.

She wanted fun.

She didn't want a possessive, growly male who thought it was his right to claim her time and body—even if he was pretty.

"We've been together for three months—"

"Not together."

"We've..." He trailed off, probably realizing where he'd gone wrong.

"What?" she asked baldly, though not cruelly. She knew she needed to be firm in order for this to be a clean break. Clear boundaries. Not bending or giving in because that just made everything worse when it inevitably came down to this. "What?" she repeated when he didn't speak. "You thought you'd change my mind, even though I've made it clear I'm not interested in a relationship?" Catching herself fussing with the tie on her robe, she forced herself to stop, to not reveal this was uncomfortable, that she didn't like doing this. No cracks in her armor for him to slip back in. "We have fun together. I like your cock. I like *you*, but I don't want a boyfriend, and that's what you're trying to be. So, it's gotta be done, Adam."

"I—" He broke off again, and she pointed to the clothes. His shoulders straightened, and his expression went from hurt to mulish and—sigh, he was going to make this even harder. "You like me. We could be good together. I love—"

Panic washed over her, and quickly she shook her head, throwing her hand up, cutting him off with a sharp order. "Get dressed." Then she moved to the bedroom door, cloaking herself in sharp words before he got the rest of that statement out. "I'll clue you in," she said, zipping up the shroud of bitch jacket, pulling up her bitch pants, slipping her feet into bitch socks and shoes for good measure. "You're just upset because you're the one who usually ends things, add in that you're used to women fawning all over you because you're pretty." A beat. "And you are. You're gorgeous."

His face had changed from mulish to pained to gentle during her speech. When she called him gorgeous, that expression became determined.

Uh-oh.

"Just a little more time," he murmured, coming close and stroking his knuckles down her throat in the way that always made her shiver. He bent, trailed his lips along her jaw, and Tammy remembered why she'd brought him home in the first place.

And she almost gave in...

Almost.

Because the man had a cock that was...

"Please, love," he murmured. "I need—"

That snapped her out of it. He needed what she couldn't give him. What she wouldn't ever be able to give him. She couldn't be open in a way that would make him happy, and eventually, he would choose someone else.

It would be much less messy to end things now.

She gripped his shoulders, and though it was tempting to draw him near, to have one more time, she knew she couldn't.

Tammy shoved him back. "I'm done."

He reached for her again. "But—"

She shoved him away. Again. "*Done,*" she repeated, having done this too many times to do anything but end it here and now. Adam was a nice guy, and she'd kept him around for so long because he'd seemed on board to be a fuck buddy, but tonight...tonight he'd been different.

Tonight he'd made love to her.

Tonight hadn't been about mutual attraction.

He had feelings for her, and she couldn't let that stand. Better to cut ties now before he grew even more attached, before things got messier.

"Get dressed," she said again, exiting the bedroom and walking down the hall, moving to the front door.

It was better to be by an exit.

That made things less complicated...and easier to slam and lock the door.

A minute later, Adam emerged from the bedroom, shoving his cell and wallet into his pocket, his eyes blazing, but his expression gentle again. His lips parted as he lifted his arms, prepared to take her in his arms.

Fuck.

She sidestepped, gripped the doorknob, and opened the door.

"Bye, Adam," she murmured.

"Baby, come on," he pleaded, taking a step toward her. "We'd be good together."

"No," she said, stifling a sigh. This was seriously getting old fast. "We wouldn't."

"You like me."

She clenched her jaw. "Look, you're a nice guy, but—"

He came close, lowered his head, mouth closing in.

She put up her hand, pushed him back. "No."

"Tammy—"

"It's not you. It's me."

That finally seemed to penetrate, probably since it was such a shitty line, such a crappy thing to say. But at least it had the result of Adam backing away, his eyes furious. "Seriously?"

Tammy just lifted her brows.

He made a disgusted sound, but she was far too well-versed in this to feel guilty.

"Goodbye, Adam," she said.

A shake of his head, but he didn't say anything further, just walked down the steps.

She watched him get into his car, screech out of her driveway.

Sigh. Now she'd need to find a new source of orgasms. Rolling her shoulders, she started to turn to go back inside.

"It's not you, it's me?"

That voice was silk brushing along her thighs, dipping up to test the moisture between them. It was heat in her abdomen, fingers grazing her nipples. It was...instant sexual attraction, the same heady feeling she'd experienced the moment she'd laid eyes on Fletcher King. Eyes catching his as she'd strode to her office, desire pooling as she took in those blazing blue irises, his dark brown hair, so dark that it was nearly black. She'd clocked sexy stubble, a built body, and a great smile.

But he wanted *it.*

It being a real relationship, a girlfriend, a wife, and the picket fence. *It* being everything she couldn't give, because she wasn't a relationship, girlfriend, or wife and picket fence kind of woman. She'd heard him talk about *it* at work, heard the sadness in his words when he and his ex had broken things off.

She, on the other hand, wanted freedom.

More than she wanted the gorgeous man standing in front of her now.

"What are you doing here, Fletcher?"

"I need a favor."

The refusal was already on her lips. A favor that brought her sexy co-worker to her house on a weekend certainly didn't bode well for her.

But then he smiled, and she actually had to force her knees to lock so she didn't melt into a puddle, and...*that* right there illustrated just how much she didn't want to be in a relationship.

Because she'd been resisting this attraction with Fletch for an entire year.

Locking her knees, ignoring the melting, denying the temptation of him.

But that sexy smile, highlighted by the setting sun, the warm lights of her porch...undid her.

That sexy smile had her refusal staying lodged in her throat.

That smile had her saying...*yes*.

Eventually.

Two

It was four on Thursday afternoon.

He was half-convinced that Tammy wasn't going to show.

She'd been avoiding him all week at work like he was the plague, but when he'd stopped by her desk that morning—sneaking up on her so she couldn't snatch up her phone and pretend to make a call or haul ass to the bathroom in order to avoid him—she'd said she would meet him at his place so they could drive up to Tahoe together.

Well, she'd snapped at him that she'd made a promise and wouldn't go back on it.

So *said* was a loose description, and add in the fact that she was twenty minutes late, and he was starting to sweat it.

His mother was excited.

To meet his girlfriend.

The non-existent girlfriend he'd been pretending to have in the lead up to his younger brother's wedding. The one he'd been pretending to have because his family was worried about him after his breakup with Trina—and one had to say, the broken heart he'd ended up with. The one he began to pretend to have after he'd had a slew of almost girlfriends who'd nearly turned him off dating altogether, who made him wonder if his dream of making a family of his own that would be like the one he grew up with was something impossible.

Because he'd dated Roxy, who'd somehow managed to make a copy of his house key and then had moved her stuff into his place after three dates.

Then after he'd gotten the locks changed and her stuff back to her, he'd dated Lana. Lana had seemed normal for almost a month. Then when they'd first gone to bed together, she had declared her love...and when he hadn't been ready to express the same, she'd handcuffed him to her bed frame until he had.

Which he had.

Then he'd gotten the fuck out.

Those two should have clued him in that he was due for a time out.

But then he'd met Beth.

Gorgeous. Curvy. Pretty eyes. An ass...well, a *fantastic* ass.

She'd seemed perfect until he'd slept with her. And even the sex had been great. Explosive. Good chemistry. He'd given her an orgasm that had left her shaking...and then start crying.

Because she wasn't over her ex. And he wasn't her ex. And it felt wrong to have sex with someone who wasn't the person in her heart.

And since he knew what that felt like—to have his heart smashed with a hammer while trying to move forward, and not feeling right—he'd held her all night while she cried over her ex.

He'd willed away his erection—and one had to say his blue balls because even though Beth had gotten an orgasm, he hadn't —and wiped her tears.

Then he'd slipped out of her house and decided he was taking a break from women.

To refocus. To center himself. To not try and shove the puzzle pieces together when they didn't want to fit. Soon he'd look for someone to build a future with. Someone who wanted kids—one day. Who wanted to come home to him, and who he wanted to see at the end of the day. Someone he could have a relationship with that was like the one his parents had.

And maybe that sounded fucked up.

Because he should want his own thing, not replicate someone else, especially not his mom and dad's.

But, truthfully, his parents had it all.

Not easy. Not always smooth-sailing. They bickered over the proper way to load forks into the dishwasher, how to decorate their house, the Honey-Do list his mom loved to make. His dad's beater of a car that he was "fixing up" was a point of contention time and again.

But it was all based on love.

His dad always brought his mom a cup of coffee to bed in the morning.

His mom always made sure his dad's stash of Hot Tamales was in his desk drawer, even though no one was supposed to know about it.

They still went on dates and made out in the hot tub when they thought nobody was looking and recently, his dad had signed them up for ballroom dancing lessons because it was a dream of his mom's.

See?

Shit like that.

And Fletcher could go on for days with *shit like that*. Romantic, lovely shit that made him want something he wasn't sure he'd ever have. Especially with his track record of picking women who were—

A car pulled into his driveway, and he perked up when he saw the redhead behind the wheel.

She'd come.

He slumped in relief when she parked and climbed out of the car, her hair shining in the sunlight, her pale brown eyes glimmering like gemstones. She flounced over, the flowy sky-blue dress she was wearing billowing behind her.

"Tam—"

She continued her flouncing...right by him, walking straight for the passenger's side door of his car. "My purse is in the front seat, my bag in the trunk."

Then she got in.

And shut the door.

And...Fletcher stood there for a moment, staring at her, smelling the hint of her perfume—something that always reminded him of apple picking in the fall, floral and sweet—gaping because he'd never seen her in a dress.

She had nice legs.

Really nice legs.

So nice they were burned into his vision when he should be thinking of nothing more than getting through this weekend, playing a role, making sure that he didn't do something stupid and ruin their work relationship.

He loved his job at RoboTech.

Last thing he needed to do was create something toxic that affected his position just because he didn't want to be alone at his brother's wedding, couldn't bear the pitying looks tossed his way after Trina had broken things off with him at the rehearsal dinner. Only slightly worse would have been dumping his ass on the altar. Because she'd still done the dumping in front of everyone close to both of them. She just hadn't done it front of everyone close to them *and* two hundred other guests.

Fletcher sucked in a breath.

Get through the weekend.

Stage a breakup for this fake relationship at some future point.

Continue with his timeout from women.

Then reset and find something similar to what his parents had.

Easy enough.

Ha.

Unfreezing himself, he moved to her car, opened the door, and retrieved her purse, then walked around to the trunk and snagged the surprisingly large suitcase for three nights and days. It was fucking heavy, too.

Was she packing bricks?

Just to piss him off?

Maybe. He wouldn't put it past her, not when she'd practically made him crawl before she agreed to help him out—including letting her take over a project he'd busted to get for his department, lunch delivered to her desk for the next month, and coffee runs whenever she needed a fix.

It would have been a lot easier if they had more women in their department.

But their group was one of the few at RoboTech that had more men than women, and their department in particular had three women and nine men. One was his boss (off limits for obvious reasons). Another was seven months pregnant and happily married (and *that* would bring far too many questions, even if she did agree to accompany him). The last was Tammy, who was unequivocally beautiful, but she'd made it clear she had absolutely no interest in him.

As in, on her first day, he'd asked her to drinks—trying to be nice to welcome the new girl—and she'd shot him down with such force that he'd felt the sting for weeks.

But, look, he got it.

She hadn't known his intentions.

So, the next time inviting for post-work Happy Hours drinks was to be done, he'd made Barry—married happily to his partner of thirteen years—ask.

She'd accepted. They'd hung in groups. They'd worked together.

Peaceful friendship was eventually accomplished.

Now he might ruin it with a weekend of pretending to be dating. But he was desperate and willing to take that risk.

He just...wouldn't fuck it up.

Right.

Nothing would go wrong with *that*.

Somehow, he wasn't convinced.

THREE

TAMMY

The car shook when he dropped her suitcase into the trunk.

And yes, it was heavy.

But this pretending she'd agreed to was for a *wedding*.

She needed heels—different pairs for the different outfits she'd brought—makeup, perfume, jewelry. Along with all the normal clothes and accoutrements she needed on a normal basis. Plus, it was cold in Tahoe this time of year. She needed a good jacket.

And snow boots.

Because what if it snowed?

They were going to the mountains. It snowed in the mountains.

Snow boots were heavy and took up room in a suitcase.

Hence the car shaking when it made its way into the trunk.

Her door opened, and Fletcher set her purse in her lap. Not in a huffy way that would have made her prickle and lash out, but gently into her lap, so she'd have it for the ride up.

Aw.

He was good guy.

She knew that—even though she was pushing him and being a bit of a jerk by flouncing around and making him lug her bags around. Still, because her work experience in the Bay Area had gotten off to such a rough start, she'd been guarded around Fletcher at first.

Guarded meaning surrounded in prickly rosebushes and hidden landmines prepped to blow.

Of one might say landmines were understandable given that her direct manager had done his level best to get her to sleep with him, even though she'd made it clear she wasn't interested. Multiple times.

Coalescing in her having to knee the asshole in the breakroom.

He'd dropped, moaned, and threatened assault.

Luckily, she'd had witnesses. She'd reported him to HR, gotten his ass fired, but because that process took so long and had been so painful—complete with him fighting it every step of the way and the department eventually divided over who was at fault (him, obviously)—she'd quit as soon as she had another position lined up.

Thankfully that new position was with some really great people at a very great company.

RoboTech was awesome.

Her work was awesome.

So, Fletcher asking her to drinks on her first day at the company had triggered her.

She'd thought that she'd ended up in the same situation she'd just left, and had panicked.

Eventually, though, she'd realized that the entire department went to drinks every Monday. His invite had been as a coworker wanting to include a new employee.

So...that had been a little awkward, given how brusquely she had shut him down. But once Tammy got over herself, she started going to Bobby's with everyone else, and she and Fletcher had built a good working relationship.

But now they were...fake dating?

And she was going to meet his parents...and potentially be in someone's wedding pictures?

Who's that girl in the corner of the dance floor?

Remember that bitchy redhead who mand Fletch carry all her things?

Crop out Fletcher's (*cough* fake) *ex from the family photos. She was so weird.*

Also—note to self—avoid the photographer like a son of a bitch.

Fletcher got into the car, glanced over at her, but didn't say anything as he pulled out of her driveway and navigated his way to the freeway. Silently. Which was the point that Tammy realized the silence would be continuing for the immediate time being.

And perhaps for the entire five-hour trip ahead of them.

Whatever.

Stifling a sigh, she got out her cell, plugged it into the dash, and blared her road trip playlist. No conversation? Might as well have music.

She was about ten bars into *Walk This Way* by Lady Gaga and really starting to groove when Fletcher unplugged her phone.

And pocketed it.

Pocketed *her* phone.

The music went off—obviously.

But...he put *her* phone in *his* pocket. And seriously, what the ever-loving flying monkeys was wrong with the man? Was she going to have to institute a tuck and roll on the freeway and abort this crazy plan?

Of course, the only reason that tucking and rolling might be survivable in the first place was because they were literally inching toward the Bay Bridge and its path that would lead up to the Sierras.

It's *path?*

Freeway? Hellish four lane road crammed with everyone trying to leave the city?

Both of those since she meant the highway clogged with cars leaving San Francisco, all trying to beat rush hour—and failing miserably.

Traffic wasn't the point, though.

"What are you doing?" she snapped, wanting to reach over and yank her cell out of his pocket, but since that would involve crawling practically onto his lap—since he'd put it in the pocket furthest from her—or at the very least put her hands next to a body part she'd been dutifully pretending he didn't have—Tammy found herself clenching her hands into fists and glaring at him.

"I spy with my little eye..." he began.

Her mouth dropped open. "Are you serious right now?"

"Something green," he finished.

"A tree." More snapping. "Now give me my fucking phone."

"Wrong," he said with sparkling blue eyes. Mischief and cool ocean waves. Damn the bastard, but that expression looked good on him.

She held her hand out, twitched her fingers. "Phone. *Now.*"

He just returned his gaze to the traffic.

And stayed silent.

Sigh.

Tammy turned her glare to the cars around them, inching forward on the approach to the lower deck of the Bay Bridge. There weren't any trees around. Just cars and SUVs and trucks. Just buildings and billboards and the freeway itself. None of those were green. Except—

"That street sign," she said, pointing at the green rectangle with its rounded corners, white iridescent writing declaring the name of the street.

"Right," he said.

A blip of pride—stupid, she knew—but she still was satisfied to have gotten the answer right. Go her. She was killing it. This was what happened when she was one of four kids. Resources were scare, competition was high.

Victories even less frequent.

So, she'd take this one.

Even if it meant playing I Spy with a man who was gorgeous and had smiled his way into getting her to agree to fake date him.

With a man who still had her phone.

She extended her hand again, and gave him her patented angry eyes—the eyes that got men out of her house, the eyes that had always made her brothers quiver in fear. Unfortunately, her angry eyes didn't appear to have any influence on one Fletcher King.

He just glanced away from traffic, lifted a brow, and then turned back to stare out the windshield.

Silence descended.

They inched forward.

The silence grew heavier...along with her outstretched hand. So heavy, in fact, that she ended up dropping it to her lap with a sigh and returning her glare out the windshield.

"I spy..." he began.

"Oh, fuck you," she muttered, then exclaimed, "Ow!"

The fucker had flicked her in the ear, and damn, he must have practiced on his brother because that really hurt.

"Don't be an ass," he declared.

"*I'm* not the ass," she snapped. "That would be the person who took my fucking phone and won't give it back and—"

"It's rude to be on your phone. We're stuck in traffic with a long drive ahead of us. We should talk."

This man could *not* be serious. "Um...you're kidding, right?"

He lifted one shoulder in a shrug. Dropped it just as casually.

Fuck it. Here she went.

She was about to get up and personal with his lap and any potential snakes that might be (*were*) lurking beneath the cargos that were so lovingly encasing his thighs. Well, call her Steve Irwin because she was about to wrestle a croc. Unclicking her seat belt, she lurched across the console, shoved her hand into that pocket on the side of his leg, and yanked out her phone. He let her have it, but when she would have plugged it back into the cord, he pushed the button on the dashboard, turning off the radio completely, and then yanked that knob off, putting it in the same pocket that had held her phone.

The cord dropped to her thigh.

Her mouth dropped to what felt like the bay they'd just begun to drive over.

"I spy—" he started again.

And seriously *fuck* this. It was time for a tuck and roll. They couldn't be going more than a mile per hour. She'd be fine.

Tammy reached for the door handle.

Fletcher snagged her arm, circling her wrist, yanking it toward his lap. "What the fuck are you doing?"

"You're an asshole," she all but yelled, yanking her hand free. "We're going all of one mile per hour. I'm done. Thus, I'm getting the fuck out of here."

His mouth tipped up at the corners. "You realize I'm fucking with you, right?"

"You *realize* that I'm doing a favor *for you*, right?" she asked —okay, yelled. "And more than that, you spent the first twenty minutes of this drive ignoring me, and then the next taking away the source of my entertainment first in the form of music and then in the form of my phone. Could I have talked to you? Yeah. Am I obligated to entertain you like some circus animal? Especially when you're not willing to provide any entertainment yourself? No."

He winced.

"I didn't want to do this," she gritted out. "I *really* didn't want to do this. You laid out your case, and yes, I agreed in the end. But I'm not fucking doing *this*"—she pointed from herself to him—"for a whole weekend. I don't like people telling me what to do. I especially don't like it when *men* tell me what to do." She ground her teeth together. "Which is why I don't have, nor plan to *ever* have a fucking *boyfriend!*"

Silence.

Long, tense quiet that was so taut it seemed to fill the entire interior of the car.

Finally, Fletcher sighed and ran a hand over his face. "Fuck, Tammy. I *am* an asshole. I'm sorry."

Her brows lifted, but her angry eyes didn't fade. She didn't let them. "Yes, you are."

His gaze skated to hers then back out of the windshield. "I'm just...I'm in a weird mood."

She snorted.

Weird mood?

Fuck him.

Fuck him and his asshole tendencies. The next stop, she was getting a Lyft and getting the fuck home and—

"The next wedding I was supposed to go to was mine," he said softly.

Right. That sucked, but—

Tammy shrugged. "So, you steal my phone and try to strong arm me into playing I Spy because of that?"

Another wince. "As I said, I'm an asshole."

"And call *me* rude?"

Chagrin on that pretty face. "Yes, I believe I said I was an asshole." He sighed and shook his head. "I'm...not myself. Part because I'm not sure how to proceed with this, because you're doing me a huge favor and this whole thing could easily blow up in my face." He blew out a breath. "We're friends—kind of. But we're coworkers first, and I know your job is as important to you as mine is to me, and I don't want to fuck things up for either of us." His expression clouded and he thrust a hand through his hair. "And now because I'm a fucking coward, we're going to have to pretend to be dating and I asked you for a crazy big favor, *and* I'm already dreading the idea of lying to my family." His words finished on a whisper, and she felt some of her anger slid away.

"We don't have to do this," she said, patting his leg. "We can still go," she hurried to say when his face fell. "But we can just say we're friends. Or you can say I broke up with you and you have to go by yourself and—"

"I can't."

"Why?" she asked. Why was this so important to him?

Probably, she should have focused on finding out why pretending to be with someone had him not caring that she was extorting him for work, and instead just relieved that she'd agreed before she'd actually agreed to this charade.

A shake of his head.

"Why, Fletch?"

A muscle in his jaw twitched. "My mom—" A sigh. "She invited my ex-fiancé Trina, and Trina's new husband."

Ah.

Well, that explained part of it.

"So, you want to show Trina that you're not still hung up on her." *Even though it's clear you still are.*

That muscle ticked again. "Yeah."

"And you thought to accomplish this by playing I Spy?"

His fingers gripped the steering wheel tight. "We've established I'm an asshole. I got in my head. I panicked. I was trying to be a friend who kept his distance by doing stupid shit like taking your phone and playing I Spy rather than a man who's supposed to be dating you and liking you and enjoying your company because that felt wrong—"

"Ouch, jeez, you know how to treat a woman."

He cursed. "I didn't mean it like that." He sighed. "I'm taking advantage of you and I'm already feeling like an asshole for that. Then you played that song—"

Her brows drew together. "What's wrong with Gaga?"

A pause.

A long, long pause that had her wondering if he would answer.

"She played that song. Trina." He cleared his throat. "A lot."

Because it's fucking Gaga! And it's awesome. But Tammy didn't say that. Because she understood his reaction, got how painful those kinds of reminders could be. She didn't dwell on that, didn't add to that hurt. Instead, she just flicked *him* in the ear—and did it hard because she'd had three siblings to practice on—and said, "Next time just ask me to turn it off."

"Right," he muttered, rubbing his ear.

Ha.

Gotcha, bitch.

"And fuck I Spy," she went on. "I'm not nine years old."

"Got it." Another mutter. Another rub of his ear.

"And if I want to ignore you and look at TikTok on my phone for the next five hours," she said, "I'm going to do that."

A nod. "Understood."

"And—"

Humor had finally begun to enter his voice, the Fletcher she knew from work making a reappearance. "You're an independent woman who doesn't need my shit, is doing me a favor, and I need to get out of my own head and stop being an asshole otherwise you're bailing?"

Since that was basically the crux of the issue at hand, she just nodded.

He reached into his pocket, handed her the knob for the radio. "For what it's worth. I *am* sorry, and I'll curb the asshole."

"Good." She took the knob, shoved it back into place, and plugged in her phone again, cueing up her playlist. She played *Walk This Way* by Gaga because she was Tammy and fuck someone telling her what to do. But once the song was over, she switched to a rock and roll track that she assumed the nefarious Trina wouldn't listen to, and when that made him relax into the seat instead of clenching the steering wheel like it was a life preserver, she made sure to keep it on classics rather than her usually poppy sugary sweet songs.

Easy enough.

Her musical taste was eclectic.

Eventually the traffic cleared up, the sun started going down, and she turned down the radio. "Tell me about it," she said when he glanced over at her. "About Trina," she added when he just stared at her blankly.

"No." A cold rebuke.

"Yes," she pressed. "You told me that you needed a woman who wasn't going to get attached, someone who could take the pressure off your parents' matchmaking. You said I was the only one you knew who could help you." She nudged his arm. "You said I was in for a weekend of food, booze, and dancing. You *said* it wouldn't get complicated."

Yes, she was stupid to have believed that.

Yes, she'd already made it clear that she'd been made an idiot by his smile.

"This is getting complicated already," she pointed out. "And it's not about matchmaking, is it?"

"No." He went quiet. "And yes, I know, I'm making it complicated. I'm sorry for that. I know that's on me. I just didn't think I'd still be hung up on..." He trailed off and Tammy's cold, dead heart squeezed.

She felt bad for him.

She *shouldn't* be feeling bad for him. He'd been a jerk.

But she knew something of what it felt like to be on her back foot, to feel insecure and in a swirling maelstrom of thoughts, and to do the wrong thing.

"Pull over," she ordered.

His brows were raised when he glanced at her, but he shifted lanes and pulled off onto the shoulder.

"What—" he began.

She wrapped her hands around his head, yanked it toward hers. "Girlfriend practice time," she said, noting the shocked blue eyes.

For the record, shocked was an expression that looked good on him, too.

"Um—"

She kissed him.

Four

The car wasn't in park.

That was the first thing he thought when Tammy's lips hit his.

The next was—*holy fucking shit, the woman can kiss.*

Then the car rolled forward, and he slammed his foot on the brake, the gear shift into park, and turned, ready to haul Tammy over the console and into his lap. It would be a tight squeeze, but he'd make it work and—

She returned her tongue to her own mouth, dropped her hands, lifted her lips from his.

Patted his cheek.

Buckled her seat belt and sat casually on the leather, her fingers drumming on her thighs.

As though she hadn't just given him the best kiss of his life.

"What was that?" he rasped.

One shoulder lifted. "Girlfriend practice."

She'd said that once before, but it hadn't made any sense then, just like it didn't make sense now.

"Um, what?" he asked.

Not the most articulate of questions, but in fairness to him, all the blood had left his brain in favor of taking up residence in his cock.

Tammy was still as cool as a cucumber. "We couldn't have our first kiss be in front of Trina or your parents." A shrug. "I realized I should have thought of it sooner. We can't have a fake relationship if we've never even touched. We would look totally...well, totally *fake* and so"—she tilted her head from side to side—"girlfriend practice."

His lips were still tingling from the kiss.

His brain was hardly functioning.

That was the only explanation for why it took him so long to process her words.

Why he was still struggling to comprehend *girlfriend practice*.

But...Tammy made a fair point. Something he should have thought of well before he'd put this plan into place. His parents were observant. He and Tammy needed to come across as natural. Anything else and they'd know something was off. Plus, if he were being honest, he was game for girlfriend practice, especially if it involved Tammy's mouth on his.

Dangerous thought.

But it had been too long since he'd had sex.

"Fletch?" Tammy asked.

"Hmm?" He was distracted, thinking about how good the sex would be between them. Tammy had the typical complexion of a redhead—pale skin, freckles dotting her arms and face like a roadmap he wanted to trace with his tongue, especially the ones dancing over her cleavage.

Yeah.

He'd *love* to bury his face in her tits.

A pat on his cheek. "Focus, big guy."

He blinked, tore his gaze away from her breasts encased in

the silky blue fabric he wanted to peel away, and met her pale brown eyes. "Right," he said.

"First step of that is driving." A nod toward the highway. "So, we can get this wedding over with while making Trina jealous as hell in the process."

"I'm an asshole," he muttered, shifting out of park and gaining some speed on the shoulder. Suddenly, he didn't care about making Trina jealous. He wanted to kiss Tammy again. He wanted to get to know her, to convince her to give him a chance.

"That's been established," she said dryly.

He snorted, checked traffic, and pulled back onto the highway, thankful that traffic had lightened up considerably. It helped that they were off the bridge and out of the major city centers. "Well, it's true. I've been all twisted up and acting like...I don't know. Not myself." Not the man he knew he could be. Not the man who'd get a chance with a woman like Tammy. "I promise I won't force you to play I Spy again."

"*Or* steal my phone?" she asked pointedly.

"Or steal your phone," he promised as he changed lanes. "*Or* the radio knob."

A flash of white teeth. Then she turned up the volume on a song that was popular on the charts right then. Not one he liked, but he wasn't going to comment. Now that he recognized his inner asshole, he was going to do his best to tell him to fuck off.

"Good," she said, settling back into her seat. "So back to girlfriend training. We need to cover the basics."

"Basics?"

"The things we need to know about each other," she said. Then added, probably in response to the confusion that was no doubt written on his face, "You know, the Big Eight?"

He shook his head.

"Oh boy," she said on a long-suffering sigh. "We're really having to start from scratch with this one, aren't we?"

He rolled his eyes but didn't comment.

"The *Big Eight*, my honeykins," she went on with mischief in her eyes, ticking off on her fingers as she listed, "Favorite meal, movie, cocktail, nonalcoholic drink, color, and flower—though the last is mostly for you to know about me. Then there are the either/ors. Beach or mountains. Coffee or tea. Night owl or early riser."

"That's nine."

"I believe I said that the flower one mostly applied to me," she said tartly.

"I can't have a favorite flower?" he teased. "Men can have favorite flowers, too."

A roll of her eyes. "Yes, Fletcher, of course, you can have a favorite flower. Okay, so the Big Nine. You start. And, since you've been waxing poetic about them, why don't you start by telling me your favorite flower?"

Shit. Now he needed to come up with a flower. What were those spiky, colorful ones his mom liked? All he could think was that Trina liked roses, so he hadn't bothered to pay attention to much else.

Pointy petals. Yellow. Dark middle.

Sunflowers!

Right. Those were the spiky ones his mom liked. He supposed those could be his favorite, too. They were cheerful, and he liked that they had other shades than just the traditional yellow—or at least the ones his mom usually had on her counter did.

"Sunflowers are my favorite," he said, "in case you were wondering what you should bring me on my anniversary."

His stare was on the road so he couldn't see her roll her eyes, but he felt it, and for some reason that made him smile. Mostly because he knew it wasn't real irritation she was feeling, and also because Tammy jokingly rolling her eyes at him felt normal. God knew she did it enough at work, at all of them. An exaggerated roll, the corners of her lips turning up, as though she were including them all in on the joke.

"There should be a Big Ten," he said.

A huff. "I don't care what your favorite bird is."

He snorted. "For the record, it's a penguin. They're always dressed to party and they waddle. How can you not love something that waddles?" he deadpanned, loving the soft laugh she gave him in return. "But in seriousness," he said when she fell quiet again, "the Big Ten needs to include you telling me about your family."

"Oh, Lord."

"What?"

"You're right." She tossed a smile his direction then affected a wince. "And you know how much I hate it when I have to say that."

God, how did this woman always made him feel better, feel lighter?

Because she was Tammy.

And Tammy was pretty fucking great—okay, no *pretty* about it. She was fucking great. No qualifications. Just a smart as hell, gorgeous woman who would put her weekend on hold to do him a favor, even though it was probably the last thing she wanted to do.

His heart squeezed, and suddenly proving to Trina, to his parents that he was over the breakup seemed much less important than winning over Tammy, than learning all the little things that made her tick.

Like the Big Ten.

Like hating to say he was right.

Fletcher chuckled. "That burn going down?"

"Like habanero salsa," she said dryly.

God, she was funny. Never missed a beat. Always was ready with a quip to lighten the mood. But more than that, he *liked* her.

Sure, she'd been prickly to him at the beginning, but he'd understand why those spikes were in place after he'd overheard her telling Lisa, their boss, what had happened at her previous job.

She hadn't known they'd done Monday night drinks.

She hadn't known he was just trying to include her in the office bonding.

She'd thought he was trying to get in her pants, so had reacted in a way to keep him firmly at a distance.

And when she'd realized that Monday night drinks were a casual coworker get together, she'd joined in. Still careful about him, a firm barrier in place that he couldn't see but could feel, one that kept him proceeding on egg shells, trying to prove to her that he wasn't like the asshole from her old job.

He supposed the fact that she was in the car with him proved that he'd succeeded, at least in that respect.

Even though he'd shown up on her porch without warning, only having been there once before when he'd dropped her off after she'd drank a little too much one Monday night.

She would have been right to slam the door on his face, to go about her weekend—especially after the drama he'd stumbled upon. But she'd let him in, wrapped her tatty robe tighter around herself, and had gotten him a cup of coffee. Then had listened when he'd told her what he needed (okay, had begged her to be his date for the weekend).

Her face had been carefully blank. Her lips pressed flat.

It would have been easy for her to say no. Hell, he'd expected it.

But then she'd surprised him and agreed. Well...negotiated. *Then* had agreed.

"Your family?" he asked when she didn't say anything more about salsa, burning, or the Big Ten. "You have siblings, right? I feel like you've mentioned a brother." His gaze flicked to hers, and he was momentarily stunned by how beautiful she was with the sun going down behind them, its rays sliding through the rear window, turning her skin gold, bringing out the burnished highlights in her deep red hair.

Her smile was even more gorgeous.

Soft and full of love—so much love that he almost felt jealous that she was thinking about someone else (and not him —which had inner alarm bells blaring). He was jealous, and that was dangerous.

Friends.

Just *friends*.

Even if she kissed like a fucking goddess.

"I'm one of four," she said on a laugh. "The baby, and the one everyone loves the most"—a wicked smile that had him chuckling again—"And I have two brothers, actually. Jaime, the oldest, and Brad, and then one sister, Penny."

"Is Brad or Penny older?"

"Penny." A shrug. "For the record, the Huntington birth order is Jaime, Penny, Brad, and me." A laugh. "As I've established, the best of the Huntington brood. My parents are Andrew and Tawny, and they're awesome. Okay, your family. Go."

He went.

"Sean is my brother who's getting married, obviously. He's younger than me by five years. His fiancée is Carrie. They're a good match. Happy and have been together since high school. They were just both waiting to get married until they finished school and bought a house—the latter they managed last year."

Tammy whistled. "And they're what? Twenty-five, twenty-six?"

"Five. I just turned thirty." He gave her a rueful smile. "And I only managed to buy my townhouse last year."

"Me, too," she muttered. "The market is tough if you don't want to end up house poor. And I, for one, like to actually do things like go to the movies and on vacation." A shrug. "So, it took me a bit to save up, too."

Fletch nodded his agreement. "Well, if I didn't love Sean. I would hate him."

Curiosity filled her eyes when they met his for a brief moment. "Why?"

"His house is nicer."

She snorted. "Sounds like they had two people saving up. Bound to be nicer than what we managed to buy. But I know the feeling," she added when he made a face, "my siblings all have it together. They're married and in love, and the babies have begun arriving. Hell, my brother even has adopted a rooster, two cats, three dogs, and a trio of goats because his wife is an animal lover. Their house is like a fucking zoo—literally—but they love it."

"A rooster?"

"Sir Fuzzy McFeatherston."

"That's a mouthful."

She winked. "That's what she said." A grin paired with waggling brows that had him busting up and needing to concentrate so that he didn't swerve into the next lane. "But everyone just calls him the Fuzz for short. He walks on a leash, and wears a sweater vest. Hell, the Fuzz is almost as cute as the goats that wear pajamas."

For a second, he didn't think she was serious. But when she didn't laugh at the joke he thought she'd made, he felt his brows shoot up his forehead. "Goats that wear pajamas?"

"Yup. My sister-in-law is a nut." Another smile. "But I love her, and she makes my brother happy."

"And your other siblings, are they as happy?"

A nod. "Yup. That and more. In fact, their happiness is positively sickening." She nudged his arm. "And you? Obviously, Sean is happy since he's getting hitched. Is it just you two?"

"Just two boys," he said. "We had an older sister, but she died before I was old enough to remember."

"Oh, I'm sorry. That must have been hard for your parents."

"Yeah, it was. My mom still gets sad on her birthday every year."

She squeezed his arm. "I'm sorry," she said again.

He nodded.

"And you like Carrie for your brother?"

His eyes flicked to hers again, saw that she was looking at him gently. Sharp, fiery, didn't take any bullshit, but with empathy that was off the charts.

He'd seen it when Dawn—their pregnant coworker—had been so sick early in her pregnancy, and Tammy had brought her ginger candies and peppermint tea and the apple pear muffins from Molly's bakery that were the only thing Dawn could keep down.

He'd seen it with Lisa when her dog died, and Tammy had brought in a painting of him she'd had commissioned from Lisa's favorite picture of her and the pooch.

He'd seen it when she tried to pay for more than her fair share of Monday night drinks.

And he'd seen it with him, over coffee at her house after he'd randomly showed up on her porch, doing him a favor even though they weren't particularly close and what he was asking was a *big* fucking ask.

"Fletch?"

He blinked, pulled himself out of his head. "Carrie's great. My whole family is, actually."

"So, why the subterfuge?"

A nice way of asking why he was lying to his family about this.

A sigh. "I don't *like* lying to them. At all. We're close, and I just..." He cleared his throat. "My mom has been so worried about me since Trina, and I was in an okay place when she invited her—"

"I find that surprising," Tammy murmured.

"What?"

"Trina dumped you and hurt you deep enough that you don't want to be seen without some girlfriend armor." She shrugged. "It just seems strange that your mom invited her. Never mind that you would be okay with it."

"I pushed her to."

"Um..." She glanced at him, brows raised.

"What?"

"But why?"

It was his turn to shrug. "The moms were close. Really close." He paused, released a breath. "Truthfully, that's probably why Trina stuck with me for so long. Our moms are best friends, have been almost from the moment we started dating. Our families were so close, and...well, it took her a bit to tell me she wasn't happy. Like more than a bit."

"What does that mean?"

"It means...she told me at the rehearsal dinner it wasn't going to work."

Tammy winced.

"I know," he admitted. "I was blindsided at first. Now, I understand it more. There were things I ignored..."

He sighed.

Yeah, it had felt like shit after the wedding was called off. Not just because he'd had a broken heart and because he'd been embarrassed how it all went down, but it hurt more to lose part of his family, for his brother and parents to be feeling the same loss of Trina and her family as deeply as he had fucking. "At first everyone stayed separate, and things were really tense. But it was hurting my mom to stay apart from Trina's mom. So, I pushed and made sure the invite didn't get lost in the mail."

Tammy's question was quiet. "Why?"

"Like I said, I was in a good place," he said. "So, it wasn't all noble. I was happy, had put the breakup behind me, and was ready to start dating again, so I thought there wasn't a need for everyone to be separate." He gripped the steering wheel. "I made my mom arrange a dinner with both families, and I made it clear that I didn't want to be the reason we couldn't be close again. Trina came, we talked a lot of it out, and she agreed with me about wanting our families to stay connected. Everyone eventually got over it, and because Sean's wedding date was set, I made sure he invited Trina and her parents."

Tammy made a noise.

Surprise? Shock. He didn't know.

She asked, "Then what happened?" before he could ask her to explain.

"They agreed to come to the wedding—all of them—and Carrie didn't dismember me for daring to invite people to her big day. We had pie." He made sure his voice was even. "With ice cream." A breath. "Then Trina shared that she was married. Had eloped with the guy she'd been dating."

Shocked silence. Then, "Oh, shit."

He sighed. "Exactly. I wanted to be happy for her," he whispered. "We'd been together too long for me to not want her to be happy."

Tammy's voice was gentle. "But she was married."

"After six weeks and a handful of dates."

"Jesus."

"Yeah."

"So that's why you went warp speed with the dating."

Not a question. It still made him frown. But he gave her the truth anyway. "I definitely jumped in hard and heavy."

"And it must have been *so* hard for all those women to fall in love with you," she said dryly.

"What are you talking about?"

She fiddled with the radio. "I know about the girls. Hell, the other guys in the office can't stop talking about how hot they are, and how many of them you keep getting."

Wow.

If she only knew.

"Let me tell you," he muttered, "no amount of attractiveness could make me go on another date." A beat. "With *any* of them."

"That bad? Worse than going to a wedding alone?"

"Worse than giving up the Carter project," he said, naming the task she'd negotiated for. The project was a cool one, charting and exploring hirings, promotions, and managers—from department heads all the way up to the executive level. RoboTech was a women-owned company, and they were probably more diverse than most of the Silicon Valley and San Francisco based tech businesses. But their CEO, Heather O'Keith had never been satisfied with probablies. She wanted data. And progress. Basically, this was the type of project that would get someone noticed by the important higher ups.

Which was why it had stung to let it go.

Not as much as the pity that would be in his family's eyes, though, if he showed up to the wedding single and miserable and...

Could he get a side of pathetic?

Everyone was happily paired off.

Except him.

And the only reason he wasn't driving up alone was because he'd bribed a woman to spend the weekend with him.

Cool.

"I'm scared to ask," she said.

"Let's just say that the six weeks Trina took to elope would have been too long for them."

"Yikes."

"Yeah."

"So now you've got me," she murmured.

Said quietly, with a hint of some underlying emotion that he couldn't tease free of the words. He glanced at her, skin still golden in the fading sunlight, her features delicate and beautiful.

She was smart and kind and fierce, and a man would be lucky to have her.

Which was why he reached over the console and brushed a thumb over her jaw.

She turned, met his eyes.

"Why?"

A blink, confusion trickling into the pale brown of her irises. "Why what?"

"Why did you say it like that, sweetheart?"

FIVE

TAMMY

hy did you say it like that, sweetheart?

"Say what?"

But she had the feeling she knew what she'd accidentally let bleed into her voice. Something she didn't think about. Something vulnerable and throbbing and painful that she'd locked up long ago.

"You said, '*So now you've got me.*'" His thumb brushed over her skin once more, so light that she barely felt it. "Why did you say it like you're some bad carnival prize?"

Um.

"Fletcher," she said. "You know who you're talking to, right?"

He lifted his brow.

"You don't need to be soft with me. Don't need to think I'm one of those women saying one thing when I really want another." She'd been cured of *that* notion long ago, of wanting anything *more*. "I'm chronically single because I choose to be. I don't have the mental bandwidth to be a good girlfriend without bribery. That guy from last weekend—"

"The *it's not you it's me* guy?"

She winced then nodded. "Yeah. Him. We were fuck buddies for three months. He wanted more. I didn't. I cut it off." A swirl of guilt despite telling herself that she had nothing to feel bad about. He'd known where she stood. "I broke up with him via text."

Fletcher glanced at her, concern on his face. "And he came over to your house—"

"No," he explained. "I broke up with him by text while he was *at my house*. In the bathroom. Because he..."

Fletcher frowned. "Because he what?"

Ugh. She didn't want to talk about this. But the pain in her ass had opened up to her, had laid it out there, and she found she couldn't leave him hanging without giving at least a little. "Because he made love to me."

A pause. "You *did* say you were fuck buddies, right?"

"Yeah."

"So..." He trailed off, paused. "I'm failing to understand the problem, sweetheart."

The second time he'd called her that. Twice more than she normally would allow, but because they were supposed to be dating and *in love*—blegh—she let it slide. "We were fuck buddies. No feelings. No *love* allowed. It was about mutual orgasms and nothing more, and...he forgot that."

"Wow."

Fletcher's tone said he wasn't impressed.

"What?" she snapped, defensive now. "Men do this shit to women all the time, and no one gets on their asses for remaining unattached. Just because I'm a woman—"

"It's not that."

She waited.

When he didn't answer, she said, "So a man gets a high five

for fucking around, but I get derision just because I want the same."

"No, Tam." He glanced at her. "It's just that I think it's hard for feelings to stay separated when you're sharing your body with someone."

"Which is why I don't normally do repeats," she said. "Adam, however, convinced me to take that chance. Then convinced himself I would change my mind." She snorted. "Like he could fuck me into becoming the adorable little wifey. I want a career. I like my house and my mattress. I paid a fucking *ton* for my pillows and sheets. I'm happy with the world I've built for myself, and I don't need a man in it."

She had herself.

Her family.

Her friends.

She never felt like anything was lacking. Not anymore, anyway.

"Of course, you don't," he said.

"So, don't give me a lecture on how *women* can't keep their hearts separate of their body," she snapped. "I'm perfectly happy doing things my way."

"I'm happy you're happy." He signaled, changed lanes, and passed a slow-moving truck. "But *I* definitely couldn't hack it. I've slept with four women, and I found it difficult to separate my feelings from them, even *when* it was time to end things— case in point, me getting dumped at the rehearsal dinner."

"And the others?" she found herself asking.

"Another case in point, because I struggled to break up with them, even when it was unhealthy."

"*How* was it unhealthy?"

He told her about the trio of women who'd prompted him to take a dating break.

"*Handcuffed* you?" she exclaimed once he'd told her about Lana.

He nodded grimly.

"And the other one copied your *key?*" she exclaimed. "Without asking you?"

Fletcher shook his head. "Yup." A beat. "And she made *two* copies, which I found out after I'd ended things and came home from work to find her naked in my bed."

"Wow."

"Yeah."

They drove in silence for a bit. "And I thought the moving in some clothes was bad."

"Now you know why I'm off women."

That was a sad thing.

Because despite the bumpy start of their drive, Fletcher was a good guy. Always on time, always pulled his weight, always paid for his share when the office went out for drinks or tapas. He didn't letch on her if she wore a low-cut blouse. His gaze was always kept firmly on her face. He was funny, and she liked that he cared enough about his family to patch things up with his ex.

She'd had no shortage of good (albeit imperfect like all other humans) male role models in her life, so it was easy to know where he fit in.

Occasional douchery.

Mostly good.

She needed to figure out who to set him up with. Of course, not herself, and with only Cora single in their group of friends, it wasn't like she had a ton of resources when it came to singles who were ready to mingle. But—

"Do you date Black women?"

His eyes flicked to hers, a smile on his handsome face. "I date *all* women. Tall, short. Skinny, plump. I love them all."

Good.

She held up her phone, snapped a picture, the flash bright in the dim interior of the car.

He rubbed his eyes before turning back to the road. "What are you doing?"

"Setting you up with my friend, Cora," she said, typing out a message. "She's hot, curvy, has great hair, and is smart as hell. She's"—chef's kiss—"absolute perfection. And she's single and not going to move herself into your house after two dates."

"It was three," he muttered.

"Semantics. And"—she tapped at the screen—"sent. That sexy smile of yours will definitely catch Cora's eye."

"You do realize it's weird that you're setting me up while pretending to be my serious girlfriend, right?"

"Is it giving you thruple vibes?"

"What's a thruple?" he asked, a deep vee between his brows.

Amusement bubbled up in her, and she rubbed her hands together, evil genius style. "Oh, you sweet, innocent thing. Let Auntie Tammy educate you. A thruple is just a relationship with three people."

He rolled his eyes. "That sounds like drama waiting to happen. I could barely handle one woman."

"It's not like that. It's...when three people are mutually in a relationship. Not like you're trying to juggle two women at once."

"Still too much work for me."

She giggled. "And definitely too much for me, so I can't give you too much shit. Hell, I don't want one person, let alone two."

"Why don't you want it anyway?"

"Want what?" she asked, playing dumb.

"A person. *Your* person." Her heart—the damned misbehaving thing—squeezed at the soft way he said that. "The one who'll have your back, who you're excited to go home to every night."

A memory flashed and was trailed by a painful pulse slicing through her insides that had her forcing out a breath to keep her voice even. "I think we established that already," she said lightly. "I like sex. I don't like being tied down. No relationship necessary."

Not ever again.

Deep blue eyes on hers, studying her closely.

Tammy held her breath, kept her expression neutral.

He turned back to the road. "Right, so why don't you educate me on the Big Ten then. I know about your family, so I need the rest."

Thankful for the change in topic, she began ticking off items on her fingers. "Favorite meal—meatloaf and mashed potatoes."

"What? Really?"

She grinned. "I grew up in the Midwest, baby. Nothing more that I love than a meal that can stick to my ribs." He chuckled and she liked that, liked making him laugh. "What's yours?"

"Meatloaf and mashed potatoes," he quipped.

Tammy rolled her eyes. "What's it really?"

"My mom makes homemade pasta, simple flavors—Parmesan, pepper, and the noodles themselves. It should be boring." He shrugged. "But it's delicious, and I always beg my mom to make it for me when I visit."

"If she's anything like my mom, I bet she loves that."

She watched the half of his mouth she could see curve up, and seriously, did the man have to have such a gorgeous smile? It threatened to melt her brain—*had* melted her brain to get her to agree to this scheme. "That she does." A beat. "Though she loves to moan the whole time she's making the dough about how hard it is." His head turned toward hers, the other half of his mouth joining the first in turning up. "That way I feel guilty and knead it for her while she's telling me all the ways I'm doing it wrong."

Laughter bubbled up in her throat. "Now *that* also sounds like my mom. She's wonderful, of course, but she has a vested interest in doing things *her* way."

"Because it's the best way, obvs."

She snorted. "Obvs?"

A smirk. "It's what all the cool kids are saying."

Now her humor didn't just stay in the back of her throat. It danced over her tongue, slid through her lips. He joined in, his rough chuckles intertwining in the air with hers. She really liked that sound, liked that they could joke and laugh. It was nice. It was like what she had with Cora and Kate, Heidi, Kels, and Stef.

Friends.

She may not be down for searching for a soul mate.

But she was always down for more friends.

Next, he quizzed her on her favorite cocktail—rum and coke, *obvs*, because the classics were sometimes best. He liked a beer from a local brewery—apricot-flavored. That wasn't a cocktail, but she let it slide, especially when he told her that his favorite movie was *Die Hard*, because that was hers as well, and if she'd still believed in soul mates, she'd be all over believing that this man was hers. Because both of their favorite colors were blue, and she loved sunflowers like him, and they each preferred the beach and coffee to tea and mountains.

Pretty much the only thing they *didn't* agree on—aside from the fact that he wanted the white picket fence and woman in a big poofy dress—was that he was an early bird, and she was a night owl.

But she knew that already.

He was usually the first one to yawn and pull up stakes at Monday night drinks, the first one in the office in the morning, making sure the coffee pot was full of the steaming black lifeblood for those who stumbled in later.

For *her* who stumbled in later.

They bickered a bit about the merits of sleeping in versus getting up and at 'em early, and then they began bickering about sports—she was a hockey fan, he preferred baseball (barf). Eventually they started discussing birthdays—hers September 8th, his

October 9th—their favorite pastries from Molly's—chocolate croissants for her, the mocha chocolate cupcakes for him, the delicious fried food smorgasbord from Bobby's, and the plans for the weekend.

Cocktails and some food tonight with his family.

A morning hike and a late lunch with the fam tomorrow morning, followed by the rehearsal in the evening, dinner afterward at a restaurant right on the lake.

Saturday. Pre-wedding breakfast.

Then Fletch would go off to do best man duties, and she'd be on her own until wedding time.

Ceremony. Reception. Cake and bouquet tosses. Dancing.

And Sunday they'd have breakfast with his parents then GTFO, getting back to reality and being coworkers, and she'd get her hands on the Carter project.

"My mom can be a little much," he was saying as they wound their way up through the highway twisting through the mountain pass. "So, if I'm gone and it gets to be too much for you just text me and I'll—"

Another one of those strange pulses slid through her. "It won't be too much."

His fingers tightened on the steering wheel. "Well, if it—"

"It won't." She dropped a hand onto his thigh. "I'm good with parents. I'm *so* good, in fact, that I've got an advanced degree in pushy moms." A squeeze. "I can handle myself. You just do what you need for your brother to make his day great, and in the meantime, we'll convince everyone you're blissfully happy and get everyone off your back. Okay?"

Now his knuckles were white. "But—"

"No buts." Another squeeze. "I may not want a boyfriend in reality, but you've paid me handsomely, so I'm going to be the best fake girlfriend around."

She laughed.

And after a beat that lasted long enough for her to glance up at Fletcher's pretty face, he joined in. Then he squeezed her fingers, peeled her hand from his thigh, and set it gently into her lap. He was smiling at her, the bright, gorgeous smile, as he said, "Damn right, you are."

She couldn't help and think she'd just missed something.

But then he was talking again, and the smile was there, and they were driving down the road to his parents' place, and there wasn't time to ponder what she'd missed.

Because it was time to put her advanced degree in pushy moms to good use.

Six

Tammy was good.

Really good.

His mom—as one's mom did—practically ran out onto the porch the moment she heard his car pull into the driveway, barely waiting for him to put the transmission into park before she was tugging open his door and hugging him tight.

By the time she released him, Tammy was out of her door, her purse on her shoulder, and walking around the front of his car.

His mom released him and straightened, beaming when she saw Tammy standing near the hood. "Hi, Mrs. King," Tammy said, moving toward them and extending her arms. "I'm Tammy. It's so nice to finally meet you."

And then she was hugging his mom.

"Connie, please," his mom said, squeezing her back. "I'm so glad you're here."

Tammy pulled back. "Thank you for letting me crash the

wedding. I know it's got to be inconvenient, being so last minute and all."

Fletcher winced. He'd asked Tammy last minute, but he'd accepted the invitation on her behalf months ago.

"Last minute?" his mom asked. "But—"

Tammy's gaze flickered, going from his to his mom's and she knew she caught the error. Her recovery was swift and much faster than his would have been. "I know weddings are planned in months to years," she said quickly. "So, I'm honored to be included." She shifted slightly, reached into her purse. "I brought this for you." Her hand emerged, a small, wrapped package in her hands.

And his mom looked like she'd achieved nirvana.

"For me?"

Tammy nodded. "It's just a little something to say thank you for having me."

His mom opened the package—she was a present lover and her lack of patience was well-known in his family—revealing some sort of lotion that made his mom squeal. "I love this brand!"

Tammy smiled. "I'm glad."

"Aw, honey, you're so sweet. Come on"—she laced her arm with Tammy's—"let's get you inside. Did you eat? I have leftover lasagna if you're hungry."

"Lasagna sounds awesome if it's not too much trouble."

"It's not," his mom said. "Do you like lemon drops?"

A flash of white. "I do."

"Food. Drinks." She drew Tammy toward the house as she tossed over her shoulder, "I'll send your dad out to help with your guys' bags, honey."

"I've got it," he called as the pair reached the front door. "Though I may break my back with how heavy Tammy's bag is."

Tammy shot him a glare, but her voice was sickly sweet when she said, "Thank you, baby."

"No problem, sweetkins."

The glare softened, amusement gentling her features.

Then she went inside, his mom at her side, leaving him to haul in her suitcase—which, as he hefted it up onto the porch, he was convinced was full of bricks—into the house. He dragged it through the front door, dropping his backpack next to it.

His tux was already up here, fitted during one of the many visits he'd made over the last few months, so other than a couple of changes of clothes, he didn't need much.

Just his fake girlfriend he'd paid for handsomely.

His insides knotted themselves up tight, and he felt sick.

When things with Lana had been going well—before the handcuffing and forcing him to declare his love (and then the calling of the police and the getting a restraining order)—he'd thought he would have someone awesome to bring to the wedding.

Then, when things had soured, he'd thought Beth was the one he'd bring.

That obviously hadn't worked out.

So, two months ago, with no prospects on the line and a trio of short relationships that had told him he needed a break from women and dating, he'd intended to just go solo. Then he'd come up for a visit and had overheard his mom gushing to Trina's mom. Saying she was glad he and Trina were both paired off and happy because she'd hated seeing him so miserable.

She didn't know about Roxy or Lana or Beth.

Because he hadn't shared the handcuffs and house keys and holding her while she sobbed because he wasn't the man she loved. Instead, his mom only knew that he was dating someone, and it was going well.

And miraculously, his mom had never asked her name.

Not until a week ago.

It had always just been *his girlfriend* or *his woman*. He could only thank the stress of planning the wedding—Carrie's parents were gone so his own parents were doing double duty, and his mom was playing the mother of both the bride and groom. Dress shopping, interviewing photographers, DJs, florists. She'd eaten it up, helping Carrie plan a wedding she'd never thought to have after having lost his sister.

So, the distraction of the wedding meant that he'd been off the hook.

At least until they were making place cards last weekend and realized they hadn't known his nonexistent girlfriend's name.

Pressed, he'd said the one person he could think of who wasn't his boss or pregnant.

Tammy.

Who was beautiful and apparently good at charming parents because both his mom and dad hadn't worn smiles like that since Sean had announced he and Carrie were getting married.

Tammy was talking animatedly, a martini glass in her hand.

"Your house is lovely, and these counters"—she ran her free hand over the polished surface—"they're absolutely gorgeous. Are they granite?"

"Quartz," his dad said, his chest puffing out.

Probably because even though his parents were best friends and kept the love alive in a number of ways, they couldn't agree over any decor for the house—from kitchen counters to Christmas lights. Their biggest fights had always been over paint colors and picture placement.

And those counters had been one of the biggest fights of all.

Ending with his dad ordering them without his mom's involvement.

Timing their arrival and installation so that it happened when Fletcher's mom was off for a girl's weekend. She'd come home to a kitchen that was finally completely upgraded...and she'd been absolutely furious with his dad's underhandedness.

She'd threatened the guest bedroom.

But as always, they'd made up before going to sleep, and all had been good...until his mom had the cabinets repainted while his dad was away on a fishing trip.

For his part, he liked the color his mom had picked *and* the quartz his dad had chosen.

Not that he'd commit to either of those sentiments, since it was the surest way to get his parents' hackles up. Just like he could see his mom's lifting at the compliment that Tammy had given.

Fuck, he'd need to wade in and—

"And those cabinets," Tammy went on. "The color is to *die* for." She got up and brushed her fingers over one of the doors. "I love how it's the perfect mix of blue and gray. And these knobs"—crystal pulls Fletch's dad *hated*—"Tony," she said turning to Fletcher's dad. "I think it's so cool that you have these in the house. I always say that real men love glitter, isn't that right, baby?"

It took him a moment to realize that she was roping him into the conversation.

Dangerous.

But mostly because he really liked the way that she called him *baby*.

"Yeah," he agreed when she stared at him, deliberately lifting her brows. "Glitter is life."

She snorted softly but didn't move when he slid an arm around her shoulders and stepped close. He told himself that it was to keep up the I, but he wasn't sure it was *only* that. Which was a train of thought he wasn't going to focus on. Push it down, pretend that this was all fine and light and this was perfectly normal to be talking about glitter with his parents and fake girlfriend.

His dad laughed, shook his head. "I see you got a good one there," he said and wound an arm around his mom's waist, tugging her close and kissing her hard and long and far too deeply in front of other people.

But these were his parents.

They'd never been shy about showing their emotions—whether they were angry or amorous. He was used to it, and he wondered if Tammy's parents were like that too, because she just sipped her drink and continued admiring the cabinets and those crystal pulls.

"Are your parents like them?" he found himself asking, needing to know the answer, the gnawing urge to know *everything* about her intense. When her gaze met his, he nodded at his mom and dad still kissing on the other side of the island.

She lifted a brow. "How do you think I got my advanced degree in girlfriend etiquette?"

He chuckled.

She grinned.

A lock of hair slid forward over her cheek, and he brushed it back, tucking it behind her ear. Couldn't help letting his fingers drift down her throat following the long, silken strand as it curled against her pale skin.

Her lips parted, her breath shuddering out.

He leaned close, let his fingers drift lower. Over one collarbone, the other, then tracing the neckline where it hugged the upper curves of her breasts. Inappropriate. Not contact they'd agreed upon. But Tammy drifted closer, stared up at him with heat in her gaze, and he found himself tracing the line of that fabric again and then again—back and forth, back and forth.

Rough lace.

Silken skin.

A flush growing on those tempting globes, spreading across her chest, beneath the neckline of her dress.

He wanted to peel the fabric away, to see how far it had spread.

To kiss every inch of her skin.

Except...

Paid handsomely.

Right.

Fake. This was all fake.

Luckily, Tammy's stomach growled. Loudly. Loudly enough that his parents broke apart—well, his mom pulled back, declaring, "You're hungry! Let me feed you," as she pushed out of his dad's arms and bustled to the fridge, pulling out a couple of containers. "Sit. *Sit!*" She gestured at the stools. "Tammy, do you need another drink? Tony, get her a refill, and get your son a beer."

Drinks were doled out.

Lasagna was reheated, along with some bread.

Salad was plunked onto plates; forks were passed across the table.

And all the while, his mom beamed and puttered around, looking happier than he'd seen her in ages.

Because Tammy was great and charming and proving she had that advanced degree in wooing parents, so his mom didn't have to worry about him anymore. And his brother was getting married in two days to a woman they all loved.

Their lives were all neatly packaged.

Her boys were happily paired off.

Everything was good.

Except it was all a lie.

Seven

Tammy

He'd gotten quiet at dinner.

She'd thought it was because she and his mom were dominating the conversation, or maybe that he was worried she'd be upset he'd all but caressed her breasts while his parents were sucking face.

She should be.

But truthfully, all she'd been thinking about was how good it had felt to have him touching her.

If he wasn't looking for picket fences and engagement rings, Tammy would have been all over that, though preferably without the side of parental supervision.

Grinning, she went into the bathroom and washed her face, scrubbing off the day's makeup and slathering on her moisturizer. His parents were as bad as hers were with the PDA, but it was nice that they so obviously still loved each other. It made for a much less complicated weekend than if she had to weave her way through a mom and dad who loathed one another.

Done with her face, she brushed and flossed and mouth-washed—the lasagna was delicious, but Connie wasn't one to skimp on garlic—then quickly combed and braided her hair. Pajamas were next, and only a few minutes later she was back in the bedroom.

With Fletcher.

Who was wearing a pair of basketball shorts.

And nothing else.

And—ho, mama—she was thanking the gods of masturbation because the man was *hot*. Long and lean, pecs that she wanted to grab, biceps that would be easy to hold on to when he lifted her up and fucked her against the wall, or when he was on top of her and was pounding into her, or when—

She tore her gaze away and moved to the side of the bed he hadn't claimed, spending a couple of moments plugging in her phone and setting her hand cream on the nightstand before climbing under the covers and beginning to rub the lotion onto her skin. "Bathroom is all yours," she murmured, chancing a glance at him from beneath her lashes. He hadn't moved, was still standing there in those basketball shorts that were riding low, making it so damned tempting to...just...push...them...down.

Tammy would bet the Carter project that the man was built.

Mostly because she could see the man was *built* through the thin material lovingly cupping—

She choked.

On her own drool.

But at least the sound broke her focus, and drew Fletcher back into his, it seemed. He turned and headed into the bathroom, the door *clicking* closed behind him.

She released a breath she hadn't known she'd been holding and finished with her hand cream, sliding down onto the mattress, and tugging the covers up to her chin. Sleep coming up to swallow her down would be really good right about now, because her inner devil was urging her to follow him into the bathroom, to nudge down those shorts, and—

A knock at the door.

Not the one leading to the bathroom.

She started to toss back the covers, but before she got more than a hand on the edge of them, the door opened, and Connie poked her head in. Her eyes were closed. "I'm not looking, honey. I just forgot to bring you the extra blankets for the bed."

Tammy bit back a smile and slid out from the comforter, glad her PJs kept her well covered up. "It's okay, Connie. I'm decent." She moved to the door as Connie opened her eyes, scanning the space. "Fletch is in the bathroom," she said, taking the blankets. "Thanks for these. I'm guessing it gets pretty cold at night?"

A nod.

Then fingers brushed the arm of her pajamas. "I'm sorry," Connie murmured. "They just look so soft. And they *are,*" she breathed. "Wow."

This was a woman after her own heart.

Knew her mind, loved garlic, and appreciated a good pair of pajamas.

With that, Tammy made a decision.

She set the blankets on the edge of the bed and went to her open suitcase, propped on a small loveseat along one wall, rustling in it, and pulling out what she was looking for. "Here," she said, bringing out the set of new pajamas, their tags still on because she'd picked them up just that morning. "You're my size, and these are brand new. Try them tonight. They're yours if you like them."

"Oh, I couldn't—"

"*Could,*" Tammy said. "My mom got me hooked on these. Let me share the wealth, okay?"

"I—"

The bathroom door opened, and Fletcher strode out, still in the sexy as hell shorts, still topless and gorgeous and...lickable.

He skittered to a stop. "Mom!"

Tammy managed to tear her eyes off the flat abdomen she wanted to kiss her way down and move her gaze to his face.

His *outraged* face.

"Your mom was just bringing extra blankets," Tammy hurried to share. "My blood fails when it comes to keeping this city girl warm in the mountains." Never mind that she'd grown up with winters and snow and temperatures probably lower than they'd get here. One, she was spoiled already with her California weather. Two, Fletcher looked very close to losing his temper. He was a pretty even-keeled guy, but his mom barging in on him and his "girlfriend"—yes, with quotes—certainly wasn't making him happy. "Thanks again, Connie," she said, "and let me know how you like the PJs, okay?"

Connie sputtered. "I—I—"

"Goodnight, Mom," Fletcher gritted out.

Connie recovered and kissed Tammy on the cheek. "Night, honey. Night, baby," she called to Fletcher.

Then she was gone.

Fletcher strode to the door, flicked the lock. Then sighed and shook his head. "Pointless. She's probably learned lock-picking skills somewhere along the way."

"Want to shove a chair in front of it?" Tammy said lightly.

He scowled at her, seemed to be considering dumping her suitcase on the floor and the size of that loveseat, before sighing and rounding the bed. "You still good with us sharing?" He nodded at the blankets bundled on the edge of the mattress. "I can bunk on the couch."

Probably, it would be smarter for him to do that.

But her toes were already chilly, and it was going to only get colder. Plus, if he was right about his mom's lock-picking skills then it would be odd for him to be sleeping on the couch.

She nodded. "I'm good with sharing. So long as you're not a blanket hog."

His lips tipped up. "I'm a very reasonable blanket sharer."

"All right then." She crawled back into bed, brought the covers up again, and deliberately closed her eyes. If she could just pretend this was normal, she would fall asleep, and everything would be good and—

The bed rocked.

The covers shifted.

Heat pooled between her thighs.

Needy. She was so *damned* needy.

But...picket fences and pretending. So, she closed her eyes and concentrated on breathing, on ignoring that Fletcher was also breathing next to her (funny how that happened), on ignoring the slight bounce when he reached up to turn out the lights.

And also the quiet rustle of him getting settled.

The faint gleam of the moonlight projecting the shadows of his movements on the wall in front of her.

The...

Finally—thank God, *finally*—sleep came up and yanked her under.

———

He'd lied.

He *was* a blanket thief.

Even when she'd woken in the middle of the night and pulled the blankets from the foot of the bed over her, she'd been awakened barely an hour later, ass in the cold, her body wracked with shivers.

There'd been a battle—her trying to yank some blanket free, him dead to the world and shoving it beneath him—and she'd lost, moving as close as she dared to him, shivering as sleep took her under again.

Then had woken barely an hour after that, with *her* beneath him, his arms wrapped tight.

She should move.

But he was warm, and his grip was tight, and she knew that it was pointless to try to escape.

She hadn't even managed to secure a corner of the blankets. With his arms around her, holding her flush against him, she wouldn't make it more than a few inches.

And truthfully, he was warm, and she didn't *want* to escape.

So, she just let her eyes slide closed, snuggled up to his warmth, and fell asleep in Fletcher's arms.

Dangerous.

And yet, she couldn't bring herself to care.

Eight

Flowers and fall in his nose.

Soft curves beneath his palms.

Sighing, he shifted, hips arching forward, his cock coming in contact with a generous ass. A moan in his ears. A hand drifting up to weave into his hair. Trina. He was dreaming, but it was wonderful because it was Trina in his arms. She always did that when they first woke up, scraping her nails along his scalp, arching back against him.

And God, he didn't want to be with her again.

But he wouldn't mind fucking her just one more time.

They'd always...it had always been really fucking good between them.

In his dream, he opened his eyes, wanting to see Trina, but the room was dark enough that he couldn't see more than shadows, couldn't even see his own hand in front of his face.

But he could *feel*.

In this strange dream world, he could feel.

And it was glorious.

He dropped his hand onto Trina's side, skating up to cup her breast through her pajamas. The globe felt larger than he remembered, overfilling his palm, but he didn't stop moving. He continued stroking along her body, slipping his fingers beneath the silky fabric of her clothing.

Sliding them back up.

Over the soft skin of her abdomen, across her ribcage, and then cupping one breast.

Fuck, that was good.

Trina moaned and rocked against him. He slid his free hand down then, scooting it under the fabric of her pajamas. She didn't have any underwear on, which made something blip in his mind. Trina always wore panties to bed.

But this was his dream, and apparently it had granted him a solid by forgoing the extra layer.

His fingers slid through the narrow thatch of hair at the apex of her thighs, slipped along her labia, caressing those soaking folds. Hot and wet and—he slid a finger inside—so fucking tight.

He groaned, thrusting that finger in and out, loving the sound of her moans, her ass rocking into him.

"Fletcher," she breathed, her breath hitching. "Are you awake?"

"Mmm." She didn't sound like Trina, and it made something blip in his mind, but then she rubbed even harder against his cock and he forgot about the voice that sounded different, the slight rasp when it should be softly melodic. He thought of nothing but her body to his, her ass against his dick, and he bent, nipped at her throat, breathing in the musk of her arousal. "I don't care."

"*I* care—"

He slipped another finger in.

She gasped, rocked harder, pussy clamping around his fingers.

"I don't," he muttered, nipping her skin again.

"Fletch—"

He needed to taste her, to be inside her, to fuck her hard and deep, dream or not. Which was why he focused enough as he thrust his fingers deep to say, "I'm with you, baby."

She arched against him. "Mmm. Fletch—"

"I'm going to fuck you so good." He flicked her clit, pumped faster.

"I need—" She grabbed his wrist, yanked it out of her pants. A second later, he was on his back, his shorts were gone, and... best fucking dream ever.

A tight wet sheath surrounded his cock.

He bucked.

"*This*," she moaned.

Then her palms came to his chest, nails digging in, and Trina gave him a *fucking* ride.

Up and grinding down, her hips bucking, fingers gripping tight, she fucked him until he had to close his eyes against the swirling shadows, the sparks gathering behind his vision, had to squeeze his lids tight just to focus on the pleasure swarming through him. It gathered at his toes and fingertips, burned up his arms and legs, arrowed through his heart, his gut.

Tighter and tighter.

Her pussy clenched around him. His name tumbled from her lips.

She ground down hard, and...he exploded.

Ash and cinder overcome by bliss.

"Fuck, that's good, Trina," he groaned, yanking her down onto his chest as he thrust once, twice more, holding her tightly against him as wave after wave of pleasure flooded him. His head dropped back onto the pillows, his arms flopped to the mattress.

And sleep rose up to tug him back under.

So quickly and completely that he hadn't noticed the woman go still over him.

Nor that sunlight was starting to peek in through the windows.

That the shadows of his dream had warmed into the soft glow of the rising sun.

Nine

She held still.

Perfectly, absolutely still.

After the best orgasm of her life, his cock still hard and inside her, Tammy had ice flowing through her veins.

The sex had been incredible.

She'd thought it a dream for a minute, but then she'd woken up and it had been the best part of waking up (yes, she sang that —at least mentally). But she'd hadn't been sure he was awake, so she'd asked, and he'd said he was with her, that he was going to fuck her good in a low, rasping voice that had skated over her skin, flooded her pussy with heat and moisture.

His fingers inside her.

His mouth on her skin.

His hand on her breast.

And...she hadn't thought about it further. Or hadn't thought of anything except chasing the orgasm he'd been building within her, the one that threatened to reduce her to ash, to melt her into a puddle of goo. With all that not-thinking, she'd climbed on top of him, yanked his shorts down, and shoved the monster he had between his thighs inside her—and *God* that had felt good. She'd never been with a guy who made her feel almost uncomfortably full. Fletcher's cock was magnificent.

Which meant that riding them both into oblivion hadn't been difficult.

She'd gotten there.

He had been right on her heels.

And...then he'd called her Trina.

Now his cock was still in her, still hard and pulsing, his cum slowly leaking out from inside her, leaving her pussy and the tops of her thighs sticky from the mixture of their releases.

"Fletch?" she asked when she realized he'd gone still, gone limp.

A snore greeted her question.

What the fuck?

She poked his chest, but he didn't so much as move, as miss a beat of snoring.

"Fletcher," she hissed, gripping his shoulders and shaking him roughly.

The fucker didn't move. He'd ground up into her, held and stroked and plunged into her. And...he'd called her Trina.

"Fuck," she whispered, climbing off him and making a fucking mess of her pajama pants, yanking them up, waddling to the bathroom. She'd given her spare set to Connie, and now this one was stained with cum and—

"Fuck," she whispered again, stripping out of her pajama bottoms, dealing with her business on the toilet, and then going to the sink to spot clean the expensive material.

Trina.

He'd said he was with her.

Then he'd called her *Trina.*

The sick feeling in her gut grew.

She hung up her pajamas, hoping that she'd be able to sneak them into the dryer later, or that they would dry before someone —Fletcher—realized what happened.

Realized?

She couldn't wait for him to *realize!* She had to tell him.

Right?

Maybe...

No.

She had to tell him they'd had sex. That it was his cum staining her pants, sticking to the insides of her thighs. She at least had to tell him she was clean, make sure he was, too. And fuck. Had she just sexually assaulted him? Had he been too asleep to consent?

Fuck, who was she kidding?

There wasn't even something like *too* asleep. He was or he wasn't.

And fuck, now she didn't think that he'd been awake. Which meant that she was the worst sort of person, and she needed to tell him and—

Nausea twisted through her insides.

He'd said he was awake.

He'd touched her first.

So, maybe he'd just drunk too much?

Which...wasn't any better.

Especially since he'd only had two beers and he'd been sober when they'd gone to bed, and she didn't think that he'd managed to get drunk *and* steal the blankets in the last few hours.

So...what now?

"Why?" she breathed, rubbing the ache in her forehead. God, why had she agreed to this in the first place? Now she was a fucking sexual deviant, a rapist, a—

"Okay, Tam," she said, stopping that train of thoughts before it could overwhelm her. She needed to talk to him, to figure this out. Nothing good came from spiraling and panicking. She splashed some water on her face and stared at herself in the mirror, psyched herself up. "You just need to tell him what happened. Explain that it was a misunderstanding and that you'll do whatever you can to make it right."

What if he wanted to press charges?

What if—

Fuck.

Okay, yeah. She was freaking out. She needed to take another breath and to go back into the bedroom and just tell him, to ask him if he remembered and it would be okay. They were two adults. Things had just taken an odd turn. Tomorrow she'd sleep on the couch because there was no way she'd be going back to sleep that night, even if light wasn't already creeping in through the windows, and she wasn't stressed to fuck and back.

She needed to wake him up right then.

No delaying. No more spiraling.

She walked into the bedroom, poked him in the side, hissed his name.

Fletcher didn't move.

She grabbed his shoulders, shook him hard.

Still, he didn't move. What the fuck? How deep of a sleeper was this guy?

"Fletcher," she said, loud enough to wake the house. Or so it seemed.

But he just snored softly, as though she wasn't shaking him like a rag doll.

Okay, so the man could sleep. What to do? What to do? What to—

Shower first.

Clearly, he wouldn't be waking up anytime soon. She could take a minute to get organized, get her thoughts together, game-plan with how to wake him up.

Blaring her cell phone by his ear? That might truly wake the house, and despite the light drifting in through the windows, it was still early.

Licking his nose? No. Licking was definitely a bad idea.

Glass of water on his face? Then she'd get Connie's sheets and pillows wet, and it would create more laundry she needed to sneak around to do. Because how was she going to explain wet sheets?

Oh, sorry, Connie. I'm just a squirter.

Or a grown woman who still wets the bed.

Or I'm—

Right. Enough of that. She should shower first. They were all going on the hike in a couple of hours. Tammy should clean up and then go down and make breakfast for everyone. The smell of bacon and coffee might rouse him, and then they could talk about this.

There. That was a plan at least.

And one that meant she could shower first, remove the evidence of their—*her*—actions.

Right.

She grabbed some clothes from her suitcase—jeans, boots, a thermal, and a hoodie. Layers were best because she wasn't the most outdoorsy girl. She'd probably be panting and sweating and peeling her clothes off in no time. Which was clearly a problem she had around Fletcher.

Not that she'd even taken them off.

Not *all* the way off, anyway.

"Ugh, Tammy. Just stop." She cranked on the shower, cleaned up, then got out and dressed quickly. A quick fluff of her hair. A bit of mascara and lip gloss and a couple of strokes of blush so she didn't look like the snow gathered on the tops of the mountains—pale as hell and camouflaging it with the bright, powdery white stuff.

Then she was slipping out of the room and down the stairs.

It didn't take long to get the coffee brewing and even less

time to pull out ingredients for her famous breakfast sandwiches (famous because she'd declared them so). Hopefully, Connie wouldn't need the ingredients she was planning on using for anything. Though, Tammy had seen a grocery store not far away.

If she used something that Connie needed, she would do a food run.

She lined cookie sheets with foil, placed the bacon in neat rows on top of it, and then popped the two trays into the oven.

Next was potatoes.

She sliced them thinly, coated them with salt, pepper, and olive oil, and placed *that* tray in the oven. Instead of having to cram a third tray inside the heated chamber, like she'd have to do at home, she had a second oven to load up.

Double ovens.

The height of luxury.

And yes, evidence that she was just a girl from the Midwest. Well, so what? Small things like double ovens excited her.

So did the fact that she could easily get a Baby Yoda martini at Bobby's.

See?

Small things.

Focusing on shoving down her squeeing over the double ovens, Tammy cut thick pieces from a loaf of crunchy-crusted sourdough, prepping them with a little melted butter and layering slices of cheddar cheese on top of them before putting them—and yet another cookie sheet!—into the bottom oven.

Four cookie sheets.

Double ovens.

Yeah, someone could *cook* in this kitchen.

And based on the lasagna and other leftovers from last night, Tammy knew that Connie cooked like a beast in this kitchen.

Right.

On to the eggs.

She cracked them into a skillet, scrambled them with salt,

pepper, milk, butter, and cheese. Normally, she'd take orders, ask her eaters how they liked their eggs—over easy, scrambled, sunny side up—but it was early, and she was tired and scrambled was the easiest route.

Humming to herself, she waited until she'd flipped the bacon and it was nearly done before turning on the burner and starting the eggs.

Nothing worse than cold eggs, so she liked to time her breakfast sandwich goodness so all the components were ready at nearly the same time. Plates out, then toast out, the cheese melted, the bread crunchy. Then she layered on the bacon—*lots* of bacon. A heaping scoop of eggs, another slice of bread, and the sandwiches were complete.

But...the kitchen was silent.

And as she stared at four loaded plates, she realized that she might have underestimated the Kings. If his parents slept as deeply as Fletcher, then it would be unlikely that coffee and bacon smells would tempt them out of bed.

She'd practically shouted in his face, had gone full earthquake in his bed.

So why would—

"Is that bacon?" a raspy male voice asked.

Whirling around and nearly upending the plates she'd so carefully made, she watched as Fletcher stumbled his way into the kitchen. No shirt. Those pecs and arms on full display. His hair a fucking mess. He looked thoroughly fucked.

Because she'd fucked *him*.

He blinked, rubbed a hand down his chest. "Tammy—" A shake of his head. "You cooked?"

"I just threw something quick and easy together," she said, picking up a plate and shoving it at him. "Here. Sit. Eat." She pointed at the island, watching as he made his way toward a stool. "Look, Fletch, we need to talk—"

"Is that coffee I smell?" Connie asked, stumbling into the room.

She looked just as wrecked as Fletcher—her hair askew, the pajamas Tammy had loaned her buttoned wrong. Fletch's mom appeared thoroughly fucked as well, and the smirk on Tony's face as he trailed her into the kitchen added credence to Tammy's mental assessment.

"And bacon," Tony said, inhaling deeply. "Oh, my God!" he exclaimed, his gaze coming to the plates in her arms. "Breakfast sandwiches and coffee? You're an angel." He ruffled Tammy's hair. "Thanks, sweetheart. You didn't have to go to any trouble. I usually take the AM cooking shift and Connie the PM."

That hair ruffle made Tammy feel oddly pleased.

But since she couldn't stand there, smiling and pleased with herself because she threw together a couple of breakfast sandwiches, she asked. "What do you guys do for the lunch shift?"

Connie shuffled to the coffee pot and began filling the mugs Tammy had set out. "Fend for ourselves," she said sleepily.

"Lunchables," Tony shared, looking much more chipper than his wife. He moved to the fridge, opened a drawer Tammy hadn't looked in and revealed...

Good grief.

It was *packed* with Lunchables—turkey, chicken nuggets, nachos, ham, the little hot dog ones—and if she'd thought they were joking, that notion had been quickly erased.

"Wow," she breathed.

Fletcher came and took the other plates from her arms, setting them around the kitchen island. "Yup. My parents are elementary school kids at heart."

"Rude," his mom said blearily.

"Because I have a palate?" he teased.

Tammy smiled as Connie handed her a filled coffee mug. "For the record, the chicken nuggets are my favorite," she confided in Fletch's mom.

Connie grinned. "I knew I liked you for a reason."

More pleased feelings. More standing there grinning like a loon.

Her own family was great. There had never been a moment where she didn't know she was loved, that they didn't have her back. But...she was the youngest, the one who often felt like an afterthought. The accident. The unwanted fourth sibling.

Not fair, she knew. Her parents loved her.

But it was also the truth.

Tammy *had* been an accident. She'd heard that stated more than a handful of times over the years, the baby that came after her dad got snipped. The baby who made her mom cry when she'd found out she was pregnant because she didn't want another kid. The fetus responsible for making her mom vomit every single day—several times a day—for the entire nine months (or the *eternal* forty weeks, as her mother liked to declare) of pregnancy.

It was a family joke.

It...didn't feel good.

Oh, boohoo, Tammy, her inner voice said. *You have a loving family who teases you occasionally. Such a tough life.*

Right.

She pushed the bit of moroseness aside, focused on the shirt-less man she'd just fucked, and wondered again how in the hell she was going to tell him what had happened.

And yeah, that made her feel *so* much better.

But then Connie patted the stool next to her. "Come sit and eat, honey. Before it gets cold."

And Tammy knew she could stay in her head, could continue to worry about what went down with Fletcher, or...

She could eat her sandwich while it was hot.

She could...procrastinate.

Yeah, that sounded better.

Tammy took her plate and sat next to Connie.

Ten

Fletcher

The breakfast sandwiches were the best thing he'd ever put in his mouth.

His parents seemed to feel the same, devouring their eggs, bacon, and butter-and-cheese covered bread with relish.

The only one who was moving a little slower was Tammy.

She picked at her sandwich and when he came enough out of his Hoovering haze to be aware of anything except that he was still half-asleep and his stomach was rumbling because he'd smelled bacon, he saw that she had dark circles under her eyes.

Tired.

Because she was regretting this?

A wave of guilt flowed through him.

He'd dragged her up here, brought her to a strange house where clearly, she hadn't slept well because she was up before the sun was fully up and cooking for his family.

No wonder she was tired.

Tammy seemed to realize they were all done—all except her,

anyway—picked up her half-full plate, and started to carry it to the sink.

"No way." His mom hopped to her feet, snagged the porcelain circle. "You two shoo. Go do fun, coupley things."

"Like getting ready for the hike Carrie is going to drag us on?" Fletcher teased.

"She wants to do some sort of woo-woo prewedding ceremony in the woods," his dad muttered, "and drag us on a seven-mile hike while we commune with our inner nature spirits."

Tammy choked. "Seven miles?"

"In snowshoes," his dad said, still muttering.

"Snow," she squeaked, "*shoes?*" Her eyes flew to Fletcher's, and she whispered, "I brought hiking boots, but I didn't bring snowshoes."

Fletcher fought back a grin. "Dad's joking about the snowshoes. At least I think he is. We're only hiking—"

"Seven miles?" she whispered as his dad joined his mom in beginning to wash dishes. "He's joking about that, too, right?"

"Um," Fletch began.

Tammy's face fell.

Shit.

He took her arm, guided her from the kitchen, out through the French doors that led to the small deck that overlooked his parents' back yard. "You can stay—"

"*Seven miles?*" she asked—or rather squeaked—again.

He winced. One could never tell with Carrie. She tended to get a little excited where nature was concerned. Sometimes it was two miles, sometimes it was ten. And he was willing to bet that no one would be begging her to stop or cut the hike short like tended to happen when she usually got carried away. Not when it was her wedding weekend.

"Seven?" Tammy whispered.

All he could do was try to keep his face neutral and shrug.

Tammy groaned.

He'd started to open his mouth to tell her that they'd figure it out, that she could skip out on the hike and he'd cover for her.

But then he heard that groan.

And everything inside him stilled.

That *groan*.

That breathy, soft groan that rumbled down his spine, gathered in his dick, making blood pool there like it had—

In his dream.

In. His. *Dream*.

Oh, holy fuck.

"Tammy," he whispered.

"Seven miles," she was saying again, his grip having slackened to release her arm as she paced away. She shoved her hair out of her face, released a sigh, and straightened her shoulders. "Okay. Seven miles. I can do seven miles. It's fine. I'm going to be fine. Yup, I'm—"

Slick heat.

A tight pussy clamping around his dick

Lush breasts.

That. Groan.

"We fucked."

In the middle of her pep talk about surviving the seven-mile hike that Carrie had planned—hopefully sans snowshoes so as not to make him a liar—his blurting out, "*We fucked,*" froze her in almost comical fashion. Her mouth dropped open, her eyes went wide, and she spun so fast that he was surprised she hadn't rolled up the deck beneath her feet like in a cartoon.

"I—*what?*"

He stepped toward her, closed the distance between them. "Last night. This morning. We fucked, Tammy." Her cheeks went bright pink, and then her face went pale. "I was inside you. Your nails"—he tugged the neck of his T-shirt to the side and glanced down. Sure enough, there were nail marks there, ones he hadn't noticed in his stupor earlier—"marked me. I—"

She clamped a hand over his mouth. "I didn't mean to."

He frowned, peeled her fingers away, starting to ask her whatever the hell that meant.

But she kept talking, and he soon learned.

"You"—a shake of her head—"I asked if you were awake, and you answered. You said you were with me, and I thought... well, I guess I didn't realize how heavy you sleep so when I'd asked..."

He shifted closer. "Was it good?"

She paled further. "I—" Another shake of her head. "Why the hell does that matter?"

He snaked an arm around her waist, tugged her flush against him. "It matters to me. I thought it was a dream"—she winced —"but I thought it was the best fucking dream of my life."

"Right," she murmured and there was something in her tone, something dark, something pained. "With Trina."

His brows drew together. "What?"

"You called me Trina."

Fucking hell.

She smiled, and it was forced. "Well..." She cleared her throat. "Anyway, that's not the point. I'm...I'm sorry that I didn't realize you weren't awake. I feel horrible, and I—"

"It's okay," he whispered.

Her ponytail snapped behind her when she shook her head. "It's not."

"Tam—" he began

"It really isn't okay," she said, stepping out of his arms and shoving a hand through her hair, clenched it tightly. "I should have realized you weren't actually awake—"

"How?"

She blinked. "What?"

"How would you know that I wasn't really awake?"

A frown marred her brow.

"Would you ask me if I was awake?" That frown deepened.

Those lips parted. "Of course, you would," he said before she could speak again. "And you'd expect me to answer. Which I did." He cupped her cheek. "I remember every moment. *Every* moment."

"Except you thought it was a dream."

"Like I said, the best one of my life."

Her words were quiet. "Featuring Trina."

"Yes." He had. He wasn't going to lie. "I did think you were Trina." He stifled a grimace. Though he knew the bigger question was why he thought he'd been dreaming of Trina in the first place. He'd had sex with other people. But...not sex that meant anything.

Because they weren't Trina.

And he was startled to realize that none of them were...*Tammy*.

His gaze flicked up in time to see hurt dance across her face. "I...um...I should go get ready for the hike."

"Sweetheart," he began as she backed away.

"No, really." Her smile was forced. "If I'm going to hike seven miles, I'd better put on my good socks." A chuckle that sounded painful. "And find some snowshoes."

He reached for her. "Tam—"

A quick movement had her darting around him, her fingers wrapping around the door handle and pulling.

"Tam—"

She slipped inside, her red hair fanning out behind her, and the door closed with a soft *snick*.

And he was left alone in the quiet on the porch—the sun shining, a gentle breeze shifting the cool air through the tall pines, rustling the needles, drifting across his skin. He'd loved growing up here, loved being able to disappear into the trees (keeping an eye out for bears, of course), but just getting lost in the sensation of being small amongst big, unimportant in the grand scheme of nature.

Usually, it brought him peace.

But that morning, he was left thinking that, once again, he'd fucked everything up.

———

Seriously, how had he never noticed that Tammy had the best ass?

Rounded, the perfect size to be cupped, stretching that denim in a way that made him desperate to peel down the fabric.

Usually, he saw her in slacks, and not that he hadn't noticed Tammy's ass—he'd be lying if he said he hadn't—he just usually kept it professional and dutifully averted his gaze if he happened to catch a glimpse of...well, *ass.*

Now Tammy had been hiking in front of him for the last hour, and he was having a lot of quality time with her ass in his face.

Add in that it was encased in tight jeans...

And yeah, well, he was just lucky that it was cold outside.

Of course, he'd also like to see her pretty face, those gorgeous eyes, *along* with that lush ass. She just...wasn't showing them to him.

Instead, she was avoiding him.

And doing it in a very sneaky way that had him not realizing she'd been doing that avoiding until they were three miles into their hike.

First, she'd been getting ready, and he wasn't an idiot. She'd obviously been upset over the whole calling out Trina's name thing, upset that he hadn't immediately remembered they'd had sex because he was a fucking bastard and in his head and a heavy sleeper. So, at first, he'd given her space.

Space to dress.

Space to get ready.

Then she'd been commandeered by his mom to help select her Lunchable for the hike.

To which Tammy had countered the Lunchable selection and sent him to the store for supplies. She'd said she would take lunch duty while she was visiting and had proceeded to make enough chicken salad sandwiches with fruit salad for an army.

Prepping and packing those had taken time—not a surprise—and then they'd left to meet Carrie and Sean and their respective bridal parties of honor at the trailhead.

Much exclaiming had commenced about the sandwiches and fruit.

Then they'd gotten on with hiking...and Carrie had claimed her.

Then Sean.

Then she'd claimed his dad.

Then struck up a conversation with Hayley—Carrie's maid of honor.

Right about the time she'd began talking to Jim—Sean's best man—was when he finally clued into the sneaky avoidance. Yes, he was slow. Yes, he'd spent too much of the hike fantasizing about that ass and all the things he wanted to do with it.

So, finally, he stopped enjoying the view and started thinking.

Something he should have done before beginning this whole charade, something he definitely should have done before all the ass daydreaming. And something he certainly should have done after seeing the hurt on her face that morning.

Because Tammy was all talk about not wanting a relationship.

She had to be.

Because otherwise, why would she have been hurt over what had happened that morning?

Because you thought you were dreaming while you fucked her, and—oh—because you called her another woman's name?

Right.

There was that.

But he still thought that she wasn't as firm on not wanting a long-term relationship as she tried to convince everyone she was. Yeah, she wanted to focus on her career—and he wholeheartedly supported that—but she also liked people. She had good friends, was connected to everyone in the office, and her family seemed as loud and brash as his was.

She wasn't a woman who liked to be alone.

No, she wasn't.

And just because she has friends, a good job, and a family means that she wants a boyfriend?

Right. There was that, too.

But maybe she just hadn't met the right man?

And that man is you?

Damn his inner conscience was a brutal motherfucker.

One that spoke the truth, of course, but one that was still brutal. Fletcher had no business thinking that he could change her mind about wanting a relationship, about wanting him. Hell, he should be running from the complication of dating someone from work.

But he didn't *want* to run.

He wanted the complication, wanted to be a stubborn asshole and to be the man to change her mind about wanting to be tied with someone.

To be the right man for *her*.

He smothered a wince at the caveman thoughts and focused on hiking, but between his wince-smothering and his ass-watching he missed the branch flying back toward him—Tammy having pushed it to the side as she hiked.

No sooner had he spotted the branch flying toward him than it was whipping him in the face and knocking him to the ground.

"Fuck," he muttered, rubbing his cheek, lifting his fingers to see them painted red with blood.

If he ended up with stitches for the wedding pictures, his mom was going to kill him.

Tammy and Jim spun around, and he noticed it was several moments after he'd decided to warm the cold soil. It was hard not to be resentful of that delay, especially when he was bleeding and he'd noticed Jim checking out Tammy's ass, too—the bastard.

Yes, he was fully aware that it was hypocritical of him.

But Jim was single and had a roving eye and a love for keeping things light and unconnected with women...and Tammy had herself convinced she wanted that.

More asshole, caveman tendencies.

But he couldn't bring himself to care, not when he finally got a glimpse of those pretty pale brown eyes—along with her kissable lips, her pert nose, her cute chin—as she turned to see what had happened—or more likely, why he'd been grunting and cursing. And then he realized there was a perk to getting knocked on his ass.

Mainly that it got her close to him, eliminated that sneaky avoidance she'd been practicing.

"Shit, Fletcher, are you okay?" She knelt by his side and began running her hands over him. And yeah, that was nice.

And yeah, that made him a caveman asshole.

Regardless, he wasn't about to stop her. No fucking way.

Not when her hands felt good. Not when they were clearing the fog from his mind and making him remember how good those hands had felt on him in his dream—or rather, how good they'd felt during their early morning interlude.

"Damn," she murmured, "it's deep."

That's what she said.

Great. Now his inner voice was turning him into a comedian.

"I'm okay," he said.

Her eyes flew to his, held. "You're *bleeding*."

Concern.

He couldn't lie and say he wasn't eating it up, but Carrie and Sean were slowing ahead, his mom and dad following suit. Soon the hoards would be descending and as much as he liked Tammy fussing over him, he didn't think he'd be able to handle Tammy *and* his mom *and* Carrie fussing.

"I'm good, sunshine," he said, covering her hand and taking it in his own, holding it as he stood, drawing her to her feet at the same time. "Just rub a little dirt in it and call me good."

Tammy scowled. "That is neither sanitary nor funny."

He kissed the top of her head. "Maybe not the first, but it's definitely the second."

"What's the matter?" Carrie called.

"He—" Jim began.

Tammy tugged his arm, turning Fletcher so he was facing away from the bride to be and cut Jim off before he could summon the masses. "Fletch just wanted to show me something about this...um...tree!"

His dad started laughing. Sean got a shit-eating grin on his face. Jim seemed to realize he'd lost any chance of flirting with Fletcher's girlfriend. Carrie and his mom just smiled and started hiking again, his mom calling out over her shoulder, "Be sure to show her the ones just off the path."

Fletch smothered a laugh.

"I'm not going to hear the end of that one, am I?"

"They'll be calling you an arborist before long."

"Hilarious."

"Damn right."

Tammy sighed and shook her head, but as the rest of their group disappeared out of sight, she slipped off the small back-pack she was carrying and reached in to pull out a first aid kit.

"Prepared," he murmured.

"Former Girl Scout," she said softly, her fingers gentle as she opened a wipe and swiped at his cheek. It stung, and he hissed out a breath, but then her grip tightened as she held him in place. "I like to be prepared."

"And here you were worried about hiking seven miles," he teased.

"*Still* worried about hiking seven miles. It's been more than two decades since someone got me on a trail. I was much more into the weaving and cookie consuming part of scouting."

"Consuming?" he asked. "I thought the whole point was to sell."

"That's true, but have you ever surrounded yourself with a hundred boxes of Thin Mints? They're impossible to resist. You're like, I'll just have a couple and the next thing you know, you've eaten the entire sleeve."

"Why does that sound dirty?"

Pale brown eyes narrowed. "Because you're disgusting?"

He winked. "There are worse qualities."

A bright red brow arched. "Really?"

Another shrug.

"What are they?"

He paused, pondered that, knowing that she had him backed into a corner as he struggled for a witty reply. Obviously, pedophiles and murderers and war lords were worse than being disgusting and those were just the top three that came to mind. But he didn't want to take the conversation somewhere dark.

She swiped his cheek again.

He hissed again.

She leaned closer, her breath coming to his cheek as she blew lightly on the cut. Then he was hissing out another breath that had nothing to do with the sting of the cleaner and had everything to do with Tammy's mouth, her body being very close to his.

"I win," she whispered, smoothing a bandage over the cut.

"Mmm?" He took the wipe and kit from her, shoved them into her backpack, zipped it closed, and tossed it over his shoulder.

"I win," she repeated, a smirk dancing on her lips. "I made the unflappable Fletcher King speechless."

"Hmm." He fought back a smile. "Not speechless for long."

A shrug. "Length doesn't matter."

"That's what she said."

Tammy rolled her eyes. "Hilarious."

"Why do you think I'm unflappable?" She was enjoying her so-called victory—either that or she didn't appreciate his humor (rude!). Regardless of the scenario, she didn't protest when he laced their fingers together, nor when he started them walking forward again...only this time it was to guide her casually off the path.

"Because you *are* unflappable," she said and shrugged. "Nothing much ever seems to get to you."

Except her.

Tammy got to him.

But he was a mess—or at least felt like a mess—every time he was around her, Fletch considered that supposed unflappable-ness a victory of his own...

And then he guided her a little farther off the path.

Eleven

TAMMY

"Things get to me," he murmured, squeezing her hand, and drawing her forward.

She rolled her shoulders, and they finally weren't aching.

Mostly because Fletcher was now carrying her backpack.

Also because she was still hopped up with adrenaline. When she'd turned and seen him on the ground, worry had knotted her insides. And then when she'd seen the blood on his cheek, her pulse had sped, becoming bullets in her veins, thrumming against her skin.

Scared for him.

Stupid, right?

It had been a small cut. Yes, it was deep—or at least deeper than she'd expected. Yes, it had bled a fair amount.

But she'd been able to wipe the blood away and fix everything with a Band-Aid.

So, it hadn't been bad enough to warrant the fear that had slammed into her.

The relief that had trailed the fear had been a tsunami crashing into her other side.

And now she was reeling when she should still be upset and avoiding. Upset because she wasn't Trina and he'd thought she was, upset that she'd spent the morning thinking she was the worst sort of person for fucking him when he hadn't been aware of what he was doing, and then upset because he remembered.

And...upset because she'd been triggered.

Because she wanted to be the person someone picked.

Which made her feel...

Icky. Weak. Stupid. Pathetic.

Ugh.

She sucked a breath in through her nose, realized she'd been quiet and in her head for too long—something she hated. It was a scary place, her mind. Which meant she needed to get the hell out of it, and—funny story—step one of that was to stop thinking she was weak, stupid, and pathetic.

Ding. Ding. Ding.

Folks, we have a winner!

Releasing a breath slowly, she rewound—rapidly past the negative thoughts—and halted at the last thing that Fletcher had said.

Things get to me.

"What kind of things?" she asked.

"Hmm?" he asked, nudging her slightly so she didn't run into a tree.

And speaking of trees, the path seemed to have closed in on them. The trees were taller, the air cooler, and contrary to where they were hiking before, snow was gathered in little pockets. It coated the base of the trunks, encroached on the narrow trail.

She shivered. "What sorts of things get to you?" she clarified.

Look at her go, staying on target.

Fletcher tugged her hand, but instead of avoiding an obstacle, this time the tug was drawing her to a halt, turning her to face him.

"What?" she asked softly, suddenly aware that it was really quiet.

Had the others picked up the pace so much that they weren't going to catch up?

A thread of concern threaded through her. "Do you know where you're going?" she asked.

Silence had her glancing up and seeing a satisfied smile trail across his face. "I know where I'm going," he said when he caught her staring, the words a heated rasp that slid over her skin. "And"—his voice went a little hard—"one of the things that gets to me is hurting a beautiful, sexy woman." He lifted his free hand, tucked a strand of hair behind her ear.

She shivered again when his fingers trailed over the shell of her ear, down the column of her throat.

"Cold?" he murmured.

Now that she thought of it, she *wasn't* cold. Not in the least. Not even with the snow accumulating along the path. Instead of little pockets around the trees, it was collecting into larger banks, connecting the trunks like a frozen Connect-the-Dots. If it kept up, they were going to need to strap on the snowshoes Fletcher was carrying for both of them.

"Tammy?"

His voice was like silk.

Why was his voice like silk? And why did it make her feel like she was burning up inside? Like she'd melt the snowbank if she sat down in it, ending up soaked and doggy paddling in a puddle.

"Tammy?" he asked again.

Still like silk...but with a touch of velvet that made her thighs quiver. "Hmm?"

"Are you cold?"

A shake of her head. "No," she said. "I'm not cold."

He slipped his fingers free, slid his arm around her shoulders, drew her close.

She squirmed in his hold. "I said I wasn't cold."

He just held her tighter. "Your lips are blue and you're shivering—"

"I—"

"—and plus," he said like it was no big deal. "I like you in my arms."

Warning. Warning, Tammy Huntington.

"Fletch—" she began.

But didn't finish the -er.

Because suddenly her back was against a tree trunk. Or rather, she was pressed to Fletcher's hands, which were pressed to the tree trunk, and his front was pressed to *her* front, and all that pressing was pretty fucking nice.

Really fucking nice.

Incredible even.

But he was looking at her with gentleness in his eyes, with concern and something that might be longing on his face. It sure as shit wasn't lust or molten heat or whatever the smutty romance novels she preferred called it. This wasn't the face of a man who wanted a quick fuck, something hard and fast and mutually satisfying. Instead, Fletcher's face was *soft*.

More warnings.

More danger.

She was Tammy Huntington, and she didn't do soft or gentle. She wanted to be respected, for sure. To be treated with common courtesy, definitely.

She didn't want soft.

No, because then *she* would feel soft in turn, and that would inevitably end up with her feeling like shit.

She tried again. "Fletch—"

"I see you, Tammy Huntington," he murmured, bending

close, his lips on the exposed skin of her throat, the words damp puffs of heat that had her shivering again.

Not because she was cold. Again.

He stepped closer, and cold was the last thing on her mind. Instead, it was the hard heat of his body, the impact of those words on her heart.

I see you.

Her breath shuddered out, and she did the only thing she could. Distraction.

She reached down and shoved her hand into the waistband of his jeans, wrapped her fingers around the hard length of his cock, and—

Found herself jostled as her hand was tugged free, nearly dropped, and then she was pinned again, her hands trapped between their chests, Fletcher's face mere centimeters from hers —so close that she could feel his breath when he said again, "I see you."

And then his mouth was on hers, his body so gloriously close, his tongue in her mouth, his arms wrapped tight as he kissed her until she forgot where she was, forgot the terror of those words, forgot that they had more miles ahead of them. She forgot her name, forgot the cold that wasn't cold. But she didn't forget the feel of his lips on hers, the need that touch invoked, the desire that left her shaking and needy, how good it had felt to have him inside her.

"Fletch," she moaned when he released her lips and began kissing his way across her jaw.

"I see you," he murmured into her ear, tongue laving the lobe, goose bumps prickling along her nape, her arms. He shifted and suddenly, she was straddling his hips, the hard length of his erection rubbing against just the right spot, pressing the seam of her jeans against her clit.

And fuck the man had rhythm.

He'd had it in a dream state.

But it was even better like this—with their breaths rasping through the cool air, his boots crunching in the snow, his mouth nipping and licking and kissing his way from behind her ear, down her throat, and then back up to take her lips again. And not once did he stop the slow grind between her thighs. Not once did he falter in that steady rhythm that was steadily driving her insane.

With pleasure.

So really, there were worse places to be.

"Fletch—" Her voice broke just as she was considering shoving him back, reaching between their bodies again, and getting that hard cock inside her again.

Her voice *broke* because he did something with his hips that should have been illegal.

Something that had her throwing her head back, barely noticing the pulse of pain that came from her skull colliding with the tree.

Fletcher noticed though, his hand snaking up, cupping the back of her head, protecting it, even as his hips continued grinding, and the movement paired with that blip of protection that was fucking kryptonite to all of her shields, sent her flying over the edge.

Need was coiled taut in her womb, and she cried out when it detonated, exploding from her center and filling her with pleasure, making her limbs go lax, her body slump in Fletcher's arms.

His mouth found hers as she tried to catch her breath—making that really difficult—but then she was kissing him and the man was a fantastic kisser and as much as she liked her orgasm, she was feeling very empty and wanting another courtesy of that glorious cock he was hiding in his pants, and—

He shifted, lowering her to the ground for a second, hands on her hips to steady her when she wavered. She was still blinking, still trying to pull herself together when he let her go and she heard fabric rustling. And seriously, thank fuck, the man must be getting naked. But by the time she managed to catch her breath, to peel her lids back, it was to see Fletcher fully dressed, the backpacks strapped to his front.

"I—"

He knelt, turned, and gave her his back. "Up you go."

"Um..."

His fingers wrapped around her wrist, tugged her toward him—or rather, practically over him, since she ended up stumbling forward and falling over his back. Before she could right herself, she was wrapped around him, his palms beneath her thighs, her arms around his shoulders.

"Fletcher, I—"

He gripped her a little tighter, stood, and started walking back toward the trail.

"I see you, Tammy," was all he said.

Those words.

Why did they settle over her like a warm blanket? Why did they make her melt when she should be launching herself out of Fletcher's arms and demanding she walk?

It would be easier to say it was because the orgasm had left her feeling lethargic and weak and too tired to continue with however many miles they had left.

But that would be a lie.

And Tammy might be a lot of things, but she wasn't a liar.

She liked the words.

Liked that he was taking care of her.

Liked...Fletcher.

TWELVE

"**M**ussed hair, swollen lips," Sean said under his breath, and it was a fucking wonder that the bastard was even able to speak with how big his smirk was. "All you're missing is the misbuttoned clothes."

"Shut up." Fletcher socked him in the arm.

Hard. Though not hard enough to warrant his brother's reaction.

"Ow," Sean whined, clutching his biceps. "I'm going to tell Mom on you."

Fletcher just glared. "You're fine. You're *going* to shut your mouth and not fuck up things for me with Tammy."

"*Did* you fuck things up with Tammy?"

He glanced over his shoulder, stared at the woman who had become his obsession. Her color was high as she talked to Hayley, probably less from the orgasm since that had been nearly an hour before, and more from the fight she'd given him to put her down before they'd caught up with the group.

For close to twenty minutes, it had been perfection.

She'd held tight. He'd enjoyed the hike, the quiet, the feeling of peace and satisfaction of having her pressed to him.

Then she'd seemed to come out of the haze of pleasure.

She'd squirmed. Then she asked to be let down. Then demanded it.

So, he had.

And then she'd taken two steps and nearly ate it.

So, he'd scooped her up again. Cue more fighting, more demanding, more...kissing.

As in, he'd found himself spinning, pinning her to a tree again, and kissing her senseless. Kissing himself senseless in the process, finding himself very close to forgetting why he hadn't fucked her against that tree, even though she would be open to it, even though she *wanted* it.

Even though *he* wanted it just as much. Maybe more because he wanted to prove to her that he wanted her and not Trina.

That Tammy was more and special and—

"No," he said, more to himself than to his brother. Mostly because he'd forgotten that Sean had been talking at all. He needed to rein it in and focus on winning Tammy over.

She wanted him.

She wasn't as allergic to relationships as she made herself out to be.

It was in the pain on her face that he'd caught a glimpse of on the back deck. It was in the way she interacted with his parents, with Sean and Carrie, with Jim and Hayley. It was the regret in her eyes when she'd worried that he hadn't been aware enough to consent. It was the way she was so fucking capable at everything—work, cooking for his family without a blink, getting along easily with this group even though she didn't know them. It was stepping into a situation to help someone that she absolutely didn't have to.

Tammy was attached.

She was just spending a lot of time pretending she wasn't.

"So, why does she look like she wants to throttle you?"

Blinking up at Sean, he frowned as the words processed then turned to glance back at Tammy.

Yup.

Daggers might as well be flying from her eyes.

"None of your business," he muttered.

"Hmm."

"Shouldn't you be paying attention to your soon-to-be-bride?"

"She and Mom are busy."

And they were—spreading out a blanket, unpacking the sandwiches Tammy had made earlier, setting out utensils and the container of fruit salad.

"Don't be an asshole," he muttered. "Help your almost wife."

Carrie glanced up and smiled at his brother. Sean quit with his tormenting and took a step toward his fiancé. Whipped.

Just as bad as Fletcher was.

Attempting casual—and probably not looking casual at all —he sidled his way toward Tammy.

She smelled like fall.

She personified temptation.

She was everything he'd ever dreamed of wanting.

He slipped an arm around her waist, slid close, and though she went stiff, she didn't push him away. Probably because Hayley was there, because his family was surrounding them, and maybe it made him an asshole, but he was soaking up any inch she was giving him, so he didn't move away, just held her a little tighter, inhaled the scent of her hair.

Narrowed eyes on his. "Did you just sniff me?"

A shrug. "Maybe."

More narrowing. "Why?"

"Because you smell good."

She snorted. "You've lost your mind."

"Maybe." He sniffed again.

Her eyes were wide when she gazed up at him. "Fletcher," she said on a chuckle.

He bent, nuzzled her ear. "I like you, Tammy Huntington. A whole lot." Straightening, he saw the panic in her eyes, dipping into the lines of her face, watched the shield slide in place over her features. "Don't worry," he said.

A deep V between her brows. "About what?"

About so many things—the least of which being the fact that he wasn't going to stop liking her, that he was going to get Tammy to like him too, that he was going to maybe do more than just liking—and do that soon—but because just him declaring he liked her had her freaking out, he was going to keep that last bit of information to himself.

"Anything," he murmured. "Don't worry about anything."

Her frown deepened. "I—"

And just because he could, because he couldn't stop himself, because he thought he might die if he didn't do it, Fletcher closed the distance between their mouths and kissed her.

Deeply.

Her lips were unmoving against his.

At least until he touched his tongue to the seam of her mouth. Then they parted and he found himself drawing her closer, tangling his fingers into her hair, deepening the kiss. She released a breath, or maybe it was a moan. Either way, it flowed from her mouth to his, dancing across his tastebuds, overfilling them, marking them, scorching them, changing them forever.

Tongue and teeth and lips.

Soft breasts, firm thighs, sharp nails biting into the muscles of his arms.

Silken hair, breathy moans, and...

A sharp smack on the back of his head.

"Didn't you get enough alone time in the trees?" his dad muttered.

Fletch was slow to emerge from the fog that only Tammy seemed to be able to create, even slower to process the words his dad was saying. But the hardest thing was to tear his mouth free, to release her, to keep his fucking hands and tongue to himself.

They had witnesses.

He couldn't fuck her here.

As much as he wanted to.

"Go on," he murmured when he was finally able to break away, nudging Tammy toward the blanket and the food that was laid out, somehow able to make his voice sound almost normal, even though his lungs were screaming and his dick felt as though it had been turned into some robot dick that never got soft, or like he'd OD'd on Viagra. "You should eat."

She glanced up at him, lips swollen and tempting him. He wanted to kiss her again. Especially when she asked, her expression a bit befuddled, her eyes soft, her pupils dilated, "Eat?"

"Go have a sandwich, sweetheart," he whispered, taking her hand and bringing her to the blanket. "Then it'll be time to get the snowshoes on."

The haze began to clear. "Oh, God. The snowshoes."

His mom took Tammy's hand, tugged her down onto the blanket—yes, they were having a picnic in the middle of the woods in early winter, snow just up the mountain ahead of them. But then again, this was Carrie and Sean's weekend and if there was anything the two of them loved more than each other, it was nature. They'd met on a ski lift as kids. Been best friends for years—hiking, boating, rafting, backpacking, rock climbing, mountain biking. If there was an outdoor activity to be tried, they did it.

And every year they skied every day they could.

Which was why Fletcher's brother had proposed at the top of their favorite black diamond.

"The snowshoes sound scarier than they are," he heard his mom say as he grabbed a sandwich and slipped from the clearing. His dick was throbbing, pushing against the zipper of his jeans, and since he really didn't want to be sporting a boner in front of his family, he slipped away and leaned against a tree, well away from the circle, soaking in the cool air—and hoping it would all go to his cock so the fucking steel rod in his pants would go away—and tried to settle himself.

Because the one thought raging through him was that Tammy Huntington needed to be his.

Only slightly tempered because *he* also needed to belong to her.

Not because of Trina or the chemistry or the most erotic dream/experience of his life.

But because now that he'd gotten a glimpse of the unguarded vulnerability in Tammy's heart, the sweet and caring center, the way she could charm and joke and slide so easily into his life...he couldn't imagine a future without her.

It was funny. He'd known he'd liked her, known he'd respected her, but after that first day at the office—the way she'd reacted when he'd asked her to the work crew Happy Hour—there had understandably been a wall between them.

Reinforced by steel and concrete and barbed wire on her side.

Solid on his because he didn't want to overstep.

Now there was a door in that wall.

One he could unlock, could push open.

Thirteen

Tammy

She sniffed.

And wiped a tear away.

Seriously, why did she always get so emotional at weddings?

Well, truthfully, this wasn't a wedding. It was a centering ceremony complete with sage burning and candles being lit and placed in the four cardinal directions. The ceremony itself was more meditation than actual pomp. But it was still beautiful—Carrie having them all sit down on the blanket again, breathing deeply, and then closing their eyes and soaking in the nature around them.

At first, Tammy had only been able to soak in the fact that her ass was freezing, sitting on that blanket.

It had been cold when they'd stopped for lunch, but there hadn't been any snow where they'd eaten, and though the ground had been cool, it wasn't like sitting on snow.

Eventually, she came to terms with the fact that the cold wasn't going anywhere, but also that the cold wasn't a wet cold.

It didn't soak through the blanket. Her ass may be frozen, but it wasn't wet.

Winning.

And then, as Carrie continued talking, it became less about the cold and her frozen limbs and more about love and joy and happiness—of a present that was so jam-packed with those things that it threatened to explode the confines of reality, of a future filled with life blasting past that reality time and again.

She spoke of tough times and easy ones, of a love that sometimes hurt.

But even those hurts were made easier because they had each other.

Most times, Tammy didn't miss having another half—especially when she understood the risks that such a partnership wrought—but weddings were always tough, the prospect of happy marriages even more so. She had the example of her parents, her brothers, knew that HEAs could happen.

Just...it was a scary fucking idea.

And the one time she thought that she might have found her person—

Fingers on her cheek.

Her eyes flew open, and she saw Fletcher's hand, his thumb glistening with another tear she hadn't realized had escaped. He reached forward and wiped again, this time the other cheek, and then lightly brushed his lips over the damp skin.

Goose bumps on her nape, a strange pounding in her heart.

Something like...longing.

Oh fuck.

She couldn't think about that right now. It was just...yeah, no, she couldn't think about *that* without freaking the fuck out, and she didn't think Carrie would appreciate that during her centering ceremony.

Running screaming through the snow, knocking candles over, potentially starting a forest fire in her idiocy?

Yeah, that wouldn't be the greatest.

Fletch slipped an arm around her shoulders, brought her close to his side.

And somehow that quieted the panic.

Loosened her lungs, slowed her pulse, made it so that her skin didn't feel like it was three sizes too small.

This was stupid.

She should pull away.

But by then Fletcher's warmth was soaking into her side, and it felt so good that she didn't move away.

Instead, she found herself giving him more of her weight.

Leaning into him and closing her eyes again.

And listening to Carrie's soft words of love and fulfillment.

Until they flowed over her with such force that she began to wonder if perhaps such a thing was possible for her after all.

Began to *wish* it was.

———

"And then you'll stop here, Hayley will fix your dress, and take your bouquet," Connie was saying, having stepped into the role of wedding planner extraordinaire.

Hayley pretended to take the bouquet, to fluff the wedding dress Carrie would be wearing the next day, and then stood in the spot indicated for her role of maid of honor. The other woman did it with joy in her eyes for her friend, and Tammy couldn't help but miss her own friends.

Connie propelled the ceremony forward and the happy couple proceeded through a shortened version of the "We have gathered here todays" and the vows they would be exchanging.

"Jim," Connie said once that was done. "Do you have the rings?"

"I—uh—right this moment?" he replied, clearly missing the

part where he was supposed to be pretending this was the real thing.

Hayley rolled her eyes, the nonverbal, *Men, sigh,* obvious.

Connie sighed, and her *Men, sigh* wasn't kept in her mind or on her face. It was spoken out loud.

Jim cringed.

"You'll have the rings tomorrow?" Connie asked sharply, and the only answer one could give—and still want to live—was yes.

Luckily, even though Jim might not be keen for pretend play, he was a smart cookie.

He answered without preamble. "Yes."

See? Smart man.

Connie stared at him with narrowed eyes.

"Yes," he repeated. "I'll definitely have the rings tomorrow. I—uh—" He patted his pockets, pulled out a keyring, and quickly shifted the keys around until he had two of the silver rings free. "I have these now!"

Connie's eyes softened slightly as he handed the silver keyrings to Sean.

Who grimaced.

"Thanks, man," Sean stage whispered, "don't worry about her. She'll chill once I get a couple of lemon drops in her at the rehearsal dinner."

Connie huffed. "I will not—"

"And *that's* enough, sweetheart," Tony said, swooping in and winding an arm around her waist. "You guys will do the ring exchange thing"—he waved a hand with a casualness that Connie wholly didn't support based on the outraged gasp she released (and that Tony caught on his tongue with a kiss that was very much not wedding appropriate)—"then you'll do the kissing thing—"

"Hopefully with as much passion as you two," Hayley whispered, and Tammy had to bite back a giggle because she'd been thinking the exact same thing.

She wanted someone to love her as much as Tony and Connie loved each other.

With love and passion and bickering and joy and...

With everything.

It was just...no one had ever truly chosen her.

Not *her*. Not Tammy.

Not as a baby or a young woman.

Not now.

Because you push them away.

Maybe she did.

No. She *knew* she did. Other women were fine. Co-workers —not the sleazy trying to get in her pants type—were fine. Men were fine. So long as they didn't get too close. So long as they didn't get attached.

So long as *she* didn't get attached.

Right. *That* was the truth she preferred to keep tucked down. *Way* down.

Buried in the Mariana Trench down.

"And then we'll all cheer and high five," Tony declared, "and you'll walk down the aisle as man and wife—"

Connie swatted him. "Husband and wife," she grumbled. "Women aren't the only ones with the title."

"Husband and wife," Tony corrected without missing a beat. "Then pictures and food and drinking all the lemon drops you want." He kissed the tip of Connie's nose.

Connie swatted him again. "Then pictures, cocktail hour, food, speeches, dancing, bouquet toss, garter toss, cake cutting, and *then* drinking all the lemon drops."

Tony, in all his infinite husband smartness didn't roll his eyes —though his expression seemed to be indicating that he wanted to. Still, he held it back and just nodded. "After all of that," he agreed, "then lemon drops. But for tonight, we're done with this, and it's time to go to dinner."

Connie's eyes went wide. "We really should go over everything one more time—"

"It's just walking up and down the aisle," Tony began. "The kids have it."

Connie started sputtered. "It-it's ju-just *walking?*" Her jaw clenched. "There's the music they have to time their steps to, and the flower girls have to know the proper way to distribute their petals, and I still haven't taught Sean the proper way to hold Carrie's arm so he doesn't step on her train and—"

Carrie stepped down off the altar and leaned close to the side Tony hadn't sidled up to. "Connie?" she asked, linking their arms together.

"Yeah, honey?" Connie asked, sweet as pie.

"I'm really hungry."

Connie snapped to attention—or rather, since she'd been at full attention from the moment they'd all entered the small church, she relaxed marginally.

Okay.

She didn't relax. Not in the least.

Instead, she turned off wedding planner extraordinaire and turned on Mom Mode Extraordinaire.

One movement had her wrapping a hand around their linked arms. Another had her drawing Carrie down the aisle. "Let's go!" she called. "No more delaying. The bride is hungry, and we need to go before we're late for our reservation! Hustle, people. Hustle!"

"She's a loon," Fletcher whispered.

"I don't know if I should be proud or amazed or frightened," she whispered back.

He stepped closer, and she had had bite back a shiver. Or maybe it was a groan, especially when him being near meant that she remembered the orgasms he'd given her. Dangerous,

dangerous man. "All three," he murmured, and when he spoke the words in her ear, she found that this time she couldn't hold back the shiver that rolled through her frame, not when the words puffed over her skin, not when he was so near.

She tried to step away, but he merely followed her, his arms coming around her, his mouth staying near her ear. "We should catch up to them."

Teeth on her lobe. "In a minute."

Her lips parted on a moan, fingers somehow finding their way to his hair. Holding him to her.

When she should be backing away.

Dammit!

His tongue slid out, caressed over her ear.

More shivering.

More dammit.

"You're overstepping, King," she muttered.

"Your fingers are in my hair, holding me to you," he murmured against her jaw. "You like it."

"I don't," she said immediately because...pride and all that.

Another flick of that tongue. "Admit it, Huntington. You. Like. It."

It took everything in her to hold back her shudder, and she had the feeling that he knew she was practically biting her tongue off in order to not melt in his hold. She sniffed. "You wish."

A nip to her throat. "I *know*."

Cocky. So damned cocky.

And why was all that cocky so damned attractive? Hmm? Probably because she'd had the damn man's *cock,* and it was fucking good and—

Fuck it.

She tore away from him.

"Tam—" he began, his eyes filled with concern.

Concern she didn't bother addressing. Instead, she grabbed

his hand, and began dragging him toward the side door. She'd been in and out that door more than a half dozen times as she'd helped Connie bring in various things for the wedding the next day. Those boxes were currently stacked in the hall she was dragging Fletcher through.

Because though she wasn't particularly religious, she drew the line at liaisons in a church.

And she and Fletcher were damned well going to have a liaison.

Right this moment.

Just not in a house of God.

She pushed through the door, led him through the vine-covered arbor and into the trees, to the bench she'd rested at in between one of her many trips.

"Sweetheart," Fletcher said, his brows furrowed, "is everything—"

No. *Nothing* was okay. This was supposed to be a silly pretend weekend with no strings, and instead it had become something more. She liked him, and not just his body. He had flaws and owned up to them. He was easy with affection and praise and his family was really fucking cool. It was easy to pretend she fit in here. Easy to acknowledge that she wanted more.

But it was going to end. And she didn't want to think about that, didn't want to think about wanting something that was more than sex.

She wanted an orgasm, a fuzzy mind, to get lost in the bliss of the moment.

And then, come Monday, to pretend that none of this ever happened.

FOURTEEN

FLETCHER

He didn't even finish asking if she was okay before Tammy launched herself into his arms, mashing their mouths together so hard that he nearly bit his tongue off.

But before he could pull away, her fingers slid into his hair, angled his head and the kiss went explosive.

Maybe it was the ache in his tongue.

Maybe it was the answering ache in his cock.

All he knew was that Tammy kissed him until he couldn't see straight, couldn't feel anything except the lush curves of her body, couldn't process the cold, the darkening sky, the whisper of the breeze.

It was Tammy and *only* Tammy.

She pushed him slightly, and he found the backs of his knees against something hard. Another push had him dropping onto a bench, Tammy's mouth still pressed to his, her tongue delving deep, her fingers gripping tight.

His lungs were on fire.

His hands had somehow found their way to her ass, were pulling her toward him, trying to get Tammy into his lap so he could do all the things he wanted to her.

But she was slipping out of his hold, loosening her fingers from his hair, and...

Dropping to her knees in front of him, her hands going to the waistband of his jeans, flicking open the button and tugging down the zipper.

He reached for her. "Tam—"

She pulled out his cock and sucked it deep into her mouth.

"Oh, fuck," he groaned, gripping the bench, using every bit of his control to not thrust into her mouth. He could feel himself hitting the back of her throat, didn't want to gag her, but fuck, it felt incredible, and he wanted more, wanted deeper, wanted—

She dragged her teeth up the length of his cock, laved the underside with her tongue.

His groan was torn out of him and probably loud enough to echo through the granite of the mountains, but he was beyond caring. Not when she added her hand, twisting and gripping tight. Not when her tongue and teeth continued working him.

Not when—

More teeth and then suction.

And Fletcher knew he was a hairsbreadth away from losing it.

Somehow, he summoned the inhuman strength to reach for her, to tug her off his cock when he wanted desperately to come in her mouth. But he wanted to come inside her more, *needed* to come in her.

Awake.

Not in a dream.

Just him and Tammy and—

He brought her toward him, sending her clambering onto his lap. Her dress pooled around their waists, and he could feel the heat of her pussy through the dampened fabric of her panties as they brushed over him, once, twice—

Fletcher snaked his hands up and yanked at them, tearing the delicate lace material off one hip, bunching the fabric to the side so she could rub wet heat over him.

Teasing.

Desperate.

Her. *Him*.

Grabbing at her hips again, drawing her up enough to position himself at her entrance. Then he shifted, lifted his hips at the same time he brought her down...and he was home.

They both froze, moans tumbling off their tongues.

Tight and hot, clasping him in a rhythm that threatened to send him out of control, the urge to thrust and fuck and pound into her nearly overwhelming. But he wanted her to know this meant something to him, that he was with her, and her alone.

So...slow and gentle.

Rocking first, grinding into her. Holding her close and guiding her into a rhythm that was controlled and easy, like they had all the time in the world, even though they obviously didn't. Even though someone could easily stumble onto them. Even though they shouldn't be doing this right now, not with the rehearsal dinner happening, not with Sean and Carrie's day being more important than an orgasm.

But this wasn't just an orgasm.

This was Tammy.

This was him showing her that he wanted her. *Her*. Not someone else.

Just the sexy, sweet, funny woman who he liked a whole hell of a lot.

So, he went slow. One hand on her hips, holding her as she moved on him, the other cupping her cheek, running a thumb across her bottom lip. "Tammy," he murmured and bit back a groan when she clenched around him, began rocking faster. "*Baby.*" He dropped his mouth to hers, kissed her deeply. "Fuck, you feel so good," he told her when they broke apart to breathe. "You're so fucking good, baby—"

He choked.

Because she all but leaped off his lap. The cold air hit his cock—hence the choking—and then he was watching Tammy back away from him.

Dread began coiling in his stomach, but before it could truly gather, before he could even ask if he'd been wrong, if she didn't want this, if this was too much too fast, she was bending over the bench. One hand on the cool stone. The other reaching for the hem of her dress.

Tugging it up.

Baring her ass and spreading her thighs, giving him a glimpse of a swollen, glistening pussy.

"Well," she said, glancing back at him over her shoulder, "are we both coming?"

His breath caught. His cock somehow grew harder.

"Come back here and we will."

"I'm tired of doing all the work," she teased and tugged her dress a little higher, spread her legs a bit wider. "I want you to come here."

And like he could deny her anything.

He pushed off the bench, closed the couple of feet between them.

"Inside," she ordered, thrusting her hips back, getting his cock wet again.

Fletcher slid home, and fuck she was tight from this angle. She squeezed him almost painfully and then began moving against him, shifting forward, slamming back hard.

"Fuck me," she said, another order. "Fuck me now and hard, Fletcher. I need it. Please," she said and the intensity, the command had disappeared. Instead, it was full of pleading. "Please, Fletcher. Please, fuck me hard."

He slid an arm up her front, shoved his hand into the bodice of her dress, massaging her breast, pinching her nipple.

Probably a bit too hard, but she wanted hard.

And when he used his other hand to grip her hip, when he began fucking her furiously, obliging her when she demanded he go deeper, thrust faster.

It wasn't soft and sweet and gentle.

It was rapid and brutal and intense.

It was still the best sex of his life, but it wasn't emotional. It wasn't deep.

Well, he was fucking her deep, but he didn't feel this in his heart, was hard-pressed to capture anything other than sensation, pleasure, desire, and need. Primal, basic need that had him forgetting about emotion, about soft and sweet.

Tammy was moaning, her head tossed back, red hair flowing over her shoulders, pale brown eyes hooded and filled with fire, bright white teeth biting into a lush bottom lip.

"Fuck, Tammy," he gritted.

She was so fucking beautiful. "Yes," she moaned, bucking her gorgeous ass against him, "*fuck* Tammy."

So, he did.

He massaged her breast, rolled her nipple, continued to pound into her. And it didn't take long for him to focus on nothing other than giving her the best fucking orgasm of her life.

Sliding out, slamming back in.

Releasing her breast and slipping a hand between her legs.

Vision going blurry as he sought the spot, the rhythm, the touch that made her squeeze even tighter around him, that had her crying out, her head thrown back, moans tumbling from her lips. "Yes. *Yes.* Right there"—she reached down, pressed his fingers more firmly against her pussy, coaxing them to circle her clit—"Oh, God. Yes, Fletch. Right *there.*"

He kept his hand where she wanted it, continued pressing and circling, moving in and out, feeling his own release creep up his spine, start to spiral outward.

Fuck.

It was spiraling fast.

Sweat prickled down his spine, his lips went numb, and he felt almost dizzy as he focused on one thing, and one thing only: getting Tammy to come before he did.

"Fletch—*oh, God.*"

His vision began to blur, his fingers cramp, and—

She went ramrod stiff for a heartbeat and then melted as she came, his name a gasp, her pussy a tight clasp around his cock, milking him and drawing him that last little bit of the way over the edge as his own release surrounded him.

For a second, it felt as though he'd been swimming and was tugged sharply underwater—a la scary as shit *Jaws* vibes —vision blacking out, lungs without air, body feeling like it had been yanked beneath the surface of reality. But just as quickly, he emerged, propelled up through that viscous layer of thoughts, flying through into fresh air, into real life, into wave after wave after *wave* of pleasure crashing into him.

He'd been wrong. It wasn't just physical, even though she tried to make it that way.

It was the dream.

It was so much more.

It was *everything*.

"Tammy," he said, reaching forward and turning her head so he could meet her eyes. "*My* Tammy."

Something flared on her face, in those pale brown depths, and then her lids slid closed, her lips parted on a breath as she slumped down onto the bench.

Fletcher caught her, dragged her close to his chest.

His heart thundered, absolutely thundered against his

ribcage, and his skin felt like it was on fire. Every single muscle in his body was strained, having long since gone limp.

Except the ones keeping her to him.

And the muscle working the hardest?

His heart.

FIFTEEN

TAMMY

This had been a mistake.

A serious miscalculation on her part.

Why had she thought fucking Fletcher would cure her of any feelings she had for him?

Oh yeah, because it had always worked in the past.

Seriously, she was a dumb ass. None of her usual tactics were going to work when it came to Fletcher King. She should know that by now. Nothing had been usual. Nothing had gone to plan. It was all fucked, had been from the moment she'd agreed to help him with the wedding, pretending it was just doing a favor for a coworker.

Fletcher had always been more than a coworker, even though she'd tried to tell herself otherwise.

It was in how she reacted to that invitation the first day.

The coldness she'd treated him with after that.

If she were being truly honest, she'd known he wasn't a creeper, even newly meeting him. It was just safer and more convenient to despise him.

Especially when he made her feel...

All the wrong things.

But now, after sex in which she'd tried to deliberately erect some distance between them, she found herself falling even further in with him.

Because it had been hard and fast and intense as hell.

And it had been perfect and soulful and...the way he'd rasped out, "My Tammy," his fingers on her jaw, his eyes boring into hers...it had shattered right through any protections she'd erected. She'd wanted him to continue doing that forever.

He'd looked at her like she was worthwhile.

Like she could be his forever.

She...wanted to be.

Fuck.

He was still inside her and instead of wanting him to leave, to give her space, to pull out so she could put herself to rights and pretend that what had happened between them was just an absolutely scorching orgasm, she wanted him to stay inside her, to keep pumping, to extend the moment. She wanted to not have an IUD, to not have used condoms because they were building a family, a future, rather than just because she was stupid and too turned on to think straight.

And *that* more than anything had her drawing away, closing her eyes, and feigning exhaustion.

Even though fight or flight hormones were pumping through her veins. Even though adrenaline coursed through her —because she was so fucking stupid thinking about making babies when she should be thinking about her job, about making a name for herself, about proving she was just as much of a Huntington as her mom, her siblings.

Not just an HR clerk.

But someone who was changing the landscape of her company, of the industry.

She wasn't saving animals' lives or taking a company public or starting a billion-dollar company like her siblings or mom.

Her life was great. She worked hard.

But at the moment, she wasn't doing anything spectacular.

She wasn't making that difference she wanted to be making.

She was just Tammy, an assistant HR specialist, who was just starting to get her career where she wanted it to be.

Which was why she shouldn't be thinking of making babies.

Tell that to yourself when you're not being ridden bareback, the man's sperm dripping down your thighs.

Smothering a wince, she forced herself to acknowledge that, yes, that had been stupid, and that, no, she wouldn't be doing that any longer.

That being fucking Fletcher King within an inch of both of their lives.

Work first. Career first.

No entanglements.

Said while the man who was creating *all* the entanglements was still hard and inside her.

Never let it be stated that she wasn't hypocritical.

Cute.

"Sweetheart." Warm, calloused fingers on her cheek. How did he have callouses? He worked in an office just like her, and it wasn't like she was getting roughened fingertips from typing on her computer all day and night.

And *that* was an aside she shouldn't be thinking about.

Not with him hard and inside her and—

God, seriously. She needed to stop thinking about the man's cock and the man's hands and the man himself and—

Those fingers drifted down, and he wrapped his arm around the front of her chest and slowly tilted her so she was upright. Then his other stayed at her hip, and she released a sigh of displeasure—

Fuck, come on!

Displeasure? *Really?*

But he was so fucking gentle when he pulled out of her, and when that made a bigger mess between her legs, he simply released her, and set her on the bench. Then he tugged his sweater over his head, dragged off the T-shirt he wore beneath, and then used the material to clean her up.

"I should have used a condom," he said, leaning back on his heels and staring up at her. And God, why did the man have to look like a fucking movie star? She wanted to count his ab muscles like a toddler practiced their numbers—*one, two, three-four-five, I wish I caught a fish alive, six, seven, eight-nine-ten, then I threw him back again.*

No, he didn't have a ten-pack, but he had six yummy squares she wanted to trace with her tongue.

One, two, three-four-five-six.

That didn't have quite the same rhyme to it.

And—oh God—she was really losing it.

One cock, three glorious orgasms, and a man being nice to her, and she was losing her fucking mind.

Buck the fuck up, Huntington. This weekend means nothing. Fletcher means nothing.

It will all go back to normal on Monday—

"I'm sorry I didn't protect you."

Crack.

She practically felt the wall around her reverberate with the impact of his words.

It teetered on the edge of a precipice, its top wavering, the once solid concrete transforming into a stack of bricks that had lost their mortar, lost their combined strength. That undulation began at the highest portion, and it vibrated through the height, shuddering, shifting, and...

Collapsing.

Her heart, along with the noise of that collapse, were both so loud in her ears she was surprised Fletcher didn't hear it, shocked that it didn't blow back the branches of the trees, knock the pine needles off and onto the ground.

It was like an explosion had happened.

Only it was just inside her head.

I'm sorry I didn't protect you.

How? How did he know that was the thing she most wanted to hear?

My Tammy.

Maybe the second most thing she was desperate to hear.

Because *My Tammy* took the cake.

"I'm clean," he said. "I just had my had my physical last week. All the blood work came back clear, but if you're not on birth control—"

"I have an IUD. I'm clean. Got tested just this week. After —" She cleared her throat as he finished wiping her thighs, bunching the T-shirt in his hand. "After the scene you saw at my house, I knew I needed to start fresh, and I always do that with a clean bill of health." She lifted her chin as he straightened the skirt of her dress, half-expecting all the soft and protective to have disappeared, derision in its place. "I also don't normally have sex without a condom."

Never.

She'd never had sex without a condom.

Except with Fletcher.

The remains of the wall inside her mind, her heart, shifted, burping up dust and debris like a dragon breathing fire.

"Smart," he said, stroking his hands down her calves before reaching for his sweater and pulling it over his head. "And I'm glad. Not that I wouldn't take care of you if that happened, but I'm not normally a man who does this without checking that you're protected." Fierce eyes on hers. "So, I'm sorry."

"It's my fault—"

"It's not like I tried to stop the event from happening," he said.

"I instigated."

A shrug, one half of his mouth tipping up. "I happily went along with what you were instigating."

"I've slept with a lot of people," she pressed, not sure why she was pushing this except that she was probably trying to find another angle to retreat, especially with her heart so open and vulnerable. "I should know better."

This is where the derision should circle back and return in full force. But instead, his eyes stayed fierce and his expression soft. "*I* should have known better."

God, why did this man make it so hard to push him away?

Because you don't want to.

Judgy bitch in her mind.

She sighed, glanced out toward the trees. The arbor had tiny twinkling lights woven through it, glimmering in the evening. It had grown quite dark, the sky more navy than sky blue overhead, the planets and the stars shining—though clouds hung over the half-sphere of the atmosphere like diaphanous curtains, softening the light. The entire scene had become ridiculously romantic and if not for the chill creeping into the air, sinking into her bared legs, her exposed arms and chest, she might have thought about a round three.

Only this time, soft and gentle with Fletcher taking her on a bed of pine needles, condom or not.

Or not.

She might as well make it a trifecta.

See? Losing. Her. Mind.

"Come on," he murmured, tugging her up to her feet, slipping an arm around her waist, and drawing her into his side. "Let's get your coat and go meet everyone for dinner."

She groaned.

"What?" he asked, leading them back down the path and toward the church.

Also, side note: now that she wasn't writhing with desire,

with a desperate need to pretend nothing inside her had changed, she realized that she was probably going to hell for fucking in the churchyard, even though she hadn't actually boned Fletcher in the church itself.

She was pretty sure that God didn't appreciate premarital sex anywhere on her (yes, *her*—Tammy said it, okay?) grounds.

"What?" Fletcher asked again. "What's that groan for?"

"They're all going to know what we were doing," she moaned.

"You mean because you have just-been-fucked hair?"

Another groan. "Yes, because of *that* exactly."

He lightly tugged a lock of her hair and tucked it behind her ear. "They'll know. They won't care."

"But they'll still know," she muttered as he tugged open the church door. She hesitated on the threshold and carefully stepped over, half-expecting to be smote (smitted? smitten?) Ah, fuck it. That didn't matter. Not when her sinning foot had already hit the pale red carpeting. When she wasn't reduced to ashes, she walked forward with Fletcher, bypassing the altar and the pews as he led her to the closet where they'd stored their coats earlier (and seriously, good man for remembering them because she was freaking freezing now). "And now," she whispered as he held up her jacket so she could shrug into it—whispering because the priest might still be around and she didn't need another religious crisis on her hands if he overheard their sexual escapades, "we're missing part of the rehearsal dinner because I needed an orgasm courtesy of Fletcher King and—"

He tugged her hair again.

"What?" she snapped.

"They'll know," he said again. "They won't care."

"I—"

He bent enough so their gazes could meet, his eyes close to hers, his expression equal parts amused and intense. "They. Won't. Care," he repeated. "You make me happy. That's the only thing that matters. So, we miss some appetizers. Locata's fried cheese is delicious, but you're a thousand times better—"

"Fried cheese?" she moaned. "Everyone's going to know we were fucking like bunnies on the church's grounds, *and* we're missing *fried cheese*?"

That wasn't quiet at all.

Hell, she was practically shouting about their boning good time. She might as well have hollered for the priest and confessed there and then. She was so freaking smooth. And yes, she was mentally rolling her eyes. So much for her trying to be discreet.

Fletcher shrugged into his coat. "I don't think fried cheese can compare to a Fletcher King orgasm."

"You don't know how much I like cheese."

His fingers were on the collar of his jacket, and her statement had him freezing.

Then something wonderful happened.

Something that made a giant vacuum appear in her mind— or maybe a huge sinkhole opened up. Either way, all that debris and dust and crumbled remnants of that wall disappeared.

And she was left wide open.

But his laugh—that wonderful laugh—it rolled over her, filled her up, encased her exposed and vulnerable heart in a protective bubble.

Open.

Exposed.

Safe.

That was her with Fletcher King.

Sixteen

Fletcher

"Dance?" he murmured into her ear.

The wedding was over—or at least the ceremony was. Jim had remembered the rings. Hayley had fluffed Carrie's dress perfectly. His mom was on her third lemon drop and finally had chilled the fuck out.

The garter and bouquet had been tossed.

Cake had been consumed.

Now Sean and Carrie were draped over each other on the dance floor, the slow thump of a song resonating through the heated tent.

Twinkly lights and cool air.

Reminding him of the night before.

Of the distance and the wall, and how things had shifted afterward.

How Tammy had softened.

She'd held his hand as they'd walked out of the church, didn't shrug off his arm when he'd cautiously slid it around her at dinner—after the teasing had subsided and their entrees (along with an extra appetizer of fried cheese his mom in all her detailed glory had ordered for them) had arrived. Teasing Tammy had endured with just the barest hint of pink on her cheeks as she drawled a diffusing, "Oh, the power of young love," before turning the conversation to her parents and their penchant for PDA.

Which then Sean, Carrie, and he had picked up, teasing Fletcher's mom and dad about all of *their* PDA.

It had been light and easy, just like so many of his other interactions with Tammy.

Even though his heart had pulsed when she'd talked of young love—

Yes, he was falling hard and falling fast.

No, he didn't care.

Fried cheese had been consumed. Tammy hadn't seemed bothered in the least by the chicken Parmesan that his mom had ordered for her, nor by the teasing.

Nor by his arm.

She'd relaxed into his side, and at one point, she'd even rested her head on his shoulder.

They'd cleared a hurdle.

He wasn't entirely sure what that hurdle was. He only knew that she seemed to be unable or unwilling to push him away, and he was going to go with it.

He was going to charm the shit out of her.

He was going to keep clearing hurdles.

He was going to get her to like him so much that she wouldn't erect more walls, throw up *more* hurdles.

He was going to make it so she couldn't kick him out of her house, her heart. That this would continue to be more than a booty call, more than just physical chemistry and a couple of great orgasms. Fletcher was going to win her over.

And step one of his plan was dancing.

Now, he was a shit dancer.

But it was just one step in his plan to win Tammy.

Keep her close. Take advantage of the chemistry between them. Claim her heart.

"Come on, sweetheart," he murmured when she didn't move, probably because the song blaring through the air was critically romantic, "dance with me."

Conflict on her face. "Fletch—"

"I won't step on your toes, I promise," he told her, nipping lightly at her ear, hoping that he could keep that promise.

"It's not that," she said, turning her head slightly, as though offering her mouth to him.

He took that offering, slanting his mouth over hers. The kiss quickly escalated, as was typical when any part of him was touching any part of her.

But he did manage to summon some control and pull back.

Fletch extended a hand, tugged her to her feet when she dropped her palm into his.

She winced.

He froze. "What's wrong?"

"It's nothing." She started to take a step toward the dance floor.

Catching her around the waist and stepping up so his front was to her back, her perfect ass pressed to his pelvis, reminding him that it had been more than twenty-four hours since he'd had her, and as much as he'd liked holding her as they slept last night, it wasn't the same as being inside her. She'd been tipsy and sleepy and had crashed nearly the moment her head had hit the pillow —which meant he'd been able to cuddle up without her reverting to distance. A victory in and of itself, but obviously that couldn't compare with being inside her, with the passion and the heat, the way she looked at him when he was sliding home.

Because that's what it felt like.

Finding home.

The cuddling was...just another piece of the puzzle.

A big one. Or maybe a corner piece—the beginning of two directions, the building blocks for something bigger.

And *that* was enough time in his head.

He needed to focus on the present, on why Tammy was grimacing.

"What's wrong?" he asked again. "Why are you wincing?"

She took a step toward the floor, trying to pull away from him, but he kept close, continuing to enjoy the feel of her body pressed to his. "I'm fine," she muttered.

"That's not what I asked," he replied, shifting a little nearer, bringing his mouth to her ear again.

He was slowly finding all her spots—or quickly, he supposed considering he was on day three of being in a fake relationship and able to touch her, and slightly more than twenty-four hours of being in whatever type of strange in-between limbo they were currently residing within. Regardless of the timeline, her neck was sensitive, her jaw even more so. But the spot that had her melting against him every single time?

The delicate patch of skin just behind her ear.

As it did in that instant.

"Why, sweetheart?" he murmured, brushing a kiss to that spot.

A sigh, her body melting against his. "Stubborn," she muttered, but gave it up. "It's nothing. My feet are killing me, that's all. These shoes"—he flicked out his tongue, tasted her again, made her melt even more against him—"look sexy, but they're hell on my tootsies."

He smiled against her skin. "Tootsies?"

"Yup. Toot—*oh!*"

He'd scooped her up in his arms, careful to make sure the skirt of her dress didn't lift or slip to the side and flash everyone. Because her squeal had garnered attention.

"What are you—?"

"Saving your feet," he said, carrying her toward one of the open sides of the tent.

"Oh, and are we going to dance like this, too?" she deadpanned.

He kissed the tip of her nose, smiled at the sparks in her pretty brown eyes. "Do you want to?"

She shuddered. "God no."

"Good." He stepped out of the tent, and as he took off for one of the tables that was clustered under an outdoor heater, the output of which was barely cutting through the night air—and long since abandoned as people sought the warmth of the tent— Fletch heard his brother quip, "I'm supposed to be the one doing the threshold carrying."

Fletch spun and shifted enough to raise a hand, lifting his middle finger.

Sean just laughed before returning his focus to his bride.

Fletcher didn't waste any more time or energy. He just kept walking, heading for that cluster of tables, setting Tammy down in one of the chairs. She shivered, and he draped his suit jacket over her shoulders, shifting around her to button the fabric over her front. It dwarfed her and for the first time, he realized how small she was.

Strange.

Her personality. Her *heart* always made her seem larger than life.

But she was tiny.

"You're like an adorable elf," he told her. "All you're missing are the pointy ears and the *Lord of the Rings* robes."

A roll of her eyes as she shoved her hands into the pocket of his jacket. "I'll have you know that most of the *LOTR* elves are tall."

"Really?" he asked, shifting to kneel at her feet. "How do you know that?"

"I don't." Said with such confidence that it took a beat for
him to process the words. Then he burst out laughing, a longer
pause as he struggled to control himself. Then, "But I choose to
believe that elves are tall and slender. Thus"—her chin lifted—
"they are everything I'm not."

"Well, good thing I like short and curvy."

She smiled even as she shook her head.

He reached for her ankle, started to undo the strap on her
shoe.

Tammy yanked her foot away. "Wh-what are you doing?"

"Your feet hurt."

"I—"

He calmly grasped her ankle and unbuckled her shoe,
slipped it off her foot. Not thinking, he leaned in and pressed a
kiss to the sole of her foot.

"Fletch!" she gasped, trying to tug it back. "That's disgusting. They're probably all sweaty and—"

He held tight and kissed her toes. "Mmm," he hummed,
"smells like peaches and cream."

She sputtered, asked, completely aghast. "Peaches and
cream?"

"Yup." Not really. They did smell a little fruity, like the
lotion he'd watched her spread over her skin that morning in the
bedroom before they'd pulled on their clothes—him jeans and a
tee, getting ready to meet his brother for all the groom things,
her sweatpants and a purple sweater, her dress on a hanger that
also had a toiletry bag hung over its hook. She'd been commandeered to go to the church and decorate with his mom before
they'd met up with Carrie and Hayley. "Your skin is delicious, no
matter the part."

More sputtering. "That's—"

"How did you get my mom to leave the decorating to you?"

Her mouth dropped open. "I—how did—?"

"How did I know that you somehow got my mom to relax before the lemon drops?"

Her nose wrinkled. "Yes. *That*."

Tartness in her tone.

"I heard her telling my dad about it," he told her, reaching for her other shoe, starting to tug open the buckle, slide out the strap. "Just so you know, she's baking you *all* the things once the wedding weekend is over. Be prepared for a huge delivery, and she won't scrimp on the sugar."

A shrug. "I love sweet things."

He'd already noted that, along with her obsession with fried cheese, but since it was important enough for her to reveal to him, it was important enough for him to underline that note in his mind. "You'll probably go into a sugar coma."

"I'm fine with that." He chuckled and bent to kiss her other foot, her toes. She didn't squirm this time, but she didn't exactly look thrilled for his mouth to be down there. Also, good to note: no foot fetish.

"What's your favorite treat?" he asked, skimming his fingers along her feet.

She scowled at his movements, but since she'd stopped fighting his hold, Fletcher considered that to be a victory.

"Chocolate? Fruity?" he asked.

Her lips pressed flat, released, and he felt her relenting, especially when she said, "An easier question to answer might be what *don't* I like?"

He began massaging her feet, and *that* she liked if her slumping back into her chair, her lids sliding closed was any indication. "What don't you like, sweetheart?" he pressed.

"Coconut," she breathed, her eyes sliding closed.

"No piña coladas?"

She waved a hand, eyes still shut. "Alcohol is a separate category from sweets." Fletcher disagreed with that statement, and if he didn't want Tammy relaxed and soft above him, he might have argued, just to watch the bright red flush of annoyance spread on her cheeks, to see her eyes spark with irritation.

But she was relaxed.

Soft.

Sweet.

Gentle.

And he wanted her to stay that way, so he continued massaging, asked, "No macaroons then?"

A flutter of her eyes, and she shook her head. "Somehow I'm not surprised that you know that I don't like macaroons and that it's macaroons that have coconut and not macarons."

He kept his voice light. "I'm a man of many talents."

She snorted, but her mouth was curved. "So long as those talents continue to be administered on my feet, I'm not going to argue with that."

With that bit of sass, he couldn't resist pushing her buttons, at least a little bit. "Next time I make macarons I'll be sure to whisk the eggs with your toes."

"First, ew." Tammy's nose wrinkled, even though she didn't open her eyes. "Second, that seems impossible. I've watched *Great British Bake-Off.* I know how much elbow grease it takes to get enough air into those egg whites." He snorted. "Third, how do you know how to make macarons?"

"I watch *Great British Bake-Off.*" A dry statement that had her eyes slitting open and glaring down at him. He added, "Despite the Lunchable lunches, my mom actually *did* cook a lot when we were growing up. In fact, she cooked and baked all the time. Used to run a little bakery and restaurant in town when we were growing up." He shifted slightly, began massaging her calves. "We learned how to bake a lot of things just by hanging out."

"Like what?" Tammy asked, flexing her toes.

It drew his gaze, and he actually looked at her feet for the first time, not just the oblique glances to see where his hands were, to see her toes distinguished from the sole and the heel. He saw her pink polish, the tiny freckle on the top of her right big toe. He saw that there were freckles in a pattern all along the top. Including beneath—

He took his hands from her legs and gripped that right foot, brushed a deep red groove that marred that delicate patten of freckles.

"What the fuck?" he whispered.

Tammy jerked slightly and he managed to tear his eyes from her injured foot to meet her stare. "What?" she asked, brows drawn tightly together.

He glanced back down at her feet.

"Wh—" she started to say again, then, "Oh." A sigh. "It's stupid," she said. "Like I said, these shoes are the devil. They're gorgeous but abuse the hell out of my feet every time I wear them."

He didn't think.

Just grabbed both shoes, stood, and walked over to a trash can, launching them into the depths of wedding waste.

"Wh-what the fuck, Fletcher?"

He leaned in, pushed her gently back into the chair when she started to stand, gripped her chin, and promptly lost his temper. "Never again will you be so casual about taking abuse, even from yourself."

She swatted his hand away, shoved him back. "Fuck off, King. I can do whatever I want." She hopped to her feet. "If I want to abuse myself, my feet, my body or heart or mind, that's my prerogative."

A curl of fury slid through him. "No."

Her brows lifted. "*No?*"

It was a dangerous question. Well, not the word itself, but the tone she used when she expressed it. *So* fucking dangerous. Answer wrong, and he'd be screwed.

But...fuck it.

She could be pissed at him all she wanted. There was no way he could back down from this.

She'd hurt herself. For a pair of fucking shoes.

A pair of shoes she was currently trying to retrieve from the trash can, walking across the ground—where she could step on a stick or a piece of glass or a burning cigarette or...or *something* that might hurt her, however improbable—and reaching into the can.

Then nearly toppling *into* the can.

Fucking hell.

The woman needed a keeper.

Yes, that was caveman. Yes, that was stupid as hell. No, he didn't give a fuck at that particular moment in time.

He marched across the clearing, scooped her up, and carried her back to the table. "Stay," he muttered, plunking her into the chair.

"St-stay—" she stammered, steam all but flying out of her ears, her gaze so intense, he might as well have been skewered with lasers. He plunked a hand on her shoulder to keep her in place, held her there for a moment, and then he straightened, released her, knowing that she probably wouldn't stay in that chair—hell, he *knew* there was no way she'd stay in that chair.

He just needed a head start.

And he had it, making it to the trash can first.

Scooping up the shoes first.

Launching those shoes into the dark forest surrounding them...first.

Okay, he couldn't reasonably say that she'd been planning on launching the shoes into the forest.

But he still got there first.

And off they went.

They both watched them sail off amongst the needle-lined branches.

And then...*then* Tammy turned to him, her face filled with such absolute fury that for the first time in a long time, Fletcher felt as though his life were in danger.

Or if not his life, then at the very least that his balls were in grave, *grave* danger.

Seventeen

Tammy

Was there smoke coming out of her ears?

It fucking should be.

Or maybe actual flames because she had just watched the man—watched him in a cloud of absolute fury—as he threw her fucking expensive shoes into the goddamned forest.

One.

Then the other.

"What the fuck are you doing, King?" she growled, ready to do violence.

Like that TikTok trend, looking into the camera and mouthing, "I choose violence."

He merely turned to her and scooped her up, carrying her to the chair and plunking her ass down into it.

All over again.

More steam from her ears.

Enough flames to start a forest fire.

"Oh, is the asshole from the car ride making a reappearance?" she snapped, shoving him away. "I thought you promised me you weren't actually *like* that. Or at least, that was the bull-shit you tried to sell me on the way up here."

Fletcher straightened, towering over her, his hands clenched at his sides. He was shaking, literally shaking, as he slowly inhaled and exhaled.

He was pissed.

Perhaps as pissed as she was.

And that...well, probably it shouldn't have, but it did anyway. Because the fact that he was furious had her anger tempering, fading, softening.

Curiosity took the place of fury.

It made no sense.

But that was the truth.

"Why are *you* so upset?" she asked and instead of ice, her question was almost gentle.

Time to turn in her feminist card.

Well, okay, she'd do that...right after she got the answer to her question.

"You're hurting yourself," he gritted out his head turned away, his jaw tight. The intensity in that statement surprised her, made her forget about cards and feminism and questions and answers. "I don't want you to be hurting."

Tammy tilted her head to the side, tried to understand why this is so important to him. "But...why?"

He turned, and his expression was so aghast that the remnants of her anger tamped down, slid away, poofed off into space like fucking fairy dust or something. "*Why?*" he snapped.

"Yes," she said and stood, placed her hand over his heart.

It thundered beneath her palm, and more curiosity trickled through her. "You're hurting yourself."

"Fletcher"—her nails dug lightly through his T-shirt—"Why. Do. You. Care?"

"I—" His hands unclasped, one warm palm dropped over hers, dwarfing her hand, the roughened skin of his callouses having her wonder once again where he'd earned them. "I care, sweetheart. You maybe don't want to hear that I do. Maybe it'll scare you and make you run. Maybe I intended to charm the fuck out of you so you wouldn't want to kick me to the curb when the weekend is done, that maybe you'd keep me when you don't keep anyone else—"

"Fletch—"

"I like you, Tammy. I know this is supposed to be pretend, but if I'm being honest with you, it's *never* just been pretend." Her throat tightened, heart pounding, pulse throbbing in her veins. "I've liked you from that first day in the office, and I like you now even more. You're smart. You're gorgeous. But more than anything else, you have a huge, kind heart."

Why did his words affect her so much?

They were just words, and she knew that words couldn't be trusted, not when there weren't actions to back them up.

But...hadn't he given her the action?

The realization had her feeling tingly from toes to top, her heart beating so hard in her chest that it felt like she was going to pass out.

Why did his words affect her so intensely?

Because they were everything she had ever wanted to hear, to believe in, and the way he was staring at her, the earnestness of his tone, the way his heart was pounding just as hard as hers was, just beneath her palm, made her believe in him.

Believe those words were more than just a talking point.

Believe they were more than some line of bullshit he was giving her when he intended to fuck her over later—fuck her over like Calvin—

No.

She blinked, and pulled away, turning her back on him as the memories sliced right through her.

Cold. She was so fucking cold in an instant.

Her feet suddenly felt frozen, soaking up the frosty ground. Her heart was a block of ice and—

No.

She couldn't think about Calvin, about how it had changed everything. About—

"I'm not worth it, Fletch." The words flew out of her, sharp painful slices on the way up her throat, over her tongue. "I'm messed up inside. I'll never be a woman who can—"

"You can." No hesitation. No room in his tone for negotiation.

She froze. "I—"

Fingers on her jaw. "You. *Can*. You're scared. I don't know why, and I don't know that I care." She choked as those fingers traced down her neck. "I want to know if and when you're ready to tell me. I want to know what is making your eyes fill with shadows, what makes you think that you're messed up and not worth it. But I don't care." His fingers closed lightly over her throat. "I don't care about those fucked up thoughts, the painful memories. Because knowing them won't change one damned thing about the way I feel about you."

"Stop talking," she whispered.

"Because they're bullshit. Those thoughts are bullshit. Because you *are* worth it. You aren't messed up—not any more than any other human on this planet." A gentle squeeze, drawing her gaze to his when all she wanted to do was allow it to flit off into the distance, to remain unfocused and distant, to not let the words affect her.

But they had already affected her.

They added a layer, a *thousand* layers to that bubble of protection he'd erected the night before.

"You have to stop talking," she said softly.

Begged.

"You can tell me on your own terms," he said, ignoring her, still talking, each of those words colliding with her, filling her up in a way that she'd never experienced before. Because this man made her feel things she shouldn't. Because he was stubborn and pushy and...he liked her, even with the chip on her shoulder, with all the barbed wire and concrete that was her attempt to keep him, to keep everyone safely at a distance.

"You have to st—"

Another squeeze, this time accompanied by the "I won't push you for answers," he went on. "And yes, I fucking want to hear all the things that make you, *you*. But I won't sugarcoat it, babe. Whatever—*who*ever—made you feel like shit is a fucking idiot, and nothing you tell me will convince me otherwise." He released her. "Because I've seen the woman you are inside, and you are *incredible*."

Finally, it was too much.

"Fuck," she whispered, stepping away from him, her hands going to her hair, panic slicing through her.

Run.

Run.

Run.

A gentle hand on her shoulder.

"No, Tammy," Fletcher said softly. "Stay, honey," he murmured, and she realized with a start that she'd spoken aloud. "Stay and reach for what you deserve. Even if that's not me. Even if it's not a relationship or a boyfriend or *more*. Stay and grab on to someone who sees you for the wonderful person you are in here." He tapped her chest, just above where her heart thundered below.

"I'm..."

Scared.

Terrified.

Torn to shreds and pieced back together.

But not by Fletcher. Who got furious when she hurt her feet just because she wore uncomfortable shoes. Who encouraged her to find someone who saw her as wonderful.

Wonderful!

Fletcher, who thought she was worth it.

And...why should he be the only one who thought she was worth it? Why shouldn't she look inside and see herself as worthy? Maybe she didn't want to be in a relationship, but that should be born of preference and choice and not of a fear of getting too close.

It shouldn't be because of Calvin.

Of the way he'd left her with no choice but to erect those walls.

No. That wasn't fair. He hadn't been the only cause. She'd fallen into that trap because it was easier to keep out than to let in, because, yeah, Calvin had hurt her. But lots of people got hurt, and it was her own pain and insecurity that made it safer to just keep her distance.

Heat at her spine.

But Fletcher didn't touch her.

Just stood near enough to let her know he was there.

And that closeness made the words come. Not the deepest, most buried truth. Not everything about Calvin, not yet. She had to unpack that in her own brain first. But the rest of it. The pain that she'd shared with her siblings, her parents.

"My mom had cancer."

Now his hands came to her, his arms wrapping around her, his body coming flush against her back. "I'm sorry."

"She's better now," Tammy whispered. "Has been in remission for years."

"That still leaves a mark."

She nodded. "I'm the baby. Barely old enough to remember her in the hospital, but even though I was the baby, I remember in other ways."

He waited as she gathered her thoughts, just holding her tightly, securely.

Protectively.

And the words came again.

"It was silly. She was—*is*—the glue that holds us together. Always at every school event, driving us to sports, asking us about our day at dinner. All the typical Mom stuff."

"And that changed when she was sick?"

"My dad is amazing. He tried to pick up the slack, and we had great family friends and neighbors who stepped in. It was just...with four kids and one parent missing, others trying to pick up the slack...things got forgotten." A beat. "Understandably," she added quickly, feeling guilty for even bringing this up. "It's stupid," she hissed. "It's not important—"

"Except it *is*," he countered. "What happened, love?"

"I got forgotten."

A long pause. "What do you mean?"

"I mean there were four kids in our family. We all played sports or were in school clubs or had playdates with friends, and...it was a lot to keep track of."

His fingers spasmed, digging into her torso for a second before gentling. "You were forgotten." His voice had gone a little rough. "How often, sweetheart?"

The music inside the tent changed, an upbeat song blaring through the speakers and Tammy finally remembered where they were at, what they should—and shouldn't—be doing. "We should go back inside," she said. "You're missing your brother's—"

"Carrie already told me that she's going to dance until her feet fall off—"

"Don't have a problem with her wearing uncomfortable shoes, do you?" she asked, trying to change the subject.

He brought it right back to her. "Carrie's not you, is she?"

Tammy sucked in a breath.

Fletcher turned her in his arms, cupping her jaw and tilting her head up. "No," he said. "I can answer that one for you. She's *not* you. Not by a long shot."

"And Trina?" she asked. "You care about her. You—" She cut herself off.

He went still, his hand flexing on her face. "Some part of me will always care about her."

Why had she brought Trina up? Probably because Tammy had seen the other woman, the beautiful other woman who'd introduced herself to Tammy and been nice—fucking *nice!* Tammy hated the woman for hurting Fletcher, wanted her to be a mean troll who sniffed at her and treated everyone with disdain.

But Trina was nice.

As was Trina's mom.

She saw why Connie had found it difficult to let them go.

Hell, Trina had brought her a plate of appetizers when Tammy had missed the chance at them because she'd packed up decorations at the church—not wanting Connie and Tony to have to worry about it that night, especially when they were taking family pictures, and especially not wanting them to have to get up early like Connie had told her she was planning on doing.

And then after Tammy had downed the plate—more fried cheese and delicious stuffed meatballs and a piece of cantaloupe that had the serving of food masquerading as something sort of healthy—Trina had fixed her hair and nudged her toward Fletcher, telling her that she would finish up so that Tammy could enjoy the rest of her night.

Trina had brought her food and fixed her hair!

What the actual fuck of a universe had she stumbled upon?

Fletcher's ex was as nice as he was.

And it was a good thing that Trina had fixed Tammy's hair because Tammy *had* ended up in some of the family pictures.

Fake relationship to family pictures.

Insanity.

Tammy released a breath. "Trina seems really nice," she whispered. "I want to hate her for hurting you, but…"

"She *is* nice," he admitted. "I mean, it would be nicer if she hadn't gotten married to someone else so quickly." He huffed out a laugh. "Her finding someone she saw as husband material so soon after we broke up was hell on the ego."

Tammy winced. "I'm—"

"But the truth is that even though it took me a bit to get over her, I can see that she made the right decision in ending our relationship. We…" A sigh. "We wouldn't have made each other happy. Not in the long term."

"I'm sure it still sucked."

He slid his hand into her hair. "So did yours." He brushed his lips over hers. "Should we talk more about how much our past traumas sucked? Or should I tell you that after Carrie's feet fall off, she's apparently taking my brother back to their place so she can ride him like a show pony."

Tammy froze. "You're kidding."

A shudder wracked his strong, muscular frame. "I wish I was," he muttered. "I don't know why Carrie insists on telling me these things."

"Because she sees herself as your sister and likes to torture you?"

A shrug. "Probably."

She laughed.

He did too, for just a moment. Then his face went serious again and she stiffened, lungs stilling, pulse picking up again. "I know that's not everything," he whispered. "I know that's not the only reason you're good at keeping your distance."

Tammy sucked in a breath, battened down the hatches.

And it was a good thing she braced herself.

Because his next words shook her to the core.

"But know this," he said, "I won't forget you, Tammy."

"Fletcher," she whispered.

"You're imprinted on my heart and soul." Another brush of his lips over hers. "And you're staying there."

Her breath caught. Her eyes stung. She opened her mouth to say...

Something.

Then the DJ's voice came onto the speakers scattered through the tent. "Join me for saying goodbye to the newest Mr. and Mrs. King!"

"So much for her feet falling off," Fletcher muttered. "I guess show pony time has—"

"Come on!" Tammy hissed. "We can't miss waving them off!" Reaching for his hand, she snagged it and then dragged him forward, her bare feet flying over the ground for all of two steps before Fletcher swept her up into his arms again, carrying her toward the tent.

They reached the tent's exit, and Fletcher set her onto her feet just as Carrie and Sean were being cheered off, huge smiles and loving expressions on their faces.

She and Fletcher yelled and threw confetti made out of dried leaves.

They clapped and shouted as the car with its Just Married sign taped to the back windshield, cans dragging and making a ton of noise, streamers flying in the wind pulled away.

She sniffed—fucking weddings.

Fletcher wiped her cheeks, dashing away her tears, and then he bent and murmured in her ear, "What's the likelihood that *you'll* ride me like a show pony tonight?"

Shock had her mouth dropping open.

But only for a second.

Because then amusement boiled up and over, and she found herself laughing hysterically, laughing so hard that she had to brace her hands on her knees as she tried to catch her breath.

"Is that a no?" he asked, crouching in front of her, covering her hands with his own.

Suddenly, her laughter faded.

Need took its place.

She wanted this man and his protective words, the promise of not forgetting. She wanted the bossy and annoying and the funny man who made her laugh.

But she was Tammy Fucking Huntington.

So, she had to throw some sass, some fire his way.

Slowly, she straightened and plunked her hands on her waist.

"You find me some more of that fried cheese, and I'll ride you any which way you want."

Eighteen

Fletcher

The scent of fall in his nose.

A curvy body pressed to his.

Tammy.

He knew before he was even fully awake, knew there would be no thinking that Tammy was Trina. Not ever again.

And somehow, he was awake before Tammy.

Probably because they'd done all sorts of riding when they'd gotten back to the house last night—show pony and wild monkey sex, against the wall and on the dresser and when they'd gone to clean up, in the shower, too.

He was wiped.

She'd barely stayed awake long enough to make it to the bed. Her eyes had already been sliding closed, even before she'd made it under the covers.

And she was still out.

But he wasn't.

Weird.

He settled back down into the mattress, started to close his eyes again...and then he heard it. Heard what must have drawn him out of deep sleep, something his body had been trained to listen for because it had happened so many times over the years.

A pebble on his window.

The scratch of a branch on the glass.

Trina.

He sat up with a start, dislodging Tammy from his chest, but she was so out of it that she didn't even move. Slowly, he shifted, pulling back the covers, and sliding from the bed. Trina *was* there, scratching his windowpane with a long branch they kept hidden beneath the back porch. It was early. So early that the horizon to the west was barely beginning to lighten.

She scratched again, and he yanked open the pane.

Then nearly got impaled by the end of the stick.

He dodged, snagged the end. "Trina," he hissed, trying not to wake Tammy. "What the fuck are you doing?"

"Come down," she called.

He shook his head. "No, Tri, I'm—"

"Just come down," she said. "It's important." Her voice was too loud. She was going to wake Tammy up, and then that was going to be a very awkward conversation—having to explain why his married ex was making a pre-dawn call to the house, summoning him like she was Romeo and he was Juliet.

"Okay," he said. "Just"—he held up a hand—"just *okay*. Give me a second."

Quietly, he slid the frame closed then picked his way across the room, searching the shadows for any obstacles that might make him eat shit. And there were plenty of them. He and Tammy hadn't exactly been neat the night before, and there were shoes and belts and jackets and underwear scattered to and fro.

And seriously, *fro?*

Apparently, he sounded like a fictional fairy godmother at zero dark thirty in the morning.

Snorting inwardly, he yanked up a pair of sweats, shrugged

into a hoodie, and tugged on his socks and boots. Then made his way quietly from the room, down the stairs, and out onto the back deck.

Trina was leaning against the railing, her hair piled on top of her head.

He used to love when she wore her hair that way, loved to go up behind her and kiss the back of her neck, to do his level best to mess up that pile of hair, to send it tumbling down, to send *her* tumbling down onto any semi-flat surface around.

Today, he found he wasn't drawn to her.

Yes, she was effortlessly beautiful.

Yes, they'd once had chemistry.

But he wasn't pining to get back with her. There was affection. There always would be, but he meant what he'd said the night before.

He and Trina were over.

A happy memory, but just that. A memory.

One he'd clung to for far too long.

One that paled in the face of what he had with Tammy.

"Hey," Trina said, pushing off the railing and moving toward him. She hugged him tightly, and he was struck by how wrong it felt to have her body pressed to his.

"Hey," he said, releasing her.

She hopped up on the railing.

He hopped up next to her, watching as her feet swung back and forth. She was quiet for long enough that he began to wonder if she were actually going to speak at all, but he didn't press her. Trina always needed time to ponder, to pull together her thoughts.

She couldn't be pushed.

It would make her feel panicked, the words stoppering up in the back of her throat, and then he'd have to spend even more time waiting for her to try to gather what she'd wanted to say.

Such a frustrating habit.

He understood it, of course. Everyone had their things. But it was just really nice that Tammy didn't have that problem.

"I was jealous when I saw her at the wedding."

Fletcher inhaled sharply through his nose. "Trina." A warning to not go down this path. It was dead and gone, put to rest. He wanted to continue to look back on their time together as having some positives, and if she went down the path he was thinking she was going to go, this was quickly going to turn into a shitshow.

"She gorgeous," Trina said. "And you've always had that thing for redheads." She turned her head and grinned at him. He felt some of the tension fade. That was mischief in her eyes, in the curve of her lips.

"I have," he agreed.

More quiet, and he found himself staring up at the sky and the fading stars, their light dimming as the sun rose higher in the sky.

"We've needed to have this conversation for a while," she said softly.

"You mean discussing my fondness for redheads?"

She swatted his arm then rested her head on his shoulder. Even that didn't feel right. Because she wasn't Tammy. Because it wasn't red hair tickling his neck. Because it wasn't Tammy's scent in his nose. "You know I mean about us."

"There is no *us*."

She lifted her head. "Don't say that."

Fear churned through his body, and Fletch began to wonder if he'd seriously misjudged this situation so badly.

Her hand rested on his cheek. "Don't say that," she repeated.

"Trina." Another warning.

"There will always be an *us*."

Fuck.

He inhaled again.

"You're a part of my past," she whispered. "And that will always tie us together."

His breath sliced out of him, but she kept talking.

"That, we can't change. We have too much history—I remember the time you got lost on Steep Locket Ridge. I know that you prefer your pizza without cheese. We were each other's first kiss, first time, practically our first *everything*." She sighed. "But that doesn't mean we would have been happy."

"I know," he said cautiously. "That's why we broke up, remember?"

Soft, tinkling laughter. "I remember, and maybe I'm coming here at the wrong time, saying all the wrong things, but I stayed awake all night thinking of you."

He smothered a wince. "Trina, that's not—"

"Thinking that I'm so glad you found someone who looks at you right."

He went stiff, nearly toppled himself off the railing.

"She busted her ass during that wedding, Fletch. She was everywhere, making sure a woman she'd met only this weekend had as gorgeous of a wedding as she'd ever dreamed of. Tammy packed up the church so your parents didn't have to. She helped the florist when all the centerpieces toppled over as the florist was wheeling them in, helping to put them back together so that they looked perfect. Hayley's hem tore? She found a sewing kit and sorted it. Your Aunt Becky was getting a little sloppy after enjoying too many lemon drops? She brought her glasses of water like it was her job. She"—Trina stopped and shook her head—"was amazing."

"She *is* amazing."

"I know." Trina sighed. "And it's not fair that I felt jealous, that I still feel possessive of you. God knows I've moved on."

He snorted.

She punched him. "Even though I was feeling a bit jealous and possessive, it wasn't in the normal way. Or maybe it was. I was feeling...protective." A sigh. "I didn't want you to be hurt—which isn't fair, I know, because I'm the one who ended us and did it in a spectacularly immature way—not talking to you, pretending it was all going to be fine, that we would be fine, and it would all just work out because we'd been together for so long, because I love your parents as much as my own."

"It's not like that," he said, grabbing her hand and squeezing it lightly. "Now I see it as brave. You did what needed to be done, did it when I couldn't. Because"—another squeeze—"I was too scared to admit that we weren't going to work out."

Her expression softened. "It was...I miss you. I love you. I know I did the right thing, of course. For both of us, but part of me still misses us, you know?"

He tugged a lock of her hair. "I know."

"But yeah, I also know that even though I miss you and miss *us*, when I heard you were bringing someone, I didn't know if this woman was going to treat you—my special, amazing first *everything*—right."

His heart squeezed. "Trina."

"So, I know I hurt you, hurt both of us. I know I should have talked to you way before the rehearsal dinner, but I was so scared to ruin us. I know I've apologized before, but I really am sorry for waiting until then and for blurting it out the way I did—"

"I'm not." A beat, her shocked eyes coming to his. "Did I feel blindsided? Yes. Did I get my heart broken? Also, yes. Did it fucking hurt to see you moving on so quickly when I felt rocked to the core? Yeah, honey, it did." She winced, and he nudged her shoulder. "But then I let all of that go and realized that you'd done the right thing, that maybe we would have been happy together, stayed together, but we wouldn't have *more*."

She nudged him back. "More is pretty great, isn't it?"

Fletcher smiled. "*So* now are you going to stop apologizing for five minutes and tell me why you're really here?"

A frown. "Brute." Another wince. "No. That was me."

"Truly, I'm not sorry you hurt me," he said softly. "It sucked for sure. But Trin, it worked out for the better for both of us."

"Of course, you're not sorry. Not now," she quipped, "that you have an awesome Tammy who stares at you like you hung the moon, and you care enough about her that you're launching expensive Jimmy Choo's into the woods."

"You—" He winced. Of course, someone had seen. There had been more than a hundred people in that tent, in those woods.

"Hubs and I snuck out for a bit," she said softly. "And when we were sneaking back in, we stumbled on you two arguing. About shoes." Her lips quirked.

He winced again. "I was an ass."

A smirk. "You were." She patted his cheek. "But you never were that much of an ass with *me*." Another pat. "You never cared that my feet pinched, that I might have pushed myself too far, or that I planned on eating an entire carton of ice cream and was going to regret it later."

"I'm not dumb enough to come between you and your ice cream."

A roll of her eyes. "Dork."

"And proud."

Smiling as she dropped her hand, she said, "I'd wager that if she was going to eat it all, knowing full well she was lactose intolerant and would be in agony later, you'd launch the carton of ice cream into the woods to rest with the fishes alongside her shoes."

Since that was true, he just nodded.

"You found her, honey. You found the woman you're meant to be with, and I love you enough that it makes me so damned happy." She hugged him tight. "And I love you enough that I had to tell you that."

A flicker of movement around the corner of the house.

He glanced up to see Trina's husband appear. "Dom is here?"

"He drove me." She straightened and smiled at her husband, who nodded and leaned against the corner of the house, waiting for her to finish talking to her ex, after driving his wife to her ex's house really fucking early in the morning.

Dom was *her* more.

"I'm glad you found him, too," he murmured, tilting his chin toward Dom.

Her face went gentle, so damned gentle that his throat went tight, his eyes burned.

"I think he'd take your ice cream," he said, forcing out the words, going for teasing because it was either that or he'd start bawling, and as much as he still cared about Trina, still loved her, he'd much rather be up in bed with Tammy than freezing his ass off crying on the porch with his ex.

"He would." A beat. "He has."

Fletcher laughed, shaking his head as he jumped down from the railing, helped her down. Then he hugged her, told her goodbye, and shoved her in the direction of her husband.

Turned to go back to who was important.

Tammy.

He bounded up the stairs, pushed open the door to the bedroom, and...

Stopped dead.

Tammy was out of bed.

Standing by the window.

Looking *out* the window.

NINETEEN

Fletcher's face tightened.

With guilt?

That certainly would have been more convenient because her insides were churning like she'd been dropped into a blender. Apple slices and frozen pieces of banana and ice cubes all flying toward those blades, spinning and being chopped up smaller and smaller and *smaller* until they were transformed into liquid.

Her heartbeat was loud, too.

Echoing in her ears, roaring like those blades did when they met the chunks of fruit.

But it wasn't guilt.

It was remorse, and based on the very sweet conversation she'd eavesdropped on—yeah, yeah, she shouldn't have invaded his privacy. No, she couldn't find herself regretting it, not when he looked like this.

Not when he was worried he'd hurt her.

Not when he crossed to her, took her hands in his, and said, "It's not what you think."

"That's what someone guilty would say."

His fingers convulsed. "Tammy—"

She squeezed his hands back, knew that what she felt for him meant that she couldn't run from the swirling terror in her, just like she couldn't allow him to feel bad, not because he was worried about her.

This was shoes launched into a forest.

This was a protective bubble she wanted to erect over *him*.

Because it did something to her to see him hurting, to see him in pain.

"I heard you get up," she admitted, "and I know I shouldn't have been doing it, but I eavesdropped." A quiet breath. "I heard everything."

"Everything?"

She nodded. The entire conversation had reinforced what Tammy had thought of Trina at the wedding—a good woman. One it would have been easy for her to hate, if she wasn't so damned nice. And brave, to risk the happiness of both their families so that she and Fletcher could both find something that meant more.

Something Tammy was starting to understand the meaning of.

Because the fake part of her relationship with him had lasted all of a couple of hours. Fake had gone out the window the moment her lips touched his. It had fucking flown into space the moment she'd realized how much it hurt when he'd called her Trina in bed because even though she'd had all of a couple of hours with the man, she'd been feeling so much more with Fletcher than she'd ever felt before, even with Calvin.

The man she'd once had so many dreams with.

The man who'd nearly destroyed who she was as a person.

The man who'd made her feel more than forgotten, more

than she'd *ever* felt as a child, as a teenager, a young woman lost in the shuffle of a big family.

"We're good," she said. "I—" The protective bubble around him hardened, stiffened until she was encasing him in concrete and barbed wire and steel. "I heard it all—what she said, what you said. I'm fine, and…" She swallowed hard. Why was it so hard to say this? To open herself up? Okay, fucking fine, she *knew* why it was so hard. It was the wasteland she'd been living in since Calvin had fucking napalmed her life. "It's good. I'm good. *We're* good."

"I don't want our good to include any fakeness."

She laughed shakily. "I'm pretty sure that all the fakeness ended the moment I kissed you."

He stepped a little closer. "I'm pretty sure any fakeness was on your side, baby."

Whirling.

Terror.

Then his arms wrapped around her, and that bubble tightened, sliding closer, slipping under the spinning blades, covering her, protecting her.

She could breathe and think and *love*.

Love.

In one weekend.

Now *that* made her want to run straight into the bathroom and slam the door…and text *herself* a breakup message.

Maybe that made her a bad girlfriend.

Girlfriend.

She breathed, dodged the blades, embraced the bubble, and thought that maybe it made her a *great* one that she could finally think the word.

And maybe, say it aloud.

"No fake," she agreed and she fucking leaped past those blades and went for it. "Just a woman embracing her inner girlfriend."

His face lit. "Yeah?"

She shoved his shoulder. "That's what I said, isn't it?"

He stepped close, cupped her cheek. "Yeah, honey, that's what you said."

She opened her mouth, readying herself to snark back, but the words didn't even get a chance to tinge the air with joyful sarcasm—*ha*—because Fletcher shoved her hard. She squeaked, arms flailing, her stomach dropping, and then...

Her back collided gently with the mattress.

Fletcher came down on top of her. "Thank you," he said, cupping her cheek. "And you need to know that I'm not going fuck it up."

That made her heart squeeze, her fear transform into a gas, somehow drifting in through tiny imperfections in her walls, sliding through her bubble, invading her nose, her eyes, her mouth.

Because she wasn't worried about Fletcher fucking things up.

She was worried she would.

In fact, with her track record, it was almost certain that she *would*.

TWENTY

FLETCHER

Monday morning coffee was key.

Only this was the first time he was pouring coffee into two mugs, adding cream and sugar to his own, but not to Tammy's.

Because she apparently took her coffee like a *man*.

Laughing to himself, he thought of how she'd teased him after they'd managed to pry themselves from the bed, had stumbled down for sustenance and caffeine to hold them over until the post-wedding brunch. So much fire in Tammy Huntington, and he kind of loved it.

No, he *did* love it.

Four days together, and he was gone for this girl.

Of course, he'd admired her for much longer, had spent a lot of timing building a friendship with the crumbs she kept throwing his way. So, a lot more had happened than he'd been expecting this weekend, and he'd ended up with a hell of a lot more than crumbs from Tammy.

A girlfriend.

He'd ended up with a girlfriend.

So, all in all, he couldn't complain.

Hell, he could barely contain his smile. Complaining wasn't anywhere on his radar.

"Thanks, baby," she said softly when he set the mug on the desk of her office. He knew that she had a call in just a couple of minutes so just squeezed her hand and headed out. He knew that because she'd brought him coffee barely an hour before—with his cream and sugar—and had told him she had back-to-back meetings straight through lunch and all the way to the end of the day.

Missing Friday meant a bit more work than normal for him, though not back-to-back meetings all day.

So, he left her to it, was smiling when he heard her dialing into the call before he quietly shut the door, even as he made plans to order lunch for her. Maybe he'd put a note inside, see if he could talk his way into her bed that night.

Hell, he'd start throwing pebbles at the glass of *her* bedroom window, find a branch and scratch, pry it open and crawl in Romeo-style—

Okay, maybe not the last.

That would be creepy.

The rest of it...yeah, that he'd do. In a heartbeat.

"*What* is that?"

Lisa's voice made him jump, made him realize that he'd been standing in the corridor, daydreaming about throwing rocks at a window.

What. A. Weirdo.

He blinked and tried to play dumb. "What is what?" he asked, turning toward Lisa.

Her arms were crossed, and she tilted her head toward her office. "Inside. Door closed." And then she strode forward into her office without waiting to see if he'd obey.

Which he would.

Because that was five-feet-six-inches of fire waiting to explode on his ass.

Fuck.

This had the potential to be very, very bad.

What gave you the clue to that genius? his inner asshole muttered.

Regardless, he followed Lisa in.

He'd take his licks like the sugar-and-cream-coffee-drinking man he was.

"Sit," Lisa ordered after having shut the door. "Now," she said once his ass had hit the seat of the chair in front of her desk, "please, God, tell me why you just left Tammy Huntington's office looking like you're fucking in *love.* And tell me," she went on before he could answer, "why the fuck the same Tammy Huntington brought *you* coffee, wearing that same lovey-dovey expression barely an hour ago?"

"We're dating."

Lisa's eyes went wide. "Are you fucking with me?"

"No."

Silence.

Then Lisa groaned and flopped into her chair, her head dropping back, gaze going to the ceiling. "My department," she moaned. "My department is totally fucked."

"What do you mean?" he asked genuinely confused.

"Young fucking love," she muttered. "Young fucking love fucking up my department."

Fletcher rolled his eyes. "Didn't you marry your secretary?"

She pointed a finger at him. "Don't you bring up useless information!" Another groan, but Fletcher wasn't offended. Lisa was all bark and no bite...and she'd been happily married to her ten-year-younger man for the last two decades.

"So says the HR manager," he quipped.

Her eyes narrowed. "You know that's not what we do in this part of the department."

It wasn't. That much was true.

They were under the larger umbrella of HR yes, but they didn't deal with employee complaints and conflicts, or help new hires coordinate resources. Their department was focused on diversity, and they were making real changes and doing real research in the tech industry.

"I'm just saying, you and Jon work together, and it's not an issue."

"Because he doesn't report to me," she said. "Because even though he's technically in the HR department, he's not under me. Not any longer." Her eyes met Fletcher's. "And we had to make that choice. It was either I move positions or he did."

Change jobs? What the fuck?

His brows yanked down. "But Tammy doesn't report to me."

Lisa sighed. "She's technically beneath you. You're management. She's just a human resource officer."

Tammy wasn't *just* anything.

She might be the newest member of their team, but she was one of the brightest people he'd ever worked with. Smarter than him, that was damned sure.

"You need to register your relationship with Rubil," Lisa said, "fill out the proper paperwork, and then as much as it pains me, one of you needs to transfer out of my department." Sighing, she rubbed her face. "Maybe we can put Tammy under Philip's management. Then I can still have her on a contract basis, and—"

"Wait," he said. "Just...promote her. You said she's one of your best employees. Then there wouldn't be the issue of different management levels."

Lisa rubbed her forehead. "Fletch. You've been here six years. Tammy's barely coming up on her one-year anniversary. I can't just promote her outside of normal channels. That's not fair for anyone else in the department."

"I—"

"So, you need to decide, Fletch."

He frowned. "Decide what?"

Another sigh.

A long pause, but before he could ask her again, her office lane rang. "Decide if she's worth it, Fletch. You have to decide if Tammy is worth all the trouble you're going to bring to the team, to the important work that we're doing here." The phone rang again, and she reached for the receiver.

Her eyes locked onto his.

"You have to decide if it's worth all the trouble a relationship with her is going to bring to both of your careers."

Twenty-One

TAMMY

I t was Thursday night, which meant dinner and prickly pear margaritas.

Now Tammy was a girl who liked a margarita.

But the prickly pear variety was her favorite.

"What's the deal with the empty chair?" her friend Cora asked from her other side.

Probably because Tammy had been ultra-protective of the seat as their crew had tumbled in from outside the restaurant, everyone lingering in front and talking about their weeks while they'd waited for stragglers to show up. Tammy had missed last week's friends' dinner because of the wedding—something she needed to hold over Fletcher, she decided.

She'd bet with she could get him to make her his chocolate chip cookies again.

They were, perhaps, the best thing she'd ever put in her mouth, and that included the arrangement of sweet things that Connie had overnighted for her. They'd arrived in the office Tuesday morning, and though she didn't want to share once she saw the muffins and the homemade chocolate croissants and the cranberry white chocolate chip cookies, she had gone around the office and let her coworkers have some.

Some meaning one.

A single treat each.

And that was it.

Fletcher had bemoaned what he'd called the baked treat one-upmanship—even though he had quickly reached for a streusel-topped muffin, and even more quickly consumed it. That night after work, he'd showed up on her porch—like he had the evening before and the evening after, for that matter—with grocery bags in his hands. He'd made her dinner, whipped up his chocolate chip cookies, then had joked that he would crumble them over her naked body and lick them up.

She'd laughed.

He'd laughed.

Then she'd taken that joke and made it a reality.

It wasn't chocolate syrup, but his cookies were a hundred times tastier, so they'd made it work.

And made it work *good*.

Ha.

"Earth to Tammy," Cora called, and Tammy felt her cheeks heat. Not good. Cora was going to know something was up, even without the empty chair that was becoming the elephant in the room because that's what everyone kept looking at.

Kate and Jamie. Brad and Heidi. Stef and Ben. Kelsey and Tanner. And her and Cora.

The two single ladies.

They always joked they were the outcasts, the only two untethered ones. Tammy because she'd been allergic to relationships forever (a convenient lie she realized now, but one she'd clung to since her family didn't know about Calvin and how he'd shattered her into a million pieces). Cora was single because she wanted that happy ending, but had six overprotective brothers who had made it their mission to prevent their baby sister from dating anyone who wasn't worthy of her.

And, for the record, they had decided that *no* man was worth her.

So, for ages Tammy and Cora had been the only single ones at the table.

Now there was an empty chair next to Tammy, and Cora was giving her the Eye. Their coupled-up friends were all just looking somewhere on the scale of smug to all-knowing.

Cora was part of the friend group because she had always been—Kate, Kels, Heidi, and her had been friends forever (well, since college). Stef worked with Heidi and was amazing and smart, perfect for the talented, brilliant women at the table. Tammy, on the other hand, had been enveloped in because she was Brad and Jaime's sister.

Oh, she couldn't deny that the women had been great friends, and she loved them.

But she was biologically related to half of the couples at the table.

She'd had an in, and they hadn't had an easy out.

It just would be nice if...

Sigh.

If they'd picked her. Not because they were trying to be nice or wanted to please their significant others, but because they'd looked at Tammy and wanted to be her friend.

But...Fletcher had picked her.

Fake start or not, he'd made it clear he saw her, wanted her, *picked* her.

"You're dating someone!"

Tammy's eyes flew open when Kate exclaimed that loudly enough to bring down the entire restaurant, and Tammy realized she'd been sitting there fantasizing about Fletcher and all the good things he'd brought into her life instead of recognizing that she—not the chair—had become the center of attention.

God, she was acting like a dope.

Like a dope who'd just revealed everything.

As if the empty chair hadn't already revealed...what she hadn't actually announced yet. Ugh. Her inner monologue was giving her a headache.

"Look at her face. *Of course,* she's dating someone," Heidi exclaimed. "She's got lovestruck written all over her."

"And she *likes* him," Kels crooned.

Tammy got it together when Kelsey extended the *likes* to schoolyard proportions. "Kels," she snapped. "Be a grown up."

"Yeah, hell no," Kels said. "Being an adult isn't any fun. I'd rather find out about the guy who's making your cheeks turn that pretty shade of red."

"Yeah," Jaime muttered. "I'd like that, too."

Uh-oh, protective older brother alert.

"Jaim—" she began.

"Me, too," Brad said, his eyes narrowed and gleaming.

A deadly gleam.

Protective older brother times two alert.

"Uh-oh," Cora murmured, and Tammy's stomach clenched. She wasn't used to being on the receiving end of brotherly attention—hell, she wasn't sure if Fletcher was either. Maybe she should text him, tell him to abort.

They were all of a week into this.

Meeting her brothers was a terrible idea. Hell, one of them was probably already texting her mom, and then her parents would be calling her for details—chances were that they might even show up here tonight.

A risk now that they lived in town.

Oh God.

What had she gotten herself in to?

But when she'd told Fletch she wouldn't be home this evening, and had seen the disappointment on his face, she'd spontaneously invited him to this dinner with her friends. They got together every Thursday they could, the whole group of them. It was loud and fun and filled with prickly pear margaritas and tacos.

Best night of the week usually.

Now that top spot had been taken over by nights with Fletcher.

So, she'd extended the invitation and he'd surprised her by agreeing—no, that wasn't fair. Truthfully, he *hadn't* surprised her. She'd known he would agree to come.

Because he wanted to be with her.

Because he liked spending time with her.

Because she wanted him to meet her friends, for them to see...

Him picking *her.*

"I'm—"

The doors to the restaurant opened and she knew...*knew* that it was Fletcher. Was it some sixth sense she now possessed? A unique Fletcher pheromone she detected in the air?

The ball of dread in her stomach?

His gaze came to hers unerringly, and he started toward the table, eyes locked on hers, the rest of the world not existing. Just him. Just her. Just them.

And then he was there. Shoving the empty chair away, crouching down next to her, cupping her cheek with one hand. "What is it, baby?"

Her throat was filled with chalk, choking her, making her feel like she had to gasp and cough.

But then Fletcher leaned in and whispered, "Do I need to pull out the chocolate chip cookie I have stashed in my pocket?"

That chalk cleared.

Her lungs unstuck, and she felt herself go soft. "Do you really have a chocolate chip cookie in your pocket?"

He grinned and rocked back slightly on his heels, reaching into his pocket, and pulling out a zip top bag. Inside was a slightly worse for wear chocolate chip cookie. He opened the top, and she reached in and yanked out the sweet treat, shoved an insanely large bite into her mouth.

"Better?" he asked on a laugh.

She nodded.

"Now, why the panic?"

The cookie was on the way to her mouth, her lips parted and tongue flat, readying for another huge bite, but his question reminded her that they had an audience.

Cheeks heating, she turned back to the table.

Everyone was staring.

Not one of the lot of them were making any effort to hide the fact that they were openly watching her interact with Fletcher.

"I never thought of taming her with cookies," Brad quipped. "Come on man, you're shirking on your eldest brother duties. How did you miss that?"

Jaime snorted. "Did you forget about the bags of Chips Ahoy Mom used to carry around?"

Heidi smacked Brad. "Stop being obnoxious," she snapped. "Or should I talk about what I carry around to tame *you?*"

Brad flushed.

"Oh now, *this* is more interesting than Tammy being tamed with chocolate," Cora—bless her heart—said. "It's not like all of us don't know that she has a sweet tooth. Heidi, what—"

Brad covered his wife's mouth with his hand. "Don't finish that question," he said, stabbing a finger in Cora's direction. "Otherwise, I won't use my connections to get you that discount in the Maldives."

Cora glared. "I don't need your discount, Brad Huntington."

"But it's a nice perk," he countered. "Plus, I can get you upgraded to an ocean view suite."

A huff and Tammy knew he'd won. Cora's expression was

murderous, but she turned the topic of the conversation to what other perks Brad could secure for her in exchange for her not pushing the topic of what had made him blush like that.

In the meantime, her brief respite in place, she turned to Fletch, eyes wide, panic no doubt written onto her face.

"What, sweetheart?"

"I forgot you coming here tonight means that you'll have to meet my brothers."

"I didn't, Tam," he said, tucking a lock of her hair behind her ear with a gentleness that made her heart squeeze. "You mentioned that your brothers are married to your friends. I knew what I was getting into."

The larger conversation had turned to Jaime, to trying to get Kate to dish on what made her older brother blush.

So, Fletch still had a chance to flee.

"Fly, you fool," she hissed.

He grinned, bopped her on the nose. "Quiet, Gandalf." He shifted so he sat in the elephant of a chair next to her and took her hand before saying, "Need another bite of cookie? Or are you ready for me to introduce myself to your brothers?"

"Oh God," she moaned, and shoved the rest of the cookie into her mouth.

Fletch kissed her cheek then stood and while she was chewing—and couldn't protest—he rounded the table and started for her brothers. He was shaking Jaime's hand before she swallowed, then Brad stood and gave him a glare that should have withered Fletch's balls.

Everyone always thought Jaime was the one to watch out for because he was the oldest brother.

But it was Brad who was the most protective.

Brad might have traveled for many years, been out of the country more than in it, but he'd never missed important events, he'd always had his finger on the pulse of the family. He was the one to watch out for.

Fletcher seemed to pick up on that, too.

He extended a hand. "I'm Fletcher."

"Brad."

A clipped-out word.

"What makes you think that you're good enough to date my sister?"

Tammy swallowed the remnants of the cookie and winced, started to stand. Yeah, no. They weren't going to do this.

But Heidi beat her to it. "Bradley Huntington, can the toxic masculinity and sit your ass down, or I really *will* tell the entire table what I carry in my purse for you."

"Tammy can take care of herself," Kate said. Her eyes slanted toward Fletcher. "Not that we won't stab a bitch"—Tammy almost choked again, hearing Kate, who was the sweetest one in their bunch, calmly threaten Fletcher—"if you hurt her. But she'd probably beat us all to it."

Fletch glanced at her and winked, apparently not in the least bit put off by all the threatening. "I *know* she would."

She glugged down some of her margarita. "How do you deal with six of them?" she grumbled to Cora.

Her friend didn't miss a beat. "I moved across the country."

Tammy laughed. "Poor, poor baby."

"Damned right. *And* they scared off the latest guy I was dating when they visited. Now I have no one but me and my vibrator and you guys."

"Hopefully the vibrator is only put to use when you're *not* with us."

A wink. "Wouldn't you like to know?"

"Eww." But Tammy was grinning, and she'd relaxed enough that her gaze drifted away from Fletcher, who was now introducing himself to Tanner, and studied her friend whose expression was mischief personified in that moment. "Please, tell me you're joking."

"Dude. We've spent enough time together that I think you'd

hear my panties vibrating, or at the very least know my O face."
Cora drew her features into something so comical it should have
been straight out of a choreographed Hollywood sex scene.

"I say again *ew.*"

Cora grinned. "How're the nerves?"

Fletcher was chatting with Kate and Kels, and both women
were clearly charmed. Jaime was watching him, but his expression was neutral, and she knew that Fletcher had probably
already earned his approval, what with the cookie and his
looking out for her. Brad would take a while, especially since
she'd never brought a man home. He'd know that Fletcher was
important and there would be extra consideration for that,
which along with overprotectiveness, would mean that Fletch
had some hoops to jump through.

But...Fletcher would.

Even though they were new, she understood that, *trusted* in
that.

It was heels sailing into trees and carrying a cookie in his
pocket for her.

It was gentle touches and kisses to her jaw and the soft way
he said her name when he slid into her.

It was Fletcher and fake not being fake and his family and
Trina.

Which was why she smiled at Cora, picked up her glass, and
took a sip of her margarita. "The nerves are just fine."

Twenty-Two

Aside from Brad shooting daggers at him the entire meal —they never did find out what was in his wife's purse —Fletcher had a great time hanging out with Tammy's friends.

They were a tight group, and though there were plenty of inside jokes—mostly about a show called *90 Day Fiancé: The Other Way*—he didn't feel isolated or on the outside during the couple of hours they sat around that table.

Tammy drank her margaritas, and pretty soon her embarrassed flush became an alcohol flush, but no one got sloppy.

It was Thursday, after all, and these people seemed to know their limits.

And not that he would be pressured to drink when he didn't want to—he had to drive Tammy home, after all—but he had an important meeting in the morning, so he didn't want to be off his game.

The meeting was key for him and his plans to talk his way into her bed every night.

He wanted forever.

So, he couldn't fuck it up.

They'd wrapped up dinner, ordering a final round of drinks and several more plates of sopapillas layered with honey and powdered sugar (and seriously, he needed to buy those items for his pantry and lick them off every inch of her body) because magically all of the alcohol and sticky, sugary desserts had been Hoovered. Then arguments had been made over paying the bill —apparently it was Tammy's turn to put the total on her credit card while everyone else Venmoed her, and her brothers didn't want her to have a big charge on her card.

To which she rolled her eyes, ignored them, handed her card to the waiter, and paid for dinner.

Everyone had sent her their share, and now they were all standing out front of the restaurant gabbing about work and life and Kate and Jaime's pets. Apparently, their goats had chewed their way through a fence in their back yard and had eaten their neighbor's prize-winning roses.

"Then Mrs. Davidson comes up to our porch, throws the stems at Jamie's feet, and declares, *This is war!*"

Jaime winced. "Never thought I would be terrified of an eighty-year-old woman."

"Well, she *did* have a cane," Kate pointed out.

"And was swinging it," Jaime muttered.

"Good thing you're excellent at dodging," Stef teased. "Gotta watch out for all those dangerous kitties."

"Hey, their nails are *sharp*," Jamie grumbled. "Plus, it's the roosters you have to watch out for."

"The Fuzz is an angel!" Kate protested. "He would never attack anyone with a cane."

"Only because he doesn't have opposable thumbs," Ben said quietly. The businessman, famous enough in tech circles that Fletch had recognized the man with just a glance, was quiet. Not exactly standoffish, just more of an observer rather than joining in on the teasing.

So the quip made laughter bubble up in Fletcher's throat.

Tammy grinned up at him, kissed his jaw.

Kate—maybe one margarita too far into the evening—pointed her finger at Ben. "It's the quiet ones you have to watch out for."

"You'd know, Red," Jaime murmured, kissing the top of her head. "Come on, you two," he said to Brad and Heidi, who he was driving home. "I think talk of roosters and opposable thumbs means it's time for this one to go to bed."

"If there was ever a rooster who could manage to swing a cane at someone, it would be The Fuzz," Kate said, tossing her hands up.

Jaime chuckled, kissed her head again. "Of course, he would."

Stef snagged Ben's hand. "I have to stop by the lab on the way home, so we should probably go, too."

Kels, Tanner, and Cora all hung for a few more minutes, walking with Tammy and Fletcher toward their cars as they talked about the trip Kels and Tanner were planning for the following month and Cora's visit home in a couple of weeks for one of her brothers' weddings.

It was easy, and though he had friends here in town, they weren't like this.

There was a closeness that spoke of hours and hours together, of lives being intertwined and connected and overlapping.

He loved that Tammy had that.

They reached his car—Tammy having taken a Lyft over because they were going back to her place afterward—and said goodbye to the others. Then they were inside and driving down the road, heading to Tammy's house.

She was quiet for a long time, and he thought that it might

be the alcohol and all the food making her sleepy, but when she spoke, her voice wasn't sleepy in the least. "I hated him."

He frowned, glanced over at her. "Your brothers?"

Was it left over from growing up? From feeling like she was forgotten?

"No," she said. "I was jealous of them for a long time, of the attention my parents gave them and feeling like I was lost in the shuffle. But looking at it from the perspective of a grown up, of having someone I know sees me, I'm almost thankful for it." She fussed with the strap of the seat belt, running her fingers up and down the fabric. "It let me become my own person. Did it sting and hurt? Yes. Does it still hurt sometimes, and did I feel isolated? Of course."

"I'm sorry, honey," he said, "That must have been very hard."

"I'm not trying to say my parents weren't great," she said. "They were and are and it would probably break their hearts if they knew I felt this way, so I've never told them."

"Why not?"

A pause. "Why what?"

"Why haven't you told them?"

She went quiet again. "Did you not hear the part about breaking their hearts?"

"I heard it," he said, "but based on your brothers' planned disembowelment of me if I step a toe out of line, I know your family loves you, and I think it would kill them if they found out you were holding something this big back. I don't think they'd want you to be hurting when they could do something about it."

"I—" She blew out a breath. "I know it seems like a big thing," she whispered, "but it isn't."

He reached over the console and took her hand. "Isn't it?"

"I—" A sigh.

"You ran from relationships," he pointed out gently. "You said so yourself."

"I didn't run because of that. I—or not *only* that." She sighed again. "When I said I hate *him*, I meant Calvin. My ex. He's why I didn't want a relationship. He—I told him about my upbringing, about how I felt forgotten and on the outside. I gave him everything, every bit of vulnerability, and he said all the right things." She tightened her grip on his fingers. "I was really lost and feeling like I could never measure up to my siblings—" She huffed out a laugh. "I mean, have you meant them? They're ridiculously talented and my mom just runs a billion-dollar business like it's no big deal. It's hard to feel that I'm like them, that I fit in with them—"

He was even more glad for the meeting tomorrow.

"You're brilliant," he said. "There's a reason every project you submit gets approved, why people are clamoring to work with you."

A shrug. "It's just HR stuff."

He shook his head. "It's not just HR stuff. You're gathering important information so that our company, our *industry* can change for the better. Your work—our work—is critically valuable, and you're a huge part of that."

"Fletch," she began.

"Do you deny it's important?"

"I—" She pressed her lips together. "*No*. Making this kind of difference is what I've always wanted."

"Right." He turned into her driveway and parked. "Me, too. So," he said, reaching for her and taking her hands, "what did Calvin do?"

"It's not so much what he did—or not *solely* what he did." Tammy rolled her neck. "It's how I was with him."

He waited.

"We ran away together."

That was pretty much the last thing he expected her to say. "What do you mean, honey?"

Her eyes skated away from his. "I…" She blew out a breath and dropped her head back. "God, I was so stupid back then. I was eighteen. He was twenty. I thought he was amazing and my future, and I did a lot of stupid shit with him, not the least of which was giving him my virginity and then running off to get married without letting my family know."

Fuck.

"We went to Vegas. Got hitched, and then spent a month together. I told my family I was taking a road trip and needed the time alone before college. They…let me go. I was always independent, mostly because I'd had to be, you know?" She glanced at him and he nodded encouragingly. "So anyway, they were used to me going off and doing my own thing, didn't question when I disappeared for a while." She sighed. "And I was young and stupid and in love, so fucking excited to be taking that road trip with him, spending my days with a man who made me deliriously happy, feeling like he was the first person who wouldn't forget me." She sucked in a breath through her nose. "And all the while he was playing me. When he realized that he wasn't going to get handouts from my parents—because I didn't *get* handouts from them, and because I was determined to make my own way—he stole my car and left me on the side of the road in Wyoming."

"*What?*"

Fury had him flying out of his door, rounding the hood, and pulling her out of her seat. "Are you serious right now?"

She smiled sadly. "Ask me how terrifying it was to camp out overnight on the side of the road, nothing but twenty bucks in my pocket and knowing that grizzly bears were in the fucking forest around me."

He was going to kill Calvin.

He knew people. He could take the fucker down.

Okay, he didn't know people, but he was still going to take the fucker down.

"One second, we were arguing about money and how I wouldn't ask my parents for some so we could stay in some fancy hotel he wanted to spend the weekend in, and the next he was screeching to a stop on the side of the road, yanking me out so hard that I had sprained my wrist, ended up with scrapes on my elbows and arms and knees, a lump on my head." He wrapped an arm around her, led her to the house. "I woke up, tried to walk to town and ended up not making it that first night. I made it by the second, though, and filed a police report then called my parents. But I didn't tell them about Calvin, didn't tell *anyone* about the marriage. I just Googled annulments and figured out how to get myself out of it." She nibbled the corner of her mouth, her voice dropping to almost a whisper. "And then I never told anyone what really happened, just tried to shove it down and forget it, even as I promised myself I'd never make the same mistake again."

"Oh, babe."

He wrapped an arm around her, drew her toward the front door, punched the code to unlock it, and they went inside. "What happened to Calvin?"

She shook her head. "They found the car abandoned. The police never located him." He bypassed the living room, took her straight to the bedroom and sat her on the bed. Next step pajamas. He snagged them from the drawer, grabbed the ugly ass robe she'd worn that morning on her porch with the douchebag she'd been trying to get rid of. It was holey and faded, but it was also soft and warm, and she needed the comfort. "And anyway," she said, "I was determined to pretend it didn't happen. To forget that I'd been so critically stupid. Then then annulment went through, I locked everything down, and I made sure to never be in that position again."

"Hence the boyfriends—or lack thereof," he said, helping

her get out of her work clothes and tugging on her pajamas. She smiled when he wrapped the robe around her.

"Yes. I wasn't going to ever do that again." Her nose wrinkled. "Until a stubborn as hell man was determined that I save the day for him." Her face softened. "He demanded that I ride in on my white stallion for him, so I did."

"And then he threw her shoes into the forest?"

"Pushy fucker, wasn't he?" she teased.

He laughed. "Damned right." He nudged her back, crawled into bed next to her, tugging her into his arms. "I'm really sorry that happened to you, baby." She nuzzled in. "What was Calvin's last name?"

"Why I—?" She stopped, shook her head. "I wasn't going to let my brothers get away with the big, tough man will solve my problems bullshit, and I'm certainly not going to let you do the same."

"Why not?"

She froze, then shot up, her mouth dropping open. "Fletcher, you—" Her words cut off when she presumably took in his expression—that being he was teasing her—and she shook her head. "You're in *so* much trouble."

"I know," he said. "Because I have a wonderful woman with a beautiful heart in my life who is so fucking brave and strong and smart, and I would do anything for her."

Her face went soft.

"But, sweetheart," he told her gently, "that wonderful, brave woman needs to talk to her family about this."

Soft to panicked in a heartbeat.

"I know it's scary," he said, gently stroking her hair back. "I know you've held it in, and that you were trying to push it down so you didn't have to deal with it, so that you could move on. And as a man who was great at doing that, at wanting to pretend I was over Trina and then thought a fake relationship was the solution to my problems—which, luckily for me, turned out for the better—I know that's not the way forward. So, I'm not telling you to talk to your family, I'm just...I don't know...*suggesting* strongly that you get this—Calvin, feeling like an outsider—off your chest, baby. Then we can move forward and conquer all the HR reports, change the face of the industry, and you can slum it by dating a guy who's sort of at your level."

Her brows pulled together. Her lips pursed. But her eyes were filled with love, and that was enough for him. "I'll take it under advisement."

A kiss to the tip of her nose. "That's good enough for me."

She smiled. "And I'm slumming it?"

"Definitely."

Tammy rolled her eyes. "Did you forget that you carry a chocolate chip cookie in your pocket? That you got mad at my shoes for having the audacity to hurt my feet?"

He grinned. "I'm never going to hear the end of the shoes, am I?"

"Nope." She pressed a kiss to his mouth. "And the reason I can tease you about the shoes is because I know I'm safe. With you, Fletch, I know I'm safe, know I'm seen."

His heart squeezed tight.

And he hoped she also knew she was loved.

Soon.

When they were together a little longer. When it wasn't so new and fresh, he would tell one Tammy Huntington that she'd stolen his heart.

And hope she would trust him with hers right back.

Twenty-Three

Three weeks, three friends' dinners, one weekend with Fletch's parents, and two Huntington-McLeod (Kate and her family were a hoot, and it wasn't terrible that she got to see Heidi, too) dinners later, Tammy was finalizing the last lines of the first report for her diversity project. They'd conducted some stealthy research, seeing how different email signatures—male versus female, standard English names versus some that were more unfamiliar—were communicated with.

Each reply was then evaluated on a scale they'd set up beforehand and that rating was put into a program to be tracked.

Now they had all the ratings and the replies and the report she'd just finished putting together was going to be sent over to CEO Heather O'Keith.

It was going to be awesome.

Maybe as awesome as dinner the next night.

A King-McLeod-Huntington family BBQ was happening at Kate's house.

Three families. Numerous couples. Several goats and The

Fuzz. It was going to be total chaos. But finally, all the moms were going to meet. Tammy had absolute confidence that Connie was going to join the ranks of The Moms, and the ultimate ruling power of the universe would become a trifecta.

A scary thought.

She grinned. It was going to be wonderful.

Because she was *in love!*

She spun in her chair, catching a glimpse of the skyline of San Francisco through the window as her chair turned, absolutely giddy that she was dating Fletcher, that not one moment of it hadn't been amazing, that there was no drama or doubts.

Every night they'd been together.

Every day they ate lunch together.

And though they'd played it relatively cool at work, there wasn't anyone in the department who didn't know they were together. Mostly because Lisa had been moaning about them making Lovey Eyes at each other. But really...it was because they were making Lovey Eyes at each other.

She sighed happily and spun once again.

Then nearly flew out of her chair when she heard, "Here." Lisa smacked down a file on her desk, and Tammy barely got her feet on the floor before her boss was striding out of her office, muttering about young love.

"Make sure you give *your* young love a kiss when you get home, Lis," she called.

Her boss flipped her off over her shoulder—which was normal. She was cranky and grumpy and despite the HR distinction—they were sometimes the worst offenders when it came to proper behavior—or at least with cursing and flipping the bird. But what happened next wasn't normal. Because Lisa spun around, and her face was sad.

Damned sad.

"I hope he's worth it," she said. "I hope to God Fletcher is worth giving everything up."

"Wh—"

But before she could finish the question, Lisa was gone, shutting the door behind her, leaving Tammy in stunned silence for a long moment before she remembered the file.

"What the fuck?" she whispered, reaching for the envelope.

Tearing it open.

Whispering again, "What the fuck?"

As the bottom dropped out of her world.

Twenty-Four

FLETCHER

He'd left work early to get everything ready.

His parents would be in early tomorrow morning, so he wanted this night with Tammy to be special and romantic and just about them.

He loved his family and hers was awesome, too.

But tonight, he had Tammy in his house, his bed, and it was going to be an awesome night.

There was a knock at the door, which he thought was weird, but then again, he suffered from Amazonesia, so it could easily be just a package showing up magically on his porch. Straightening the bouquet of red-tinged sunflowers he'd picked up to celebrate their favorite flower, he headed to answer the door.

Tammy was on the other side.

He felt his smile grow. "Hey, sweetheart," he said, reaching for her, "did you forget your key—"

She stepped back.

Her face went cold.

Frost slid down his spine. "Tammy, honey, what is it?"

She slapped a folder to his chest. "How could you?" she hissed. "How could you do this to me?"

He barely caught the papers before they dropped to the ground. "What is this?" he asked, shifting the file to one hand, reaching out with the other to grab her arm when she started to turn away from him, to try and stride away across the porch. "Wait, Tammy. Seriously, what's going on?"

She yanked her arm out of his grip. "Don't fucking touch me. I trusted you. I *loved* you. I put my fear aside and gave you everything I had in me, and y-you fucked me over." A shaky breath, tears pouring down her cheeks. "I thought Calvin had destroyed me, but you...you incinerated me, my heart, my dreams, my j-job—"

"Tam—" He started to step toward her, but she backed away again.

"Don't—"

"Talk to me, sweetheart. Tell me—"

A shake of her head. "No. *No*, I'm not doing this. You—you —" More tears escaped. And then she turned and ran down the steps, sprinting for her car.

"Tammy, wait!" He started to take off after her, but then remembered what he held. He flipped open the top of the envelope, pulled out the papers, and started to read. His heart sank down to his feet as he began to process the words, dread scorching through him. This was wrong. This wasn't what they'd discussed. Every bit of it was wrong. So *fucking* wrong. "Tam—"

Tires squealed in his driveway, and his head jerked up, gaze going to her car—or rather watching her car shoot away from his house like the hounds of hell were after her.

Or maybe like an asshole had broken her heart.

Again.

"Fuck," he whispered, turning and striding into the house.

The sunflowers on the counter mocked him.

"Fuck!" He growled, shoving his feet into his boots, wanting to put a fist through the wall, wanting to tear up the papers in his hands or light them on fire, to turn them to ash and pretend this hadn't just happened.

But it had.

And he needed to find a way to fix it.

———

Heather O'Keith was a scary motherfucker.

Probably because he'd just stormed into her office, bypassing the desk that normally held a secretary preventing just this sort of interaction.

But then again, it was nearly seven on a Friday evening and most sane people weren't in the office.

Heather wasn't always considered sane—or at least in business circles—mostly because she pulled insane hours. Workaholic was a weak description for her. Though, rumor had it her husband Clay Steele had chilled out her working habits, at least a little bit. She took time off, and more often than not, she wouldn't be here this late, especially on a Friday.

But he'd known she would be in.

She'd just returned from overseeing the testing on Robo-Tech's drone project, a collaboration with the Scottish billionaire, Colin McGregor. Fletcher's understanding was that it would be utilized to drop food and medical supplies in areas hard-hit by natural—or man-made—disasters or those places not easily accessible to relief workers. The whole project sounded pretty fucking amazing, and normally he'd be proud to be part of a company that was investing in that kind of humanitarian project.

What *didn't* sound amazing was that he'd had a meeting with the head of HR and Heather O'Keith three fucking weeks ago where he'd discussed his and Tammy's relationship and requested that he be the one to be transferred out of Lisa's department.

He was supposed to be taking a slight demotion, even.

Tammy—God, *Tammy* was supposed to be untouched, unaffected, not to have her position change in the slightest.

Because it was her dream, and he would never take it away.

"We had a fucking *arrangement*," he snapped, trying to hold on to his temper, because this was his livelihood, but also struggling with control because he was pissed out of his mind. He'd done the right thing, gone along the right channels. HR had brought in Heather because it was an unusual request and though she'd wanted some assurance that this was the right thing for him as her employee, she'd told him that she respected his decision.

And then *this*.

Tammy being shifted out of HR.

Completely out. She'd been so fucking excited to finish her report, so excited to share the results with Lisa, with Demi (the head of HR), with Heather.

And instead, she got a shitty ass letter telling her that she was being transferred to engineering.

Engineering?

Seriously, what the fuck was that?

Her specialty was HR.

Her *dream* was HR.

Put *him* in fucking Engineering.

"Careful," Clay said, who was a regular enough visitor at the office that Fletcher recognized Heather's husband. Well, that and the fact that he'd been kissing Heather when Fletcher had stormed into her office would have clued him in. Either way, Clay wasn't looking all that pleased at the interruption.

"Fuck careful," Fletcher snapped, stomping over to Heather's desk and slamming the file onto the messy surface.

And yeah, interrupting his boss and her husband in an interlude and snapping at both of them was probably stupid as fuck, especially if he wanted to keep his job—or get Tammy back her old one.

"Sit the fuck down," Heather said, picking up the envelope and opening it.

Fletcher moved to the chair but didn't sit down, just gripped the back of it, his fingers digging into the wood. "You assured me that everything was going to be okay. You *promised* me that Tammy would be taken care of."

Heather's eyes flicked across the papers. "It seems like she's been taken care of," she said. "Same level. Same salary. In fact, a better opportunity for growth."

"A different job description," he growled. "One that won't have her doing what she's passionate about."

"Hmm." Heather settled into her chair as she continued to read. Clay remained standing—and glaring at Fletcher. She set the file down, glanced at her computer screen. Then she picked up the phone and made a call that had his heart dropping all over again.

"Security?" she said, "I need you to..."

TWENTY-FIVE

TAMMY

Her eyes were swollen.
She could actually feel them pulsing in her skull, and her throat felt like shit.

She'd barely made it back to her house, her tears had been streaming down her face, clouding her vision.

Fucking hell.

Then she'd sat in her driveway, unable to go in, the betrayal pulsing through her.

Anger taking over.

Her tears drying.

She'd found herself backing out and driving aimlessly.

Until she'd parked in a familiar lot.

Bright lights, empty parking spaces surrounding her.

A multi-story building in front of her. It was mostly dark inside, pretty much anyone with a life having already gone home for the weekend. She still grabbed her keys and her badge.

Not picked.

Forgotten.

Those two sentiments rattled around her brain, and she let herself in and headed for the elevator, up to her floor. To the HR department. To her office.

To the report still sitting on her desk.

Because she was going to go through it one more time. She was going to make it the best fucking report anyone had ever seen.

And then she was going to look for another job.

Because *she* wanted to be the one who was picked.

Not the one who was shuffled around because someone else —because Fletcher—was more important. Not again. No more.

No—

"Ma'am?"

She blinked, halting in the process of opening her office door, and turned to see a security guard was standing in the hall, his arms crossed. "Y-yes?" she asked haltingly.

"I need you to come with me."

"I—" She held up her badge. "I work here."

"You need to come with me."

"I just want to get a report—"

"You need to come with me."

Seriously?

Maybe the icing on the cake was that she was getting fired. Not just a position shift. But canned right when she felt like she was going to live out her dreams.

Because she'd let a fucking man in.

That protective bubble surrounding her had popped—had disappeared like it never existed in the first place.

She sighed, closed the door. "Okay," she said on a sigh, "Lead the way." And she followed the guard to and the into the elevator.

Kick her out of the building.

Send her off to the police.

Book and fingerprint her. Throw her in a cell. Do whatever

they did to people who snuck in to do extra work on a Friday night.

Yes, she was being dramatic.

But fuck...Fletcher. He'd done this and—

The elevator doors opened, and she stepped off.

Then looked around in confusion. This wasn't the lobby. This was...the executive level. What the fuck?

The guard touched her elbow. "This way."

Dread settled into her, a stifling cloud, but she was on the floor, and she'd gotten the file with her new job in it. If that wasn't on the table any longer, if Heather O'Keith or some other executive wanted to demote her in person, well, then Tammy was about to get demoted—or hell, maybe even fired—in person.

The guard led her all the way down the hall, past the smaller offices, and to the one directly at the end.

Oh, joy.

Yup.

Tammy was about to see Heather O'Keith in person.

On a Friday night. Probably with her mascara running all over the place, her voice hoarse from her sobs, her eyes swollen.

Yay.

The guard opened the door, nudged her inside.

The moment Tammy saw who was within, she tried to turn and GTFO. But then the door *clicked* closed behind her.

And she was shut in Heather O'Keith's office with a man she never wanted to see again.

For the record, that man wasn't Clay Steele, the handsome blue-eyed man standing with his arms crossed behind Heather's chair, but rather the handsome blue-eyed man who'd held her heart...and then shattered it.

She spun, intending to flee.

Yes, it was cowardly.

But fuck, this *sucked*.

"Sit," Heather ordered.

"I—"

"Tammy. *Sit.*"

Ah fuck, that *tone.* It was Mom Tone or Boss Tone or Mom-Boss Tone.

Whatever it was, she found herself unable to ignore it. She found herself walking toward the chair and plunking her ass down into it.

And then waiting.

As Heather studied her and didn't say anything. And seriously, was *this* what they were doing here? Sitting in silence while Tammy's heart broke all over again?

The quiet stretched on, tense and still. Heather's eyes on hers. Fletcher a silent, antsy presence to her right. "I—"

"Fletcher met with me and Demi almost three weeks ago," Heather began before Tammy's sentence could materialize. "He disclosed your relationship and requested that he be transferred out from Lisa's department so that you could stay in your position. He was going to take a demotion so that your job description didn't change."

What?

But the question stayed in her throat, smothered by too many emotions bursting through her, a firework of hope, of pain, of longing and joy and fury.

Still, her eyes shot to Fletcher's.

He nodded, barely.

"Now, what I didn't tell him. Or you," she added when Tammy's gaze moved back to the CEO, "was that Fletcher taking a demotion just so we could hop through some HR loops didn't sit well with me. You weren't a direct report to him. There was no power disparity. If he was in Lisa's position, that would present some difficulty." Heather sighed and leaned back in her chair, steepling her fingers. "But he's not. And while he has more seniority than you, it's not enough to manifest into the issue that Lisa was so worried about."

Fletcher shifted closer.

Heather continued talking. "So, he left the meeting thinking his demotion would be happening. He'd signed the paperwork, filed everything he needed to file. But I pulled his papers before Demi could process them. Because I got wind of the project you"—she held Tammy's gaze—"were spearheading. I was excited. This is exactly the type of project I wanted to conduct when I took over RoboTech. What you're doing is meaningful and important, but truthfully, it's a better fit with the engineering department. They have the programming and data analysis experience. In fact, even though I've only seen the preliminaries for what you're doing, I think it'll mesh perfectly with the program Kelsey Scott's team is developing."

Tammy froze. "Kels?" Her friend, Kels?

Heather's face gentled slightly. "Yes, *Kels*." She stood, rounded her desk, and sat on the edge of it. "You'd be okay working with her? Doing more of what you're doing now, just in a different department?"

A bit dumbfounded, a lot relieved, and with excitement beginning to brew, Tammy nodded.

"Good." Heather sighed. "So, now I find myself in a position I hate: having to apologize."

Clay snorted.

Heather shot him a glare then turned back to her and Fletch. "As much as I don't appreciate someone"—her eyes locked onto Fletcher—"barreling into my office and demanding that I fix this. I also *really* don't like it when I fuck up. I planned on talking to you about the job next week when I was back in the office, not at seven at night on a Friday."

Tammy winced.

"However, what I didn't plan on was my very efficient

assistant being three steps ahead of me and filing the paperwork before I had a chance to discuss it with you."

"I—" Tammy sucked in a breath and released it slowly. "So, I'm really not getting demoted?"

"No, Huntington," Heather said with a smile. "I want you to keep doing what you've been doing, just on a bigger scale."

"And—" Her gaze went to Fletcher's. "You really were going to take a demotion for me?"

His face gentled. "In a heartbeat, baby."

That protective bubble reappeared without warning, surrounding her in a flash, making her wonder if it had ever been gone, or if it had just been invisible. Because she was a fucking moron. She groaned, dropped her head into her hands. "I'm such an idiot."

Warm palms on her face, lips brushing her forehead. "Not an idiot. Understandably upset."

"I stormed to your house and tossed papers in your face," she snapped. "Then stormed off without even getting an explanation from you. So *fucking* stupid. I should have let you explain and—*oof*." One second, she was in the chair and the next she was in his arms.

"Tammy, honey," he said, "If I'd gotten this news without an explanation, I would have freaked, too." He stroked a hand down her back. "This is a trigger for you. You need trust and care and not to have any secrets, and your job is important to you. Do I wish you would have given me a second to have a conversation about this? To read the paperwork? Of course." His hand stroked back up. "But would I have still stormed in here and interrupted Heather and Clay canoodling?"

"Canood—"

She cut off the question, remembering where they were.

In her boss's boss's *boss's* office.

Shit.

She flew out of Fletcher's arms, gaze darting around the office, realizing that she and Fletch were alone.

"They were canoodling?" she whispered, half-expecting them to pop out from some secret hidey hole and tell her and Fletcher to stop with *their* canoodling.

He nodded. "Jumped apart like guilty school kids." His mouth turned up. "Kind of like what you just did."

She found herself chuckling...and then she found herself crumbling.

More tears.

But these ones were tears of relief.

It didn't matter, though, because the tears had barely cleared her lashes when she was in Fletcher's arms again, his arms stroking up and down her back, his words gentle and sweet. "I can't believe you stormed into our boss's boss's *boss's* office going to bat for me," she said when she could finally speak again without losing it.

"I'd do it again."

No hesitation.

No prevarication.

Her heart swelled.

Because she knew that, too.

"I'm sorry," she whispered guilt practically drowning her.

"I'm not."

Again, no hesitation. No prevarication. Just truth.

"Why?"

He stroked her cheek. "Because now you get to live out your even bigger dream.

"Oh, fuck."

Fletch went still. "What?"

"You know you've gone and made me fall in love with you?"

Somehow, he went even more still. "What?" he breathed.

She brushed her nose along his. "You heard me. How can I not love a man who throws my shoes into trees?" A smile on his gorgeous mouth. "How can I not love a man who has a favorite flower?" A kiss to those gorgeous lips—one that left her breathless, her heart racing. "How can I not *love* a man who wants to make my dreams come true?"

Even though she'd stupidly lost it on him.

Even though she'd run.

He'd still fought for her, for her dreams.

That meant more than anything else.

"Tammy," he whispered, and his throat was clogged with tears, his eyes shiny. "Fuck, I love you."

She smiled, those words strengthening the bubble, running rebar all along the inside, making it so it would never pop, never collapse.

Safe.

She was safe.

And in love.

Tammy Huntington, the woman who promised a hundred, a thousand times that she would never, *ever* trust her heart to another person, had freely given it away.

Wasn't it fucking great?

Epilogue

"And I know I should have talked to you about this sooner..." Tammy trailed off, tears glistening on her cheeks. She'd just told her mom everything about Calvin, about feeling forgotten growing up, and how those had played into her avoiding relationships with men.

"Oh, honey," Tawny said, sliding closer on the couch and hugging her daughter close. "I do wish you'd told me sooner, but I understand why you might have held that in."

"You do?"

Tawny smoothed back Tammy's hair, wiped her tears. "I should have seen through the shields, baby. You were always so independent, but I never considered that you felt that you had to be." A kiss to Tammy's forehead. "I'm so sorry."

"No. Don't apologize. It's not your fault—"

"Honey." Andrew's voice took on a sharp edge as he joined his wife and daughter on the couch. "Who's the parent in this scenario?"

"But—"

"We *should* have noticed."

Andrew slipped an arm around both of them, held them close, and Fletcher decided that was the cue for him to leave. Quietly, he stood from the armchair Tammy had asked him to sit in for moral, and left the room on soft feet.

They needed privacy and to talk it out more.

Not that one conversation would fix everything.

But it would be a start, and Tammy hopefully would feel heard and seen and like a weight had been lifted off her shoulders.

"You love her."

He turned at the cold voice, turned to face the one Huntington who'd continued to glare at him over the last months during every friends' dinner, every time their families got together, every single time that he and Brad were in the same room.

Now, it was still cold.

But there was something else in that tonight.

"That's not even a question," Fletcher said, moving down the hall and away from the conversation that was taking place in the living room. He didn't want to distract Tammy or her parents from what they needed to talk out, not when they finally *were* talking it out.

Not when his beautiful, kind Tammy had finally found the strength to share.

The demons wouldn't have any power over her.

He was still working on finding out Calvin's last name from her, determined to do...*something* to make the other man pay.

But considering that Tammy was the only woman he'd ever met who was more stubborn than he was, Fletcher didn't have much hope that he'd get it out of her.

"Who was he?"

Fletch stopped and faced Tammy's brother. "What?"

"The man who hurt her?"

Fletcher glanced back down the hall, wanting to make sure they were far enough away from Tammy and her parents. "Who says a man hurt her?"

"*I'm* saying that." Brad stepped closer, his expression so like Tammy's that it was uncanny. "Tell me so I can take care of it."

It was tempting to admit what he knew, to get an ally in the Fuck Calvin Up plan. But this was Tammy's truth, and she'd just found the courage to share it with her parents. It needed to be on her terms to share it with her siblings.

"And *I'm* saying that your sister has it handled, and you need to back off. She'll come to you if she needs help."

Silence.

Tense silence and flashing eyes.

But he'd been on the other end of that Huntington glare plenty of times before.

He knew how to withstand it.

He just held Brad's eyes and said again, "This is Tammy's life, and I'm supporting her in it, not taking it over."

"That's bull—"

"*That's*," Heidi interrupted, "perfectly reasonable, and you know it, love. Your sister is perfectly capable of handling her own life." She swept into the hall and wove her arm through Brad's. "Come on. We're heating up the pizza oven, and you need to choose your toppings." She started to tug her husband toward the backyard, but glanced over her shoulder. "For the record, Fletcher, that was the perfect answer. Tammy doesn't need a keeper, or a protector. She needs someone who loves her for the awesome woman she is."

Brad scowled. "The man threw her expensive *heels* into the forest."

God. He really never *was* going to hear the end of the shoes.

"That was sweet," Heidi said. "That just shows how much he loves her."

"So is sharing the name of the asshole who hurt her," Brad grumbled.

"Someone hurt her?" Heidi dropped her husband's arm and marched over to Fletcher. "You didn't tell me that someone hurt her. Tell me the asshole's name and I'll—"

"I love her for the capable, strong woman she is," he said. "And I would never take away her ability to take over." A beat. "Even if I've begged her to let me." Brad finally lost the fury, the first notes of humor entering his eyes. "I would take the burden if I could. But I can't in this instance. She doesn't want me to, so I have to respect that."

"And you're just going to step back and accept that?" Brad asked.

"I love her," Fletcher said. "There's nothing *but* acceptance."

Brad held his gaze for a long time before nodding, and there might have been approval in Tammy's brother's eyes.

Might have been.

Or maybe that was wishful thinking.

Or maybe not.

Because Brad clapped him on the shoulder and started walking again, heading for the sliding glass doors that led to the back yard and the pizza oven that was warmed up and ready to create deliciousness.

"Come on," Brad said before he went out. "Let's eat."

"Wait." Heidi stopped in the hall, glancing between them. "You said that someone hurt Tammy. Who is he?" She whipped out her phone, started taking notes. "What's his full name and occupation?" she asked, fingers flying. "Oh, and his social security number."

"Heid—" Brad began.

"Dish, King," she snapped. "Now."

"What happened to Tammy being capable of handling her own shit?"

"What *happened* is someone hurt my Tammy and I'm going to—"

"Do nothing because it's in the past?"

Tammy's voice slid through the hall, and they froze. Gut clenching, Fletcher turned to see her standing behind them, her parents close. All three of them had reddened eyes, but one look into Tammy's told him that she was okay, that while not everything was solved with just that one conversation, this was a step forward.

Tawny nodded at him, Andrew following suit, his expression approving.

Whether that was for sparking the conversation between them, or because of what he'd said just now, he didn't know. He didn't care either.

Tammy looked lighter and happier, despite the red eyes.

And that was the only thing that mattered to him.

Fletcher smiled. "Hi, sweetheart."

"Hi," she whispered.

She moved toward him, threw herself into his arms. "I love you."

"I will *never* grow tired of hearing you say that."

A pert smile. "Me neither."

He took the hint. "I love you too, Tammy Huntington. From the first moment I laid eyes on you, until the time comes that my lids slide closed for the last time. You're here"—he tapped the spot above his heart—"and I'm never *ever* going to stop seeing you."

"Dammit, Fletcher."

"What?" he asked.

But he knew, knew that tone, knew that curse, knew why she got so stiff.

Emotions.

Free of concrete and barbed wire. Out in the open.

Trusted to him.

And he wouldn't let her down, couldn't bear to *ever* let her down.

So, he just tugged her against his chest, wrapped his arms around her, and when she'd finished crying, wiped away her tears. The hall got mysteriously empty, her breathing slowed.

Then his strong, capable, love of his life stepped out of the circle of his arms.

Took his hand.

Tugged him toward the group of people who loved her, who wouldn't forget her, who would *see* her.

Always.

Because he wouldn't allow it to be any other way.

Bad Best Friend

Billionaire's Club #14

ONE

CORA

C heetos were really the best thing on the planet.

Okay, maybe not the *best* thing.

Because she *could* list a few things that were better than the faux cheese crunchy deliciousness—those being her mom's chocolate pecan pie, the croissants from Molly's in her new hometown (San Francisco had a lot of perks compared to the small suburban city that she had grown up in, not the least of which were the delicious treats from her favorite bakery), and sitting at home in her fuzziest socks while watching the Hallmark channel on repeat.

Those were all better than Cheetos.

But truly, they were all a close second. At that moment anyway.

Which was mostly because she had her bag of chips propped on the couch next to her, her orange powder-covered fingers— on her left hand, always, since the right hand was reserved for the remote so she could pause for a heartfelt sigh at all the perfect parts. And to rewind and watch them again.

And to sigh again.

She also had a box with baked goods on her coffee table—minus one croissant because she couldn't wait until the morning—and hell, why should she? It was Friday night. She was single since her brothers had decided to chase off the last man she'd dated.

Truthfully, she couldn't complain too much.

Six brothers equaled a lot of testosterone, and when they got it in their heads that she needed protecting, it was nearly impossible to get them to stop.

They were dogs to a bone.

Mostly because they had been protecting her almost her whole life.

Five. She'd been five years old when her dad died. The youngest. The baby. The long-awaited girl after *all* those boys. She needed to be protected. Coddled. Looked out for. It was sweet but stifling. Loving but overbearing. Coming from a genuine place but sometimes so absolutely infuriating that she wanted to tear her hair out.

Her older brothers had made it their full-time jobs—complete with benefits, plenty of PTO, and 401k plans—to watch over her.

Her dad had ingrained it in them.

Her dad, whom she loved...but—she sighed—she just wished she had the memories her brothers did, her mom did.

Everything she had was blurry on the edges, more feelings and smells than crystal clear memories.

Being tossed up in the air, flying so high that she felt like she could grab the stars twinkling overhead.

The smell of his skin, his hair.

The feel of his strong arms hugging her tight.

It was enough...and it wasn't *nearly* enough. She wanted what her brothers, her mom had, but knew she would never get it. So, she contented herself with the stories, the fractured memories, and pushed the longing she felt for all that she'd missed out on deep, deep down.

So many people had it worse.

She could suck up her daddy issues, be grateful for her family—even for the big lugs that seemed determined to mess up her love life—and enjoy her Cheetos and Hallmark.

"Exactly, Cor," she whispered to herself. "Cheetos. Croissants. Forests in Vermont where small-town girls find their happy endings with lumberjacks who have thick, bushy beards and plaid shirts that threaten to burst from the sheer size of their biceps."

Pleased with herself—go, new positive Cora!—she hit play on the remote and allowed herself to get wrapped back up in the story.

And God, seriously, those colorful leaves were *gorgeous*.

She was thinking that she really needed to plan a trip to Vermont when there was a knock at her door.

"Ugh," she groaned, wishing she could ignore it. But if it was one of her brothers, they would just let themselves in anyway, and if she wanted to protect her Cheetos from their Hoovering abilities, then she needed to be proactive.

Which meant answering the door.

After stashing the bag of Cheetos behind the pillow.

Sighing, she paused her movie, did her stashing, wiped her Cheeto fingers on the napkin she had draped over her leg for just that purpose, then stood.

A glance through the peephole had her sighing again, this time paired with shaking her head. It was so much worse than her brothers.

It was *him*.

She tugged open the door.

"Rafe," she grumbled, plunking her hands on her hips, "which of them sent you?"

Yeah, she had six brothers, but she might as well have a

seventh because Rafe had hung around Jeremy, Wyatt, and Asher—her eldest three brothers who had all come within three years of each other (her poor mother)—all the way through elementary, middle, and high school and well into adulthood.

Case in point, he just shrugged, barged into her house, and said, like it was absolutely no surprise (and she supposed it wasn't), "All of them."

She muttered an epithet, closed the door he'd just left wide open, and hurried past him, lest he try to steal her croissants.

With six brothers, she'd learned to protect what was really important.

Which was why she grabbed the bag of Cheetos right after she'd safely secured the box of pastries.

He dropped a bag on the floor—right in the middle of her living room—and sank onto the couch, picking up the remote and changing the channel, like he'd visited a hundred times before.

And she supposed he had.

He always seemed to tag along.

To *protect* her.

And yes, she was mentally doing air quotes to go along with that thought, even as she shoved his feet off the coffee table. "What are you doing here?" she growled, snatching the remote back and returning the television to its rightful place—the Hallmark channel.

But she didn't get to rewind the movie back to where she'd left off.

Because Rafe shrugged his bulky shoulders, nodded at the bag, and said—

"I'm moving in."

Two

RAFE

He plunked his feet back on the table, snagged the pale blue pastry box before Cora could complain.

She jerked forward like she was going to snatch it from him, but because she already held the bag of Cheetos and the remote, her attempts to keep her treats to herself were thwarted.

He opened the lid, snagged a croissant that was drizzled heavily with chocolate, and jammed a huge bite into his mouth.

Mostly because he knew that she'd do her level best to snatch it back.

But the blue box was from Molly's.

And he didn't pass up a chance for Molly's.

Her noise of outrage chased his second bite, and then she was tucking the bag of chips behind her, reaching for the box, and plunking it onto the side table at her end of the couch.

"You never did like to share," he teased.

She glared. "You never did like to ask before you took my things."

God, she was cute with her glary eyes, her fluffy slippers, and her ratty robe printed with unicorns that he'd seen her wear at least a hundred times over the years. "With six siblings, you're used to that."

More glaring. This one not deemed to be paired with a reply.

Or rather, the reply was that she pushed the box of pastries farther away from him, held her Cheetos tighter to her chest, and then turned the volume up on her movie.

"How's work?" he asked.

A shrug. The volume clicked up.

That sent his spidey sense tingling. Her boss was an asshole.

He didn't know why she'd left Robotech and transitioned to the startup the previous year, but he knew she wasn't happy in her new position.

Not that she said anything.

Well, *that* was why his spidey senses were tingling.

Cora was a woman who didn't limit her words. She spoke and did it a lot, and he had to admit that as entertaining as he often found her, sometimes his mind drifted a bit...especially when she talked about work.

Which she wasn't doing.

Hadn't been doing.

For several months now.

And she was home on a Friday night, wearing her ratty robe, eating Cheetos, and watching shitty Hallmark movies.

Why was that?

Why *was* that?

She sighed, and he glanced over at her. But she wasn't looking at him. In fact, her gaze was glued to the TV, and he watched her watch that lame movie.

Until she sighed again.

It wasn't Cheeto-related (she was chowing down on those like it was her fucking job to get every last crumb out of the bag).

It also wasn't croissant-related (she still had ten in the box, and yes, he'd counted...as he'd shoved one in his mouth). He didn't think it was related to him barging into her living room (even if she was annoyed, she'd had years of practice with him and her brothers doing it). She'd had years of being barged in on and because Cora was a practical woman, he just didn't see her getting exceptionally frustrated with something that wasn't going to change.

So, what else was it?

Another sigh.

"What's up, baby doll?" he asked.

Bouncing curls as she turned her head in his direction. "You trying to chit-chat and distract me isn't going to work," she said. "I've got all my treats securely protected." A shrug. "Or securely in my belly," she added.

With that, she tipped the bag up to her mouth, dumping the dredges of the Cheetos in.

Rafe grinned. He'd never seen this woman eat a salad—or not one without a slab of steak sitting beside it, anyway—and he loved that she wasn't shy about downing snacks. He *could* have done with her sharing those snacks more willingly, especially when they involved Molly's, but he liked that she wouldn't ever be the kind of woman to pick at her food just because he was in the same room as her.

Hell, she'd eaten him under the table plenty of times before.

"I'm not trying to distract you," he began.

But didn't get any further, mostly because she snorted and turned back to the TV.

The volume went up again.

She returned to ignoring him.

And the sighing continued.

And...he couldn't pinpoint why there was a niggling in his brain. Something was off with her, but he didn't know what.

And he didn't like it.

Rafe wasn't a man who didn't know things. For as long as he could remember, he understood his place in the world, and he got what he wanted—whether it was answers or respect or success. Also, yes, he knew that made him sound like a cocky bastard, but—here, he mentally shrugged—confidence was sometimes more important than actual skill.

So, Cora being off didn't please him. He wanted to know what was going on and he wanted to know right then, especially if it meant that some asshole was responsible for her being off— because between her boss and the assholes she dated, she was surrounded by a plentiful cluster of the fuckers.

It wasn't out of the realm of possibility that someone had wronged her.

So, it wasn't out of the realm of possibility that Rafe would have to get off his ass and make that wrong a right.

Cora was his, and he protected his family, would always protect them—

She sighed.

He reached his limit, snagged the remote from her, and muted the TV.

"Hey!" She lunged, tried to grab the remote back.

Which meant that he tossed it across the room.

It *clunked* against the far wall, and she turned to him, mouth agape for a long moment. "Seriously?" she muttered.

"What's up?" he asked again.

A huff, the couch depressing as she pushed to her feet. "You're unbelievable, you know that, right?"

He grinned. "Yup."

A muscle in her jaw ticked. "And by unbelievable, I mean that you're an ass."

"I *have* an ass." He grinned. "A nice one from what I've been told."

"Christ," she muttered, starting to move past him.

He snagged her arm. She twisted, her eyes hitting his before flicking down to where his fingers circled her wrist. Olive wrapped around mahogany, her skin like silk beneath his own, her bones delicate and fragile and—

Her eyes narrowed.

She yanked her arm free, stomped over to the remote.

"Is this about me moving in?"

"*If* you were moving in," she said as she bent and retrieved the remote, "I would be annoyed, but since you're not..."

She dropped back onto her end of the couch, hit the volume.

"I *am* moving in."

Now she hit mute, turned to face him, and ordered, "Spill."

"Asher thinks—"

She groaned, arm and remote flopping to the couch.

"That you need someone here in case—"

Another groan, this one paired with her other hand reaching into the pastry box and taking out a croissant. She shoved an admirably large bite into her mouth and chewed while keeping her eyes on the television.

"—you run into some trouble or you need—"

Her gaze drifted to his. "In case I need...what?"

She'd led him down a twisting path, and at the end of that winding trail was a thicket of spiky blackberry bushes.

He sighed. "Look," he said. "You know I'm firmly on Team Protect Cora, but I also get that you're a grown-up and need your own space."

She glanced from the box to him. "Oh, *do* you?"

Shit. She had a point there. See what he meant about her and words? She was too damned good at them.

So, he gave her the truth.

"It was Asher or me," he said. "And since I have a job in town for a few weeks—a job I'll be very busy at, which means I won't be here, cramping your Friday night of bad movies and carbs—I figured you'd prefer me."

Cora pressed her lips together, sighed.

"Am I right?"

The volume clicked up.

"Because otherwise I could call Asher and go hole up at a hotel until your brothers come to their senses—or until you get arrested for fratricide."

She made a face.

Or at least that was what he supposed was happening, given he could only see one-half of her expression. But the half he *could* see went all weird and crinkly, and he knew her well enough to know that she was pouting.

Or fuming.

Or raging silently while calling him every single bad name she could think of inside her head.

And since next would come raging vocally, he decided to go for the kill...or rather, the nail in the proverbial coffin that would put this argument to rest.

He pulled out his cell and started dialing.

"What are you doing?"

"Calling Asher."

"You *are* not."

He lifted his brows, held up his cell so she could see the screen...which was filled with Asher's contact info.

All he had to do was hit the green call button.

Now he got to see the face she was making. It was fucking cute.

It did not dissuade him from his quest.

Which she knew.

Because she sighed, grabbed the bakery box, and extended it in his direction. "Since you're staying," she grumbled.

Victory!

Those were so few and far between with Cora that part of

him felt like he should fist-pump, but because he didn't want to stomp on that victory that had just been won (and risk losing it), he shut his mouth, snagged a croissant, and settled in.

To watch bad movies.

Tomorrow, he'd work on gaining control of the remote.

THREE

CORA

"And *then,*" Kelsey said, "I told Tanner that if he didn't tie me up right then, I was going to—"

There was a choking noise from the kitchen.

From *Rafe* in the kitchen.

Who'd been—she leaned to the side, glared at the pass-through to the man in the kitchen—drinking out of the milk carton.

Out of the milk carton.

Her organic, hormone-free, very expensive—and very Californian—milk.

Backwash. *All* up in there.

And now milk dripping down his chin.

And wide eyes on that handsome, annoying face.

His gaze hit hers, surprise in the depths of his emerald green eyes, but she merely raised her brows. If he didn't want to be part of Margarita Night, then he shouldn't have moved into her house. Him overhearing Kels's hilarious attempts to reenact their latest co-read (they didn't have a book club because they read far too many books for that, but they did also tend to read the same books at the same time, especially if it was a spicy new release from one of their favorite authors).

Tanner—Kels's hubby—was sexy and exuded confidence, and Cora knew for a fact that he and Kels had a fulfilling sex life, so the idea of him balking slightly because Kels wanted to act out one of those spicy scenes had them all in giggles.

Kate—sweet, kind, and in the cute baby belly stage—giggled at whatever else Kelsey said.

And because Heidi and Stef both began cackling, Cora knew it had been good.

And she'd missed it.

Because of the big, annoying lug in the kitchen.

She narrowed her eyes.

He lifted a brow, took another drink from the milk carton.

"Did I tell you guys about the last guy I dated and the hand-cuff incident?"

Slowly, the milk carton lowered.

Now both brows were up, and they were paired with fire in his green eyes. Protective instincts prickled.

Right.

This was why she didn't normally talk about the "fairer" sex when her brothers were around (fairer because they were big babies about splinters and eating vegetables and man flus).

Well, in for a penny, in for a pound.

He wanted to move in?

Then he could hear about handcuffs.

"Well," she said, deliberately turning her attention from Rafe and focusing back on her friends, "you know that he wasn't packing, and he didn't know how to use it."

Another choke from the kitchen.

One she ignored this time, deliberately not looking at the interloper in the other room.

"I thought that he might get inspired if we got a little freaky."

Kate grinned.

Kels, Heidi, and Stef cackled again.

"So, I bought these handcuffs, and I had them couriered to his place, along with a key to my front door and a note telling him that I would be waiting in bed naked." She felt her cheeks go hot, was damned glad that her skin didn't show her blush because she was forgetting that this story was embarrassing and she wanted to sound nonplussed, especially in front of Rafe. "Then, because he was really dumb and I didn't think he'd get it, I added a postscript."

"Oh Lord," Heidi said in the way that only a friend who'd known her from all the way back in college could say (that being with equal parts knowing and horror).

"What did it say?" Stef breathed in a tone that said she was a newer friend and as such, didn't know the mess Cora could make of her life.

"It said that I was ready and waiting and expecting to be fucked."

This time the choke was louder.

Kels shrugged. "I mean, you're a woman who knows what you want, so I'm not seeing the problem here."

"Well, the problem is that he came over and started to use the handcuffs."

"Okaaay," Kate began.

"But he forgot the key."

Stef frowned but didn't say anything, probably wondering what the big deal was.

"And he tightened them too much."

That frown deepened.

"Which meant that my hands started falling asleep—"

Raised brows.

"And he panicked and instead of just going back to his place and getting the key like a normal person because it wasn't an emergency, he whipped out his cell and called 9-1-1 and—"

"Oh, God," Kate began.

Cora nodded. "Right."

"Please, tell me that this isn't going where I think it's going."

"You mean to firefighters busting my lock on the front door because Kenny was too panicked to answer it? Or maybe you might be wondering if the sexy men in navy blue saw me in my full, naked glory?"

"Um, for the record," Stef said softly, "I'm wondering about both."

"I already *know* it's both," Heidi announced.

"Oh, Cora," Kate murmured.

"Right," she said. "So, there's a little gem for you." She cleared her throat, added brusquely, shifting so she couldn't see the kitchen, couldn't see *Rafe* in the kitchen (Rafe, who was emanating very unhappy vibes. Rafe, who was making her feel like she was ready for the floor to open up and let her fall through in order to avoid those unhappy vibes...and she could only hope that the unhappy vibes wouldn't transform into him telling her brothers about the handcuff incident...and also, this just in, she was an idiot because she'd thought that this would teach Rafe a lesson, but really, all it was going to do was rile his protective side, make it difficult to look him in the eye, and reinforce that she always opened her mouth far too soon and way before she thought things out), "Anyway. My brothers might have run him off, but, truthfully, I wasn't sad to have an excuse to wave goodbye."

"Yeah," Kate said, quipping in a way that was totally not Kate, but also totally awesome, "that's bound to happen when a sexy fire brigade sees your hoo-ha."

Cora glanced at Heidi.

Heidi's lips twitched. Then she glanced at Stef. *Her* lips twitched.

Then Cora lost the battle, and embarrassment gave way to laughter because laughter was the best medicine, and even though she was hopelessly single and spent her Fridays alone in a ratty robe with Cheetos and croissants, she still had her friends and margarita nights and Thursday dinners and...a lovable, albeit annoying septuple of men who cared about her.

Even if they were cock-blocks.

Even if one of them was currently pondering investing in chastity belts.

"Hoo-ha is never allowed to pass through your gorgeous lips again, m'kay?" she teased, when she'd managed to get herself together.

"As long as you know that you're not allowed to play with handcuffs again," Kate countered.

Sassily.

Apparently, pregnancy hormones brought the sass.

Cora liked it.

Even though it was Sass Lite. Even though she knew it was less baby-related and more because her friend had found a partner who'd given her the confidence to be herself. Not that Kate hadn't been herself...it was just that Kate had been hurt and there had always been something a bit fragile and vulnerable about her.

That meant they'd all been careful with her, and she'd been careful, too.

This wasn't careful.

This was confidence and teasing and a woman comfortable in her own skin.

And Cora *really* liked that.

Which was why she nodded and then because she was no stranger to sass herself, she added, "At least not without a skeleton key within reach."

Stef hooted.

Heidi grinned. "Why do I think that you've bought a half dozen of those keys and have them stashed around the house?"

Cora waggled her brows. "Because you've known me for a solid decade?"

More laughter, and then Cora reached for the blender that was sitting on the table, virgin margaritas (for camaraderie with the baby-making machine) mostly depleted. She made her way into the kitchen, half expecting Rafe to still be standing there with disapproval on his face, the contaminated milk carton in his hand.

But he wasn't in sight, and the carton of milk was back in the fridge where it belonged (she knew because she checked).

And she wasn't disappointed that he'd gone.

She was happy that he was giving her privacy.

Well, either that or he was calling her brothers and sending an SOS to the entire Hutchins clan to descend upon their sister who'd been corrupted by romance novels and mildly kinky sex.

Maybe he was doing that along with buying stock in chastity belt companies.

Next thing she knew, she'd get all *Robin Hood: Men in Tights* up in there.

"Fun," she whispered as she dumped ice and margarita mix into the blender. Her life was so freaking fun.

"We all know that Jaime was ready with those restraints," Heidi teased, referencing Kate's hubby's profession—as a vet, he'd had to restrain a fair number of tough customers. "And Tanner balked but followed through."

Cora bit back a laugh, doubly so when Kels's cheeks went bright pink.

"So, what about Ben?" Heidi asked. "What did he think of our last book?"

It was Stef's turn for pink cheeks.

And for eyes darting away, even as a satisfied smile creased her expression. "Let's just say that Ben was thoroughly inspired."

They cackled. There was no other word for it.

And Cora joined in.

Because it was a cackle-worthy moment, and because she was so fucking happy for her friends to have found the people they loved and just because she was single didn't mean that she wasn't thrilled they had that.

It was just...

She was lonely.

FOUR

RAFE

Handcuffs.

Fuck.

He really shouldn't be thinking about handcuffs and Cora.

Hell, just the two words near each other in a thought should send his gut churning, bile burning the back of his throat.

Instead, he felt...weird.

The same weird he'd felt when he'd suggested that he stay in Cora's spare room. The same weird that he'd felt when he'd watched her creep of a high school boyfriend grab her ass before they'd left for prom.

Protective.

But not simply that.

And *that* was when he cut the thought off in its tracks. Danger led down that path, and as an honorary member of the Hutchins family (and a dishonored member of his *own* family), he valued his place, wouldn't do anything to fuck it up.

Sighing, he cracked the door, listening for any sound of

cackling.

The women had quieted down earlier, but after the handcuff speak, he wasn't taking any more chances.

Yes, he'd hidden.

No, he wasn't ashamed of that.

Probably, he should have informed Cora's brothers of the handcuff incident, but since he'd been part of the "intervention" (a.k.a. the intimidation) to scare off the asshole who was a bigger asshole than Rafe had previously thought, he figured that letting sleeping dogs lie in this case was better for everyone.

Because they really didn't need to revisit the fact that she had handcuffs, was apparently a little kinky—

Sweet Christ.

He cleared his throat.

Her brothers didn't need to know that apparently, the entirety of the local fire department had seen her naked.

After a few minutes of not hearing any cackling or the reverberations of any bad reality TV, he crept into the hall and—

"*Oof!*"

Fuck, that was a tackle.

He stumbled back a couple of steps, his lower back ramming into the doorknob as a lush, warm body threatened to take him to his knees.

"Shit!" Cora hissed, losing her balance and falling into him harder.

The door slammed back into the wall with a crash. His hands closed around her, holding her tight, catching her against him when she would have fallen to the floor.

She smelled spicy, like cinnamon and apples.

She *felt*...

Curves. Soft. *Woman.*

Shit.

He dropped his hands.

Then immediately had to grab her again when she stumbled

and would have hit the hardwood floor.

He hit it instead, his ass plunking down onto the floor, a sharp burst of pain radiating up his spine. She dropped onto his thighs, her breasts hit his chest, but he didn't let her go this time, even though she was basically straddling him, and his hands were full of woman.

Of Cora.

Fuck.

He reacted without thinking, shoving her off him abruptly.

She landed with a pained grunt, and guilt swarmed him. "Shit, Cor," he began, "I'm sorry—"

"It's fine," she said, shoving to her feet.

He reached to help her...and encountered skin.

Bare skin.

His fingers grazed her thigh, silken fabric fluttering over the back of his hand.

He jerked back like he'd been scalded. And maybe he *had* been. Because that skin beneath his palm had been softer than the hem of the short robe she was wearing. Because that touch had been...he could still feel it, his fingers tingling, a bolt of heat shooting south, shooting toward an appendage that shouldn't be in existence when he was around her.

"I'm sorry," he said again, scrambling to his own feet and lurching for the switch by the door. He flicked it on. "Are you...?"

His question stoppered up in the back of his throat.

Because that robe.

That robe.

It was white and shining and...*sheer.*

Hips and ass and when she spun to face him, blinking, probably at the sudden brightness of the overhead light, his gaze wasn't caught on her pretty brown eyes. It was on...

Breasts.

Large, round globes pressing against silk.

Hardened nipples perfectly outlined.

His cock twitched.

Fuck. *Fuck.* He needed to burn out his retinas.

He averted his eyes, swallowed hard, and determinedly focused on the door...and the knob that had wedged itself into the sheetrock behind it.

"Shit," he muttered, tugging it forward and wincing at the puff of dust that emerged.

That was a decent-sized hole.

"Good thing you're in construction," she said. He hadn't heard her approach, hadn't heard her get close to him, and her words made him jump.

And glance down.

Breasts.

Fucking *hell*, she had *breasts.*

"What?" he croaked.

Cora lifted her brows, the edges of her kissable mouth curving up.

Kissable—

Wait, *what?*

She nudged his shoulder with hers, and fucking heaven help him, but her breast brushed against his arm. He was *so* a breast man. He lived to touch and squeeze, to lick, suck, and nibble the delicious globes, but Cora wasn't supposed to have breasts.

And she definitely wasn't supposed to have breasts that he noticed and—

"Did I break you?" she teased. "I *said,* it's a good thing that you're in construction."

She went to bump him again.

He backed away, returning his focus toward the hole, but not before he saw the flash of hurt cross her face.

Fuck.

"Right," she whispered, "I'm going to get my hot chocolate and head to bed."

"You still do that?" he asked, turning to face her, unable to *not* look at her.

Growing up, he'd slept over at her childhood home so many times that he'd begun to understand the ebbs and flows of the Hutchins family. He knew them as well as his own breath, his own preferences and habits.

Cora was a night owl.

God, he couldn't remember how many times he'd made her a cup and they'd sat on the couch in her mom's basement when she couldn't sleep, playing *Mario Kart* or watching some borderline inappropriate movie for her age (think: *Speed* and *Die Hard* when she was eight or nine).

They'd watched or played until her eyes began to droop.

Then he'd swept her tiny body up into his arms, carried her up into bed, and tucked her under the covers more times than he could count.

But she didn't have a little girl's body now.

She was a woman, and he was desperately wishing that was a fact he hadn't noticed.

Her eyebrows lifted nearly to the black silk of her hair wrap, but she just shrugged. "Hot cocoa is still the best drink on the planet."

"Because you still don't sleep well?"

Those brows relaxed, her shoulders rose and fell on a shrug —and fucking hell, her breasts jiggled with the movement.

He skittered back another step, dropped his stare to the ground.

Sweet, sweet baby Jesus.

"I sleep fine."

He watched her feet, watched them turn for the hall. Watched them pause, just on the threshold of the door.

"Goodnight," she whispered.

He stared at the opening long after she'd gone.

Which was why he knew that she hadn't gone down to the

kitchen, that she hadn't gotten her hot chocolate, that she probably wasn't sleeping, even though the house was still and quiet, even though there wasn't one bit of noise from her end of the hall.

And as he stared, he replayed that flash of hurt, the soft goodnight, over and over.

He replayed it long after the sound of her footsteps disappeared, long after he should have gone to sleep.

He replayed it so long that eventually he found himself listening to the sound of his own footsteps descending the stairs, padding across the floor into the kitchen. The clink of the mug, the beep of the microwave.

The creak of the cabinets as he searched for the good chocolate, because he knew she had to have some stashed somewhere.

Cora without chocolate was...unfathomable.

And there it was. A large stack of expensive bars. He opened one, broke up half into small chunks, and dropped them into the warm milk, microwaving it again to get it all to melt.

A stir. A dollop of marshmallow cream. A heavy dose of caramel syrup. A vigorous stir. Plenty of whipped cream and chocolate syrup and more caramel syrup on top.

Her special comfort hot chocolate. From him. From the recipe *he'd* created for her.

Then he was walking up the stairs.

Then he was walking down the hall, carrying the steaming mug with its whipped cream melting on top.

Carrying it to Cora's room.

Knocking on the door.

Waiting, his heart hammering against his ribs, knowing that something had changed and yet understanding that *nothing* had.

No answer.

He knocked again, beginning to wonder if perhaps he'd misjudged the quiet, misconstrued the silence and the direction of her footsteps.

Maybe she'd fallen asleep.

Maybe she'd already gotten the—

The door swung open.

Cora stood there in her robe, her skin glistening like she'd been in the bath, or maybe like she'd just been thoroughly fucked—and fucking hell, that thought shouldn't be passing through his mind, it *should not* be in his mind at all. Beautiful. Grown-up. Tempting.

But her eyes were cautious.

And that reminded him why he was standing outside her door in the middle of the night.

"Here," he blurted, shoving the mug at her, the hot chocolate nearly spilling over the rim. "To help you sleep."

Then he spun on his heel, ran—yes, *ran*—down the hall and into the spare room, closing the door firmly.

Probably more firmly than he should have.

But the wood between them was necessary.

The fierce *click* also required.

To remind himself who he was. Who *she* was.

He turned off the lights, slid into bed, tugging the covers over himself, even though he was sweating, even though part of him was burning up inside.

With need.

For Cora.

For his best friends' sister.

Who had lush curves, a set of breasts that a man dreamed of, an ass that should have been illegal. His dick twitched, and he groaned, rolling to the side and punching the pillows, trying desperately to forget, to get comfortable.

And knowing that he was fucked.

Because as the hours passed and he finally began to drift off to sleep, all he could think of was what her skin would taste like.

Fucked.

So. Totally. Fucked.

FIVE

CORA

She held the mug of hot chocolate, the scent of cocoa and whipped cream drifting up to her nose, making her mouth water.

But it was a distant response of her taste buds.

Because...Rafe.

Because of the flash of awareness in his eyes. Of *heat.* Before he'd spun on a heel and took off for his room—no, for the *spare* room, she needed to remember this was her house, her life, her *flipping* room.

"You're losing your mind, Cor," she whispered, turning slowly and closing her door.

She moved to her bed, her robe still sticking to her tub-damp skin, her body overheated from soaking, sleep just curling on the edges of her mind. She'd been drying off, debating between starting the newest book she and her friends were reading together, knowing that could either go really bad or really good depending on how good the book was.

Either she'd be asleep in minutes, or she'd be up until dawn, hiding under the blankets and whispering, "Just one more chapter," to herself and her Kindle.

But the hot chocolate was a surefire sleep technique. That paired with a shoot-em'up was guaranteed to have her out in less than an hour.

The hot cocoa would fill her belly, coat her taste buds, and when she pulled herself out of bed to brush her teeth—because oral hygiene was important, even for insomniacs like herself—she would clean her choppers while she was half-asleep before she stumbled back to her cozy mattress, cuddled beneath the soft blankies, listened to the white noise of explosions and gunfire, and passed out.

And Rafe had given it to her.

With heat in his eyes.

"What the fuck?" she said, or rather kept whispering, moving to the bed, trying to solve the puzzle that was Rafe, but knowing that she wouldn't, knowing that instead she just needed to drink her cocoa and watch her movie and let sleep take her under.

So, she drank her hot chocolate.

She watched Bruce Willis yippee-ki-yay.

And eventually, she stumbled to the bathroom, cleaned her teeth, stumbled back to bed.

And...sleep took her under.

———

Light was streaming through the windows when she woke, and she groaned as she rolled over, totally unready to face the day.

She hated mornings.

Hated getting out of bed when it meant that she had to start the day.

Luckily, it was Sunday, so she could afford to be lazy for just a bit longer.

Sighing, she tugged the covers up, eyes hitting on the mug—empty because Rafe could make a mean hot chocolate—sitting on her nightstand.

And she was brought back to all the weird from the night before.

The flash of horror in his gaze when he'd accidentally touched her.

God, the man made her feel like a hideous monster.

She knew he was used to seeing her as a little sister, but his reaction was more than a bit ridiculous. She was an adult woman, for God's sake, had been one for the last almost twelve years. Hell, the last time she'd seen her ob-gyn for her yearly torture of speculum and breast exams, she'd been told that her eggs were getting old.

At thirty.

And Rafe was thirty-six.

Jeremy, Wyatt, Asher, Eli, Rowan, Rome...and her.

Jeremy and Wyatt were twins, both had would turn thirty-seven shortly. Asher was thirty-six because, for some godforsaken reason, her parents had decided to try for a third when the twins were only a few months old. Her mom always said she was too sleep-deprived to know better, but she said it in that dreamy way that she always did when talking about her family.

Edy Hutchins was made for home and hearth. Her veins should have been filled with Christmas cookies and the ability to get stains out of sports uniforms.

And...she'd worked her ass off.

Jeremy, Wyatt, Asher, Eli, then surprise! Another set of twins—Rowan and Rome. Six boys under six...and then Cora.

And then...her dad gone.

Probably because of the stress of taking care of seven kids under seven...either that or having superhuman sperm.

"Gross," she whispered, shuddering as she shook that thought out of her head.

Sperm and parents.

Two things she shouldn't *ever* think about.

Sighing again—and God, wasn't this like her teenage years, sighing and shuddering and feeling a bit gross and worthless—she tossed back the covers and moved to the shower. Cleaning her body, not her hair because she seriously did *not* have the time or energy to deal with her hair today, then getting on with her normal Sunday routine.

Moisturizing—hair and body. Touching up her toenail polish, organizing her work outfits for the week.

Black pants and a coral top.

Black pants and a cream blouse with a cute, slouchy bow at the top.

Black pants and a turquoise body suit, topped with her awesome gray plaid jacket.

Black pants—

Sensing a theme here?

Except, she pulled out a surprise on Friday. Because it was Casual Friday at work and that meant she would be wearing black *jeans.*

Go her.

She paired those with a floral button-down, swirls of purple and pink alluding to roses and pansies.

Then she moved on to underwear and bras and shoes.

Because she *really* hated mornings, and though she'd been able to make her own schedule at her previous job with Robotech, her new boss was a stickler. Early to the office, late to leave. Extra hours and emails on the weekends and hustling, hustling, *hustling.*

Which she could appreciate because they were trying to get the company off the ground.

She was willing to put her sweat equity into something great, so long as there was a light at the end of the tunnel, a marker they were moving toward, a finish line to cross.

The only thing was...she'd been wondering if the company was really great.

If there would ever be a finish line, or if that line would keep moving forward, never to be crossed.

She sort of thought that she knew already, the certainty of wrongness having sunk deep into her bones, making it settle there like a second layer of marrow. The company wasn't great—or at least, not great for *her*. And paired with the control her boss wanted to exert over everyone and everything, the micro-managing of every single project that she worked on and was shaded as just making sure everything was "perfect" because it needed to be "perfect" in order for Voldcom to succeed and...she was exhausted.

Too many hours.

Too little freedom.

Too...much thinking for her free day.

She straightened the final pair of shoes for the week then stood up, stifling another sigh because she wasn't going to go full teenager on her free day.

Then she grabbed the mug from her nightstand and left her room.

The house was quiet. Empty.

The door to Rafe's room—to *her* spare room—was closed, but she knew he wasn't inside.

She had inner brother sense, an inner brother detector—and that included Rafe, because God knew he'd been around so much that he fit firmly in that category. Even if...he *was* pretty, and she could appreciate it.

Like a fine art painting.

Gorgeous. Yes. Untouchable. Also, yes. A little off-putting and too fancy-dancy for her.

No.

She liked fancy.

She *liked* untouchable.

She liked Rafe. Had liked him her whole life.

It was just better when she pretended that she didn't.

For everyone.

Six

His eyes flashed open, sleep falling away in an instant. He focused on the room—on the darkness flowing through the windows of Cora's house—and tried to pinpoint what had woken him up.

He snagged his phone, saw it was a quarter to five.

He had to be at the job site in an hour and a half, but his alarm wasn't set to go off for another thirty minutes. Mostly because he was a roll out of bed and go kind of man. Clean clothes, brush his teeth, tumbler of coffee, and call it good.

Showers at the end of the day.

Because by then he would be covered in muck and grime, with sawdust and sheetrock powder. The nature of being a contractor, even for big industrial projects he was supposed to be just overseeing—which, of course, wasn't *exactly* true. He wasn't the kind of man who just oversaw. He liked to get his hands into things, to get dirty, to feel and hold and touch and *know* that everything was put together properly.

Even if it was just putting together an estimate.

He wanted to see the area he would be working in, to just be in it, to feel the concrete beneath his feet, see the walls and judge the plumbness for himself, to breathe in the space and—

There was a noise from downstairs.

And he abruptly remembered that he'd been woken before his alarm.

Narrowing his eyes, he tossed back the blanket and stood, yanking on a pair of sweats and grabbing his phone. He shoved it into his pocket and crept toward the door, tugging it open, glad that he'd oiled the hinges throughout her house the previous day while she'd been bingeing some reality TV show that had nearly given him hives.

A murmur from the first floor had him going stiff.

He knew it couldn't be Cora.

His Cora didn't roll out of bed until at least nine. Plus—he glanced back in the hall, saw that her door was closed—she was most definitely asleep.

Which meant there was someone in the house.

His instincts prickled, and he softly padded down the stairs, phone out and ready to call 9-1-1, wishing that he'd brought his baseball bat along with him.

Lights in the kitchen had him frowning.

He turned the corner, moving into the space, and his frown deepened.

"What the fuck?"

Cora was there—full makeup on, completely dressed in a shirt that was some weird shade of pink with black pants and heels...and sitting at her computer, earbuds in place.

She glanced up at him, her brows drawn together.

She had glasses on.

They were cute as fuck, but her expression beneath them, or rather, her eyes beneath the lenses...they weren't cute at all.

They blazed with irritation.

She glared at him, mouthed, "What. *The.* Fuck?"

Then turned back to her computer, fingers flying on the keyboard, said, "No, Robert, I understand. I've reworked the 2.0 campaign and it's ready to be—"

Her shoulders went stiff.

"I'm—"

Stiffer still.

"I went over and revised that, too—"

Then those shoulders slumped.

A tendril of rage coiled in his stomach, he stepped forward, prepared to yank out the earbud and hang up on the asshole who was railing at her on the other end of the line.

"I—"

Another pause, this time paired with her whipping around and glaring at him again. A sharp shake of her head.

At him.

And that shake worked. He halted in his tracks.

And he watched as she navigated the conversation, as the glare transformed into frustration and then into defeat. Watched as the light faded fully from her eyes, as she focused on a point over his shoulder and continued the conversation.

"Right, Dale. I'll redo it." Her lids slid closed. "Yup. Of course." Her lips turned up at the corners, shifting into a fake smile that *Dale* couldn't see—and one that Rafe fucking hated. "Of course"—her eyes opened, and she glanced at her wrist—"I'll be there in thirty."

Thirty.

Rafe's gaze flicked to the microwave. It was now five to five, and she was going to be in the office in thirty minutes?

That made no sense. Or at least, it didn't fit in with what he knew about Cora.

She did *not* function in the morning.

She did *not* get up early.

She'd...grown up.

And that was...good? Working hard was important. Rising to the occasion even more so.

Except, what wasn't good was the expression on her face, the defeat in her eyes, the long, quiet sigh as she rubbed her forehead.

Her shoulders slumping.

He *really* didn't like that.

She closed her computer, pushed back her chair. Then she was moving to the coffee pot, was pouring herself a tumbler.

"Coffee?" she asked after she'd screwed on the lid.

He blinked. "What?"

"You want a coffee?" she asked, slowly, like he was an idiot.

And maybe he was staring at her like he was. "Yeah," he said, when she waved the half-full pot at him, the scalding liquid inside sloshing around. If only to get her to stop waving it around like she was about to give herself a third-degree burn.

She grabbed another to-go cup, filled it up. "Still like it black?"

"Yeah, Cor. Thanks."

A nod, and then the top was on, and she was carrying it to him, her heels clicking on the hardwood floor. "Here."

"Thanks," he said again.

Another nod.

Then she turned back to the table, tucking the laptop into a black leather satchel that was lying on the table. Another brusque movement had her jacket off her chair, then her arms shoving inside it.

"Cor?"

Her eyes hit his, and there was a cold quality, a lifelessness in those chocolate depths that he really fucking hated.

"You okay?"

Her lips turned up, forcing their shape into that fake smile, one he fucking hated even more, seeing it a second time. "I'm great," she said. "There are cinnamon French toast Eggos in the freezer, Jif in the pantry."

His heart squeezed.

She remembered what he liked for breakfast.

And she had it, even though he'd shown up without warning on Friday, bag in hand, even though she hadn't been happy about him invading.

"Cora," he began. "You didn't have—"

A shake of her head. "I was out. I grabbed some stuff. End of story." She turned for the door. "It's not a big deal."

"Careful," he said gently, "your Edy is showing."

Edy was...amazing. Thoughtful and maternal and caring for others without a second's hesitation. It was instinctual.

And it was Cora, too.

She turned back, her smile softening.

Then shook her head again. "Bye, Rafe."

———

"You hate it."

He spun, turned to see Teresa, hard hat in place, clipboard in hand, heavy construction boots on her feet that looked way too large for a woman who was all of five foot three inches tall.

But she had freakishly large feet.

Kind of like a hobbit.

Minus the hairy toes.

At least, that was what he figured.

He hadn't seen Teresa's toes, so who knew what she was hiding beneath those giant boots?

"Do you have hairy toes?"

She frowned, her chin jerking back. "What?"

Inappropriate.

He shouldn't be thinking about any part of Teresa, toes or

not. She was his colleague, his project manager, his righthand woman.

And he wanted to keep her there.

Hell, he wanted her to become his partner.

So, step one of that probably shouldn't be asking her about her toes. Step *two* of that definitely shouldn't be asking her about her *hairy toes*. Step three of that—

Shouldn't be blurting out what he blurted out.

"I hate it."

He did. The space. The work that had been completed so far. The whole feel of everything. It was all...wrong.

Teresa had busted her ass on getting the pieces in place before he'd come in to finish them off, and the work had been done properly, cleanly. The space was impeccable.

And...it was all wrong.

She sighed, slapped her clipboard against her thigh.

"I'm—"

He didn't finish the sorry.

Mostly because, as one did—or at least, as *Teresa* did—she was one step ahead of him. "I've already revised the plans," she said, slapping that clipboard to his chest.

He glanced down at the clipboard, at the paper held to the top of the stack.

Floor plans.

His eyes flicked from the page to the space, from the ideas that he knew he would have come up with eventually—eventually, because Teresa had always been smarter than him and much faster than him, and he would have come up with this, but it wouldn't have happened quickly.

And it would have taken a lot of beer, a significant amount of cursing, and then some additional help from Teresa to get to this point.

"This is good," he said.

She grinned.

"Like really good."

Her grin widened.

"Except"—he grabbed a pencil from his pocket, began sketching—"we need to move this wall so that the egress is clear and—"

"*Yes*," she said, snatching both pencil and clipboard from him. "And if we move that wall, then we've freed up space for this bank of offices and can squeeze in another bathroom."

He lifted his brows. "*Another* bathroom? How many can this place possibly need?"

"Have you ever waited in a line ten deep just to use the toilet?"

Rafe shook his head.

"Then you don't know that there really can never be too many bathrooms." She snagged a pen from his pocket, clicked the end, then outlined the square she'd just drawn—this time in pen, as though the non-erasable ink would make it come to fruition.

And it would, he supposed.

Because what Teresa wanted, Teresa got.

———

He rinsed the last glass and set it carefully in the dishwasher. Then he turned to Mrs. Hutchins, offering, "Can I make you a cup of coffee?"

Wyatt and Jer were in the family room, a hockey game playing in the background, Wyatt chattering about a new girl he was seeing, while Jer was mostly taking the opportunity to give him shit.

But he'd just gotten a free dinner from Mrs. Hutchins.

He needed to make sure he pulled his weight.

And, truthfully, he didn't mind helping wash up. Edy was funny and, for all intents and purposes, had been his mom. He could show that he was grateful for her support over the years by washing a few dishes.

Easy enough.

"You know you don't have to do this," Mrs. Hutchins said, reaching into the cupboard over her head and going up on tiptoe, trying to grab a mug.

"I got it," he told her, snagging enough mugs for everyone, "and do what?" He nudged her lightly with his elbow. "Help my favorite woman wash some dishes after she cooked us a delicious meal?"

"No, honey," she said, something like sadness crossing her face.

"Make you a cup of coffee?"

"Not that either." A pat to his shoulder. "I just—"

"Is there any pie left?" Jer asked, striding into the kitchen. "Oh, coffee? Want me to pour you a mug, Mom?"

"Rafe's got it, honey."

Jer's eyes connected with his, nodded approvingly.

Thanking him for taking care of his mom.

"Good." Jer nodded to the hall. "It's intermission, do you still want me to hang that picture in the hall?"

"Yes, baby." Mrs. Hutchins pressed a kiss to Jer's cheek. "If you have time. Otherwise, I can do—"

"I got it," Jer said firmly. "When we love people, we take care of them. That's what Dad always said, and that's what we do as Hutchinses."

Edy smiled, patted the cheek she'd kissed. "You're a good son, baby."

Jer grinned, kissed the top of her head. "That's the only kind to be, Mom."

SEVEN

CORA

Her feet ached—stupid fucking heels that she'd *stupidly* decided to wear on a *stupid* fucking Monday that had started too *fucking* early and had ended stupid *fucking* late.

But her head ached more.

Because Dale...was being Dale.

And he was exhausting. No, *she* was exhausted. Okay, well, he was exhausting, too. It was just...she was done.

So *fucking* done.

But Voldcom was so close, so freaking close, and she wanted to be part of that.

She'd just...send out her resumé and bide her time and—

Deep breaths.

Lots of deep breathing and meditation and non-virgin margaritas and—

She'd extended her hand, reaching for the knob, readying to push open the door when the wooden panel ripped open, and Rafe stood directly in front of her. His expression was absolutely thunderous, and as she stared at him, trying to process the fury, his fingers wrapped around her wrist and yanked her into the house.

"Oof," she grunted, sprawling against his chest, palms feeling...stuff she really shouldn't.

Okay, feeling muscles and man and...

See? Stuff she *shouldn't* feel.

Which he probably knew because the moment they were clear of the door, he dropped his hands from around her wrist and stepped back, fist clenching like touching her skin was akin to picking up a pile of dog shit with his bare hands.

And that made her feel...*other things* she shouldn't.

Clearing her throat, shoving down that *hurt,* she moved past him, dropping her laptop bag on the table, trying not to limp, but knowing she was because her shoes hurt physically more than the emotional hurt of Rafe acting like she had rabies.

Or maybe it was the fury in his eyes, like she'd done something to disappoint him.

Or maybe it didn't matter because she was tired and hungry and tired and—

"What the fuck are you doing?"

Her head dropped back, eyes hitting the ceiling. "Why don't you ask me a real question, Rafe?"

"Why the fuck don't you tell me why you were out of the house before five and now back after eight?" His brows arched into sharp C's. "Because by my calculation, that's a fifteen-hour day."

She huffed, kept walking. "And how do you know that I'm not getting back from a hot date?"

His laugh was sharp. "Because it's not even eight-thirty?"

Asshole.

"Yeah," he said, the words hot in her ear. Damp and warm and sending goose bumps prickling down her nape, "I *am* an asshole." A beat. "But that doesn't mean I'm wrong. I care about you, Cor. I'm *trying* to take care of you."

Fuck.

Now she was so pissed that she was yelling at him out loud instead of in her head.

Even if he *was* an asshole.

Even if he deserved to have her yell at him.

"I don't need someone to take care of me. I'm an adult and—"

"Yeah, you are, and I'm an asshole who doesn't deserve to be one of you—"

She frowned. "Wait, what?"

"But none of that means I'm wrong," he said, stepping closer. The heat of his chest coming very close to her spine, that nearness tugging at the threads of thought from her mind, scrambling and knotting them. "Because I'm *not* wrong, am I?"

Fury sparking to life, she spun on her heel, jabbed a finger in his direction. "What I'm *not* doing is spending another second dealing with your bullshit, and that includes you questioning me about my life and my job and what fucking time I come home from it."

"So, you're admitting that you've just worked fifteen hours."

"Ugh." She threw her hands up, spun on her heel a second time—and sweet Christ, that hurt. "What I'm doing is none of your...*ah!*"

One second, she was stomping away, and the next she was in the air.

Rafe's arms were around her, one at her waist, one behind her shoulders, and then she was colliding with his chest.

She shoved at that chest, his muscles bunching beneath her palms, but she might as well have been trying to push her way through a brick wall for all the good it did her. Then they were moving, or rather, *he* was, carrying her across the kitchen and plunking her onto the counter. "Sit," he growled.

"I'm not a fucking d-*ah-og!*"

She'd barely come to terms with her ass hitting the granite when Rafe backed up.

But he didn't go far, just bent and yanked one shoe and then the other off her feet, chucking them over his shoulder. She heard them collide with the cabinets behind her, one after the other.

"You better not have chipped the paint on my—"

Suddenly, his face was *right* there.

In front of hers, his lips...

She inhaled sharply.

"You're limping," he growled, "because of these dumbass shoes."

"They are *not* dumb," she growled back (because if he could growl, then so could she, dammit!). "They are expensive and sexy as hell. So, you just need to—" She started to slide off the counter, but before she could, he planted a hand on her thigh.

One big broad hand totally encompassing her thigh.

"Limping."

One *word.*

Intense. Sharp.

Sliding down her spine.

"I'm fine."

His hand convulsed. Fingers tightening, his thumb pressing against her inner thigh, sending a bolt of heat skating between her legs.

Another inhale, her lips parting and—

"Fifteen *fucking* hours." More growling.

Her chin came up. She pushed his hand away. "It's my fucking life, and if I want to work *fifteen* freaking hours, then I can."

His eyes sparked with fury, green depths flashing with gold and brown, blazing into hers. His hand returned, and then the other one dropped onto her other thigh. "You'll burn yourself out."

He was right.

Which pissed her off even more.

She *was* burned out. Because she was exhausted and ready to quit and desperate to *not* be working fifteen-hour days.

But she didn't need the overbearing asshole telling her what she was feeling and what she should be doing, and fuck, if she wanted to wear uncomfortable heels, then that was her freaking prerogative, even if they *were* giving her blisters on the backs of her heels and she wasn't sure if her arches would ever recover.

But it was *her* life.

Not Rafe's.

Not her brothers'.

Not Dale's

And, fuck, but it was way past time that she did something about that.

She shoved his hands back. "Get out," she snapped. "*Get. Out.* Get. *The fuck.* Out!"

The anger faded from his expression. "Cora, honey—"

"Get out! Get out! Get—"

He kissed her.

Just slanted his mouth right across hers, parted her lips with a swipe of his tongue, and then he was *kissing* her. Plundering her mouth, kissing her so deeply that she almost felt like the contact was bruising her mouth.

And she didn't care.

The slight bite of pain was overwhelmed by pleasure, by the sheer storm that was Rafe.

Fingers threading into her hair, tilting her head back. His tongue darting deeper, stroking along hers. His hands back on her thighs, spreading them wide. He stepped between her legs, hands sliding to her ass, tugging her forward, tugging her even closer, perching her on the edge of the counter. But she didn't fall. He had her...close.

Oh, God.

He had her close.

He shifted, hands drifting down, coaxing her to wrap her legs around him. And—*oh*—that was good. So good that she didn't hesitate to also wrap her arms around his shoulders, to arch against him, to bring her body flush to his.

To...

He tore his mouth away from hers.

One second, she was dangling in a web of pleasure, her limbs and torso wound tight in the silk, floating weightless and out of her mind. And the next...

That spider was coming close.

That spider was descending, readying to devour her.

That spider...was gone.

Leaving so fast that her feet hit the hardwood with a jar that clinked her teeth together, that her hands scrambled to grip the counter behind her, so she didn't end up on her ass.

The front door opened and closed.

Her lips pulsed.

Her breaths came in rapid gusts.

Her legs shook...so hard that she found herself sinking to the hardwood anyway, sinking slowly but inexorably down to the cold, solid surface.

And she sat there, the pleasure slowly fading, the pain in her feet creeping back in, the fatigue, the mental drain, the...

Tired.

She was so, so tired.

EIGHT

RAFE

He needed to go jump off a bridge.

Like literally, to put himself out of his misery.

Definitely before Cora told her brothers that he'd accosted her in her kitchen.

I was just trying to take care of her...by shoving my tongue down her throat.

"Fuck," he muttered, getting out of his truck—and yes —*slamming* the door shut. Luckily, he was alone on this stretch of the highway, the streetlamps few and far between on the curving road that followed the coastline of the Pacific, so no one was around to hear him have his hissy fit. "Fuck," he said again. "*Fuck.*"

He gripped his hair, tempted to yank it out by the roots, and forced out a sharp breath.

Cora didn't want him butting into her life, so he sure as shit wasn't going to sic her brothers on him, not when it would bring the full force of the Hutchins clan down on them both.

"Fine," he said, rounding the back of his truck and hopping

up to sit on the side of the bed, feet dropped onto the tire, holding him in place when he felt as though the rest of the world would crumble beneath his feet. "It's all going to be fine," he muttered to himself, staring out to the ocean, not able to see much aside from the occasional white froth of a wave breaking, even with the full moon overhead. Dark and dim.

Kind of like his brain.

He snorted, hands falling to his sides, gripping the edge of the bed of the truck, the cool metal nothing at all like Cora's skin.

Soft like silk.

Her curves lush.

Her mouth hot and sleek, her tongue a heated brand as it tangled with his.

Her moans rolling up the back of her throat, drifting across her lips. He'd swallowed it, absorbed the soft groan, felt it sear itself onto his soul. Onto his cock, his brain coming up with all sorts of pleasurable imaginings of how her lips would feel on the head of his dick, how good that warm, hot tongue would be stroking up and down his shaft, how—

"Fuck," he hissed again, slamming his palm against the metal, the loud reverberation even drowning out the waves.

Or maybe that was his pulse pounding in his ears.

Because he shouldn't be thinking about his cock and Cora, her mouth and how fucking good it had been to have her thighs wrapped around his waist.

For all intents and purposes, she was his sister.

But hell, he had never gotten so hard from a fucking kiss.

Ever.

"Why did it have to be Cora?" he whispered.

He blew out a breath, or maybe it was a sigh, or maybe it was just a fuck-his-life exhalation because he knew why.

Because *he* was fucked.

———

Rolling his shoulders, he stared up at the lightening sky, his face sticky from the damp ocean air, his eyes burning because he was too fucking old to be sleeping in the back of his pickup truck with nothing for a bed except a couple of balled-up sweatshirts and one thin blanket that he used to protect anything that needed protecting when he was hauling it around—wood, furniture, appliances.

But it didn't protect his back...

And now he was exhausted, sticky from the salt in the air, and his back felt like it had been jabbed with a million needles—and not of the acupuncture variety.

But the sun was coming up, and he needed to get his ass in gear.

Because he needed to work himself into exhaustion so that his brain all but melted, too tired to think about what had gone down with Cora.

See?

Good plan.

Muttering a curse, he pushed up out of the bed, used one of the sweatshirts to wipe off his face, snagged the blanket and folded it, stashing it and the extra sweatshirts in the cab of the truck.

Thankfully, he'd had the sense to commandeer one of the company vehicles for his use while he was in town.

Otherwise, he would have had to get a hotel the night before—

Actually, he *should* have gotten a hotel the night before.

Then he would have skipped the whole needles jabbing into his spine thing.

"Right," he muttered, rolling his shoulders, feeling the breeze from the ocean whip up and tear through his hair, the fog rather than the night sky obscuring the waves now. He stood for a minute, listening and staring at the undulating clouds, the mist gathering in places and spreading thin in others, knowing that this wouldn't be his last visit, that there was something that felt like home here.

That maybe that sense of home was more than the ocean or the winding roads hugging a coastline.

More than redwoods growing tall and strong along the shore, more than the invasive ice plants taking over the dunes.

And he worried that where he felt *most* at home was in the small craftsman Cora owned with the sturdy wooden columns, their bottoms wrapped in stone, on Cora's porch with a rocking chair and pots of cheerful flowers stashed in the corners. Walking through Cora's wide front door. Sitting on Cora's sleek gray couch and knowing that it looked atrocious but was incredibly comfortable. Opening and closing Cora's white cabinets and setting out plates on Cora's stone countertops. Padding across Cora's warm hardwood that he'd installed himself—along with Asher and Wyatt—much to Cora's fury, especially since he'd canceled the flooring contractor she'd hired. Using Cora's spare bathroom with the tile he'd installed. Striding up Cora's stairs, holding on to the handrail he'd screwed in, making certain it was secure so that she would be safe.

He got into his truck, turned on the engine, his head spinning, his throat tight.

Because he wasn't stupid. Because he could sense the theme. Because...he wanted to avoid the truth, *had* to avoid it.

But the truth kept smacking him in the face.

Cora.

Home.

And that was what worried him the most.

"Shit," he muttered, the drill slipping, the screw falling to the floor, the bit digging into the sheetrock surrounding the windows he and Teresa were boarding up.

It was dark—well past quitting time—and he knew that the only reason she'd stayed late was because he was here, doing something they could easily send a crew to do in the morning. This property had closed just before five, and so he was technically the owner (he even had the keys and alarm codes in hand, along with the requisite excitement that came from possessing something in the tens of thousands of square feet, something that would become businesses that real people used or office buildings where real people worked, and knowing that he was responsible for that).

But even with the requisite excitement and being the owner, Rafe understood that he didn't really need to be here boarding up windows.

There hadn't been issues with squatting. There weren't any break-ins or even equipment and tools on-site that someone might try to steal, and he'd already arranged for his security company to watch the buildings—and entire complex —overnight.

They were covered.

He was just...avoiding.

Cora.

He was just *avoiding* Cora.

Right. Simple. Cowardly. And...yup...good times for that.

He held the wood with one hand, snagged another screw from the belt hanging around his hips, and plunked it between his lips. Then grabbed another—because at the rate he was going, he was probably going to lose another half dozen of the pointy metal bastards—and positioned it beneath the drill bit.

This time, he was able to screw a piece of wood into the frame without creating unnecessary holes.

So, he repeated the process—screw beneath bit, screw in wall, screw from belt, screw beneath bit, screw in wa—

"You okay?"

The bit wobbled. The screw dropped.

He steeled himself, lifting his eyebrows in question when he turned his head to meet Teresa's eyes.

She'd finished her windows and was watching him with concern written into the lines of her face. "You okay?" she asked again.

"Yup," he muttered around the screw still held between his lips, turning back to face the wood, thankfully finishing the job without making any additional holes, without dropping any more screws. "Just peachy."

Of course, it was just a bonus that she couldn't really hear him, since he was still all but chewing on the sharp metal fastening.

But it also meant that she came closer, holding the wood on his next window while he screwed, coming close enough to see his expression and probably the turmoil within his brain, making his fingers rubbery, his mind fuzzy, his—

"You're not okay."

He lifted his shoulders. Dropped them. "I'm not okay," he said, telling her the truth—or the safe part of it, anyway—because Teresa could sniff out bullshit with the best of them. And, to add to that, it didn't help that he was a shitty liar. "I'm tired," he added before her concern could swirl to worrisome levels. "I didn't sleep well, and Cora isn't all that thrilled that I'm at her place." He detailed the sex talk and the margarita night with her friends.

Teresa smirked. "Sounds like fun."

"If you want to take a flamethrower to your ears so you don't hear about your best friends' sister talking about bondage during sexy time when she's supposed to be innocent and pure forever—"

Except she hadn't been pure when I'd been sticking my tongue down her throat, had she?

He gritted his teeth, shoved the thought away.

It was made easier because Teresa burst out laughing, straight bending over, holding her belly, laughing as she sputtered, "P-p-pure?" A huff. "And *in-in-innocent?*"

"Teresa," he growled.

She put her hand up, palm out. "N-no," she said, still sputtering, "no, I *can't*. You want a grown-ass woman to be pure and innocent?"

He glared.

"You've totally lost it," she said, "I know that you think of her like a little sister, but come on!" More laughter burst forth.

"I'm not seeing the humor in this."

"You *wouldn't*," she muttered, "seeing as you're a big, protective alpha who can't retain your protective alpha status unless you're rescuing poor, helpless maidens."

His glare didn't abate. "That's not fair," he said. "I've never once stepped on your toes in this job."

Gentle snatching amusement, and she stepped close, bumped her shoulder with his. "No, Rafe, you haven't." She tilted her head from side to side. "Okay, well, you did step in and threaten to shove a pry bar into that one sub's eyeball on the Kowalski job."

"He grabbed your ass when you bent over to measure the baseboard!"

Her lips twitched. "He did." Another bump of her shoulder. "But maybe the pry bar-eye threatening was unnecessary?"

"He grabbed your ass," Rafe gritted, "and couldn't keep his *eyes* off your boobs—"

A pat to his cheek—one of the ones on his face. "Which is why you're a big, proud, protective alpha," she murmured in a singsong voice, "with big, proud, protective alpha *tendencies*."

He hissed out a breath. "Teresa," he warned.

"Big, proud, protective alpha tendencies don't make you bad," she said in a tone that was so consoling, he knew it was purposely aggravating. *Gah.* Women. "It just makes you a big, proud, protective, *annoying* man." She grinned. "And I can say that because I have two annoying, proud, protective brothers *and* an annoying, albeit lovable, proud dad."

Rolling his eyes, he took the battery out of his drill, picked up the screws from the floor, and turned for the exit of the building.

The windows were done.

All that was left was to set the alarm, lock the door, and go home.

To Cora.

He inhaled slowly, silently.

Fucking hell.

"Rafe?"

He narrowed his eyes at the still smiling Teresa.

"What?" he asked gruffly.

"Carbs."

His brows pulled together.

"You're in the doghouse," she said, hitting the button on the alarm panel then holding the door closed so he could lock it. "The best way to get out of that is to invest in carbs—ice cream, baked goods, gourmet chocolates. Pick Cora's favorite and bring it home as a just because." She smirked. "Trust me, it'll be the best thing you can do to remedy your living situation."

"Right," he said, pocketing the keys. "I'll do that."

A nudge, a wave, and they exchanged goodbyes.

Then he was in his truck and on his way to invest in his body weight in carbs.

Because he didn't just have to get out of the doghouse.

He had to buy enough carbs to get Cora to forget about that kiss.

NINE

Well, maybe she'd scared him off for good.

One kiss from Cora and see how they run!

She blew out a breath, rotated her head from side to side, trying not to think about the fact that Rafe had fled after the kiss, that he hadn't returned the night before—and she knew because she'd barely slept, and most of that sleep had happened on the kitchen floor after she'd sat there in a depressed haze, feeling sorry for herself.

If he'd come across her, he definitely would have ordered her to an actual bed.

That being, *not* the hardwood floor in the kitchen, the only benefit of her makeshift bedroom being the heater vent that had blown warm air along her side, thus ensuring she didn't turn into a human popsicle.

When her stomach had finally rumbled loud enough to shake her out of her haze, she'd grabbed a bag of carrots from the fridge, a jar of peanut butter from the pantry—don't judge her, they were good together—and had gone up to her bedroom (the real one, that was) where she had consumed two-thirds of the peanut butter and the entire bag of baby carrots, listening for him to come home while doing her level best to make certain that her consumption of veggies didn't bring any actual nutritional value.

Or that her consumption's nutritional value had been completely canceled out.

But he hadn't come home.

And she'd left work at a reasonable hour—not because of Rafe and his bossiness. But because she was done. Boundaries needed to be drawn. She needed sleep. She wasn't being productive anyway, and she knew that if she was required to be creative (necessary since Dale had basically shit-canned the entire project and she had to start over), she had to be operating on all cylinders.

Dozing on the kitchen floor wasn't conducive to that.

Staying up watching action movies with the subtitles only, realizing that sound was seriously required when captions read, "intense intensity" (umm, what?) and "gunfire and explosions" (way too tame to explain an entire building turning into ash), also didn't allow for the most restful night's sleep.

Also, she was at the IDGAF point with Dale.

He wanted to fire her?

Fine.

He wouldn't be able to finish the campaign without her.

So, yeah, she'd gone home and ordered pizza (with pineapple because, fuck the haters!) and watched bad TV, and she didn't care if Rafe came back to the house. He could stay away for-*ev*-ah —or until the next family holiday...which would be coming up far too soon for her taste, especially considering that Asher's birthday was two weeks away.

Whatever.

She'd deal. And Rafe would have to as well, just pull up those big boy britches, man up, and shut his flipping mouth.

And keep his tongue to himself.

Plus, she hadn't wanted her space invaded in the first place, so if a kiss scared him off, then good.

She should have done it long ago.

"I should do it to my brothers. Then they'd stay away, too, and wouldn't eat me out of house and home—" Shuddering and processing that as she was stomping around, getting her Cheetos and popcorn and wine, and not really understanding the whirl-wind that was her mind until those words actually crossed her lips, she realized what she'd said. Kiss her brothers? "Ew," she muttered. "No. I am *so* not doing that. Definitely *not*. No freak—"

The lock clicked in the front door, screeching in the metal slot, and she froze, glass of wine in one hand, her bag of Cheetos in the other.

Her face was covered in green goop. She had her most unflat-tering pajamas beneath her unflattering and holey robe, which was fuzzy and cozy, but ratty as hell. And—she turned, saw Rafe walking into her house, bags hung on his wrist—she barely fought the urge to whirl around and run upstairs, to go and hide in her bedroom.

Because of the kiss.

Because she was in the most unflattering clothes she owned, with the most unflattering face mask in the history of all face masks globbed onto her face.

She set her wine down.

Rafe moved into the kitchen, the bags crinkling, and...

Fury filled her.

It began in her toes, sparking and prickling up through the arches of her feet, tingling along her calves, the backs of her knees, her thighs, across her stomach, and up between her breasts. Her words bunched up on her tongue, ready to whip forward, to slash and cut and wound. And her nape prickled, her arms strained, her fingers clenched tight into fists.

The bag of Cheetos crinkled as her hand tightened, but thankfully she didn't have her wine glass in hand or else the stem would have certainly shattered.

Well, there was nothing for it.

A breath, ignoring Rafe as he made his way into the kitchen. She turned back to the counter, forced her hands to relax, lest her Cheetos be reduced to dust, and after tucking her bag of popcorn beneath her arm, she deliberately picked up her refilled glass of wine and started for the family room, intending to walk right by Rafe.

And still ignoring him.

If that wasn't obvious.

Because he was evil and awful and...a really good kisser.

Ugh.

"Cor—"

Nope. Not gonna do it.

She sidestepped his outstretched arm, moved into the family room. Cheetos and wine glass on the coffee table. Remote snatched up and finger poised to hit the play button. Throw pillows plumped and—

A familiar bakery box in front of her face.

Rafe sank onto the coffee table, nudging her wine glass to the side, the chardonnay sloshing up near the rim, almost splashing over the top.

She narrowed her eyes. If he spilled so much as *one* drop, so help her God.

He settled the glass, stashed the wine safely next to her Cheetos.

Fine.

The man could live. For the moment.

He crouched, trying to intercept her gaze. But she wasn't going to let him go there, so she deliberately kept her eyes plastered over his shoulder. At least until the box rattled slightly, cinnamon wafting up to tease her sense of smell.

Cinnamon. A Molly's box with cinnamon seeping out of the cardboard.

He didn't. The man *hadn't*. Seriously, he hadn't bought her an entire coffee cake from Molly's. That was going to go straight to her ass, and she wasn't joking.

She also wasn't going to turn it down.

"Cora," he began.

No, dammit. Stay strong over the glorious scent of cinnamon and a drizzle of cream cheese. Even *if* her mouth was watering, and her stomach was definitely not on the *stay strong* train.

She clicked the play button.

A sigh, then the remote was out of her hand, the pause button pressed, her glorious reality binge paused for the moment.

"It's fine," she said, reaching for the remote. "Apology accepted. We can pretend that never happened. Now let me watch my show."

"I didn't even apologize yet."

"Consider yourself off the hook," she muttered. "I know how much you hate apologizing."

"I don't—"

She glanced up at him, lifted her brows...and that was enough to halt his denial.

"Fine," he muttered. "I don't like apologizing." He dropped the box into her lap. "But I should anyway."

And didn't *that* feel good?

Her kisses made men run *and* apologize. Joy!

"Cor—"

God, why wouldn't this end?

But all her protests and snarky response would just draw this out, so she was just going to grin and bear it and—*okay*, she wasn't going to *grin and bear it*, she was just going to *bear it*.

"I'm sorry," he said. "I shouldn't have done that."

Then...silence.

And she realized that was all he was going to say. Some apology. Shouldn't have done *that*.

"Right. You shouldn't have questioned my work habits considering that I'm a grown woman who can choose how many hours I work and what time I wake up in the morning." She lifted her brows higher, waiting for him to challenge her.

But also...sort of holding her breath, waiting to see if he was going to acknowledge the kiss.

Which felt like more than a kiss. It felt like an undoing, like the moment his lips had touched hers, every single part of her had been undone. Torn apart. Then stitched back together in a way that left her feeling changed in a way she hadn't wanted.

Ever.

There was more silence, tense this time as his emerald eyes locked onto hers. Then he said gently, "I worry about you."

Not acknowledging it.

Right.

That wasn't unexpected.

It also shouldn't hurt.

But if they weren't acknowledging things, she could wrap that pain right up in there with the kiss. Pretend it never happened. Be as good as new.

Her chin came up. "But I'm a grown woman, and I can choose how much I work." A beat. "And sleep."

A muscle began to tick in his jaw, making her confidence begin to trickle back in.

Goodbye, pain.

Hello, Cora.

She was back, bitches, and she was going to win this fucking conversation. *If* winning conversations was a thing...and dammit, yes, winning conversations was a thing. Hell, it was an *important* thing, especially with an annoying man who wanted to interject himself into her life. The good news was that she was on the precipice of winning *this* conversation because they were on the precipice of acknowledging The Kiss, and heaven forbid Rafe do *that*. Not when he was trying to get a gold medal in pretending it hadn't happened.

And know what?

She'd take that win, any freaking day of the week.

"Right?" she pressed.

That muscle continued to tick.

His eyes held hers; the air between them crackled.

"Yes," he said finally. "I overstepped, and it won't happen again."

Victory!

She was ready to dig out her pom-poms from somewhere deep in her closet and do a cheer. She was sure she could *dig* out some two-four-six-eight-who-do-I-appreciate from the recesses of her mind.

But she could be gracious.

Out loud anyway.

"Thank you." She snagged the remote again, started to hit the play button, then hesitated. "You know what would really make your apology all that much better?"

His lips pressed flat, amusement nowhere present on his face.

Except in the corners of his eyes, trickling into those emerald depths, warming and glimmering and—

He reached into his pocket, pulled out a plastic-wrapped fork. "This?"

Her heart did a pitter-patter.

Then she shoved it down, plastered a smile on her face...and snatched the fork. Yup, snatched it. Because she had an evening of Cheetos and coffee cake, wine, and reality TV, and she was going to dive right into it.

Even if her heart did another pitter-patter when he sank onto the opposite edge of the couch.

But that pitter-patter was squashed in a second when he pulled out a second fork.

TEN

I f looks could kill, he would have been six feet under when he tugged the second plastic-wrapped fork from his pocket.

But even though her brown eyes filled with irritation, and her shoulders rose and fell on a loud huff (one that nearly overshadowed the drama of the truly awful—albeit addicting—show that was blaring from the TV), she still put the box between them so he could dig into the coffee cake, too.

He should have apologized, gone upstairs.

Left her to her sugar and wine and bad TV and put some much-needed distance between them.

Except...he couldn't.

He was glued to the show, couldn't peel himself away from the coffee cake—

Lies.

Well, both of those were true.

But the lie was that he was tiptoeing around the biggest reason he'd stayed.

Cora.

Because he was glued to her, couldn't pull himself away from her riot of brown curls, the slender curve of her nape and shoulders, the way her breasts pressed against the plain pajama shirt she wore—that was made decidedly *less* plain because of those breasts—

And fuck, he shouldn't be thinking about *Cora's breasts*.

"You drop that coffee cake, and I'll impale you with this."

He snapped back into his body, into his consciousness. Realized that he had been lost in his perusal of those breasts—and other things—and so he *had* been at risk of dropping the cake. His fork was digging into the pan, tipping it slightly up, and far too near to the edge of the couch for his peace of mind.

One, because the coffee cake from Molly's really was delicious.

Two...because she might really impale him with that fork.

Quickly, he set down his fork, moved the coffee cake to a safe location.

Then he turned his attention to the show. "I'm struggling to understand how this show works."

A flick of her eyes to his. "They buy things at yard sales. They rehab them. Then they sell them, and the team that makes the most money wins."

"I get that part," he said.

Her head swiveled, gaze locking onto his. "Then *why* are you interrupting my binge TV time?"

"Because they're not rehabbing them," he pointed out. "That pair just bought a piece of glass and had the production staff build an entire coffee table around it. That's not rehabbing items from a yard sale. That's...having someone build a brand-new table and then taking credit for it because they set a piece of glass on top."

"Well—"

"And that team," he said, "that locker thing they built is so rickety, I guarantee that it'll fall apart on the drive home if someone is stupid enough to buy it.

"That's not—"

"And—Christ—look at *that!*" He tossed his hands up. "The fucking glass doesn't even fit!"

She smirked. "You're awfully invested in this show for all your moaning and groaning about how bad my choice of TV is."

He shrugged. "But am I wrong?"

"About my choice of TV or the show?"

"Neither."

When she opened her mouth to snark back, he reached around her, stole her Cheetos, managing to get a few out of the bag before she chucked a pillow at his head. Also, she had good aim. Like *really* good aim.

So good that he nearly choked on that first chip, and with all his coughing, he didn't have a chance at blocking her from taking the bag back.

Nor from snatching up the coffee cake.

"You're banned," she muttered.

"Worth it," he wheezed, still trying to not die from the Cheeto dust currently entering his lungs.

"Oh, for God's sake." More muttering, but this time it was paired with her extending her wine glass toward him, putting it up to his lips, and ordering, "Drink."

Then she tilted up the glass, forcing him to drink through his sputtering, and if it didn't soothe the burn and coughing in his throat, he would have thought she was trying to waterboard him with the red wine. But it *did* soothe his choking.

She snatched it away. Put it on the side table—let it be noted that it was well out of his reach. The chips joined it...along with the coffee cake.

He grinned.

She chucked another pillow at him.

"Shut up and watch the damn show."

————

He didn't realize that she'd nodded off until the soft snore reached his ears.

Then another little puff of sound emerged from her lips.

She still snored the same.

God, she was so fucking cute.

Carefully, he reached across her and snagged the remote, clicking off the TV and cleaning up the mess. And, since she was still snoring, he ate the last bite of coffee cake.

First, it was better fresh.

Second, he'd put one on the counter for the morning.

A total bribe, but he'd taken Teresa's advice and gone to town. There were also two more bottles of wine in her cupboard, flowers in a vase on the island, and six bags of Cheetos in her pantry.

Bribe complete.

He rinsed out her wine glass, put it on the rack, then moved back into the family room. Maybe he should just pull a blanket over her, leave her to her sleep.

But Rafe knew he wouldn't be able to leave her.

He couldn't even leave her house when it would be a hell of a lot smarter to just get a hotel room.

So, he strode across the room, scooped her gently into his arms, and carried her up the stairs.

Down the hall. Into her room. And then he strode over to her bed, tucked her under the covers.

She sighed, nuzzled into her pillow, lips parting.

He wanted to kiss her again.

He wanted to peel back the covers, to slide in behind her. To slip an arm beneath her and to tug her close. To fall asleep with her in his arms. To...wake her up with kisses. To strip off the ratty robe, the adorable pajamas she wore beneath.

To—

Sighing, he smoothed the blanket, tucked it over her a little more securely.

Then he walked from the room.

Even if he needed to force his feet to keep moving the entire time.

———

Rafe's hands were full. He was trying to carry everything from the table to the sink. His dad liked him when he did that.

Or at least he liked when Rafe did that.

Did things so his dad didn't have to.

But this time he'd tried to do too much, and as he walked to the sink, one of the beer bottles balanced on top of the stack of dishes from the meal he'd made—or the frozen dinner he'd microwaved anyway—toppled from the plate precariously balanced on top.

It fell in slow motion.

Down.

Down.

Down.

And...crash.

Remnants of the beer sloshing out, the bottle shattering, shards going in all directions.

The plates in his arms wobbled, the entire stack threatening to topple, to go down. Scrambling, he managed to keep hold of the dishes, but sauce splattered to the floor...and all over his dad's feet.

"*Fuck*," he hissed, jumping back. "*Fuck!*" he hissed again, having stepped onto a piece of the glass, and this time he slapped Rafe across the head. Hard enough that Rafe's head snapped back, and he tasted blood. "You're absolutely fucking worthless, you know that?" He lifted his hand again and Rafe closed his eyes, preparing himself for the punch.

But instead, it was a shove.

He stumbled back.

Fell.

Cried out in pain as the dishes clattered in all directions, as the glass bit into his palms, sliced through his jeans.

"Useless," his dad muttered. "Absolutely fucking useless."

"I'm sorry," Rafe said quickly. "I was trying to—"

"Try harder." He kicked a plate, skittering it across the floor, and left, leaving bloody, sauce-covered tracks across the tile. "Clean this shit up."

Rafe looked at his palm, sliced open, the floor, a pile of broken plates, at the sauce and the blood and—

He sat bolt upright, sweat pouring down his face.

"Fuck," he whispered, clamping a hand to his chest. "Fucking hell."

The clock said just after two, but he knew the nightmare would stay with him. It always did. Every *fucking* thing from his childhood always did.

Cursing again, he threw back the covers and stood.

Shower.

Coffee.

Work his ass off to forget.

Make sure the important people in his life knew, *knew* that he wasn't *that*.

Wasn't...worthless.

ELEVEN

CORA

She had her laptop bag slung over her shoulder, her coffee mug tucked under one arm, a tote with her clothes—it was Thursday Night Friend's Night (which was really just an excuse for prickly pear margaritas, bowls and bowls of chips and queso, and laughter, teasing, and hanging with the people who were most important in her life).

Aside from her brothers and mom, of course.

She also had several files she'd brought home the night before, working in her bedroom and doing her level best to avoid Rafe.

He'd carried her upstairs.

He'd tucked her in.

So tight that she'd felt like a mummy when she'd first woken up the day before...and she'd had to do a fair amount of wriggling and yanking to get free.

Her hair was a mess.

She was late to the office (because her phone had been set to silent—and her alarm turned off—both of which she knew had been done by the man who had tucked her in so securely).

Dale hadn't been happy.

She'd worked late.

So late that Rafe hadn't been up when she'd gotten home, his door firmly closed, light off when she walked quietly down the hall. Which meant that she and her folders and working late had hidden in her room with *her* door firmly closed—though she left *her* lights on.

The better to see her work.

And great, now she sounded like The Big Bad Wolf. *The better to see you, darling.*

Ick.

"You're late."

Dale.

His eyes were filled with irritation, and she found her own eyes drifting to the wall behind his shoulder, to the digital clock that was large enough to be seen from any of the cubes.

"It's six A.M."

"I pay you a salary to be available for me at all times."

Wow.

What?

"I must have missed that clause in my contract," she said, and yeah, it was snarky and a little snappish. To her boss. But honestly, she was done. D.O.N.E. With Dale. With the company.

Dale rocked back on his heels. His brows came up.

His lips parted.

And she didn't give him the chance to say something snarky in return. "I'm going to finish this report," she told him.

Then she moved toward her office.

She glanced back over her shoulder, saw that he'd started to follow her. "In *my* office."

He took another step, as though he were still going trail her.

"Alone," she added firmly.

His brows slammed down, irritation on his face.

But she didn't let that stop her.

Nope. She just moved to the door, closed it with a firm click. Then flicked the lock for good measure.

She took a moment, stifling more teenager-esque sighs, resisting the urge to slam her head on her desk. Mostly because Dale had stopped in front of her office, was staring at her through the blinds adorning her window.

But also, because she needed to have some self-respect, and she wasn't going to let that asshole bother her.

So, she ended her moment.

And got to work.

And after lunchtime rolled around and Dale knocked on her door—or really, thirty minutes before lunch because Dale was Dale—she delivered that report.

And then redid it to his *exacting standards* (which basically meant that she moved two paragraphs around and changed the font).

And *then* the moment she got the fuck out of his space, she went back to her office and spent the rest of the afternoon submitting resumés.

Done.

She was so *fucking* done.

———

"I think there might be a spot in Heather's department," Kelsey said. "I heard that Abby was looking for someone with marketing experience." She filled up Cora's pitcher with more—what else?—prickly pear margarita. "Do you want me to ask Abby? I'm sure I can get a job description."

"Oh, no," Cora said. "I don't want you to go to any trouble."

"And by *trouble,* you mean sending one email?" Kels's brows lifted. "For my friend."

Cora made a face. "Seriously, *I* left RoboTech in the first place. I don't want to be—"

"Any trouble?" Stef asked.

Innocently.

Except, her lips were twitching.

Cora narrowed her eyes, jabbed a finger in her friend's direction. "I don't want to hear about not making trouble. Not from *you.*"

Heidi grinned. "She's got a point."

More narrowed eyes. "Or *you,*" she muttered. "Ms. I-don't-want-anyone-to-lose-sleep-so-I'll-be-miserably-sick-by-myself."

"That was one time!" Heidi protested. "And during finals week. I didn't—"

"Want to be *any trouble*," Cora finished for her.

Heidi scowled. "You know, if we hadn't been friends for years, I would think you were really freaking annoying."

"That's the trouble with knowing someone for more than a decade," Cora said innocently, "I know *all* the bad things."

"What bad things?" Brad—Heidi's hubby and the man who was sickeningly in love with her—asked. "My lovely wife has absolutely *no* bad character traits."

Silence.

Then "Boo!"s all around.

Jaime chucked a chip, and with impressive aim, beaned his brother right in the forehead.

"Hey!" Brad snapped. "I'm just trying to compliment my wife here."

"I love my wife, too, but I'd be the first one to admit that she's got a problem with taking in strays."

Animals.

And people.

Which they could all attest to. Kate, her other best friend—

right along with Heidi, Kelsey, and now, Stef—was the type of person who brought people together and kept them together. She was awesome and nice and...well, *awesome*.

"You like my strays," Kate said, looking nonplussed as she sipped her virgin margarita. Jamie stroked a hand over her rounded stomach, and Cora couldn't help but think that his hair had grown out nicely. There had been an incident a few years back with him cutting his man bun because he'd wanted to make a good impression on his wife's family, and the collective of the feminine population had mourned on the altar of deceased sexy man buns (as opposed to gross, greasy ones). She wasn't a woman who liked long hair, but the way he tied it up was totally lumberjack sexy (especially with his bushy beard and bulging biceps and...goddamn, she really needed to get laid).

"You love your wives," Tanner said. "We get it."

Cora and Stef's gazes collided...and their lips twitched. Because Tanner was just as bad.

Which he proved by adding, "Plus, my girl is a certified genius, so she's obviously the best."

"Well, my wife is a mini-genius," Ben said, sliding his arm around the back of Stef's chair and pressing a kiss to the top of her head. "*And* she picks great strays."

Considering that Stef's stray was an adorable golden retriever named Fred, Cora couldn't disagree. Fred was cute. Fred was friendly. As the last single woman standing, Fred had been her date on more than one occasion.

He was attentive and sweet, albeit a bit drooly.

"Did Fred like the new bandana I bought him?" Cora asked, completely off topic and hoping that the interjection would be enough to change the conversation from the menfolk singing the praises of their womenfolk.

As the only single womanfolk, that wasn't great for her ego.

Which was probably why Kate picked up the conversation and ran with it, asking Stef for pictures. Stef produced her phone, and then it was passed around as they all properly admired how handsome Fred was in his big boy bandana.

Talk of the bandana led to talk of Kate and Stef's newest stray, an owner-relinquished chinchilla named Maggie. She was crotchety, didn't like to be held, and had a serious eye infection that vet Jamie was treating. Kate was *treating* the crotchety-ness, and Cora had no doubt that the treatment would be effective.

It wouldn't be long before Maggie would be eating out of Kate's hand.

Probably both literally and figuratively.

Kels nudged Cora's shoulder. "FYI, you pain in the ass—" She grinned. "And I say that with the most love, my darling."

Cora glared, but she knew the picture that she painted—or was attempting to paint, anyway—was ruined when the corners of her lips tipped up.

"FYI," she said again, "I just texted Abby, and she requests that you send your resumé."

"Kelsey," Cora began.

A ping, and then Kels held up her phone, showed Cora the screen. "Like *yesterday*."

"*Kelsey.*"

"Like so much yesterday that she'd love to offer you a job."

She held up the phone again, and Cora saw that Abby had indeed written that. She sighed. "I don't want to manipulate the system—"

"Fuck that."

Cora stopped.

Blinked.

Because that hadn't come out of her mouth (as was most common), nor Kels's or Heidi's or even the slightly quiet, Stef's.

It had come out of Kate's.

Sweet, innocent *Kate's*.

Who glared at everyone's gaping expressions, and even *that* was sweet.

"What?" she asked impatiently. "I curse."

Jaime's face went soft. "Yes, Red, you do."

"Except that you yelled at Tanner last week because he dropped the f-bomb," Heidi pointed out. "You said the baby might hear and have a potty mouth."

"I didn't—"

Cora opened her mouth to agree, but there was movement out of the corner of her eye. The front door opening or maybe it was just a flash of familiarity at the edge of her gaze. Or maybe it was like some part of her was in tune with some part of him.

Him.

Rafe was walking up to the hostess stand, and after a brief conversation, the young blond man there handed him a menu.

She watched his lips move as he read, both hating and loving that she knew he always did that, had always *done* it, all the way back from his elementary school days because he'd struggled with reading and his teacher had helped him and—

His head jerked up.

Their eyes locked.

Her heart began pounding. Her palms went sweaty, and she nearly lost her glass of prickly pear goodness.

"Cor," Kelsey said, and Cora quickly tore her gaze from Rafe's, released a relieved breath when she saw that Kels was looking down at her phone, that the conversation had devolved from pressing her about the job and had moved on to teasing Kate about her cursing habits.

"I've heard that puck is the perfect alternative for the f-bomb," Ben said. "Puck off. Mother pucker. Pucking hell."

"Except hell is a bad word, too," Stef said.

"To whom?" Heidi asked.

"To..." Stef shrugged. "I don't know. To a lot of people."

"I'm telling Abby," Kelsey said, drawing her focus from the curse word alternatives back to her friend's. "I'm telling her that you're sending her your resumé in the morning, so there's no getting out of it now— Wait," she said, suddenly looking up. "Isn't that Rafe?"

Oh, no.

"I don't think so."

Kels leaned to the side. "No, I think it is."

Oh, no.

Kels raised an arm, waved it wildly. "Rafe!"

Oh. *No.*

"Are you ordering takeout?" she called, probably way too loudly considering there were other patrons in the restaurant. "Don't do that! We haven't ordered yet! Come sit with us!"

Cora's eyes slid closed.

Oh. Freaking. No.

Twelve

He'd come close without really thinking about it, drawn like a bee to a flower.

Cora's friend waving and calling out just an excuse.

He'd spotted Cora the moment he'd walked into the restaurant.

Slender shoulders revealed in a sleeveless top. Laughter turning her smile warm, drawing him in. He wanted to be the one to make her smile like that. Then she spotted him. And that warmth had disappeared.

Asshole.

Him.

But still his feet had drifted her way.

Then Kelsey had waved in his direction, called him over, and though he should have turned away, forgotten his plan for takeout (and yeah, maybe he'd realized that it was Thursday night and knew she'd be here with her friends, knew that she needed space from him, The Asshole, but he'd come to the restaurant anyway).

They'd avoided each other for a few days.

He was itching to see her.

And when he'd gotten home to that empty house, remembered it was Thursday, he'd come here without really thinking about it.

Or maybe he was thinking *too much* about it.

Because he was at the table, near enough to smell the soft, sweet scent of her, and he was staring.

Not speaking.

Not quipping a funny joke or introducing himself to the people at the table that he didn't know.

Just staring.

At Cora.

Kate—who he'd been introduced to during the margarita night (and who he now knew too much about her attempts at BDSM with her husband, gross)—cleared her throat. "We haven't ordered yet. You want to pull up a chair and sit?"

He was a heartbeat away from saying no, from leaving Cora to her friends and her night.

But then she narrowed her eyes at him and brusquely shook her head.

And...the devil inside him came out.

He turned to the empty table behind him, tugged out a chair, and squeezed it in between her and Kelsey—even though there wasn't room for it, even though Cora definitely didn't want him sliding in next to her. Kels, who he'd met countless times over the years (most of those the elementary ones, since Cora and she had been friends since childhood), grinned.

As he sat, his and Cora's thighs brushed, and though Kels had slid her chair to the side, giving him more space on her side, Rafe didn't shift away from Cora. He stayed *right there*. Thighs pressing together, shoulders in contact, her curls dangerously close to his cheek, his mouth. And her scent surrounding him, dropping him straight into the Cora bubble that promptly made him lose his mind.

Or his words.

Or his mind.

Or his...*something*.

Sanity. Self-preservation. Sense of self.

All the S's.

Because he leaned into Cora's space, that hair of hers smelling like roses and fruit. Maybe it was apples or perhaps pears. All he knew was that it wasn't something tropical. No coconut and bananas and white sand beaches. It was mountains and flannel, the first winter snow, crisp air tightening on cheeks. And...he was a fucking contractor, not a poet (or a bad one since that shit was coming out of his brain). Then a curl brushed across his cheek, and he found himself capturing it between thumb and forefinger, gently tugging as he murmured, "What's wrong, baby?"

She jumped, her shoulder colliding with his, her thigh brushing over the top of his.

Then she leaned back, the curl sliding from his grip, her margarita sloshing over the rim of the glass she held. Her skin glistened with the alcohol, and his mouth watered with the urge to taste the sweet and tart on her flesh, to trace his tongue along that glimmering patch. "*You*, Rafe," she snapped, chocolate eyes sparking fire. "You're annoying and persistent and invading my space." A hiss. "So *that's* what's wrong. And I know that you're smart enough to know that, even though you're playing at being an idiot."

He smirked. "What if I am just an idiot?"

"What if you're both?" she muttered.

"Then I'd suppose I'm exceptionally skilled."

A huff of laughter, and he felt like a fucking superhero when the annoyance faded, and amusement entered her expression.

"Only you would think it's a good thing to be skilled at being an idiot."

"It takes all kinds."

She rolled her eyes. "I could do with a little less of *your* kind."

He chuckled, shifted his thigh against hers, knowing he was playing with fire and unable to stop himself. He was strapped onto the ride, the safety checks complete, and the button had been pushed.

The roller coaster was taking off.

And he was flying...

And he'd deal with the consequences—motion sickness, his friends, her brothers, the complications and anger and fists that would surely be flying—later.

All of that, *later*.

"You know what I think?"

Cora glared. "That I don't care what you think?"

He flashed her a grin, leaned a little closer. "I think you like it when I invade your space."

A sharp inhale.

White teeth pressing into pink lips.

She did. And fuck...he liked it, too.

So much that he was going to get on that roller coaster a second time.

Leaning in further, his lips brushing her ear. "And, full disclosure, I like it, too."

She inhaled again, sharp and short, and then turned her head, eyes hitting his, and her lips coming...so fucking close.

Now he inhaled, smelling the sweet tartness of the margarita, mixing with the apples and fresh snow of her scent. He wanted to taste both on his tongue.

"Rafe," Kelsey said, "I don't know if you've met my husband, Tanner?"

He tore his gaze away from Cora, turned to Kels, saw that

she was looking at him with far too much innocence. Then he glanced from her to the man behind her shoulder, one he'd met a couple of times, but only in passing. Tanner was good-looking, confident, and had been friendly enough. But his focus had been Kelsey because the man was obviously in love and not afraid to show it.

Tanner lifted his chin in greeting.

Before Rafe could return the greeting, his gaze drifted beyond Tanner's shoulder, and he saw the entire table was staring at him. Well, staring at him *and* Cora. And there were more than a few raised brows. And smirks. From the women, that was.

And from the men...

Knowing looks.

Fuck.

If one of Cora's brothers were here, he would be dead. D.E.A.D. *Dead.*

That roller coaster was looking a lot less appealing right about then.

He cleared his throat. "Hi, Tanner," he said, leaning slightly forward in his chair and extending his hand. "Good to see you again."

Kelsey glanced up at her husband, pressed a kiss to the line of his jaw. "I don't know if I told you, Rafe is staying with Cor."

At that, Tanner's brows lifted a little higher.

"In the spare room," Cora burst in, her voice high and squeaking and having those knowing looks spreading from the men to the women.

An awkward pause.

Rafe cleared his throat again. "I have a job in town," he said. "Cora was nice enough to let me crash at her place for a few weeks."

A snort from behind his right shoulder, a feminine thigh shifting against his own.

"What do you do?" one of the other men asked.

"Construction," he said, extending a hand across the table. "I'm Rafe."

"Ben," he said, shaking Rafe's hand firmly. "It's nice to meet you. Stef"—he nodded at the pretty blonde at his side, one Rafe remembered from the night at Cora's house"—mentioned that you were staying at Cora's home."

Ben.

Ben.

Ben *Bradford.*

Holy shit. Rafe hadn't processed who was sitting across the table, and he really should have. Ben Bradford was the newest, hottest tech CEO around. He'd recently taken his company public...and that company had just accepted Rafe's company's bid on a warehouse retrofit.

He mentioned that, and then they began talking shop, which the table allowed for a few minutes before he and Ben were banned from work talk.

"I love you, baby," Stef said. "But it's Thursday Night Friends' Night. Which means there is an expiration label on shop talk."

Ben's face went soft, and he kissed the top of Stef's head, murmured something in her ear that had her cheeks going pink.

"I heard that you got the full Margarita Night Experience," Tanner said.

"Not the *full* experience," Ben chimed in. "There wasn't any alcohol involved."

"It was *enough* of an experience," he said lightly. "Let me tell you that."

Heidi's lips curved. "Did we scar you with our talk of BDSM?"

"Fuck yes, you did," he said, which earned him cackles from all the women except Cora, and sympathetic groans from the men.

Tanner's ears went red. "Please, tell me my wife didn't—"

Rafe put up a hand, palm out. "Let's not go there. Suffice to say, I've bleached any memories of that evening from my brain."

"Fuck, man," he muttered. "These women—"

"Are fabulous and perfect and wonderful," Kelsey interjected with a grin and waggling brows.

Tanner mock glared at her. "And annoying and loud and responsible for sharing far too much and—"

Narrowed eyes directed at Tanner. "And going to get into *so* much trouble—"

Luckily, the server arrived then, two fresh pitchers of margaritas in one hand and a plethora of chip baskets and little cups of queso on a tray that was perched on the shoulder of her free arm. She deposited all of it with an aplomb that told him she had probably taken care of this group before. And he supposed she had, considering that Cora and her friends tried to get together at this restaurant almost every Thursday.

The back-and-forth between Tanner and Kels was halted as glasses were topped off, orders were taken, and then when the server left, her notepad full, Kate jumped right into the conversation, thus preventing the back-and-forth from resuming.

Kate changed the topic of discussion from BDSM and annoying (or perfect, depending on which side of the argument one was part of) women, right to the newest superhero film with an ease that told him both that she'd played this game many a time before and that she was also going to be a really good mom.

As time went on, the conversation was lively (and thank fuck, but there was no more talk of the ladies' sexual habits and/or appetites). They argued about the best villain, made plans to see an action flick. The way the conversation developed and molded and changed was an interesting mix that Rafe had never experienced before—or well, he'd only ever experienced it once. With the Hutchinses. Side conversations and talking across the table interspersed with discussions that included everyone.

Laughter and teasing, warmth and a comfortable familiarity that made him feel about five years old again, escaping the quiet hell that was his house two doors down, and sitting at the table in the Hutchinses' kitchen for the first time.

Cora's mom making up a plate for him without a second glance, not caring that she'd had to pull in a stool from the pantry for him to sit on so he could have a chair.

Then later, after many meals, buying another chair so that he could sit at the table.

He closed his eyes and the conversation continued to roll over him, and he knew the roller coaster had pulled back to the beginning, had come to a halt, unlatched the safety belts. He was gathering his belongings and exiting to the right.

Because...Mrs. Hutchins.

Because Asher and Jeremy and Wyatt, Rome and Eli and Rowan.

How could he move in on their sister when they'd made him one of them? How could he take advantage when they'd done so much?

He was here to look out for Cora. To protect her.

Not too long to see her naked breasts, to taste her...*everywhere*.

A slight clatter in front of him had his eyes flashing open, seeing that the server had placed his beer in front of him.

"Everything okay?" she asked.

He nodded quickly, forced a smile. "Yup. Thanks very much."

But nothing was okay.

His thigh was still pressed to Cora's, their arms occasionally bumping, and even though she had been determinedly ignoring him, he could tell by the stiffness in her frame that she was as aware of him as he was of her.

So, he gave them both a break and scooted his chair from hers, putting some space between them.

Instantly, he felt cold.

But he pushed it down.

Mostly because the conversation was still reminiscent of the Hutchinses, and he wouldn't do anything to jeopardize that.

Even if it felt like he had to shove down part of his heart to get there mentally.

Thankfully, he was helped along by the tears (also an occasional occurrence in the Hutchins household). The waterworks having been caused by Heidi tossing an envelope at Kate. She'd torn it open with furrowed brows, saw what was inside—a pass to a local wild animal park where Kate could hold a sloth (apparently, a lifelong dream for the animal lover that was Kate).

So, before the fajitas had been brought to the table there were tears, Kate alternating between sobbing and squealing and hugging Heidi and Brad (who accepted the gesture but made it clear that it was all Heidi's idea).

Jamie coaxed her back into her seat, wiped the tears away with a tissue he jokingly said that he'd begun keeping in his pocket from the moment he'd learned his wife was pregnant.

Which had earned him a swat from a still-sniffing Kate.

The tears were gone. The glares were back.

And apparently, pregnancy hormones were real.

And also, Cora had good friends.

He liked that for her.

He wished he could like that for *him,* too.

But—the roller coaster took off without him—he knew that wasn't to be.

THIRTEEN

CORA

She'd had too many margaritas.

Work was going to *suck* tomorrow.

But Kelsey had talked her into sending her resumé over to Abby somewhere between prickly pear margarita three and five and based on the text reply from Abby (*When can you start?*), she didn't think she needed to worry about keeping Dale happy for much longer.

Two weeks.

She would need to keep him happy for two more weeks—or if not happy, then she at least needed to tolerate him for those two weeks.

Because her contract required two weeks' notice.

Because...she was done.

She almost didn't care how much she would be paid or what she would be working on.

She just needed *out*.

Now she was making her careful way to the bathroom. Her car would be spending the night, and she'd ordered a Lyft

—or she'd *attempted* to order a Lyft because Rafe had given her a look, snatched her cell, and ordered her to the ladies' room.

No warmth.

All order. All distance.

Kind of like the space between their bodies. She'd felt him shift away, *seen* the mental shift in the ticking muscle in his jaw, the tension in his muscles. She'd felt the physical one.

A jerk of his chair away.

His thigh shifting from hers. Their arms no longer brushing.

And...she'd felt that distance. And that distance had felt... like a slap.

So, the copious amounts of margaritas and chips and queso, and an entire platter of steak and chicken fajitas. Grilled onions? Yup. Hell, yes. She'd load 'em up, the better to keep annoying, confusing men at bay. Charred peppers? Double hell, yes. If she was feeling a little sick, she might as well add heartburn to the mix.

And heartbreak.

And...her drunk ass was being all dramatic.

That was courtesy of prickly pear margarita five...and also, maybe the gallon of queso she'd downed.

But she was going to focus on the positive.

New job forthcoming.

And it had been the easiest interview process (that being *no* interview process) she'd ever been part of.

Other positives to focus on, however, were a struggle to coax to the forefront of her inebriated mind. Mostly, she could only think of negatives. Like how cold her thigh had felt when he'd pulled away. Like the way he'd almost ignored her after he'd moved his chair. Like the slightly impatient way he'd snagged her phone and told her he'd drive her home.

It hurt.

It shouldn't.

She *should* want that distance. It made things infinitely simpler.

But...part of her liked it when he was close. Okay, a big part of her did. No, if she were being honest, *most* of her did. Most of her wanted to climb him like a cat tower and rub her face against his. Cover him with her scent, soak in his.

And *that* was the margaritas talking.

Bathroom.

She'd come into the bathroom to *use* the bathroom, and that meant she needed to stop staring at herself in the mirror and actually do her business.

Not think about how much she'd liked the kiss and the gruff way he'd wanted to protect her. How he'd chucked her shoes and made her hot cocoa because he knew it would help her sleep. How he'd gotten mad about the long hours and then kissed her in a way that had her not feeling like a boring little sister.

But like a woman.

Heart-pounding, lungs screaming, a hear-her-roar *woman*.

And a melting puddle of desire.

That too.

"Bathroom," she told her reflection. "Get on it."

She concentrated—because margaritas—on her business then washed her hands and pushed out into the hall, nearly plowing into Rafe.

"Easy," he said, his hands coming to her hips as he steadied her.

She stiffened.

Because she knew what was going to happen next.

And yup—the moment he processed that he was touching her—he jumped back, clenching his hands into fists at his sides.

She hitched her purse up higher on her shoulder, feeling more and more sober by the second. She wanted to order another pitcher of margaritas, to allow the pleasant fog of alcohol to suck her under again.

Anything was better than the slice of pain those clenched fists wrought.

Anything was better than feeling *this*.

God.

Pathetic.

She needed to grab on to her inner Cora. The tough, badass who didn't put up with any shit, and who knew her own head and heart. Lifting her chin, she pushed past him. "I need to get my bag out of my car before we go."

Then she walked down the hall, pushed out the back door, and strode across the back patio.

It was one of her favorite places with twinkly lights and a dance floor and had been the perfect space for Kate and Jaime's wedding.

Smiling, as she thought about that night and how happy her friends had been, how much fun they'd all had (despite an unfortunate cake disaster wrought by Heidi and Kate's trouble-making rooster, nicknamed The Fuzz), she moved quickly across the quiet space.

It was late and the tables had been bussed, the chairs stacked along the edge of the dance floor.

She pushed through the little gate on the far side of the space and bleeped the locks on her car, Rafe a thundercloud of a presence behind her left shoulder.

She tugged open the driver's door. "I can just—"

"You're *not* driving."

A breath through her nose. "I didn't say that I was going to drive." She snagged her bag from the passenger's seat, straightened, slinging it over her shoulder. "I was going to offer to get a Lyft."

"To the same house?" He grabbed the bag from her, slung it over *his* shoulder.

And that was it.

He spun, walked toward his truck, crammed into a spot in the far end of the lot, opened the passenger's side door.

Waited.

Cora stood there, debating walking the miles between there and home versus getting in that damn truck...and knowing there was no point in debating because he would get her ass in that truck.

Plus, it was cold, and she was tired, and she didn't *want* to walk home.

Which was why she walked over to the truck.

Okay, maybe she stomped, but just a little bit.

One foot on the running board, another inside the cab. She reached for the handle, started to draw herself up and in and—

Then her lungs froze.

Because he was touching her again.

Lifting her into the seat. Then jerking back his hands like he'd just completed the most disgusting action ever, like he needed to go dunk himself into a bucket of bleach.

Nice.

The door closed.

And so did her eyes.

At least if her lids were shut, she could pretend her world hadn't gotten so twisted and tangled, could pretend there wasn't hurt woven into every breath of her interactions with Rafe. She didn't even *like* him. He was an adoptive brother and nothing more, so it shouldn't hurt that he wasn't touching her like a woman he wanted, as he had in her kitchen.

Except...it did.

It hurt down to the marrow of her bones, felt like a stake in the heart, acid in her stomach...or well, an acid that didn't belong there. One that burned and had the contents churning and made her hate herself.

Because fuck him.

She didn't allow any man to drudge up those feelings in her.

Not now, not ever.

Not. *Ever.*

———

The last she remembered was feeling like shit.

Then she woke up, floating through the air, bouncing against something uncomfortably hard.

Spice in her nose. Strong arms surrounding her.

And for all her pretending to hate the feelings Rafe brought out, to despise the annoying, over-the-top way he was trying to shove them into the brother and sister roles...she liked it.

Nothing was better than when he was holding her.

Nothing.

Which made her a total pathetic weakling, she knew.

Something else that added to that weakling status?

The fact that she closed her eyes and continued to pretend to be asleep. Through the walk up to the house, through his bumbling with the lock and up the stairs. Her eyes stayed closed as he carried her down the hall and tucked her into bed.

Gentle fingers removed her shoes, tugged the covers up, and smoothed them lightly over her shoulders.

The light clicked off.

The door closed softly.

His footsteps padded away.

But her heart, as stupid as it was, her heart went right with him.

———

They met in the kitchen and squared off like enemies on opposite sides of the battlefield.

She threw up the white flag.

Mostly because she hadn't been able to sleep after her catnap in the car, and during her sleepless hours, she'd decided (and maybe it had been delirium that fueled this decision) to take a page out of Rafe's book.

She'd pretend.

She'd pretend he was just another one of the big lugs that were her brothers, and then everything would be fine.

So, yeah, she was totally ostriching.

But sometimes a girl had to be an ostrich.

"Coffee?" she asked, even though she was already making him a to-go mug.

Silence, as though weighing if this were a trap.

Then, footsteps growing closer, "Yeah. Thanks, Cor."

She shrugged, snapped the lid on, and set it to the side, filling her own mug and adding copious amounts of sugar and creamer because...she needed the sugar and creamer to deal with this *and* the forthcoming interaction with Dale.

Abby had emailed her early that morning with a formal offer.

Cora had signed it, sent it off, and in two weeks' time, she would be a RoboTech employee again. (Also, this just in, fuck startups run by middle-aged, mediocre men, she'd take Heather O'Keith as a CEO any day of the week).

"This one for me?"

Cora blinked, glanced from her mug to the one Rafe was reaching for and nodded.

"You need to run off to work or you got time for breakfast?" he asked, his eyes searching hers, probably looking for something that wasn't there. Okay, hopefully, it wasn't there. It being the longing, the revisiting the kiss and the shoe toss in her mind at increasingly inconvenient times.

Like right then.

She shoved it down. "I need to go get my car."

He rested a hip against the counter, arms lazily crossed, one hand gripping the mug where it rested against the shelf of biceps.

Convenient, that.

And, yes, she was also aware that thinking about Rafe's biceps went against her thinking of him as an annoying lump of older brotherness.

But...best intentions.

But...baby steps.

But—

"No, you don't."

She blinked, her hand gripping her own mug. "Um, did you forget that you drove me home last night?"

"Nope." He took a long drink from his cup, and no, she definitely didn't watch the strong lines of his throat work as he swallowed, didn't note his biceps flexing and shifting as he lifted it.

"So, unless my car is like an errant puppy finding her way home..."

He lowered the mug, reached one hand into his back pocket, and tossed her...

Her keys.

"I went and got it last night."

Her brows were drawn so tightly together that she could actually feel the furrows imprinting themselves on her forehead, but he enlightened her before she could ask.

"Caught a Lyft to the restaurant, drove it here."

How had she not heard the garage door open or the car pull up?

She hadn't slept...or at least she hadn't thought so. Maybe the man had ninja skills. Or maybe she had just been so lost in the tornado of her brain that she hadn't heard him.

It didn't matter.

What did was that her car was here, she had a new job on the docket, and...in front of her was the perfect opportunity to reinforce to her stupid, stupid brain that Rafe was nothing more than a brother.

So, she nodded. "Thanks."

And then she accepted his offer for breakfast, sat at the island while he made her favorite cinnamon sugar toast, and when he plunked the plate down next to her before plunking his butt up onto the counter by her elbow while shoveling plain buttered toast into his mouth telling her about his job and asking her cautious questions about hers (then more excited ones when she mentioned the job Kels had basically maneuvered for her), she could almost pretend that he *was* just Rafe.

Just another brother.

If only her heart didn't skip a beat when he slid down, his hip brushing her shoulder.

FOURTEEN

Teresa's gaze scanned the plans, and he waited to see what she would come up with.

They'd spent the day with the construction team from Ben's company, going over supplies and timelines, and then they'd popped over to the warehouse.

For his new pet project.

This would become something that was his, something he'd get to make all the decisions on from start to finish.

Well, all the decisions that weren't changed or nixed by Teresa.

Right.

Anyway.

He did the big jobs with businesses so he could do the passion projects that fed his soul. And since Teresa always seemed to get exactly what fed his soul—at least in a business capacity—he was fine with her nixing the ideas that wouldn't fit in with his plans for the project.

"You know," she said, tracing her finger over the layout of

what he'd envisioned would be the gym area, "between this and our other current projects, plus the bids that have been accepted, you're looking at more than two years of work here in the Bay Area."

That was his goal.

Or, well, he wanted to shift things from the Central Valley and SoCal to the Bay Area.

One, because he was tired of traveling.

Two, because his foreman for the SoCal jobs, Cabe, hadn't been nearly as effective at finding work as Teresa and Steve (his lead in the Central Valley). That had been before Rafe had let him go, having caught him giving kickbacks to shoddy subcontractors. He'd managed to relocate most of the crew to Steve and Teresa's teams as he finished off the contracted jobs, but that meant he'd spent a lot of time in the Valley lately.

And he wasn't a fan of the traffic and smog and *traffic* of Southern California.

Not that there wasn't traffic in the Bay Area.

It was just...it felt more like home.

And it was closer to the Hutchinses. Or at least, closer to Cora's mom's new house at the foothills of the Sierras, and since whatever Hutchins were in town tended to get together on the regular (and since he was an honorary Hutchins himself), he wanted to be close to the action.

Or Cora.

He clenched his jaw.

Cora was a Hutchins. *That* was why he wanted to be close. Not the only reason, but definitely near the top of the list.

"That's a good start," he said, ignoring that thought. "Between this and the jobs Steve pulled, the company is going to have its best year ever."

"Right."

He waited for her to say more or to comment on the *best year* thing.

But the only thing she did was look at him expectantly.

"What?" he finally asked.

"You realize that this means you should probably start looking for your own place, right?" One side of her mouth kicked up. "I know you said you bribed your way back into her good graces with wine and baked goods, thank me very much"—she blew on her knuckles, buffed them on her shoulder—"but I don't think she'd be down with letting you live in her guest room for two-plus years."

"I'm going down to finish up the job in a couple of weeks," he pointed out.

Teresa nodded. "Well, all I'm saying is that when you come up a few weeks after that, you should probably have a plan to live somewhere else." She made an X on the plans, sketched out a new layout of a few offices. "And, no, that's not me offering up *my* spare room."

"I'm only staying there because her brothers..."

The look she shot him had the rest of his words drying up in his throat.

"Only because of her brothers?"

"Well"—he reached over her, used his pencil to expand on what she was doing with the offices—"because of her, too," he said and added before the triumphant look Teresa could send his way could manifest into something that took over the conversation, or more than it already was, anyway—"You should have heard about the last guy she dated. He pounded on her door at midnight, demanding another chance. What if he'd gotten inside? What if—"

"She'd just call the police and take care of her own shit, like she is very capable of doing?"

He stopped, closed his mouth so fast that his teeth clicked together.

"I know you and her brothers have this weird sense of protectiveness that should have gone away like, fifteen years ago, but I've met Cora. Many times over the last few years. She's fully capable of running her own life without you guys meddling in it."

"I know that, but—"

"Do you?'

He frowned.

"Do you actually know that?" she asked. "Because it doesn't appear that way to me and coming as a woman who is the baby of the family with an extremely overprotective brother and sister herself, all I know is that sooner or later Cora is going to lose patience with all this."

"She already has." More times than he could probably think of.

Usually, this resulted in her calling in Mama Hutchins, who did some threatening—mainly involving food, because the Hutchins boys loved their food. Hell, one year, she and Cora went to Tahoe for Thanksgiving without telling anyone and left them to try to rustle up their own meal for the holiday.

That was the year that Rafe had learned how hard it was to cook a turkey.

They'd eaten Chinese food.

Because it was the only restaurant that was open and had shared a store-bought pumpkin pie that Asher had managed to wrestle away from another desperate man.

"Well, if she has, and you guys haven't listened, then watch out."

They finished sketching, so he rolled up the plans, tapped the end on his thigh to even it out. "What do you mean?"

"I *mean*, at some point, all this meddling is going to cause Cora to lose it, and then you guys are at risk of losing *her*. Forever."

A sick feeling exploded in his gut, spiraling up and out until the back of his throat burned.

"That scares you."

Of course, it did. "She's like a sister—"

Teresa snorted.

"—to me."

She huffed out a breath, patted him on the shoulder. "Right," she said. "So, if that's truly the case, then why do you look like you're going to puke right now?"

He inhaled sharply, but she didn't give him a chance to answer, just shook her head, called out a goodbye, and then she was gone.

And all he could think was, if she could see what he was trying to hide, even from himself, then what would Cora's brothers see?

Useless?

Worthless?

And even if not that, then how painfully would they kill him for daring to touch her?

———

He stayed in the warehouse long after Teresa left, walking the space, using the excuse of needing to feel the vibe with the changes in the layout they were making, but truthfully, he wasn't noticing the vibe or anything else.

It was all white walls and emptiness.

And Cora.

And Asher and Jeremy and Rome and Rowan and Wyatt and Eli.

Would he lose one or the other?

Or would he lose them all?

But if he continued pretending he didn't have feelings for Cora, what *else* would he lose?

And maybe, maybe if he really worked at it, proved his worth, did all the right things, he could make both work?

Sighing, he eventually sank down onto the floor and rested

his head against a wall that was soon to be taken out, looking at the space and feeling absolutely disgusted with himself.

For myriad reasons.

But really, it all came down to one thing.

Was he going to be able to shove down the feelings for Cora, to only see her as a sister? Or was he going to risk it all and tell her how he felt?

He knew it would be good.

That kiss had been...

And he wasn't risk averse. Rafe had done more than a few stupid things, starting with jumping off really big rocks into a questionably deep lake as a child and ending with moving his business up into a competitive market because he missed his real family.

(That being the Hutchinses).

It was just...he had a family that was bad, and he was part of one that was fantastic. So, knowing how bad *bad* could be, and how good *good* could be, how could he even think of risking being part of the Hutchins family on something that was probably a fad, a weird out-of-the-blue urge that would go away as quickly as it came on?

He couldn't.

He just...couldn't.

Further that, he was going to take Teresa's advice and make sure the collective brothers—himself included—stepped back the overbearingness and stopped interjecting themselves into Cora's life. They needed to let her live it.

Because he couldn't lose her either, even if it meant keeping her in a way that was a sad facsimile of what he really wanted.

Of course, what he *didn't* know as he sat there, making those plans, was that the moment he got back to her place, all of that would go to absolute shit.

FIFTEEN

CORA

Breakfast that morning had told her one thing.

She needed to keep living her life.

Lunch in her office with Dale alternating between firing her and begging her to stay had prompted her to lose herself in her phone.

In the *apps* on her phone.

And she wasn't in Safari playing Wordle (which, btw, she'd kicked ass by getting it on the second guess that morning, so bam!).

She was dusting off her dating apps.

Refreshing her profile, swiping, and...matching.

Messaging. With a guy who was cute, lived in the area, and had adorably asked if it was too soon to take her out for a drink that evening.

Not in a pushy way either.

But...endearing and making her smile and considering Dale's alternating fury and pressure and mood swings that had her seeing stars, *and* Rafe's deliberately brotherly distance, endearing and eager was much appreciated.

So was the drink.

If it went well, it could turn into something more.

If it went poorly, she could peace out.

If she wanted to bust out the handcuffs and rock Donovan's (cute name, right?) world, then she could do just that.

She was a grown woman—or maybe that was *groan* woman because the moment she had opened her garage door and was making her way to her car, Rafe pulled up to the curb. She was meeting Donovan at a local bar because she was a grown (not groan) woman and didn't want a strange man showing up at her house or knowing where she lived.

His truck turned off, and she heard the door open and close.

And yeah, she hurried for her car, to open *her* door, to get inside before he saw what she was wearing.

Which was short and tight and paired with high, high heels and red lips and smoky, shimmering eyes.

She looked hot.

She *looked* ready to fuck.

And she just might. If Donovan were cute enough and nice enough and she felt like it.

But she really didn't want to deal with Rafe.

This dress, these heels would ensure that she would be dealing with him.

His footsteps reached the garage just as she tugged the handle and started opening the door.

"What. The. Fuck?"

She glanced over her shoulder, ignored the heat that began bubbling through her middle, dripping down to gather between her thighs when she saw his gaze on her ass, as it traced slowly up her legs. And she knew a lot of them were on display with the short hem, just like there was a lot of the *rest* of her on display in her backless dress.

His stare was almost a physical caress. She felt it hit the bare skin between her shoulder blades, caress over her hair (curls on display and looking fucking good, thank her very much).

Then the air in her lungs went solid.

Because his eyes had hit hers.

Fire.

Need.

He stepped closer. No. He stepped *close,* pinning her between the car and his chest, hot breath on her nape, scorching words in her ear. She shivered, and he leaned more heavily against her. The cool metal of her car. The heat of his chest.

Thunk.

She turned her head, saw one broad hand plunking onto the car's frame.

Thunk.

The other boxing her in on the other side.

Thunk.

His body shifted, his knee closing the door, his body shifting even closer.

"Where are you going?"

Her body was practically vibrating with awareness, but she managed to get an answer out. "I have a date."

Still.

He was so fucking still.

Then he was leaning a little closer, his head dropping to her throat as he inhaled deeply. Her gaze was still facing forward, and she watched his hands tighten, the knuckles standing out in sharp relief. Why? Why was that so fucking sexy, that show of obvious strength?

She shivered again, and with him so close, the movement brought her ass in contact...

With him.

With *all* of him.

Sweet Jesus, she'd had some cock in her life, *good* cock. But

Rafe was packing, and the way that he rolled his hips, just a slight press, a rhythmic motion, she knew he knew how to use it.

Instinct drove her to arch back, not slightly this time, but to get the full feel of him.

And for one glorious second, he moved into her, made her wonder if angels were singing, or if it were actually possible to come from a man just thrusting into her ass and not touching any of the pertinent parts.

With Rafe and his clenching hands and big cock nestled right between her cheeks, she thought it might just be possible.

Another thrust.

Not exactly gentle, but she liked the edge of rough, the thought that he might be losing just the slightest bit of control.

It was hot.

So fucking hot that with the next thrust, her arms wrapped around his, palms gripping his wrists, ass up, spine arched, a moan tumbling from her lips.

So good. That felt so fucking good that she didn't notice the change in him, not right away.

Not until his hips shifted away.

Not until he'd tugged his arms free of her grip.

Not until his mouth had dropped to her ear again.

"Have a good time on your date," he whispered.

Cora blinked, desire having made everything go slightly fuzzy, trying to process those words, the meaning, and when she did, hurt slicing down her spine, tangling in her middle with shame and self-chastisement, she pulled away, smacking her front against the car.

She stumbled, caught herself just in time to see him climbing the two stairs that led into the house, moving like he wasn't the least bit affected.

And, right then, she hated him.

Just a little bit.

Just—

He pushed open the door, glanced over his shoulder. "And don't forget a jacket," he said, tone so neutral it had her teeth clenching together.

Then opening, a retort on the tip of her tongue—

"It's cold out tonight."

The door closed.

Her retort stayed on her tongue.

And, right then, she hated him, more than just a little bit.

———

She was turning into an alcoholic.

And it was all Rafe's fault.

Donovan was a nice guy. He was as cute as his picture, polite, and not pushy. And he was into her. Into her in a way that didn't have him clenching his fists and running away from her.

So...she'd accepted his offer to drive her home when one drink had turned into three, along with appetizers and desserts while sitting at Bobby's.

He turned off the engine, spun to face her. "I'll walk you up."

"You don't have—"

"I know I don't." He grinned at her. "But if I don't, I won't get a chance at a goodnight kiss without the console jamming into my side."

That made her giggle. Not solely because of the drinks—though she could freely admit that the drinks encouraged it—but because Donovan had been making her laugh all night. He was a manager at a popular club in town, and he had *all* the stories about people behaving badly (which, not ironically, was her favorite subReddit ever).

He grinned, popped open his door, and strode around the hood, getting to her side just as she started to push out, catching her hand and drawing her up. He closed the door, looped his arm around her side, and said, "Nice house."

"Thanks."

"I'm more of an apartment guy," he said as they wove through her planters. "Mostly because I have a black thumb."

She smiled up at him. "This"—she waved a hand at the planters, perfectly lit, exactly as Kate had planned—"is courtesy of my brothers and my friends."

"Nice friends."

"Yeah," she said softly as they reached the porch.

"Nice night," he said, just as softly.

Her lips curved. "That's a lot of *nices*."

"Truth?"

She nodded.

"You're so beautiful that it's hard to think sometimes, and that goes double for trying to think up adjectives."

Cora inhaled, her eyes prickling because that was...*nice*.

"Cora?"

"Yeah?"

"Okay if I kiss you goodnight?"

She nodded.

His lips curved, and then he lowered his head, brushing his mouth over hers once. Twice.

Oh, that was...nice.

But just *nice*, just nice and a little boring, and nothing at all like she felt when Rafe had kissed her—

Don't think about Rafe.

Right. No Rafe.

Just her and Donovan and his mouth and his tongue that was a little *too* much tongue. But the way he held her was *nice*, and it didn't leave her any doubt that he liked her, liked what they were doing and was excited by it.

The problem was...her response was only slightly better than lackluster.

"Donovan." She tore her mouth from his. "This isn't—"

The door opened.

They both jumped, and she glanced to her right to see—sigh—*Rafe* silhouetted in the light from the hall, his arms crossed over his chest, his expression thunderous.

Donovan froze, his hands still gripping her ass, his mouth still close enough that she could feel his breath puffing on her lips.

"Really?" Rafe asked, eyes on hers.

"This is none of your business."

Donovan's hands started to drop, brows shooting up. "Is this one of your brothers?"

Considering she was black and Rafe was white—very white—she thought this was a pretty dumb question, but she didn't say anything because it was late and she was tired, and hell, he might as well have been her adoptive brother, so what the hell did she know?

"No," she said. "Rafe isn't my brother."

Donovan's brows went higher. "Your roommate?"

She pressed her lips together. "Not exactly."

"So...is he your man?" he asked.

"It's not like that," she began. "He's—"

Donovan grinned, shrugged, and said, "Hey, no judgment here. You're a beautiful woman with needs. If he's game for an open relationship, who am I to complain?" His hands tightened, drawing her closer, his pelvis brushing hers.

And for the record, what he was packing didn't compare to Rafe.

"That's not what—"

"I'm just saying"—his hands dipped down again, drew her even more tightly against him—"I'm happy to join in whatever activities are on the table."

She turned her head away, and unfortunately, that meant she met Rafe's stare.

His brows lifted. "*This* is what you want?"

Like she was sexually attracted to dog shit.

And look, she was all for the *you-do-you* mentality, especially when it came to what happened between the sheets.

But she wasn't much for sharing, and yeah, maybe she'd read more than her fair share of MM or MMF books, and she couldn't say she hadn't had the odd fantasy here or there about being with two guys at the same time. But that was just it. Those thoughts were a fantasy, and despite Donovan's offer, she couldn't imagine trying to tackle two men at once.

"Hey, man," Donovan said, his fingers kneading her ass in a way she probably would have liked if not for the offer in the air, if not for Rafe and the way he was staring at her (the dog shit sexual attraction). But Rafe was there, so when Donovan went on, she was ready for the floor to open up and swallow her whole. "I'm just here for the lady, but I'm also good to just watch or be watched or—"

"Shut up."

Donovan shut up.

"Cor?" Rafe asked.

Her gaze shot up to the man standing in the doorway, now staring at her expectantly.

Wanting her to answer the question.

Waiting for her to give that answer.

She *should* want Donovan. Okay, maybe not *should* want him. She *wanted* to want him because that meant she wouldn't want Rafe. And maybe it would also rub in his face that she was a sexy and desirable woman and—

Her sigh was silent.

Attraction and chemistry couldn't be faked, and as *nice* as Donovan was, the draw just couldn't compare...

"*Cor?*"

To Rafe.

His green eyes glimmered.

"Do you want him?" he asked bluntly.

And her answer was just as blunt.

"No," she whispered.

Donovan's arms jerked.

She winced, not because it hurt, but because she wasn't the kind of woman who brought one man home, only to drop him for another. "I'm sorry," she said softly.

To his credit, Donovan didn't get mad. "Nice plants. Nice house. Nice woman." He cupped her cheek. "No guilt." A kiss to her cheek, whispered words in her ear. "But I don't think you're one for an open relationship." He straightened slightly, tilted his head in Rafe's direction. "And I don't think he is either."

Her gaze went to Rafe again, to the rage emanating off him.

"Bye, Cora." There was an edge of disappointment in Donovan's voice, but that was as far as it went before he released her, nodded in Rafe's direction, and left, his car zipping off down the road mere moments later.

And...silence.

Tension. Anger.

Waves and waves of it pulsing off Rafe, coursing over her.

And all the while, he just stared at her, those eyes as effective as stakes pinning her in place. Which was why she didn't move into the house, didn't do anything but watch Rafe's hands open and close, open and close.

But eventually, the silence got to be too much.

"I had to leave my car again," she whispered.

"I know," he said, eyes flicking behind her then coming back to hers.

"I'm not drunk." Still whispering. "I'm just...not sober."

Her gaze dropped to his hands again, saw that they'd clenched into fists again. Tight skin, white knuckles. Strong capable hands that had helped her with her house, held her tight, but were also gentle to tuck her into bed, to make her cinnamon toast.

Silence had her gaze drifting up to his.

"I'm not drunk," she said again.

"I know," he said the moment their eyes connected.

"I—"

The rest of whatever she'd been about to say was caught up in a gasp because suddenly Rafe was there, and by *there,* she meant he was in her space, sweeping her up into his arms, and...and...

Those hands went to work, holding her tight.

Pleasure slid through her.

No.

It consumed her, set her on fire, burned through her nerves, set her heart skittering. Had *her* hands going to work, gripping his shoulders, sliding up so that one covered his nape and the other shoved itself into his hair.

"Cora," he groaned.

"Rafe." A whisper.

A plea.

And finally, finally he obliged.

His mouth covered hers, tongue thrusting deep.

One of his hands went to her ass, slid down her thigh, coaxing it around his hip, and she quickly wrapped both legs around him, lungs screaming, head spinning, tongue doing its level best to keep up with his.

Then they were moving.

Into the house, up the stairs, cool air on her legs, a hot palm dipping under the hem of her dress and cupping her bare ass cheek.

Warm rough hands.

Fingers dipping just slightly into her crack.

And seriously, thongs for the win.

Down the hall.

Into her room.

Onto...she squealed when her ass collided with cold granite.

Into the bathroom apparently.

His emerald eyes blazed with need, his lips were swollen, his chest rose and fell like he'd run a marathon. But all he did was reach for her toothbrush, slap some toothpaste on it, and order, "Wash him off."

She shivered.

And not from the cold tile.

But she didn't grab the toothbrush.

A spark of fury, fueling the desire coursing through her. It dripped down her thighs, had her pussy absolutely aching.

She grabbed the toothbrush. She scrubbed her teeth. She spat and rinsed and—

Another squeal as she was in his arms again. But it was only a millisecond long because then his mouth was on hers again, and she wasn't thinking about Donovan or how much she liked bossy Rafe in the bedroom.

She was flying through the air, landing with a slight *oof* on the mattress—

And Rafe was between her thighs.

A jerk brought her ass to the edge of the bed.

A rough movement to spread her wide.

He gripped her panties, yanked, and...they were gone. The silk fluttering to the floor somewhere behind him. She hadn't even known it was possible to do that. Hell, she didn't think it *was* possible to actually tear someone's panties off.

But Rafe had and...

Wet.

She'd been wet before, dripping down her legs. Now...now she was practically melting for him.

And he was kneeling before her, lips parting, eyes glued to her bared pussy.

Sixteen

Rafe

He was going to hell, and he couldn't summon a fuck to give about it.

Glistening folds, shorn curls, lush legs spread wide.

And Cora in that dress that revealed more than it covered, the hem dancing around her ass, the top so low cut that her tits were nearly bursting free as she lifted herself up onto her elbows and stared down at him.

With mischief in chocolate eyes.

"You just going to look at it?" she murmured.

He was tempted to.

"It *is* the prettiest pussy I've ever seen," he said, stroking a finger through her folds.

So. Fucking. Wet.

Like a knife through butter, and he knew that he'd slid right into the hot, tight clasp of her. No resistance. Just liquid silk.

Cora's head tipped back, her throat on display and calling for his mouth.

But the part in front of him was calling louder.

He drew his finger back down, tracing patterns through her labia, slowly making his way back up to her clit, pressing lightly.

A gasp. A curse. Her thighs shaking. Her hips thrusting up.

His head dipped. He inhaled.

And...he lost control.

Hands beneath her ass and drawing her close, yanking her against his mouth, thrusting his tongue deep inside, his thumb sliding up, circling her clit, pressing firmly.

And...Cora lost control.

She bucked against him, thighs clenching around his head so tightly he almost couldn't breathe, the mattress bouncing when her elbows gave way and she caught his hair, holding him to her. Fine by him. He was prepared to drown in her.

But first, he needed to get her off, to see her come apart for him.

He needed to know everything about her.

What touches sent her soaring. What words pushed her over the edge. Did she like his tongue—

Oh yeah. She definitely liked his tongue there.

Firm kisses and gentle circles.

But suction. Suction was where it was at for her.

"Shit. Rafe. Oh fuck!" Her hips ground against his mouth, her hands gripped tighter. Hell, that stung. He would be surprised if he had any hair left when he was done, and truthfully, he wouldn't give one fuck if he ended up with two bald patches by the time he made her come.

Not that he gave a fuck.

Because he'd be making her come.

Because...

Thoughts left him as he became a machine focused on making sure she reached the precipice, that she toppled over the edge. He drank her up, sucked her harder, deeper, pressed a finger home at the same time as he hauled her closer to him.

Her breath caught.

One breast popped free from her dress.

The sight of her nipple, beaded and calling for his mouth had him doubling down, moving faster, circling and licking, kissing and sucking and—

She came apart on his mouth, a gush of liquid on his tongue.

Tart berries, sweet Cora.

Her hair was splayed around her shoulders, her eyes were half-mast. Her other breast was threatening to escape, and fuck yeah, when she took a deep breath, his wish came true, and it popped free. Dusky nipples. Jiggling breasts. Glistening skin.

The *fucking* best.

"Rafe," she whispered, lifting her head enough that those heavy, half-mast eyes collided with his. "Please."

He moved, lifting her up as he shifted onto the bed, her head hitting the pillow, lips parting on a gasp. He wanted to taste that gasp, but his fingers were already working on more important things, tugging down the rest of her dress, leaving her bare to his gaze, and fuck, she was gorgeous. Breasts and hips and skin that demanded to be kissed.

"Wait," she said as he started to climb over her, intending to start with her mouth and then kiss her all the way down.

"No?" he asked, knowing he'd stop, but really not wanting to.

His cock hurt it was so hard. His hands shook and his mouth watered and sweat had broken out on his spine. He needed her, and he needed her *now,* and he needed to have her before the rest of the world intruded.

Before he thought about that fucker who'd escorted her up onto the porch, about their family, and her brothers and—

"Yes," she said, "I just—"

Her hands went to the hem of his shirt, began tugging it up, and he understood.

Rearing back, he yanked it over his head, shifted so he could shove off his pants, his underwear.

Her gasp, her eyes widening in approval, lips parting, and what he wouldn't give to have them parting because she was taking his cock between them.

The thought had barely formed before she was up on her knees, her hands coming to his chest.

A shove had him falling back, narrowly missing the footboard, but then she was on him, straddling his middle, hands on his shoulders as she bent and kissed him deeply. Her tongue was in his mouth, tangling with his. Her pussy was splayed across his stomach, the damp heat of her arousal soaking into his skin. Hands in his hair, breasts on his chest, nipples hard and dragging across his skin.

And that was enough for his control to splinter.

He flipped them, coming on top of her, and finally, *finally* got his mouth on her breasts, and hell yeah, he discovered that she loved suction there, too, drawing on her nipple, rolling the other between thumb and forefinger. Then palming her breast, caressing and squeezing lightly, before dragging his palm down her side, dipping his fingers between her legs again.

A hiss as he brushed his thumb over her clit.

Her thighs clenching around his arm, but he didn't stop.

Just continued stroking as he kissed his way to her other breast, lavished it with attention until her hips started working against his hand, until liquid silk began to gather on his palm, his fingers. Her hands came to his head, tugged him off her breasts, drawing him up, slanting her mouth across his and kissing him so deeply that he felt as though his heart was going to pound out of his chest.

"Now," she broke away, gasping. "Now, Rafe."

He didn't think.

Didn't *think*.

Just spread her thighs and thrust deeply.

Oh fucking hell. Tight and wet, her pussy clasping around his dick. She arched against him, wound her legs around his hips as he moved once, twice, felt his orgasm coil at the base of his spine. That was the moment he knew he'd better get her there and fast, because if she wasn't *there* with him, then she'd be shit out of luck.

So, he needed to figure out what she liked.

And he needed to do it quickly.

Hitching her leg up, he thrust several times, clenching his teeth to hold back his desire as he found out what she liked, what angle had her gasping, what pressure had her neck curving as she *thunked* her head back into her pillow.

"Oh God, baby," she moaned. "Just like that. Like *that*."

Thank fuck.

He kept like *that*, thrusting deep and hard and clenching his teeth, and feeling sweat drip down his spine and her lips parted, his name toppling off her tongue.

"Come, baby," he ordered. "Come for me."

Come before he did.

A hard thrust, deeper than before.

Her pussy convulsed, a moan bubbled up in the back of her throat, and...*there*. Thank fuck, she came, gripping him so tightly that his orgasm barreled forward, that he exploded, pounding into her, barely able to make sure he wasn't hurting her, that the thrusting was extending her pleasure and not hindering it.

Then he wasn't thinking of anything else.

Then he was *feeling*.

Then he was lost in the sensation of Cora.

How good it felt to have her wrapped around him, how perfect this moment was, how perfect *she* was.

And then...he lost sense of himself, of the world, of time and place.

Seventeen

Cora

Her heart pounded against her ribs.

Sweat coated her skin.

And every muscle was lax and loose and like putty.

The best sex of her life, and it hadn't even involved handcuffs.

A giggle bubbled up in her chest and burst through her lips. The man was still on top of her, still inside her, a hot, hard brand (and hey, giggling with him deep inside her felt great, no lie).

He stiffened.

And reality intruded.

She went stiff, the pleasure that had been inundating her faded away. Because...reality. Certainly, it was hitting Rafe, too, and any moment he was going to be pushing up and off her, pulling out and leaving her cold and empty and—

He shifted, pulled out, slid off her.

Cora's heart squeezed, and she mentally braced as he pushed to his feet.

Waited for him to go.

But then his fingers were around her wrist, and he was tugging her to the edge of the bed, scooping her up into his arms, carrying her to her bathroom. He set her on her feet near the toilet (and seriously, the man was going to protect her against UTIs as well?) then faced the shower stall, turning on the water.

"I'm going to get you some hot cocoa," he murmured, starting for the door.

Panic.

Now he was going to leave, or worse, say this had all been a mistake—

"Rafe?"

His eyes held hers. "I'm not going anywhere." A crooked smile. "Well, I'm going to the kitchen, but I'll be back, okay?"

Her breath shuddered out of her. "Okay," she whispered.

She did her thing then wrapped up her hair and stepped into the warm steam of the shower, letting the water stream over her, not really bothering to do anything but just stand there and enjoy the heat.

A *clink* drawing her focus, and she saw Rafe, still buck naked, setting a mug on the counter.

He turned, met her eyes through the glass.

And she found herself holding her breath.

Then releasing it as he strode toward her, opened the door, and stepped into the shower with her. His hand slid down her spine, turned her to face him, his emerald gaze locking with hers. "One night," he whispered.

"One night," she agreed.

Heat in his gaze, his cock hardening and pressing into her stomach. Then...they both moved at once, and it was...effortless.

He seemed to know exactly where to put his hands to drive her absolutely wild.

She knew instinctually where to touch him that had him

groaning and shaking, his grip tightening on her, his kisses growing more and more desperate until he was lifting her up, the tiles a cold shock on her back, but only for a second.

Because then he was inside.

Her head plunked back, and he slipped a hand in between her skull and the tiles, stopping her from hurting herself, protecting her even as pleasure sucked her under.

He moved.

She moved.

They came together in a rhythm that was jerky and inelegant, filled with the sounds of water and skin sticking together, with the slick noise of desire, of his groans rumbling up in his throat, her heart pounding, his name an epithet on her tongue.

And when the pleasure had been wrung out of her, when he'd come apart, his forehead resting on her shoulder, his breath coming in rapid gusts, his body shaking from the exertion, but still he rallied himself to soap her up, to turn off the water and dry her gently, then tucked her under the covers, handed her the mug of cocoa and turned on *Die Hard* she knew...*knew* that this one night was going to absolutely destroy her.

———

The sounds of gunfire woke her up.

She stretched, body deliciously sore, feeling like she'd run a marathon, but one that actually made her feel great (and minus the runners' shits).

Wincing, thinking that was probably the wrong thought to have when she was naked and had just had the best sex of her life, and was still in Rafe's arms.

It wasn't night.

Their night was over.

But...he was still in her bed.

And it was all she could do to smother the hope in her heart.

One night. One. Night. This was...just a continuation of that one night.

His arms tightened, his nose was in her throat, and he inhaled deeply, pelvis rocking against hers. A hand snaking down, fingers slipping between her thighs, his lips pressing to her neck, and then he was rolling her to her stomach, lifting her up onto her knees.

A kiss on the back of her neck, drifting down along her spine. On one cheek and then the other.

She jumped when his teeth met flesh, when his fingers fluttered over her clit.

She gasped. "Rafe."

"Cor," he murmured, stroking through her folds, the head of his cock pressing into her. "Tell me you're ready."

She was ready, damned ready.

She nodded.

He thrust home.

"Fuck," she hissed.

"Too much?" he rumbled, sliding a hand down her spine, pulling out slowly, until just the head of him was inside her.

She shook her head. "No, baby."

And then there was no more talking, his hips flexing, his cock moving deep inside her. A slow drive forward, an even slower withdrawal. He fucked her like he had an eternity to drive her up and over the edge, to be inside her, to coax her to orgasm. Then when she was getting close, he froze, flipped her onto her back, rocking deep and slow until she felt like she was going to come apart at the seams.

"Wait, baby," he whispered.

She pressed her head back into her pillows. "Rafe, I need—"

A jerk of movement, him rolling them so she was on top, and then coaxing her into that final sprint. Slow and steady gone. It was fast and intense and—

"*Oh God,*" she moaned.

It was there. Right there.

Then she was over, Rafe's big hands clamped onto her waist guiding her through, guiding *him* through as wave after wave of pleasure hit her, leaving her sprawled across his chest like a limp noodle, and maybe *that* was the best sex of her life.

It hadn't been the furious coupling of the shower, nor the snap of control roughness after her date.

It was slow, steady, meaningful.

That tendril of hope blossomed inside her. She shouldn't have allowed it to. She knew that, knew that Rafe would never truly accept this change in their relationship. Not when he was supposed to protect her. Not when it would mean choosing her over her brothers.

Wyatt...fuck, he would freak out.

Asher...he wanted to pretend she didn't have a vagina, or if she did, it was safely ensconced behind a chastity belt.

Jeremy was the worst.

But Rome, Eli, and Rowan were just as bad when it came to the men she dated.

But maybe...maybe it would be different if it were Rafe.

He was a good guy. He was one of them. He—

A knock on the front door.

The heavy pounding knock of one of her brothers, followed by the worst sound in all the world—a key scraping in the lock.

Followed by an *even worse* sound.

Her brothers' voices in the hall.

One second, she was sprawled on Rafe, his warm arms around her, his hand tracing lightly up and down her back. The next she was dumped onto the mattress, her robe chucked onto her chest.

"Get dressed," he hissed as Jeremy's voice echoed up the stairs.

"Cora! You'd better be awake! It's Hike Day."

Hike. Day.

Fuck her life.

She scrambled into the robe, tying it securely at the same time as Rafe disappeared into the bathroom, his clothes bundled into his arms.

And then...they descended.

Jeremy popping his head in first, his expression tightening when he saw she wasn't dressed. "You forgot?"

She slung a hand on her hip, tried to pretend there wasn't a naked man in her bathroom. "You mean, did I forget the event I swore I would never *ever* go on again after the last time that you guys dragged me on a six-mile hike without even knowing the path you were supposed to be taking?"

"Meh," he said, shoving her arm to the side and sweeping her into a tight hug.

"Paths are for pussies," Wyatt, her second oldest (by a few minutes anyway, but definitely her tallest brother) declared, sweeping into her bedroom and dislodging Jeremy so he could steal a hug.

Then her room was invaded by Asher and Eli, who nearly knocked her over with the exuberance of their hugs (and thank God she managed to keep her feet because she was naked under the robe). Rowan and Rome were a little quieter, but then again four had come before them, and as Cora knew intimately, there was only so much air available.

And noise their ears could take.

"Sorry, peanut," Rome said, when he hugged her. "I tried to convince them to leave you out of it."

"Let me guess," she muttered, "you were outvoted, four to two, with you and Rowan being the only two voices of reason."

He pulled back, bopped her on the nose. "Got it in one."

"Look, guys," she said when she'd finished hugging Rowan, and because she needed to get them out of her room before something disastrous happened, like one of the big lugs needed to use the bathroom or something. "I'll go on the damned hike, but I need to shower first, and I need Asher to make me his oat—"

A crash in the bathroom.

"—meal," she finished, clearing her throat, hoping that her voice had drowned out the noise.

Except, six gazes had turned from her, had focused on the door to the bathroom.

Tension filled her bedroom.

She opened her mouth to say *something,* maybe to scream bloody murder about there being a spider—that had worked when she'd been a teenager—but Jeremy whipped toward her, eyes flashing as his gaze drifted from her (presumably taking in her short robe cinched tight) over her shoulder (more presuming, since he was staring in the direction of her very mussed bed). "Do you have a man in there?"

Oh, fuck.

But she was Cora Hutchins.

She'd dealt with these idiots for thirty years—and she was *thirty years old,* dammit! If she had a man in there, it was her prerogative.

"I'm a grown woman—" Or really, a *groan* one again, because Jeremy ignored her, walking toward the bathroom and reaching for the doorknob. "I can make my own—"

The door opened.

Fuck. Her. Life.

EIGHTEEN

RAFE

The door whipped open, but he was ready.

Even though his heart was fucking racing and his palms were sweaty and he was mentally spiraling.

Disaster.

Disaster.

So fucking stupid.

The best night of his life and the worst morning...because he wouldn't ever have her again.

"What the fuck, man?"

Jeremy. Of course, it was his best friend. And, of course, his other best friend was on his heels. Wyatt's eyebrows slashing down, fury on his face.

Time to play it cool.

Even though his dick was still drying from being inside *their sister.*

He rolled his eyes. "One of you fuckers want to fix the showerhead?" he asked, stepping out of the stall and holding the piece he'd unscrewed.

This being after he'd pulled on his clothes.

Pants. Shirt. Jeans. Two shoes. Two socks. No underwear. Because he hadn't had time to find it, and he was praying that Cora's brothers didn't accidentally spot it.

Jeremy's face relaxed.

Wyatt watched him closely. "Why didn't you come out when you heard us?"

"Because I was elbow deep in showerhead?" he asked, setting it on the counter and drawing his friend into a slapping hug that made him feel both at home and like total shit, all at the same time.

Jeremy slung an arm around Cora's shoulders. "Told you it would be a perk to have a contractor staying with you." He glanced at Rafe. "Chase off any assholes?"

Cora glared. "I'm a grown woman, I can chase off my own—"

"One," he said, knowing that he was one of the assholes that should be chased off, either by Cora herself or her brothers, or probably both.

The things he'd done to her...

The things she'd done to him...

His cock twitched and...

Asshole.

Jeremy grinned, kissed the top of Cora's head. "Get dressed," he ordered, shoving her into the bedroom. The hem of her robe dancing around the tops of her thighs reminded Rafe of...*too much*. He tore his gaze away.

Not going there.

Not ever again.

"What's wrong with it?"

He frowned. "What?"

Wyatt nodded at the showerhead he'd set on the counter. "What's wrong with the showerhead?"

Rafę froze, knowing he should have an easy excuse, but unable to come up with one.

The silence stretched, too damned far, too damn dangerously.

"It's not spraying right," Cora said, having righted herself after the shove. She stood in the doorway, looking sick, but determined, probably very similar to his own expression. The sick part, anyway.

Because the only thing he was determined about was getting the fuck out of this house and away from Cora's brothers, from his friends, until he got his head on straight...and found a new place to stay.

Clearly, this could not go on.

A breath as he pushed by Wyatt. "Did I hear something about oatmeal?" he asked. "You fuckers can cook me breakfast while I soak this showerhead in vinegar and baking soda."

He strode from the room, weaving his way through a sextuplet of men who would die for the woman among them, who would cheerfully murder him if they'd known he had just finished enjoying himself with their sister when they barged into her house.

He did it pretending that nothing had changed.

He did *it*, casually nudging his missing underwear under the bed on the way out.

———

"I'm so going to change the locks on you assholes," Cora grumbled from ahead of him, her ass swaying as she climbed the incline on the six-mile hike Rowan had picked for them.

For *them*.

Yup. Them including Rafe, even though he'd tried to get out of it.

Because as much as Cora protested about their pushiness, Rafe wasn't immune, even though he'd attempted the excuse of needing to work.

They'd strong-armed him into the hike.

And now...now he was in hell.

And the self-flagellation was real. He'd been in an inner spiral of panic and disgust, one that kept being sparked because now that he'd had Cora, he couldn't look at her and not see the rich brown skin he'd kissed, breasts he'd had in his hands, nipples he'd tasted, a pussy he'd had on his tongue.

And he was with her brothers.

Which then meant the cycle started right back up again.

So, the self-punishment was real.

Ceaseless.

God, he had to think about something, *anything* aside from the way it had felt to cup Cora's hips and thrust deep inside her hot, wet puss—

"You good?"

He nearly skidded off the trail, and considering it was a hill on one side and a sharp precipice on the other (anyone want to guess which side he nearly toppled off?) there were a few good seconds there where his life flashed before his eyes.

He didn't hate that the last night of his life had been spent with Cora.

Which...presented a problem.

A hand gripped his arm—a hand that belonged to Wyatt. "You good?" he asked, studying Rafe closely.

Rafe cleared his throat. "I'm fine."

"You're not yourself."

He wasn't.

Because he'd *fucked their sister!*

"Yeah," he said, "my mind is on my new projects. Got a busy schedule coming up, and it's going to mean a lot of travel between here and L.A. until the job down there is complete."

"That sucks, man." Wyatt nodded ahead and they moved to catch up, Rafe thankful they were at the back of the pack and the other brothers couldn't give him too much shit about his near-death experience.

"Still planning on moving up here?" Wyatt asked.

Rafe nodded. "Yeah, that's another thing. The L.A. job is the last one, and then we're going to have two years of busting our asses until we finish our current contracts. So, I need to find some time to find a place to buy or rent, considering that I can't stay in Cora's spare room forever."

"She wouldn't mind."

Laughter in his chest. "You've either lost it, or you don't know your sister. She barely let me stay *this* time."

"Meh. Cora's bark is worse than her bite. She always relents."

That reminded him of what Teresa had said, about the warning she'd given. "Maybe, Wy," he agreed. "But at some point, she's going to be done relenting and you guys might actually end up with more problems than her dating a guy you don't approve of."

Furrows in Wyatt's brows. "What the fuck are you talking about? Did Cora say something? Is she dating—"

Rafe shook his head. "You know I'm a lifelong member of the Protect Cora fan club, but I'm just saying that she's a grown-up, and she's going to start resenting the interference in her life at some point." A beat. "If she hasn't already."

The grooves on his forehead were deep. "Did she say something?"

"No." He shook his head. "I just—my foreman, Teresa, mentioned something. She's got brothers, and the overprotectiveness strained their relationship."

Immediately, the worry left his face. "Well, that's Teresa. Cor's different."

"I don't—"

A cry.

Cora cried out.

And Rafe stopped thinking and spiraling and trying to make Wyatt see reason. He heard Cora was in pain, and...

He reacted.

Nineteen

Cora

One second, she was grousing about the hike and huffing and puffing as she followed Jeremy, Rome, Eli, and Rowan up the hill, and the next she was falling, seeing Asher's eyes go wide in horror.

He'd nudged her, a playful brotherly push, telling her to stop her complaining.

But she'd been between strides, and the push was ill-timed.

She caught her foot on a tree root...and tripped.

Fell sideways.

Right over the edge of the path.

Her hip hit something hard—a rock, another root—and then she was sliding, rolling. Pain through her temple, her cheek as she was caught by a branch.

She heard a shout, but she didn't know which of the males it belonged to.

Not when she was scrabbling, nails breaking as she tried to claw at the hillside, trying to slow her descent.

But it was all loose rocks and leaves and crumbling dirt and—

A jarring pain shooting up her back.

It took a moment for her to realize that she'd come to a halt, mostly because rocks and dirt, leaves and sticks kept sliding by her for long moments.

She lifted a hand, saw it was covered with blood, deep gouges dug into her palm, several of her nails broken, blood seeping. Then she tried to move.

Everything hurt.

Her toes in her boots. Her ankles, calves, shins. Her knees felt like they'd had a run-in with a rototiller. Her thighs and ass were on fire. Her back was oozing. Her arms on fire. Her face…it felt like her nose might be broken.

"Fuck," she hissed, trying to lift her head then promptly freezing and lying back down.

"Cora!"

Movement above her, rocks and dirt, leaves and sticks tumbling down again, bumping into her, creating a whole new net of pain as they collided with her.

"I'm okay," she whispered.

"Cora!"

"I'm okay," she managed to say a little louder.

"Cora, fuck. Cora, baby." Rafe skidded to a halt next to her, nearly going over the edge himself, having to grip the trunk of the tree to stop himself. "Shit." He extended a hand toward her, pulled back before he touched her. "*Fuck.* Baby, oh my God.*"

"I'm okay," she whispered again. "I just—"

More rocks and sticks, dirt and leaves began coming down again.

Rafe lurched forward, blocking the flurry, covering her body with his own, somehow without smushing her. "Stop!" he yelled. "You're knocking shit down onto Cora."

Curses, but the flurry stopped.

"Is she okay?" Jeremy called.

"I'm fine," she called back...and winced because her ribs, her ribs didn't like it when she raised the volume of her voice.

"She's not fine," Rafe yelled. "Get the first aid kit ready. I'll get her up to you."

She shifted her leg, stifled a pained groan.

"Stop moving," Rafe ordered, turning to face her.

She ignored him, kept going until she managed to get both of her legs on the same side of the tree. A hiss of air when she put her hand beneath her, but before her arm gave out and she collapsed back down to the ground, Rafe's arms were around her.

"Stop," he ordered.

Her teeth clinked together, sending a bolt of pain along her jaw. "I'm—"

"You're not *fine*," he growled. "You're hurting and bleeding from a dozen different places. It's a god damn miracle you're conscious, and I'm not even sure you don't have broken bones or a fucking skull fracture."

Miserably, she lifted a hand to her head, trying to smother her wince at the movement. "Don't yell at me."

"Then don't fall off a fucking cliff," he snapped, gently lifting her up.

She cried out.

She *hated* that she'd cried out, but it had just slipped out.

Rafe cursed. "I'm sorry, baby."

Concentrating on breathing, it took her a long minute to be able to speak without crying. "It's not your fault."

"Yeah, it's fucking Asher's fault," he muttered. "And I'm going to take care of *him* later."

He shifted her, and the gentle movement had her teeth clenching, had pain shooting along her jaw again, had fire shooting through her torso. Fuck, that really hurt. She didn't know how she was going to stand being carried up this hill.

All she knew was that she wasn't going to be able to walk up it.

So, she *had* to stand it.

"I'm sorry in advance for this, baby," he warned, arms tightening slightly. "But I've got to get you up this hill."

"Just do it," she ordered.

Rafe's eyes hit hers. They were gentle, with deep regret in their depths. "Sorry, baby," he whispered.

"It's—"

But the rest of her words were cut off on a pained breath.

Because he was moving up the hill, arms wrapped tightly around her as he climbed the slope. His body pitched forward so he wouldn't fall. Occasionally releasing one arm so he could grab onto a root or rock to heft them higher.

All of it hurt.

Every jar and movement. Every heft and shift of his grip.

They were agony.

But then there were more arms around them, hands grabbing onto Rafe as they hauled them up and over the edge.

"Put her down over here," Jeremy ordered.

Rafe carried her across the trail, set her gently on a pile of sweatshirts.

The moment his hands were off her body, he stood, spinning and cold-cocking Asher.

She gasped. Then whimpered.

"Save that shit for later," Jeremy snapped, and then he was bending over her, hands fluttering like he didn't know how to touch her without hurting her. And he probably couldn't. As previously established, she hurt everywhere. "Fuck, Cor, you're a mess," he said gently.

"I'm fine. Just bandage up the worst of the cuts and wrap my ribs so we can get out of here."

His eyes flared when she said ribs, but he didn't get up and punch Asher in the face again like she half expected. Instead, he sucked in a breath, released it slowly. Then he began cleaning the worst of the wounds, his jaw clenching so tightly that she was worried he was going to crack a tooth. He startled slightly when Rafe knelt beside them, shaking out his fist. His fingers were gentle when he slowly pulled up the hem of her shirt, probing gently at her ribs.

"You'll need an X-ray," he said softly.

Movement at her feet, Rowan's voice terse as it reached her ears. "And here." Fingers loosened the laces, gently tugged off the boot. "It's already swelling."

Rome crouched at her other side, grabbed a wipe, and began cleaning her face. "Maybe a CT Scan."

If she weren't hurting so much, she'd be losing her shit. Four of them hovering over her, three others bare feet away.

But for the moment, she just wanted to lie there long enough to summon the energy to get up and make her way back to the car. She knew they'd barely made it a mile on the trail, but that mile back was going to be hell.

So, she didn't freak out about the hovering.

She closed her eyes, rallied her strength, and vowed, "I'm never fucking hiking again."

———

"I swear to fuck," she growled as they argued about who was going to carry her into the house, "if all of you don't back the fuck up and let me hobble my ass into the house..."

Asher was feeling guilty and was being over-the-top protective.

Jeremy was the oldest, needed to feel in control.

Rowan and Rome were hanging back, but they'd both offered to help.

Wyatt had already moved to the door, had it wide open.

And Eli was trying to make the case that he was the biggest, the strongest, so *obviously,* he should be carrying her into the house.

Then suddenly, her brothers were pushed away, and Rafe was there.

"Arms on my shoulders, baby," he whispered in her ear, leaning close and crouching down so that she could grab on. "One. Two. *Three.*"

Her teeth clenched, but she managed to hold back her groan of pain.

"Easy now, baby," he whispered. "Okay?"

She swallowed hard. "Okay."

Then they began walking into her place, slower than a granny using a walker, and probably more painfully.

Definitely more painfully.

"Brace," Rafe said.

He barely gave her the time to do that before he was bending slightly, scooping her up into his arms. She gasped, the pain still there, but it wasn't the worst sort, not when he was moving so gently, holding her so carefully.

And it was a hell of a lot better than the slow, painful trudge up her front walk with Rafe holding her, carrying her up the stairs and into her house. Then she was on the second story, moving into her bedroom, and he was pausing, waiting for Jeremy to pull back the covers before he set her gently onto the mattress.

Her shoes off.

"Let me get you some pajamas," he said softly, kneeling at the edge of the mattress and squeezing her wrist lightly, one of the few spots on her that wasn't scraped to shit.

"On it already," Rowan said. "Why don't you all step out and I'll help her?"

There was some shuffling, some movement that told her they'd all followed Rafe into her bedroom, and she knew they were worried, so she did her best to smile even though she was ready for a pain pill and to sleep for a hundred years.

"I called Kate," Rafe said. "She, Stef, Kels, and Heidi will be here in the morning. I told her not to come tonight." He pulled a bottle of pain pills from her pocket, shook out one and handed it to her. A glass—from Eli—appeared at his elbow, and he helped her sit up enough to swallow the pill. "Figured you'd just want to sleep," he said once he'd helped her lie down again.

She nodded. "Thanks," she whispered.

"Anything for you." He stood, started for the door.

"Rafe?"

He stopped. "Yeah, honey?"

Her heart skipped a beat, but she kept her voice neutral. "I..." Her gaze drifted around the room, to her brothers stationed like sentinels. "I...just...thanks."

A nod. Then he was gone, and everyone but Asher and Rowen following him. Rowen took one look at his brother, set the pajamas on the bed, and said softly, "I'll let Asher help you."

"Okay," she whispered.

"Rest easy, sweetheart," Rowan murmured. "I'll check on you later."

Big, annoying, protective lug. No. *Lugs.* Because they were also *her* big, annoying protective lugs. "I love you," she said.

"Love you too, Cor." He squeezed her ankle—the uninjured one—then disappeared into the hall behind the rest of the lugs.

And that left Asher.

Whose eyes were swollen. Both of them. And not from crying.

She winced.

He hurried over, hands flapping. "What is it? What's the matter? I can—"

She reached for his hand, caught it, and tugged him lightly toward her. "Your face." Her lips twitched. "I don't mean that as a bad sister joke. Your eyes. I-I'm sorry Rafe and Jeremy punched you."

He crouched down next to her, head hanging. "I deserved it."

"No, honey"—a squeeze—"you didn't. We were messing around, and it was an accident." A shitty one, but still an accident.

Gently, he tugged out of her hold, hands clenching into fists. "I pushed you off a fucking cliff, Cor."

He had.

He really had.

And for some fucking reason—perhaps the pain pill they'd given her in the hospital joining with the one that Rafe had just given her, with the floating feeling just beginning to creep in and soften the edges of her hurt—she found that funny. She let out a giggle, clutching at her ribs because, Christ, that hurt, even with that pleasant fog just beginning to drift in. "You *did*," she said, tears forming at the corners of her eyes, more giggles bursting out of her in little cascades of pain. "Oh my God, you so totally did. Mom is going to *kill* you."

His face went comically scared, and her laughter got louder and slightly more painful.

But that was okay because after a few moments, he began chuckling softly, the guilt abated—slightly, she figured, since if *she* had pushed someone off a cliff, she definitely would be feeling real guilt, and feeling it for a good long while.

Still, his expression eased, and he laughed with her, agreeing, "Mom definitely is going to kill me."

She loved the big lug, especially because he took her teasing on the chin, and she knew that while the guilt might not ever completely go away, it *would* get better.

Because they had to laugh about it.

That was what Hutchinses did.

They cried, they laughed, they moved on.

Then they brought up the story at every family dinner, every holiday, every birthday...*forever*.

TWENTY

He hadn't slept the night before.

By the time they'd gotten home from the hospital, and he'd managed to calm down Jeremy and Wyatt and the others—with beer and DoorDashed BBQ—Asher had come downstairs, announcing that she was asleep.

The guys had stayed late, taking turns checking on Cora until he'd managed to send them home, reminding them her friends would be there in the morning, and that he could cover her for the few hours remaining between then and when they would show up.

So, by three in the morning, the Hutchins clan had gone off to get some rest, and he had sat in Cora's bedroom, back against the wall by the door, watching her sleep, unable to close his own eyes.

Because he couldn't stop thinking about that moment he'd seen Cora go over the edge.

Her eyes going wide, a scream piercing the air.

Asher frozen in horror, arm outstretched.

He didn't remember moving, just suddenly, he was next to her, and she was bleeding and hurt and—

"Fuck," he whispered, shoving a hand through his hair.

He knew that would be a nightmare he would have for the rest of his life.

Now, he was trying not to hover. Cora was still in bed. Her crew had arrived with bags in hand and what he assumed were the proper accoutrements for a friend who'd fallen down a fucking cliffside. Now there was chatter and quiet laughter, and he knew they'd take care of her.

But he couldn't stop himself from taking care of her either.

Which was why he was hovering in the hall, a cup of cocoa in hand, her bottle of pain pills in the other, and knowing he could have lost her.

Could *still* lose her in so many ways.

If they—

He shook his head, not willing to go there. Not right then. There would be plenty of time for guilt later.

Now, she needed her pills.

Cautiously, he stepped into the doorway, knocked on the door, the pills rattling in the container.

Five female heads turned in his direction.

Cora was still in her pajamas, the blankets folded around her middle.

She looked tired, like she was feeling worse than the night before, and he suspected that the next couple of days would be the worst, as far as the aches and pains went.

And that made sense.

Two bruised ribs. A sprained ankle. Three cuts that had required a total of twelve stitches. Glue on her temple and the side of her scalp.

She was banged up.

She was hurting.

He hated that.

So even though he should probably take the time to back up and erect some distance between them, he couldn't. He just... couldn't.

He walked to the bed, hovered by the edge since there wasn't room to sit on the edge, not with her friends perched on top of it, food and books and beauty products spread between them. Kate was dabbing some sort of cream on Cora's scabs. Heidi was smoothing an oil into the ends of Cora's hair, and Stef was gingerly painting Cora's toes. Kels was next to Cora, pillows propped up behind them both, and had been showing her something on a tablet.

"Sorry to interrupt the spa party."

Stef smiled up at him. "Please, interrupt," she said on a laugh. "Save Cora from my horrible pedicure."

"I think it looks nice," Kate said.

He glanced at Cora's toes, knew that generally a pedicure meant keeping polish on the nails and not the toes, but kept that comment to himself.

Stef bit her lip, tightened the lid on the nail polish. "I just know when I broke my ankle, I liked my toes to look pretty."

"Stef?" Cora asked.

Her friend shifted her gaze to Cora's.

"Thanks," Cora said.

His heart squeezed, lungs going tight. Good friends. Good people. And Cora, the girl he'd grown up protecting and loving as a sister, had become such a good *woman*.

He cleared his throat. "I just have your pain pills," he said softly. "And some hot cocoa." He felt the women's gazes on him when he put the mug on her nightstand, shook out a couple of pills and handed them to her.

Then watched, probably creepily, while she took them.

After she was done, he had a hard time leaving the room, but he forced himself to turn around, to walk into the hall.

But the whole time he did so, he felt like he'd left part of himself in that bed.

————

"Hey."

He glanced up from his laptop, saw Kate standing in the living room.

The rest of the women had gone home an hour earlier, but Kate had insisted on staying and baking Cora's favorite chocolate chunk cookies before Jaime came to pick her up. She winced and rubbed her belly.

"Hey," he said, closing the laptop and standing up. "Is everything okay?"

Her brows pulled together. "You mean because I'm eight million years pregnant?"

More like eight and a half months, at least that's what he thought based on the dinner conversation the previous week. "Yes, Kate. Because of that. Is the baby coming?" he asked. "Because I think Cora would be pissed if you ruined her rug by having a baby on it. I'm not even allowed to wear my shoes on it."

She laughed then broke off and winced again, rubbed her belly again.

And he had to admit, he might have been joking, but all the wincing and the belly-rubbing had him more than a little freaked out. He hustled over to her at the same time as he pulled out his phone. He was going to call Jaime—

A hand covered his.

"It's fine," she said. "Just the baby trying to get comfortable when there's not a lot of room in here."

Yeah, that didn't exactly make him feel better.

Because less room meant that baby was almost done being cooked.

Which meant it might come out.

While he was here.

A nudge. "Sit down," Kate ordered. "I'll get you a cookie, and..." His ass hit the couch and then his eyes opened, connected with hers. "I...um...I'm guessing this is yours, and that you...um...don't...um...want Cor's brothers to accidentally find it."

"I—"

Fuck.

He took it, shoved it in his pocket. "Right. I—"

She turned around and disappeared into the kitchen.

"Right," he whispered again.

His underwear. How the fuck could he have forgotten—

"Here."

Kate was back and shoving a half dozen cookies at him, along with a beer. When he frowned at the combo, she sank down next to him, munching on her own stack of cookies. "Jaime says it's a weird but good combination."

Since the cookies smelled delicious and the beer was cold, he shut up and started eating and drinking.

Learning that the combination *was* good.

Learning that the conversation was going to bring up a bunch of *not* good.

"It's in the way you look at her."

His eyes shot to hers. "What are you talking about?"

"You love her," she whispered. "You love her with your eyes."

"I—" He shook his head. "Um, no, that's not—"

"Rafe." Just his name, said in a way that was gentle, but also threaded with steel. "Don't bullshit me," she said. "I've experienced that look plenty. I've been around you and her enough over the years to know. The look in your eyes is no longer just that of a protective brother."

He inhaled.

"It's possessive," she said. "You want her. And not like a sibling." A beat. "You want her like a man."

"That's not—"

But he stopped. Because...Kate, with her sincere brown eyes locked onto his, her caring expression holding him in place...and he couldn't lie.

But he also couldn't admit the truth.

Because of what it would mean. What it would change.

So...he just didn't say anything. Didn't agree or disagree. He just looked down at his beer, ate his cookies, tried to pretend that he wasn't watching Kate's expression change from caring to disappointed.

"I know," she said after a few minutes of eating and drinking in silence. "I know that things are complicated with Cora's brothers, but if you really love her, if you're really willing to fight for her—"

"I'm not."

Kate sucked in a breath. "If you fight for her, they will accept it. Accept you."

They wouldn't.

"I'm not going to fight for her."

"Rafe," Kate began. "I know you're—"

Heart pounding, he stood up. "You don't know anything." Her fingers caught his. "*Anything*." Not wanting to hurt her, he gently extricated himself. But after he'd rinsed his beer bottle and put it in the recycle bin, he didn't go back into the family room, didn't wait for Jamie to get there, even though it was kind of a dick move.

Instead, he bypassed the room altogether and snuck up the stairs.

And hid.

From the truth. From the reality.

From the future.

Twenty-One

She had freshly painted toes, cuts that were hurting a whole lot less thanks to Kate and her magical ointment (which, maybe Cora should have been pissed about, because it was for animals, though according to Jaime, none of the ingredients could hurt humans), and she'd slept for what felt like an eternity.

So long that her eyes were crusty.

Sighing, she rolled over and glanced at her phone, knowing that there would be a plethora of messages from Dale.

She'd given her notice, and now she was "conveniently ill."

His words.

Not hers.

And not that she was saying she wanted to be hurt and laid up in bed with a sprained ankle, two bruised ribs, stitches, cuts and scrapes and contusions all over, and miss her last two weeks of work. She wasn't a hero.

She didn't like pain, so waking up hurting like this meant that she was pretty miserable.

Not miserable enough to wish she were at work.

Who said there weren't small victories in life?

Especially if the consequence of her slide down a hillside meant she worked remotely and didn't have to deal with Dale?

She'd consider that as a win.

Now, however, as she reached for her phone, all she encountered was a naked nightstand. Her phone cord was still there, attached with a little clip she'd bought online to stop it from falling to the floor all the time.

But the part that plugged into her phone was empty.

Frowning, she gingerly sat up, holding her ribs which still hurt like hell, and though she was still cut and bruised in other places, she was happy to report that it hurt less than the day before.

Once vertical, she saw that her nightstand wasn't completely naked. There was a napkin with a few crackers and her pain pills on it, and sitting alongside that was a bottle of water.

Rafe.

All Rafe.

He'd been wrangling her friends and her brothers, popping in to check on her a few times as the day went on, and considering that the girls had been there all day, and then her brothers had come to check on her in intervals (and not all at once, descending like locusts and staying to eat the crops...of cookies Kate had made), she knew he'd been playing doorman, too.

After eating the crackers, she made short work of the pills and was debating whether or not to get out of bed and risk hobbling on her crutches by herself to the bathroom when she heard it.

Rafe's raised voice.

Frowning, she opted for the hobbling, only instead of to the bathroom, she was hobbling to the hallway, to where Rafe was standing, his back to her, one hand clenching her phone, the other in a fist at his side.

"I don't really give a fuck what *you* want, Dale," he snapped. "Your employee had a serious accident this weekend and needs time to heal. *If* she feels up to working from home in a few days —which I'm sure she will because Cora isn't the type of woman to not fulfill her responsibilities, then she will do so when she feels up to it. She will *not* do it just because you keep blowing up her phone and are acting like an asshole."

Silence.

Listening.

Then, "Did you not hear what I said about the whole *acting like an asshole* thing?"

More silence.

Then, "Nope. I guess you didn't. So, if you don't get your head out of your ass, I'll report you to your HR department, and if that goes nowhere, then I'll make sure to contact the Division of Labor and the Better Business Bureau to report your company for not allowing employees to use their sick time they've *legally earned*."

A beat of quiet this time.

"Yeah," Rafe said. "I will. So don't fuck with me or Cora. Shut up, sit tight or that report will include a complaint on the forced overtime Cora's also been pulling." A pause. "Yeah," he said. "I will definitely go there." More silence then, "Uh-huh. My advice? Chill the fuck out, trust the employee you've hired to get the work done, and then thank your lucky stars that she's not the type of person to fuck you over. *Then* do some soul-searching, asshole, and change your management strategy. Because I don't give a fuck how good your product is, if you can't manage people correctly, you're going to crash and burn."

He went quiet again, listening.

Then he sighed. "Yeah, unfortunately, I can see that you're not going to take my advice. Cora will be in touch when she feels up to it. Good luck in the future, dick bag."

He jabbed at the phone screen, holding the cell in his fist, tightly enough that she had to wonder if he was going to break it, but then he sighed, relaxed his grip, and turned around, startling when he saw her.

"Cor?" he asked.

She smiled, heart skipping a beat for some reason.

No.

Not for some reason, but because he didn't have a shirt on, and his chest was yummy, and she'd kissed her way across it and—

She wanted him.

Not right that instant, since her ribs were aching, and she really wasn't feeling the whole hobbling around on crutches thing.

"How much did you hear?"

A shuddering breath that hurt coming out. "Of your verbal smackdown with Dale?"

He winced. "Right," he said, "so all of it."

"Most of it," she corrected. "I...thanks for standing up for me. You didn't have to."

"He called your phone a good fifty times," he muttered. "And that was before seven o'clock. You need your rest."

"Still," she said. "You didn't have to do that."

"I did." He stuck her phone in his pocket. "And now you need to get back into bed. You need your rest, Cor."

"Honey"—she reached for his hand as he came close, wobbling slightly on the crutches because she'd taken one hand off the wheel, so to speak—"I'm fine. I just—"

He lifted her up, her crutches falling to the floor.

"Rafe!"

"Bed," he repeated.

And when he got all growly and demanding and started talking about bed, she remembered their night and she...

Yeah. Hot damn. One night hadn't been nearly enough.

He stepped over the crutches, strode down the hall, and

started to deposit her on the mattress. "Wait," she said before he could release her. "I need to—" She tilted her head in the direction of the bathroom.

A flick of his gaze from her to the door. "Right," he whispered, hefting her up again and walking into the bathroom, setting her gingerly on her good foot. "Do you need—?"

"So help me God, if you ask if I need help using the toilet, we're going to have problems," she muttered. "I don't care how sweet you've been to me."

Emerald eyes on hers. "Right," he said. "I'll wait outside until you need me."

"Good plan."

Snorting, he moved from her—after he made sure she was steady on that good foot—and then left the bathroom, though she didn't miss that he didn't latch the door completely.

She did her thing—

Also, this just in, having bruised ribs did *not* make it easy to sit her ass onto the toilet. But she managed, did her business, hauled herself up, and hobbled to the sink to wash her hands, brush her teeth, and tame her hair.

Then she reached for the bathroom door.

Which barely missed her face as Rafe pushed it open.

"Jesus," he muttered, halting it an inch from her nose.

"Yeah," she grumbled. "Tell *me* about it."

His fingers brushed over her cheek. "Sorry, honey."

Ouch.

The endearment had her inhaling sharply, longing filling her, and that—shocker of shockers, that hurt her ribs.

His gaze had been on hers, but her response had him looking away, that muscle in his jaw ticking all over again.

"Come on," he said, lifting her up, carrying her, and putting her into bed. "You need anything?" he asked after he'd tucked her under the covers.

"Yeah."

He paused, glanced back at her, question in his eyes.

"Are we really just going to do this?" she asked.

That question grew.

"Just going to pretend it didn't happen?"

His expression clouded. "Cor—"

"I know," she whispered. "I know you said one night, Rafe, but...how? How do we do just one night when our night together was..." She pushed up, sucked in a breath, and just told him what had been in her heart since the night he'd first kissed her, from the moment she realized that he might be feeling a little of what she'd been feeling for ages. "It was the best I've ever had. *Ever.* And I mean *ever.* And I know you're a good guy and I've"—a breath—"and truthfully, I've had a crush on you forever. I just never thought we'd...you'd know—"

She bit her lip, struggling with the words, hoping he would say something.

But he didn't, didn't say anything. He just stared at her, his expression unfathomable.

Her heart was on a slow sink.

Just an anchor hooked into her, drawing her down and down and *down*. Until she was going to drown in those cold green eyes.

"I mean," she finally said, "was it not good?"

"*No.*"

The anchor was joined by a dozen more, yanking her under the surface of the water, the cold liquid gushing into her nose, down her throat. Choking now. Choking on hurt and despair and...maybe just the slightest bit of bitterness.

"Right," she said. "I think you need to find somewhere else to—"

"It was the best. Hands down."

She blinked, but then he was there, sitting next to her on the bed, fingers smoothing back her hair, brushing lightly over the cut there. "What?" she breathed.

"The night. The morning. Us together"—he took a breath, released it slowly—"it was...I've never felt like that, never had that, never—" He sighed and shook his head. "But I can't do this. I can't—"

Her heart had been drifting up, nearing the surface.

But his words sent her sinking again, a slow, downward drag.

"Why?" she asked.

He was still. Like a big, handsome statue.

"If it's the best and, fuck, I mean we've known each other our whole lives," she said, knowing she was blabbering. "We get along for the most part, and we know each other. You get along with my mom, with my brothers—"

"Cora."

"And it's not like I'm saying we should walk down the aisle" —though she couldn't lie and say she hadn't written about it in her diary at the ripe old age of fourteen...and fifteen...and sixteen —"I just, we could see how things go and—"

"*Cora.*"

"And my brothers love you. You'd be the first man they couldn't run off and—"

His eyes slid closed. "Honey," he whispered. His forehead rested on hers. "Honey," he said again.

"Just try, baby," she murmured. "We can just try. No expectations, just...us."

She watched his nostrils flare as he inhaled. "I—we could—"

"What the *fuck?*"

Rafe stiffened and straightened, head jerking as he looked over his shoulder.

Jeremy was there, expression thunderous.

"What. The. Fuck?" he snapped. "What are you doing to my sister?"

Fucking Jeremy.

Rafe had hopped to his feet like a goddamned whack-a-mole, his face going pale. He looked like he'd committed the most grievous of crimes...and maybe according to the bro code, he had.

Which was why she gave him the out.

"Chill, Jeremy," she snapped before her brother freaked out even more completely. "He was checking my stitches. A piece of my hair got stuck in one of them, and I was worried that it got pulled out."

Rafe had turned back to face her, and the relief in his eyes made her sick.

God, what was she doing?

He didn't want her or didn't want her enough to deal with her brothers, so really that was the same thing.

She'd all but thrown herself at him, and he...

Didn't want her enough.

So...the sex was incredible, their night was one that might ruin her for all future men, but...he wasn't going to take a chance on her. So, she wasn't going to do this, wasn't going to draw it out, to make herself feel like a reject over and over again.

He'd done it with the kiss.

He'd done it when her brothers had shown up announced.

He'd done it just now.

So now it was three times that he'd made her feel like crap.

Three times was three times too many.

She was Cora Fucking Hutchins. She didn't get her heart trampled by men. She didn't sit and feel hurt and sorry for herself just because she wasn't woman enough for a man.

Wasn't enough for Rafe.

So, fuck him.

And fuck her brothers for that matter. It was beyond time for them to stop interfering in her life. She'd given them far too much leeway in her life, hadn't set boundaries or had set them and let them keep busting right through them. But she'd had enough.

Of them.

Of Rafe.

A free place to stay. A free fuck.

But not worth fighting for. Not worth standing up to her brothers for.

Not worth *enough*.

So...enough.

Rafe could just get the fuck out of her place, and her brothers could as well.

She was changing the fucking locks—and getting one of those automatic locks where she could give (or revoke) a code at will.

Seemingly satisfied, Jeremy turned to Rafe. "How is she this morning?"

Like Cora wasn't *right there*. Conscious and wholly capable of sharing about her own health.

"I'm fine," she said before Rafe could answer for her.

Which seemed to bounce off the walls and through the space, remaining totally unheard.

And seriously? What. The. Fuck?

"She's stiff and still can't put weight on the ankle, but I think overall a little better."

She tried again. "I'm—"

"And the ribs?"

"Still very tender from what I can—"

"Out!"

It was a yell, so loud and intense she practically scared herself. But it had the desired effect. Both Rafe and Jeremy turned to her.

"What's the matter?

A snapped out question from her brother...and seriously, the wrong thing to say. What was the matter? *The matter?*

"You mean despite the fact that I've let you assholes butt into my life for too fucking long?"

Their brows lifted, almost in unison. Then Asher popped

his head in, followed by Wyatt. And she knew—*knew*—that the rest of them were just down the hall, ready to invade and take charge, and the worst fucking part of that was that *she* had allowed it.

And that just pissed her off more.

"It's my fucking life," she snapped. "My life, and I swear to God, I need you all to back off and let me live it."

"Cor—" Jeremy began in a condescending tone.

"No! You need to stop. I didn't even *want* to hike, and now I'm laid up in bed with bruised ribs, stitches, and a sprained fucking ankle. I didn't want you to run off my boyfriend or interfere with my job"—she glared at Rafe—"I don't want you to just show up at my place without calling or texting first. I don't want you to act like I'm still six years old and need to be looked after! I'm a grown woman with my own life, and you are only in it because I allow you to be—"

"Cora, honey," Rafe began.

She jabbed a finger in his direction. "No," she snapped. "You don't get to have an opinion either."

He reared back.

Wyatt opened his mouth.

Her finger went in his direction. "Neither do you!"

"You're our sister—"

"I know!" She tossed her hands in the air. "Your baby sister who never pushes back, but I'm done. *Done!* D.O.N.E. *Done!*" The last she punctuated with another finger jab. But apparently it was too vigorous because pain shot down her side and the rest of her words were cut off on a gasp.

Rafe started toward her. "Cora—"

"Don't," she yelled.

"And I think it's time for you all to go."

Her eyes shot to the door, seeing Heidi and Kate pushing their way in through the mass of her brothers, Heidi's calm but firm words having her brothers turning in her direction.

"But—" Jeremy began.

Kate's expression turned mulish. "That wasn't a request, Jeremy Hutchins. It was an order. Cora has had enough, and you guys are messing up her recovery."

Heidi nodded. "So you need to go, and you need to stop smothering her."

"And not come back until she tells you she's ready," added Kate.

Collectively, her brothers began to shake their heads, and Cora braced for a refusal.

But then, surprisingly, Rafe took her side.

"We all need to go," he said. "Well, all of us except Heidi and Kate."

"But—" Jeremy began.

"Wyatt?" he said, lifting his eyebrows pointedly.

Wyatt's expression was hard, but after Rafe had held his eyes for a few seconds, he blew out a breath and sighed. "They're right." The words were begrudging. "We need to go."

"I—"

"Jer."

Her brother stopped, stared at Wyatt.

And then he sighed as well. "Right," he said. "We'll go." With that, he crossed to her, kissed her cheek, and left the room, her brothers saying their goodbyes and doing the same. Kate and Heidi followed them out, and she could kiss them for making sure they left.

But Rafe didn't follow them.

"Cora."

Twenty-Two

Rafe

His heart squeezed tight when she turned away from him, her eyes closing.

"Honey," he said again.

Those eyes shot open. "No," she said, and the hurt threaded through her voice tore him to shreds. "No, you don't get to call me that."

"You know why we can't—"

"I know why you *think* we can't." Vulnerability and pain and tears in the corners of her eyes. "But what you need to understand is that every time you say that we can't be together because you don't want to mess up things with them, don't want to lose them, what you're actually saying is that I'm not worth enough to take that risk."

His heart had moved beyond squeezes. Now the organ had been tossed into a blender and the puree button had been pushed. She didn't understand. He cared for her, loved her, but he felt so much of both emotions and it was all tangled up with his past. He'd worked so hard to be part of the family, tried so hard to be a Hutchins.

What if he fucked it all up?

What if they looked at him like his father had and—

"You keeping your distance, saying you want me, but that want isn't enough means that *I'm* not enough."

Oh, fuck. That was the last thing he ever wanted her to feel. *Ever.* "It's not like—"

"Cut the bullshit. It's *exactly* like that. You're attracted to me. You want me. But not enough to stand up to my brothers. Not enough to tell them the truth and bear whatever fallout might come from it."

The worst part?

He couldn't deny that it was the truth. He wanted Cora. From the moment he'd kissed her, everything had changed. He couldn't think of anything else, of *anyone* else, hadn't been able to stop wanting and needing her. He'd been pretending that his living at her place was because of her brothers, but he knew it was because of *him*.

Because he hadn't wanted to leave Cora.

Because he wanted her.

Just...not—

"I get that I'm not enough," she said. "And that's the fucking truth. So, you can play at being protective, but I know it's a fucking joke because the one you're actually protecting is *you.*"

———

"Women," Jeremy said, drunk as hell, but still drinking.

They all were.

Rafe included.

Rafe *especially.*

He lifted his beer to his lips, taking another long swallow.

This was beer...five...six...fuck, he'd lost count. All he knew was the edges of Wyatt's house were looking fuzzy and every single one of Cora's brothers were as drunk as he was.

Because Cora had kicked them out.

Because—at least for him—Cora had flayed him to the very core with her words.

No. With the truth.

Because what she had said was true, and the moment he'd realized that was the moment she had told him off, he had realized she was right.

He was protecting himself.

Because he was scared of being alone again.

Scared of not being enough, and in all that fear he'd allowed to rule him, he'd made Cora feel like *she* wasn't enough.

He'd hurt her.

He'd hadn't protected her heart.

He'd stomped on it, and then thrown it in the blender alongside his.

"Can't live with 'em," Rowen muttered.

"Shut up," Wyatt said, turning to Rafe. "He warned me." A nod at Rafe. "I didn't think that it was a real possibility."

"What'd you tell Wyatt?"

Jeremy's eyes locked onto Rafe's.

"My friend, Teresa, warned me this might happen. That we were overstepping and might burn some bridges. I mentioned it to Wyatt because, staying at her place, I've seen her frustrated. I thought it might be something that could happen at some point. I just didn't—" He sighed, drank deeply. "I guess I didn't think it would really happen."

"Fuck," Rome said. "Yeah, who would? We've always been there for her."

"Kind of feels a little ungrateful," Eli muttered. "I mean, it's not like we did anything really bad."

Asher snorted. "Except, push her off a fucking cliff."

Rafe clapped him on the back. "Accident, man. Remember?"

Asher's gaze dropped to his hands, to the bottle clenched between them. "Yeah," he hissed. "I remember." But the anger was self-directed. They all knew it, and though tempers had exploded on the trail, the fury had passed, and it would never be as intense as Asher's own at himself.

Because he'd hurt Cora.

And they'd all vowed that would never happen.

She'd missed out on a lot. She didn't have the same memories of Tom, of the great father he'd been. She'd missed out on the fun vacations, the new clothes, the big birthday parties. They'd been a family of seven on a single mother's salary.

And the only memories she had of that time were fuzzy and more feeling-based than something actually concrete.

Rafe wasn't even part of the family, and he had memories of Tom, of Mr. Hutchins.

And they were good ones, good enough that they nearly eclipsed the bad ones of his own father. The fists and the bruises. The harsh words and the way they seemed to always cut him to the core. There were arguments at the Hutchins'. Loud voices and fights over toys and bickering and pushing each other's buttons.

But at the end of it, it was all coming from a place of love, and they always found their way back to it.

That's why Cora exploding had thrown them all for a loop.

Because they'd all—even part of Rafe had, too—had expected there to be a phone call apologizing for the outburst, telling them she had ordered some pizza and beer and that it was all good. To come back.

But she hadn't.

And now hours had passed.

And she still hadn't.

"It was all of us," Rome said. "We all know that she wasn't

happy with us barging in. We just didn't think that she would ever really get mad at us."

"She never has before." Jeremy sighed, studied his bottle. "Not really, anyway."

"Right," Wyatt said. "But this is different, and drinking all night isn't going to make it better."

"She's hurt and needs—"

"She's an adult," Rafe interjected, "and as much as it pains me to admit it. She can take care of herself."

"With bruised ribs and a sprained ankle?"

His fingers clenched on his beer. "Yes," he said, even though he hated the idea of her struggling on her own. "And she's adult enough to ask for help if she needs it. Plus," he added when it seemed like Asher was going to protest, "she has Kate and Heidi there."

Six sighs of relief.

No. Seven. Because he was relieved, too.

It wasn't going to be easy to step back and not jump into protective mode, but he knew they needed to figure out a way.

And that way couldn't be just drinking themselves into oblivion every night while watching *Die Hard* on repeat. Because it was Cora's favorite, and they were feeling sorry for themselves and—

The door to Wyatt's place slammed open.

They all jumped. Every last one of them. Beers jerking, splashing over the rim, dotting Wyatt's carpet. Then they were moving, jumping to their feet, and for Rafe's part, at least, that ascent was shaky.

So much beer.

But before he could summon his white knight to save Wyatt and the others from whoever had barged into his house, he realized who was there.

Who. Was. There.

A woman who looked very much like Cora.

But one who was infinitely scarier.

Cora's mom. Edy Hutchins. The woman who'd singlehand-edly made his childhood bearable. And she was *scary*.

Scary *pissed*.

"What the fuck all have you been doing to my baby?"

————

It had taken them a long time to calm Edy down.

Mostly because she'd apparently come from Cora's place, where her beloved daughter had spent the day crying her eyes out.

Because of her brothers.

Which Edy grouped Rafe into.

He deserved it, but he also knew that he'd probably hurt Cora the most.

And that felt...like absolute shit.

"We're just looking after her," Jeremy said. "Like Dad made us promise."

Edy shot him a look. "Smothering your sister is not looking after her." Her eyes narrowed. "As you well know, since we've had this conversation before."

Jeremy sighed, but he didn't argue further, and none of them argued when she took over Wyatt's kitchen and whipped them all up some food that didn't come out of a box, bag, or can. Since this—and getting yelled at for the second time in one day by a woman who didn't make it a habit to yell—meant that the drinking had stopped, the sobering had commenced, it was finally safe enough for them to make their respective ways home.

With promises made to let Cora reach out first.

"You cool if I crash on your couch tonight?" he asked Wyatt. "I'll grab an Uber or something in the morning." And hope that Cora would let him in long enough to grab his stuff.

"Of course, man."

Edy was at the door, shrugging into her coat, but that exchange had her crossing over to him, poking him in the arm with her finger. "Oh no, buster, you're not getting out of it that easily. You're coming with me."

"I—" His eyes hit Wyatt's, who shrugged, seeming to say there was no sense in fighting it.

Which was exactly what Rafe had been thinking.

So, he nodded, grabbed his coat, and shoved his feet into his boots. "Okay, Mrs. Hutchins."

"Edy," she corrected, as she always did.

Rafe didn't bother arguing with that either, just nodded again and followed her out the front door to her car, a small red sedan she'd had from the moment Cora had left for college and she hadn't had to schlep kids around any longer.

He had to cram himself into the passenger's seat, his knees practically in his armpits.

Then they were on the road, zipping along the highway, making the forty-minute drive back to Cora's place.

"It's late," he said, eyes finally hitting on the time. "Are you going to be okay driving all the way to your house after dropping me off?"

Her gaze flicked to his. "You just can't help taking care of us, can you?"

And that was enough for him to make a study out of his hands. Oh look, he had a new scar across his knuckles. *How did that happen?*

"Me."

The blinker clicked as Edy changed lanes.

"Cora."

"All because your dad didn't take care of you."

He inhaled sharply. "I...he wasn't capable of giving me what I needed."

"Which is a very mature way to think about it, to spin it." She tapped her fingers on the steering wheel. "Unfortunately, it doesn't mean anything when you're still a scared, hurt little boy inside."

A sharp burst of pain.

"I'm—" Another breath, but he didn't know what to say to that, so he fell silent.

"You know, the first time Wyatt and Jeremy brought you home, I couldn't believe how tiny you were." She released a breath. "They were right around your age, but at least four inches taller and fifteen pounds heavier, and at six, that's a lot of inches and pounds." Her lips curved as she glanced at him. "But you've certainly filled out now, haven't you?"

"I'm not skinny and wearing youth extra small anymore, at least."

More curving before her eyes went back to the road. "Did you know that you were the first of the boys to hold Cora when we came home from the hospital?"

"I was?"

"Yup. You were."

He...thought he remembered holding her, but God, that was a long time ago.

"Quiet."

"What?"

"Always the quiet one," she said. "You were always so quiet and yet so protective over my kids. When you should have just been a baby, a little kid without any worries, you were always in your head, weighing every action, as though there were some scale in your mind and you thought that if you stepped out of line too much, did something we didn't like, and you'd tip it so that we didn't love you anymore."

His pulse picked up, palms going a little sweaty.

"But what you didn't understand, what I think you *still* don't understand, is that we love you. And love isn't something that is weighed out on a scale, one side filled with your good qualities, the other with your bad. Nothing will change that."

Another glance, just a bit of humor in her eyes. "Not even pushing my beloved daughter off a cliff."

He winced. "Asher is—"

"Going to beat himself up for an eternity, and then when he finally stops feeling guilty about it, will then be subjected to the torture of his brothers for another eternity?"

"That," he agreed.

She laughed. "Yup. I know my boys." Her eyes came to his again and she reached over, squeezed his hand. "And I love my boys. *All* my boys."

Fuck.

Now his eyes stung.

But she wasn't done.

"And I'll love them even if they don't make a choice I agree with, even if they make one my other boys don't agree with." She took the exit for Cora's place, halted at a signal at the end of the ramp and turned to him, gaze boring into his. "Because if they've made it with their heart and their mind, I *will* support them."

Sweat prickled on his nape. Did she know—?

"Because I trust my boys' hearts." The signal turned green. "And in case that wasn't clear, I consider you one of my boys, too, Rafe."

"Mrs.—"

"Edy," she corrected.

"I've always loved you all," he said, "you know that. I wouldn't do anything to jeopardize that."

Eyes so much like Cora's connected with his, but only for a moment before they were back on the road.

And that sweat continued to prickle.

"But honey, you know the others trust you, that if you made a decision"—eyes to his again, for just a second—"and if that decision was made with your heart and your mind...you know they'd come around, too."

What the fuck?

Did she know?

"I—"

But now her damned eyes stayed on the road, and when she began talking again, it wasn't about Cora or the boys. It was about arrangements for Jeremy and Wyatt's birthday dinner the following month—he was dating a woman and she wanted the scoop to see if it was going to last long enough to make it to a family dinner.

Spoiler alert: the woman was lovely and sweet (at least when they'd met up over drinks) and…she probably wouldn't because Wyatt was Wyatt.

And then they pulled into Cora's driveway.

"Is she going to hobble down the hall on her crutches and point a shotgun at me?"

Edy grinned, lifted her chin in the direction of the front door. "Only one way to find out." A laugh. "You feeling lucky?"

Twenty-Three

CORA

The knock at her door was tentative enough that she knew it belonged to one of the males of her family.

Whether that was a brother or a Rafe, she didn't know.

She *suspected* Rafe, since he was living at her house—not that she'd seen him since the blow-up on Monday—and not her brothers because her mom had apparently joined in on Cora's outburst and had given them *her* version of the riot act.

She'd gotten exactly one text from each of her brothers.

An apology and telling her they'd wait to hear from her.

All a variation on the same.

Which told her they'd gotten together and drafted up something together, and maybe that should have annoyed her, but she was already feeling more than a little guilty for yelling at the monsters—ungrateful much?—and yeah, she knew that she needed to continue to reinforce the boundaries and really, they couldn't just keep barging into her house and her bedroom.

And they needed to stop freaking out if she was dating someone.

But...she loved them.

So, she didn't want her life to not include them.

Rafe...well, unfortunately, she didn't want it to not include him either. She just needed...to figure out how to steel her heart so that it didn't hurt.

Brother and sister and that was it.

The knock came again, even more tentative this time.

But unlike before, the door didn't open, and no one popped their head in. Whoever was on the other side—and she should face it, it was Rafe, it had to be—just waited.

So, she called, "Come in."

The door opened slowly, and, yup, Rafe poked his head in. "Dinner's here," he said softly, holding up a bag of food.

Since she hadn't ordered anything, that was confusing, but because one of her siblings or friends probably had, she just shrugged and said, "Thanks."

Kate had left a tray for her, so she could eat in bed, and honestly, Cora was taking advantage of it. Her ribs still ached, and her ankle was feeling better, but she didn't think that she would be strutting around in heels any time soon.

Rafe grabbed the tray before she could, putting the food out on it, and pulling a can of soda from his pocket. "Need anything else?" he asked.

Yeah.

She needed him to get his head out of his ass.

But since he wasn't going to do that...

She just shook her head and thanked him again, but as he set the tray over her, their eyes locked, and her lungs...they froze.

"Cor," he whispered, leaning closer, his spicy scent filling her senses. "I'm sorry about before."

"I know."

His fingers stroked along her jaw, dipped down to trace along her throat. "I just—"

She covered his hand with her own. "Rafe. Just—"

His head dipped, mouth coming close enough that she felt his breath on her lips. Heat and need, desire and—

"No."

He blinked, straightened. "I'm—"

"God, please don't say you're sorry again."

"I wasn't going to."

Her brows lifted. "Bullshit."

He winced. "Okay, I might have been ready to apologize. It's just...you're Cora. I've loved you forever." Her heart began skipping around, tap-dancing along her rib cage. "Since you were a baby," he added quickly, and that sent the tap-dancing to a halt.

"Right."

"And I just don't like knowing I'm the one to hurt you. And I know your brothers feel the same way."

"I've already talked to Asher," she told him. "I put him out of his misery this morning."

"I know."

Of course, he did.

"And what, you thought he paved the way, so you would try for forgiveness, too?"

"Yeah," he muttered. "I just want us to all be okay." His expression told her that she was at least partially correct. Because there was something else in his eyes, in the line of his jaw that spoke to the inner conflict. Probably the same attraction and desire that had her skin prickling, her body so freaking aware of his, her breathing had elevated, her fingers tingled, her pussy ached.

"Right," she said. "Well, the good thing is that we are already okay. You made it clear what you want, and I'm not going to fight you on it." She forced a smile. "Brother and sister, right?"

He'd been lifting the tray up and over her, but her question had his hands shaking, the soda can tipping over. Thankfully, it hadn't been open. "Sorry." He set the tray down and righted it. "I...uh...thought we could eat and then I'll make some popcorn and hot chocolate and we can watch that new action movie with The Rock."

"As brother and sister," she repeated.

His fingers flexed. "Yup," he croaked. "Because I see you as my sister."

Cora rolled her eyes. "Right."

"So food, movie, and popcorn?"

"Don't you have anything better to do on a Friday than hang out with your sister?"

He chuckled. "Honestly? No."

That had her laughing, too, and good news, that actually hurt less than the day before. So...winning.

"What do you say?" he asked.

Besides that, he was a stupid man who was apparently determined to punish them both?

What *could* she say?

Either she could avoid him forever—difficult considering he was an integral part of her family and she'd have to deal with him any time she was around them, not to mention he was currently living in her freaking house—or...

She could accept what he was willing to give.

That one night.

And now, friendship.

"I say..." His shoulders went stiff, probably expecting her to tell him to fuck off. But she wasn't going to, she couldn't. "I say," she said again, "that movie night sounds good."

The relief on his face shouldn't have been so grand.

But it was.

And that made her feel...confused, weird, and...fuck this week had been a freaking whirlwind. She just wanted to feel normal, and movie night with popcorn and hot cocoa felt very normal (so did the longing for him, but then again, she'd had decades to get used to that, so that was new?).

He settled the tray over her, disappeared a few minutes later, and reappeared with a plate for himself.

Then he sat at the end of the bed as they ate, and eventually they paused the movie for hot cocoa and popcorn preparations, for him, and bathroom needs, for her.

It wasn't until buildings were exploding that he relaxed and didn't go stiff every single time their hands brushed in the popcorn bowl. It wasn't until the end credits rolled and he gathered everything up, that it felt like the old days, like they were sitting on a couch in the basement of her mom's old house, and she was going to doze off before he carried her up to bed.

But instead, Rafe was already *in* her bed.

"Right," he said, his hands full of cups and bowls and trash, "I'll just let you get some rest."

"Yeah." She studied his eyes, wondering if this was all it would ever be.

Knowing it was.

"Night," she whispered.

With a nod, he slipped out the door, mugs rattling as he closed it behind him, and she was left with the sounds of the credits playing, trying to figure out if she felt sad or resolved or numb...or all three.

Then she saw the bag leftover from dinner, sitting on the floor next to her nightstand.

Then she saw the name on the receipt tacked to the *outside* of that bag.

Rafe.

He'd ordered her dinner.

He'd orchestrated the whole thing.

And...then she was as confused as ever.

And...then she woke up, and Rafe was gone.

And yup.

Confused.

She should buy stock in it.

————

She cursed as she began to drag the coffee table across the room, ribs screaming and stitches pulling.

And itching.

"You know, honey…"

Cora froze, whipped around—fucking stupid, she knew—and bit back a wince as she faced her mother, leaning against the wall, arms crossed, and watching the scene.

It had been a week since her injury.

A week since Rafe had disappeared in the night and not come back.

But who was counting?

Not her.

Nope.

No way.

She shook that off, internally, not physically, because she was not about that rib pain. "Hi, Mom. I didn't know you were coming. Do you want something to eat? Or some coffee?"

Her mom's lips twitched, probably because she had instilled all those good host merits into Cora.

"No, honey," she said, then straightened, inclined her head to the kitchen, "but I *did* bring you lunch."

She held up a Molly's bag, and Cora could have kissed her.

Hell, she was Cor's mom, so she *could* kiss her.

So, she did, limping over and pressing one to her cheek. "Thank you."

Her mom smiled, wrapped her arm around Cora's waist and led her into the kitchen. "You're my baby," she said by way of explanation as they pulled out stools and started to sit. "You *know*," her mom began again once her ass hit the chair, and Cora braced. "You don't have to do it *all* on your own."

Cora gritted her teeth, knew exactly who'd told on her. "Kate."

A shrug. "Kate did call me after you sent them all away yesterday, but that's not what I meant, honey."

"They did enough," she said. "They have lives and partners, and Kate is like nine million months pregnant. Plus, Kelsey bent over backward to get me a job back at Robotech—"

"And by *bent over backward*, you mean she had one conversation with Abby...who's her friend and clearly wanted you back with the company." Her mom lifted a brow. "Because *you're good at your job*."

"I—" She sighed. "She *got* me a job, Mom. I was unhappy, and she pulled some strings to get me a job like she was ordering a Happy Meal in the drive-through—"

"*She* reconnected you with someone who was sad to see you leave the company and very happy to bring you back on to do a job you're very qualified for?"

"*Mom.*"

A tap to the tip of her nose. "What I'm saying is that you don't always have to do everything on your own."

"I know."

Her mom unrolled the top of the bag, began pulling out containers, setting them on the island. "You *know*, except for the fact that you push everyone away who tries to do something for you."

"Mom—"

"Especially Asher, baby, you know that he's feeling guilty. You know that he would feel better if he could help you out a little bit—"

"It wasn't a big deal. You know it was an accident, and that I'll be fine—"

"Yes, honey. You know. *I* know that, but Asher is going to

eat himself alive for a while yet." She let out a long, slow breath and squeezed Cora's hand. "Baby, what you need to understand is that sometimes being so strong and on your own and isolated and tough and taking no prisoners can hurt you." Another squeeze. "And sometimes it can hurt more than yourself."

She inhaled.

"Because, baby, sometimes it hurts the people who we love, too."

Cora stared down at the salad in front of her, the small cup of soup, and saw the care in this small gesture. The *love* in it. And...a curl of guilt sliced through her. Because—fuck—what kid liked to know that the nonsense their mom was spouting was right?

And she *was* right.

That curl of guilt tightened.

"I see you're getting me."

Because ugh. Yeah, she was.

Which was why she reached into her pocket, tugged out her cell, and made a call.

He answered on the first ring.

"Ash? Do you think you can come over? I could use a little help."

Twenty-Four

Rafe

He was exhausted, covered in sawdust, and had spent the last month busting ass in L.A.

Now he was back in the Bay Area, had spent the day at the warehouse, and finally, *finally* he was going to go to his new apartment.

It was small, and mostly empty, the stuff he'd shipped up from SoCal not having arrived yet.

Tonight was the air mattress night.

Tomorrow his belongings would arrive.

And tomorrow night...he would see Cora again.

It was Jeremy and Wyatt's birthday—he'd already wrapped the signed puck from his favorite Gold player, Brit Plantain, and left it in Edy's care—but they were all getting together tomorrow night for meatloaf, potatoes, and Edy's homemade red velvet cheesecake.

Family tradition said it was the birthday boy—or girl's choice—of meal and Edy-prepared dessert.

Then they'd play board games until curse words were exchanged.

Which happened sooner or later, depending on which games were chosen.

UNO? Within five minutes (which meant that it was just a night of curse words that Mrs. Hutchins pretended not to hear).

Ticket to Ride? They might make it ten before the cursing commenced (also ignored by Edy).

Munchkin? Basically, from the beginning.

So, really, it was a lot of cursing, a lot of games, a lot of competitive spirit...and a lot of Edy ignoring the misbehavior of her grown children.

But it was fun, and he wouldn't miss a Hutchins Birthday Get Together.

Even if he knew it was going to churn up everything with Cora all over again.

Even if there was nothing to churn up because it was already in the front of his mind. Because it hadn't gone anywhere.

Because he'd spent nearly every waking moment working his ass off, trying to *not* think about Cora.

And failing anyway.

He'd had more wet dreams...

"Packing up?"

He nearly impaled himself with his hammer—and not the one that was misbehaving and waking him up with soiled boxers like a goddamned teenager.

Clearing his throat, he turned to face Teresa.

Who looked like she was fighting a smile.

He glared.

She stopped fighting it and *just* smiled. "You know how I gave you advice that you told me was correct a while ago. About Cora," she added, like he hadn't known exactly what she meant.

"Uh-huh," he muttered, shoving his hammer into his toolbox.

"Well, I also have some advice about a stubborn man with the woman he's in love with."

His heart clenched, but he didn't say anything, just snapped the latches on his toolbox and started for the door.

"See you later!" Teresa called. "You know, unless you get your head out of your ass and run away with Cora!"

He stopped, turned around. "You know what?"

She sauntered over, punched him lightly in the shoulder. "What?"

"You're fired."

Laughter in the air, her arm lacing with his as she led them both out the door. "You know you would never fire me. You love me"—a grin up at him—"just not in the same way that you love *Cora*." She extended the -ora in Cora for a good five seconds.

"I swear to God, T—"

A beatific smile. "Also, Mrs. H invited me tomorrow, and you know I'm not going to miss one of her dinners—"

"Or the chance to torment Jeremy by beating him at Monopoly."

Teresa laughed. "That, too. But you know that I've seen you two together, and you know that I was right about the other stuff"—she wagged her brows—"just like I'm usually right about *everything*."

He sighed. "Teresa."

She blinked up at him innocently. "What?"

"I swear, sometimes I wonder why we're friends."

"No," she said. "You sometimes wonder how empty your life was without me, and then you get on your knees and thank the Goddess that—"

He covered her mouth with his palm.

And...she licked him.

"Ugh! Gross!" he exclaimed, wiping his wet palm on his thigh. "You're disgusting."

"And you love me." She pursed her lips, blew him a kiss. "You know it."

He did. Spit and all. "Shut up, T."

She smirked, hit the code for the alarm, and he locked up, right as she glanced up at him, still smiling beatifically. "Also, can I have a ride to Mrs. H's tomorrow?"

He sighed.

But because Teresa was Teresa and he was him, all he did was shake his head.

And she knew that was a yes.

Because he cared for the people in his life and took care of them...

Even if that meant part of him didn't get the same care.

———

More exhaustion, this time paired with a sense of satisfaction.

No air mattress tonight.

His whole bedroom was set up, as was his kitchen and family room. He still had a closet full of stuffed duffles and suitcases instead of clothes that were hung up or put away, but the toughest areas were moved in.

Tomorrow, he'd deal with the clothes.

Tonight, he was girding his loins.

Cora would be there, and he had to forget about their night. Had to go back to her just being Cora, his little sister and—

Bullshit.

They *couldn't* go back.

So, his new strategy was ignoring that night, the attraction, and pretending that everything was great!

Yup.

With an exclamation point.

Because it all *was* great. He had a place to stay. His business was on to bigger and better things. He had friends and the family he'd built.

So, it was all perfect.

Or as perfect as he could ever hope for, especially with his doorbell going. And the knock. And the woman standing on the other side of his door.

"I'm ready for my Uber, baby!" Teresa called.

He sighed. "You're riding in the front seat."

———

"And then," Teresa said, scooping up a truly huge bite of red velvet cake and shoving it into her mouth, somehow speaking clearly despite the mass of frosting and baked good, "just because I'm me, I made him chauffeur me all the way out here."

Rafe rolled his eyes.

Cora giggled.

And all six brothers looked relieved. Because Cor was laughing and hadn't kicked them out or yelled at them again. Probably because Wyatt's girlfriend, Tiffany, was there, so she was on her best behavior, but also maybe because she'd forgiven them.

At least forgiven her brothers.

She wasn't giving him the cold shoulder exactly. But...she was distant.

And he didn't like it.

Which was fucking stupid because, of course, she was distant. He'd erected that space between them when she wanted more.

It was just...

He didn't like it.

Fucking moron.

Quietly, he got up from the table, slipped from the room. Teresa was in full story-telling mode, so they wouldn't notice if he took a few minutes to himself. The back deck had twinkly lights crisscrossed overhead that he'd installed a few years back, and he'd put in a sunken fire pit that Edy had found a picture of on Pinterest just a few months before.

Weekend projects for his mom.

Because his own was dead and gone.

Because he'd never even known his mother, and his father becoming a single parent without warning hadn't gone over well. Rafe's dad had died a couple of years back, and maybe it made him a bad person, but Rafe hadn't cared. Hell, he would have been happy for the miserable asshole to depart the earth a few years before that.

He'd had no problem making it known that Rafe was a burden.

But then again, he'd had no problem taking Rafe's money or becoming Rafe's burden. Because as much as he'd wanted to treat his dad the same way he'd been treated, Rafe hadn't been able to.

He'd paid for his in-home nurse. Hell, Rafe had paid for *all* of it—electricity, mortgage, cable, internet, new clothes, fucking *diapers,* and bedpans.

And never once had he been made to feel like a son.

Just a burden.

Just a cash cow.

"Hell," he muttered, walking by the fire pit that was blazing and moving to the railing, leaning his elbows on it. "Fucking hell."

"I know what's the matter."

His head jerked, and he saw that Jeremy was in the shadows. "Avoiding Teresa?"

One half of Jeremy's mouth turned up. "Of course, I am. That woman—" He sighed and shook his head.

Rafe let that go.

He didn't need some next-level Teresa ESP skills to know

that Jeremy was into her (even though Teresa's skills seemed to exclude her interactions with Jeremy and how much he was into her, and...see? She did have limitations...and they included her being closed to any sort of relationship that involved her heart).

"But that's not who I'm talking about."

A thread of cold down his spine.

He'd caught himself watching Cora far too much that night. Had needed to force his gaze away from hers many times over the evening.

Too many times.

Jeremy ambled over, leaned on the railing. "I know, Rafe," he said. "It's all good. We don't have to talk about it, but I know that it's a rough time with the anniversaries."

He glanced out over the darkened back yard, struggling for a moment to come up with what anniversaries Jer was talking about. Then he got it...and maybe he should feel like shit because he'd just been thinking about the old bastard kicking the bucket. But he hadn't thought about his mom too much.

Not ever.

She was dead because of him.

Okay, so he was old enough and mature enough to understand it wasn't exactly because of him. His mother had suffered from postpartum depression and had committed suicide.

Because she hadn't gotten help.

Because people didn't really talk about it, or his dad hadn't helped her get the help she needed, or her doctors hadn't seen—

She was gone.

It was Rafe's fault.

Those had been the words from his father. Those had been the words that defined his childhood. Those had been the words that had defined *him*.

Until Mr. And Mrs. Hutchins had changed his mind.

He wasn't a burden. He was a gift.

But...he didn't know if that was something he would ever

truly believe. Because otherwise, he would just go for it with Cora, wouldn't he? He wouldn't be such a coward, too worried to gain the disapproval of her brothers.

Because Edy...she knew.

She'd caught his eye enough times that night, and paired with the conversation in the car, he knew she knew, and he knew that she would support him.

It was just Jeremy and Wyatt, Eli and Asher, Rome and Rowan.

How could he risk them?

But he was starting to think...how could he not?

How could he sit with Cora, eat and drink, talk and laugh with her and know what they had and know what they *could* have...and know he was taking that away from them?

Because he was scared to try.

"Fuck," he muttered, rubbing a hand over his forehead.

What a fucking mess, and it all seemed to be moving toward this inevitable conclusion. Like what was going to happen when he couldn't resist her any longer, when he couldn't resist.

This was all just going to blow up and—

Jeremy bumped him on the arm. "I'm sorry, man."

"I'm okay," he said. "It's not my parents. That's just...reality. I mean, I never knew my mom, and my dad was my dad." He blew out a breath. "Truthfully, if I'm being honest"—he glanced up at Jer—"the anniversary of your dad dying is a hell of a lot harder on me."

Jeremy was quiet for a long time. "I'm sorry your dad was such a dick."

"I'm sorry your dad wasn't and that my asshole of a sperm donor got to live a long life and your dad didn't."

"He was as much your dad as he was all of ours, you know that, right?" Jer cleared his throat, gaze on the yard. "My dad...I don't know how he did it, but he never made us feel like we were missing out, not even when there were more of us."

Rafe watched the trees rustle in the distance, the cool evening breeze starting to pick up. "I don't know how I was lucky enough to become one of you."

Jeremy went stiff then punched Rafe hard in the arm. "What the fuck, man?"

"Ow." Rafe rubbed the spot. "What the fuck to *you?*"

"*Lucky to become one of us?*" Jer shook his head. "You know that we love you, right? You know that we're the ones who feel lucky to have *you*, yeah?"

"I—" Rafe sighed. "Look. I know what I bring to the table, and I know what you guys bring—*ow!*"

Another punch. This time harder.

"Dude, what the fuck is going on with your head?"

"I'm fine. I just—"

The door slid open behind them. Asher and Eli sauntered out, took one look at him and Jer and lifted their brows. "What's going on?"

Jer shoved Rafe lightly. "This one is being a dumbass."

Asher grinned. "What else is new?"

"Let it go, Jer," he muttered. "Let's have our heart-to-heart another time."

Jeremy bent close, studied him closely with narrowed eyes. "I'll let it go. For tonight only. Because next time I see you being a dumbass, we're having the heart-to-heart, even *if* I have to tie you down and force you to listen to me."

He forced a grin. "Kinky."

"Idiot." Another punch. "Come on, let's go have another beer and enjoy our time before Teresa destroys us all in *Ticket to Ride.*

TWENTY-FIVE

CORA

Her shoulder was aching, absolutely aching, but then again, she'd been pulling some long hours at her computer over the last month.

Partly, because she felt obligated to complete the promised projects for Dale, even though it had taken her longer than her final two weeks, since she'd been laid up for most of them. Partly because she'd hit the ground running at RoboTech, helping them kick off the marketing plan for their newest children's robot.

The Hunter Five was wicked cool.

It could be taken apart and put back together. It could be coded to complete simple tasks.

And for every robot sold, RoboTech donated one to schools.

Epic, right?

She thought so. And she especially thought it was epic to have a boss that respected work hours. No emails expected to be replied to in the middle of the night, no six A.M. starts in the office. No staying late or working through lunch.

After spending almost a year without that, Cora had almost forgotten what it was like to have a normal life.

Especially, the last couple of weeks.

And now...family dinner time and Rafe pretending that nothing had happened and...yeah, it sucked, but that was the way it was going to be, so there was no point in flogging that dead horse.

"Are you all right, honey?" her mom asked.

Cora frowned, coming out of her own head (it was easy to get lost in it when she was drying the various pots and pans that her mom had used to cook dinner, not to mention the special cake plates and forks that were absolutely not allowed to go into the dishwasher), and realized she was rubbing her shoulder again, the towel dragging across the exposed skin of her throat.

"Cor?" her mom asked again, putting down her own towel, brows drawing together.

She shook herself. "Honestly, I'm just a little fuzzy headed. This last month has been a lot, and my body isn't fully recovered."

"Your ribs?"

Cora nodded. "Yeah, they're tender, and then my ankle still feels a bit weak." She shook her head when her mom got that worried Mom Look and put her hand up before her mom could really get going. "I'm not pushing it too hard, Mom. I promise. Dale's in the rearview, and you know the climate at RoboTech is a lot better. The hours and workload are reasonable. It's just... going to take some time for me to recharge."

Her mom came close, leaning back against the counter next to her and wrapping an arm around Cora's shoulders.

Which hurt.

She bit back a hiss.

"Baby," her mom began.

She shifted, rolled her shoulder. "It's fine, Mom. I promise. Just too much time on my laptop and my brother pushing me off a cliff." Her mom rolled her eyes and sighed. "Plus, my period is about to start. I'm so crampy. Actually," she said. "I'm going to get some ibuprofen from your bathroom, then I'll come back and finish these up."

Her mom kissed her on the cheek. "I'll finish up here and then get the heating pad."

"You're a goddess."

A grin. "If only you'd known that when you were a teenager."

Cora chuckled...then winced.

Her mom nudged her toward the stairs. "You just get your pills, and maybe a pad, you know"—her mom made a face—"just in case nature decides to bless you."

"Ew," Cora said.

A shrug. "Well, you're the one who wore white pants."

There was that.

"Anyway," her mom pushed off the counter. "Pills, pad, and then go out and get the boys. I think Teresa is getting restless." A nod toward the family room where Teresa was setting up *Ticket to Ride* (Wyatt's choice) with Tiffany helping her, and considering that Teresa was practically vibrating out of her skin, her competitive nature well-known and already showing.

"Right," she murmured. "I'm on all of it."

"Good." A kiss to the top of her head.

Cora draped her towel over the edge of the sink and hit the hall, climbing the stairs, and hating how weak she felt.

Ribs. Shoulder. Ankle.

She needed to heal because it really shouldn't be this difficult to climb one flight of stairs. Hell, she was puffing like she'd run a fucking marathon by the time she reached the top, and the shoulder pain eclipsed everything else.

Well, everything else except for her cramps.

Her mom was right. She'd better get a pad, too. Last thing

she wanted to do was ruin these pants. They'd cost over a hundred dollars and were dry clean only.

Rolling her eyes at her idiocy—because she was an idiot who'd spent over a hundred dollars on white pants when she spilled on herself at regular intervals—she huffed her way into the *en suite* attached to her mom's bedroom and helped herself to the medicine cabinet.

Pad. Check.

Ibuprofen. Check.

Water from the tap to take said ibuprofen. Check.

Head still slightly muzzy and cramps increasing in intensity? Check.

Perfect.

Sighing, she left the bathroom and made her way down the stairs, along the hallway, and out the slider onto the back deck.

The boys were gathered around the fire pit, deep in discussion, and they didn't hear her.

And what *she* heard had her feet freezing, retreating, taking her back into the shadows.

"Admit it," Asher was saying, "you like Teresa, and you don't really care when she beats you."

Okay that wasn't the part that drew her back into the shadows. In fact, hearing that, she grinned, started forward, mouth open and ready to join in on the teasing.

That was one thing about growing up with six brothers.

She had gotten damned good at dishing out teasing.

And the not-so-secret secret that Jeremy liked Teresa was the perfect topic for that teasing.

"Fuck off," Jeremy muttered, swigging out of his bottle. "What's more important is that one"—he nodded at Rafe— "being an idiot."

"*You* fuck off," Rafe muttered.

See? She needed to be in the shadows for this. Because if what he was being stupid about was *her,* then she shouldn't be hearing this, shouldn't be part of this conversation. She should turn around and come back in five or come back dragging her feet loudly so they'd hear her.

But all she did was stand in the shadows and idly rub her aching shoulder, hoping the pain killers kicked in soon.

"He thinks he's lucky to have us."

Rome snorted. "And let me guess, he doesn't get that we're lucky to have him, too."

She inhaled sharply.

Lucky for *her*, the boys were too busy yelling at Rafe to hear her.

"Seriously, man?" Eli said.

"What the fuck?" Wyatt.

"Dumbass." Asher.

Only Rowan was silent, studying Rafe in the quiet way he had. "You know, Rome and I don't have a ton of memories of our dad, because we were the youngest besides Cora when he died."

"She has it the worst, but...it was hard," Rome said. "Especially those of us who had less time with him."

Cora bit her lip.

"But we remember enough," Rowan added in that twin way of theirs, smoothly finishing each other's thoughts. "We know he taught us that when you love someone, *you're* the lucky one."

Great. Now her eyes burned.

Because her brothers had told her that so many times over the years, and to know they meant it, that'd they'd get all gushy without reservation to make sure Rafe knew they meant it...

Yeah, tears were imminent.

Things might not have worked out between them, but he deserved to know that he was loved.

Especially since his dad had been so abusive, had messed him up deep inside, had him questioning the love, thinking that he wasn't good enough for it, that he could lose it if he stepped out of line.

And that was the crux of the problem between them, wasn't it?

She'd always known that her brothers would love her.

No matter what.

And Rafe's foundation of love was based on a mother who'd committed suicide (left him) and a father who'd been abusive (emotionally with plenty of gaslighting thrown in).

Her stomach clenched. Hard.

Because she realized she'd pushed him in the wrong way.

She'd asked him to choose because she'd known that her brothers would always love her, would love him. That they might be pissed and grumpy and maybe a punch or two would be thrown, but she knew they would come around.

Because Rafe had a big heart, and the love he gave to them all was beautiful.

Because they loved him in the same way.

But it wasn't fair for her to push him to give something when his past was...bad. That was the simplest word for it, and also the most basic because that kind of trauma didn't just go away, even being folded in the Hutchins' clan couldn't cure it.

"You wouldn't think that if you knew."

Silence.

At least, she thought her brothers had fallen silent because it was hard to hear anything, not with her pulse pounding in her ears. Her breathing seemed loud, too, not that anyone else seemed to hear it.

Then Jer spoke. "What do you mean?"

Rafe rubbed a hand over his face, and she knew, *knew,* he was going to sabotage this, try to prove to himself that see? He'd never deserved it. The love wasn't stable. It was something that could be ripped away, used to punish.

Just like his dad had done.

God, she was an idiot.

She'd thought that because he'd been one of them for so long that he would know their love for him wouldn't go away.

But clearly, he didn't.

Because he'd reached some dead end in his mind, and he was ready to just...implode it all. To end it. To impale himself on his sword and destroy everything he'd held so tight.

He sighed. "I didn't mean for it to happen. I want you to know that."

Wyatt frowned. Rowen looked retrospect. The rest of her brothers were in various stages of confusion.

And she was standing in the shadows, stomach cramping, hyperventilating, and feeling dizzy.

"What are you talking about?"

Rafe's gaze went to Wyatt's. "Shit, man. It's your birthday. I shouldn't—"

"Dude, I don't give a fuck about my birthday. I want to know what's put that fucking look on your face."

"I slept—"

She couldn't let him do this.

Heart pounding, she lurched out of the shadows, pain ricocheting up her side. "It's time to play *Ticket to*—"

Seven gazes whipping her direction.

"Cora?" Rafe said. "Are you—?"

His gorgeous face went unfocused.

He moved toward her. She took another step, so terrified he was doing this that she was shaky and out of breath.

"Don't—"

Her legs gave out.

Twenty-Six

RAFE

"Look, I slept with her, okay? I had sex with Cora, and I'm fucking in love with her and—"

Those were the words flying through his mind.

But he didn't see Cora coming, didn't expect to see her lurching out of the shadows, her expression odd, her skin a sick, sallow color.

What the fuck?

"Cora?" he said, moving toward her. "Are you—?"

She clutched her side. "Don't—"

She collapsed.

Cursing, he moved toward her, trying to grab her before she hit the ground. Her legs had crumpled beneath her body, splayed at strange angles, and her lower half...

His gut seized.

Because her lower half was stained with blood.

———

He'd pushed his way into the back of the ambulance.

Anyone else probably would have been a better choice, a saner choice.

But Cora had collapsed.

She was bleeding.

A lot.

A first, Edy had thought it was just her period, laughing off their shouts. But then when she realized Cora was unconscious, saw the amount of blood soaking her clothes, she'd yelled for someone to call 9-1-1.

Everyone had moved.

Jeremy had already been making the call before Edy had freaked, and the rest of them buzzed around, grabbing towels, clearing some space, doing...stuff—

He'd lost track.

Because he was holding onto Cora's hand, talking to her, telling her everything that had been going through his head from the moment he'd decided to just tell her brothers and fuck it all, because he couldn't keep the secret any longer, couldn't keep pretending—

Not with Cora.

She deserved better.

She deserved to be more than a secret.

She deserved for him to choose her, above all else.

But he hadn't gotten to tell her that. Not while she was conscious, and he had no way of knowing if she could hear him.

He did know her brothers had heard him. That Teresa and Edy had as well.

So, the cat was out of the bag.

And he didn't give a fuck.

Because...her hand had been limp when they'd rushed her through the double doors of the emergency department, sliding from his so easily.

She could be gone, just that easily.

He might not—

A sob bubbled up in his throat, but he choked it down, dug his fists into his eyes. He'd wasted—

A hand on his shoulder had him looking up.

Jeremy was crouched in front of him, and the look that was in his eyes told Rafe everything. "Breathe."

Movement at his side, Wyatt sitting next to him then at his other, Edy taking the other seat and weaving their hands together. "Has the doctor come out?"

He shook his head. "No."

She squeezed his hand. "So, then we wait."

So...that was what they did.

For hours.

And still, they heard not one word from the doctors and nurses in the back.

———

"Cora Hutchins?"

His eyes had slid closed, but the sound of Cora's name had him lurching to his feet, along with the rest of her family.

The young doctor who had called, saw the movement, and wove her way toward their huddle. "Cora Hutchins?" she asked again.

He nodded.

"That's my daughter," Edy said, clenching his hand.

"Cora is out of surgery."

He inhaled sharply. They hadn't even known she was *in* surgery. It had all moved so fast in the ambulance with them getting an IV in, rushing down the roads to the hospital, taking her through the doors.

"Do you know what an ectopic pregnancy is?"

Rafe frowned, shook his head, but Edy's breath in was sharp, and she nodded. "Oh no," she whispered.

"From what we could see, she was about six weeks along. But the good news is that she's stable for now," the petite brunette said, "but she lost a lot of blood and one of her fallopian tubes burst—that was the source of the bleeding. Unfortunately, we had to remove it, but her other tube is intact, and she shouldn't have any issues getting pregnant again, though they'll want to watch her closely when she is ready to get pregnant again."

Pregnant.

Pregnant.

"Can we see her?" Edy asked, and thank fuck for that, because he was spiraling and doing the math and realizing that he'd nearly killed her.

He'd nearly killed her.

He'd hurt her and *nearly killed her.*

"All family here?"

His head shot up.

He opened his mouth to say he was just a friend, but Edy just clamped down on his fingers and said, "Yes."

The doctor nodded. "They'll be transferring her from a recovery room to a normal bed, and once she's settled, two of you at a time can see her. I'll send someone out with the room number and visiting hour information soon, okay?"

"Okay," he whispered.

"Now," she said, "the events will have been quite traumatic, and she may need some counseling. I'll make sure the social worker rounds on her, but I want you to keep that in mind and to be open to some for yourselves as well."

He nodded, not knowing what the rest of the group was doing because he was hearing the doctor, but he was also spiraling and in his own head, and all he could think was because he'd slept with her, because he hadn't used a condom, because—

A rough hand on his arm, dragging him from the waiting room of the emergency department, through the automatic doors, and out into the cold evening air.

All the air was squeezed out of him when he was shoved against a wall, his back colliding hard with the brick of the building. Pain shot up and down his back, along his skull, his legs, and then the fist was coming for him.

He watched it get closer.

Braced for impact.

Readied for the pain to increase. Hell, he was *dying* for that pain, desperate to feel it.

Anything so that he wouldn't be feeling *this*.

Guilt.

And like he'd truly fucked up the best thing he'd ever had.

But that fist didn't collide with his face as he'd expected. Or not hard, anyway. Instead, it tapped against his nose lightly. "*That's* for fucking my sister and knocking her up. This—" A breath. "*This* is for loving her like she deserves."

Rafe's eyes shot open.

Too late.

But it wasn't another punch—a real one. This time, Jeremy yanked him into a hug, clamping his hand onto the back of Rafe's neck and holding him tight.

And fuck if his eyes didn't tear up.

"Dude," Jeremy said, releasing him from the hug, though he kept his hand on the back of Rafe's neck. "If it was anyone else, *anyone*—"

Rafe swallowed, eyes shutting tight.

"But you and her make sense. And..."

He opened his eyes again, saw Wyatt had stepped close. "We knew."

"What?"

"We've known you love her for years," Jeremy said, leaning on the wall next to him. "It just took you long enough to realize it."

"I—" He frowned. "*What?*"

Wyatt rolled his eyes. "Dude, the way you jumped to stay at

her place? How you were always the first one to run the assholes off? The guilt on your face whenever you looked at her the last weeks?"

"But you got all in my face in the bedroom—"

"Yeah," Wyatt said, "because she's my *sister*. I'm going to get in the face of anyone who wants to get into her pants, even if that man is my brother."

Asher shuddered. "Fuck, man, don't say it like that."

Eli smirked. "How else is he supposed to say it? It's like some fetish film—"

Rowan clamped a hand over his mouth then shoved his bigger, older brother away, pushing by him and coming up to Rafe. "She's going to be okay. *You're* going to be okay. We're all going to be—"

"Let me guess," Eli muttered. "Okay?"

Rome punched him.

"The point is, we know that you'll love her the way she deserves."

"Yeah," Asher said, "and if you hurt her, we'll just push you off a cliff."

That got smirks, all except for Rafe, who had just been dropping into an alternate fucking universe. "I—" He shoved a hand through his hair. "I don't understand what's happening right now."

Jeremy squeezed his shoulder. "What's happening is that you treat our sister right, it'll all be good, whether you two work out forever, or not. As long as you love her and treat her right, then the rest we'll figure out."

"Like not punching you in the balls because you want to fuck our sis—"

"Jesus," Rowan muttered. "Treat her right, and we're good, yeah?"

Rafe blinked. "I...um...I...yeah. I want to give her the world."

Another squeeze from Jeremy. "That's all we want for her, too."

"So just breathe, and let's all be there for her, okay?"

He still felt like he'd been dropped into an alternate universe, but Cora was inside in a hospital bed and her brothers weren't killing him, so that's all he knew for the moment.

Fuck. No. He knew more than that. Because he knew that he needed Cora to know how much he loved her and, fuck, he needed to find a way to make up for leaving her, for just walking out and not contacting her, for pretending their night together, their time at her house, the years they'd spent building their friendship, their love (even though it hadn't been romantic until recently) hadn't been enough.

He needed to make up for making her feel like she wasn't enough—

Fuck.

He needed to grovel.

And he needed to do it big.

TWENTY-SEVEN

CORA

There was a weight at her side.

And heavy ones on her eyelids, making it nearly impossible to open her eyes.

Had she fallen?

Had she...ouch, it felt like she'd been run over by a Mack truck...had she been pushed off another cliff?

Except...it was quiet.

And if she'd fallen at her mom's house, it wouldn't be quiet. They'd be fussing all over her and—

There was the sound of a door scraping open, and her brows drew together, mostly because the scraping was followed by... someone touching her.

What the fuck?

Her eyes flew open.

"Oh, hey there." The nurse at her side had frozen. Then she carefully smoothed the blanket she'd been lifting. "Do you remember where you are?"

Cora shook her head.

"You're in the hospital, Cora."

She frowned, trying to remember. She'd been so dizzy at her mom's house. "Did I fall?"

A nod. "Yeah, honey. You fell and were transported by ambulance. You've been in the hospital for a little over twenty-four hours."

"I—" What the hell?

The nurse patted her hand. "Let me get the doctor, sweetie. She'll be able to answer your questions."

"I...okay."

The door opened and closed again, and then the nurse was gone, but she hardly noticed because she'd finally focused on the heavy weight at her side.

Rafe.

Of course he was there, dark circles beneath his eyes, stubble on his cheeks.

And waking up, as though some part of him had realized she was finally awake.

"Cor?" he asked, lacing his fingers through hers as he sat up. "Oh, my God," he whispered. "You're awake. Are you okay? How are you feeling—?"

The door slid open, and a short brunette walked in, a stethoscope hanging around her neck. "Hi, I'm Dr. Philips."

And then, after greetings were exchanged, Cora felt the world shift beneath her feet.

She'd been pregnant?

But she wasn't now and...how could she be grieving for a baby she hadn't even known she'd had?

The world closed in on her, reduced down to the doctor and her words, the pain in her side, and the strength of Rafe's fingers around hers.

And then the doctor was gone.

And then she was crying.

And...

Everything was the same, and yet everything was different, and...it was all wrong.

———

She'd fallen asleep again.

There was a weight all along her side, one that had her opening eyes, much more aware this time around.

A baby.

Part of her was grieving for a baby she hadn't even known existed...

God.

Why was she doing that? She hadn't even known, didn't even *want* to be pregnant, and—

And her mental asshole just needed to chill the fuck out.

Because it was part of Rafe and her, and she was allowed to grieve and—

She stopped.

Nearly bolted upright in the bed.

Because it was part of her and Rafe. Because *her and Rafe.* Because...

"Oh, my God," she whispered, eyes flying open, and she didn't quite bolt upright, but she did slowly push herself into a seated position, which then jostled that weight slumped behind her on the bed on her uninjured side.

Which jostled *Rafe.*

Because Rafe was there.

Next to her. *In bed* next to her, his arm carefully tucked around her shoulders.

Fuck.

Rafe was there, and suddenly everything she'd been hearing and thinking and realizing and panicking over before she collapsed slammed right into the forefront of her mind.

Rafe. Her brothers. They couldn't find out. She knew it would all be fine, but Rafe didn't, and if he thought he would lose—

"Rafe," she hissed, shaking him. "*Rafe!*"

He bolted upright, nearly clocking her in the face with an errant hand, controlled just in time. His dark circles, which she'd made a brief study of before her world had come crashing down, were even darker, even deeper, heavy grooves inching up the sides of his mouth, curving outward along the corners of his eyes.

Exhausted.

He looked so exhausted, she nearly had him lie back down and go back to sleep, fuck her brothers and their inane urge to protect her from men.

She'd tell them and—

Voices in the hall.

Voices she recognized because they belonged to the big protective lugs that were her brothers.

Voices that were going to murder, death, kill Rafe if they found him in bed with her.

"Rafe," she hissed again. "You've got to get up, to get out of this bed."

His arm tightened slightly, but then to her great relief—or maybe disappointment, because she'd had this man's name in her diary so many times over the years, so having him hold her like this was...magical.

Magic—

Fuck.

She needed to get her brain working.

"Rafe!"

He blinked and slowly moved his arm, shifting it out from

behind her and climbing out before gently helping her lie back down onto the mattress.

"What the hell do you think you were doing?" she asked, as the door began to open.

Then halted, voices gathering out in the hall.

He'd been turning away, settling into a chair at the side of the bed, but her question had him freezing, spinning back toward her, and cupping her cheek in his palm, leaning close, enveloping her in his spicy scent all over again.

"Cor—"

Her pulse raced. Her heart got a little fluttery.

And then...

The door opened a little farther.

She jerked away, slamming her head into the—thankfully— soft bed, the pillow that had been thoughtfully fluffed. "Rafe, you can't—" A sharp shake of her head. "They— I know that you can't lose them—"

His face changed, emotions scrolling rapid fire across his face.

Too fast for her to process.

But before she could press him, ask him to slow down and explain the flurry in his expression, the door swung wide, and her family rolled in.

All of them.

Descended.

Hugs and crowding around her bed, and it was overwhelming and too much and...perfectly Hutchins.

Once the guys had settled in, and she'd gotten the explanation that Rafe had bribed the nurses on the floor with treats so they could all come in together, at least for a few minutes, the big conversation settled into smaller, side conversations, with Jer sitting at her side, stare locked onto hers.

He squeezed her hand. "You scared the shit out of me, Cor."

She squeezed back. "I'm the only girl. I've got to go big or go home."

"About the—" His eyes flicked down. "Are you okay?"

"Honestly? I didn't know I was...pregnant." She sighed. "But I'm sad anyway."

"Cor," he whispered. "I'm so sorry."

She forced a smile. "Me, too. But I'll be okay."

"You don't have to be tough, honey. We can talk about it, about what you're feeling," he said, glancing around the room. "We're all willing to discuss and—" He broke off, frowning.

"What?"

A shake of his head. "Nothing."

"*What*, Jer?"

"Rafe—"

Her gut clenched. "He's got nothing to do—"

A chime blasted through the speaker behind her head, the same slightly musical tone she'd heard several times over the past couple of days, announcing that someone should return a page or was needed in a patient room or at the nurse's station.

She winced, started to ignore it, and finish her thought.

But the voice came on.

And it was a voice she recognized.

"Attention. Attention, Hutchins clan."

"What th—" Jeremy's eyes went to the speaker in the wall.

She was already sitting up, and she twisted, which hurt less than she expected. Probably because the man was still talking and what he was saying had her even more on edge.

"That's—" She began loudly.

Jeremy leaned over, gently covered her mouth with his hand.

Normally that would have sent her straight over the edge...or at the very least, she would have licked his palm for the indignity of covering her mouth.

But Rafe was still talking.

And the room...the room fell silent.

"...Attention, Hutchins clan," he said again. "This is Rafe, your resident adopted son and annoying older brother, and the man just trying to be the best friend possible, and...I love Cora. I love your daughter, and your sister, and I need to make sure she knows that because she is the most important thing in my life."

Her pulse had sped up, thundering in her ears so loudly that she could barely hear all of what Rafe was saying.

"I made her think otherwise. I made *you* think otherwise, baby, and I was so scared of my feelings that I hurt you. But I love you, and I'm going to tell you that every day for the rest of your life, and I'm not going to waste another moment to show you that."

She wrenched her gaze away from the speaker, somehow knowing...

Knowing that he'd be in the doorway, that he'd be staring at her.

"But," she whispered, "my brothers—"

"Love you," Jeremy murmured, "and him."

Her eyes flicked to her brother's, saw that his eyes were warm, that he was smiling, not looking ready to murder the man she was in love with.

Gently, he pushed her cheek to the side, and she inhaled sharply.

Because Rafe was there.

His fingers came to her jaw, brushed lightly over the skin there. "I love you," he whispered.

"I—"

"And I love you enough, you *are* enough for me to make sure the entire world knows it." He leaned close, cupped her cheek. "Especially if that world includes your overprotective brothers."

She laughed. "But—"

"But nothing," he said. "I was a coward, like you said. I was too scared to see you, to see what we could be, and worse, I made you feel like shit because I made you feel like you weren't—"

"Enough."

His fingers flexed lightly. "Not enough. Not nearly enough. This"—he snagged her hand, brought it to his chest, pressed it to the spot over his heart—"is yours. *This*"—he used his free hand, tapped his temple—"has finally got itself together, and so if you still want to give us a chance, still are willing to give *me* a chance, I—"

"Yes."

He blinked. "I didn't even finish the statement."

"Were you going to say I'd have your eternal servitude and I can always put my cold feet on yours and you'll always be the one to get out of bed to turn out the light when we forget? And—"

"Yes."

"Dude," Asher warned.

Her mom swatted him.

Hard.

"Ow," he muttered, rubbing his arm.

And Cora looked back at Rafe, saw his mouth had curved up. "Yes," he said again.

"You don't even know the rest of my list."

He leaned close, mouth brushing her ear as he spoke. "No," he murmured, "but I know *you*."

She shuddered, fingers threading into the hair at his nape, some part of her unlocking when he stayed close, when he nuzzled lightly at her throat, when his lips brushed hers.

"Get a room," she heard Asher mutter.

Then she heard him yelp and a laugh bubbled up in her throat.

"Unfortunately," she said, loud enough for their audience to hear, "I think my list also includes a half-dozen idiots who are related to me."

"Hey!" Rome declared.

"Trouble is," she declared, ignoring him, "I love the big, protective lugs, and so I can't imagine my world without them."

"The thing is," Rafe said, "I love the big, protective lugs, too. They may be annoying—"

"Truly, that's uncalled for," Wyatt grumbled.

"But the funny thing is, I owe them my life," he said softly, and the room grew quiet, the muttering silenced, the air going just the slightest bit tense, "because they taught me how to accept love, and then they taught me that the biggest, most powerful gift of all is to be able to give that love to someone else."

Cora's eyes stung.

"So know that I love you, Cor. That I understand how precious of a gift it is." His lips brushed her forehead, one cheek, the other, her chin, the tip of her nose. "And know that I won't ever squander the gift of you again."

Now it was less stinging and more attempting to not sob like a baby.

"Rafe, I—" Her voice broke, and she found herself whispering. "What if my list is too long?"

"Never."

"But..."

"*Never.* Here's the thing. Someone really smart told me that as long as we love each other right that everything will be okay."

Her mom sniffed, and Cora glanced over, saw Rowan handing their mom a tissue before he glanced back at her, winked.

As she turned back, her gaze hit Jeremy's, and he grinned, mouthed, "I'm the someone really smart."

"And I know you love me right, too," Rafe said gently.

Her hand found his, squeezed tight. "Why?"

His smile hit her right in the solar plexus. "Minus the sappy stuff?"

"For this moment, minus the sappy stuff."

Gentle fingers intertwined with hers, warm, soft eyes holding hers...and then filling with mischief. "Because you shared your Cheetos with me."

The laughter and joy that had been bubbling up inside her burst free.

And the best part?

No punches were thrown.

Because her brothers laughed, too.

Epilogue

RAFE

He walked up to the house, Cora's arm tucked through his.

She'd just been discharged that morning, and surprisingly, her brothers hadn't given him a hard time about being the one to take her home.

Surprisingly, they hadn't given him a hard time about *anything*.

Right, so maybe that wasn't surprising because it was the Hutchins way. Once you were in, you were in, and he'd been in nearly his whole life.

Still, he couldn't help but keep flinching every time one of them came close, half expecting a punch to be flying at his face for daring to touch Cora.

Which Wyatt, Jer, and company thought was hilarious.

Bastards.

But he *was* touching her, and he was doing it a lot because... he loved her, and he wanted to show that and—

They'd reached the front door.

Which opened before he could reach for it, swinging wide and revealing her friends.

"We've got the full Get Cora Healthy Kit, prepped and ready," Heidi declared.

"So long as it doesn't include stories of handcuffs," he muttered.

Cora snorted then winced and grabbed at her side. "Don't make me laugh."

"Don't bust out the handcuffs then."

She smiled up at him, and fuck if it wasn't like the sun hadn't just slid out from behind the clouds. Then she patted his hand where it was wrapped lightly around her waist. "I think you'll come to have a neutral to positive relationship with my handcuffs when all is said and done."

His cock twitched.

He told it to behave.

Then they were walking into the house, and he was starting to guide her to the stairs...but she was pulling away, turning toward the family room—

And he stopped dead.

"What is this?" he asked.

The room was filled...with his things. The collection of pictures he'd unpacked the other night and set on the mantel at his apartment, were hung on the wall. A blanket that Edy had bought him—blue and green plaid—was folded and laid over the back of Cora's couch. His TV had been swapped for Cora's and he knew that was the result of Rome and Rowan, who were standing in the corner, fiddling with cords, Cora's old—and much smaller—TV, sitting on the floor and propped against the wall.

His signed Gold hockey puck was perched on one of Cora's shelves, propped up by a set of thrillers he'd had signed by his favorite author.

He spun, saw his shoes lined up on the shoe rack, his jackets on the coat tree in the corner.

His coffee pot on the counter.

Keys on the little plate she kept on a table in her hall.

"What is this?" he asked again.

Cora was there when he turned back, smiling gently at him.

Then her hands were on his arms, his shoulders, his face. "This isn't an announcement over a hijacked call system"—she grinned, and he knew, *knew* the bribe donuts he'd given the nurses had really paid off, when she brushed her lips over his— "but I love you, and"—a sweep of her arm—"this is me showing it."

"By stealing your stuff," Asher said. "I don't know that—"

Wyatt socked him.

He shut up.

Cora ignored them all. Her eyes were on his. Her mouth turned up. "I stole your stuff, because your home is here, is with me, and my pain-in-the-ass brothers—"

"Hey!"

Laughter in her gaze. "My lovable and extremely sweet, but still giant pain-in-the-ass brothers, who aided and abetted me from my hospital bed—"

"And while we love you"—Jer called—"we don't want to live with you."

"Yeah, Cor," Wyatt added. "Watch out. He leaves his dirty socks on the floor."

He chuckled, shook his head.

Cora rolled her eyes.

"Just so you know, bro," Rome chimed in, "Cora's hair gets *everywhere*."

"Boys!" Edy snapped.

"And, if we're going for full-disclosure, if you're living here, you're going to have to deal with us over all the time," Heidi said.

"We're not over *all* the time—"

"She's lying," Kels stage-whispered.

Cora rubbed her forehead. "Why did I decide to do this in front of an audience?"

He grinned, wrapped his arms around her waist. "Because they're our family."

"Because we're awesome!" Heidi hollered.

"Children," Edy snapped.

Their audience quieted.

"For the record, I also leave my dishes in the sink without washing them for a ridiculously long time."

"For the record," he murmured, smoothing back her hair, "I already know that."

"And I don't promise to always share my Cheetos." A beat. "Especially if I'm on my period."

He grinned. "That's fine." His lips found her ear, pressed lightly. "I don't even really like Cheetos, anyway. But your croissants, those you'll have to always promise to share."

A sigh, her hands on his jaw, one drifting down to cross over his heart. "You drive a hard bargain."

"I'll do the dishes."

She grinned, leaned up on tiptoe, whispered. "Just saying, Rafe baby, I don't really care about the dishes."

He turned his head so that his lips met hers for a brief kiss. "And I don't really care about the croissants."

Laughter and love in her eyes before she kissed him.

Before she pulled back and said, "Are you ready for this?"

"Ready for what?"

"Ready for the rest of our lives." She grinned. "And that starts with…"

"Game night!" Asher said.

"Our families. Us," Cora corrected. "And copious amounts of competition."

He leaned close, rubbed his nose against hers. "And yelling

and sabotaging and cheating." A beat. A kiss to her jaw. "Oh, and maybe love, too." Another kiss to the tip of her nose. "Because in this family, they go hand in hand."

Cora released him, weaved their fingers together, and tugged him toward the dining room.

Where there was a stack of board games a foot tall.

Waiting for them.

Waiting for him.

Waiting...

No.

He was done waiting. He was ready to live.

Which was why he grabbed *Catan* from the middle of the stack and declared, "You're all going down."

Catcalls. Boos. Hisses and shit-talking.

And family.

BAD REBOUND

ONE

JEREMY

"Fuck, yes, I win!"

God, she was frustrating.

Gorgeous. Smart. Funny.

And frustrating.

Teresa tossed her head back and laughed loud and deep, showing off the innate confidence she had. She was a woman who liked what she liked, who lived big and unafraid.

And she was fucking intense when it came to any form of competition.

Brutal.

As in, she took an opponent down with precise strategy and absolutely no sympathy.

Case in point...

His utter destruction at her hands in Spoons.

"I'm out," he muttered, tossing his cards—and let it be noted, he couldn't toss his spoon on the table because he'd lost...again.

Teresa had shown up about the time the board games got really serious and had jumped right in, just like she always did.

During the three years she'd worked for Rafe, his best friend and brother, for all intents and purposes, she'd become an honorary Hutchins.

At Sunday dinners.

At game nights.

At family events and holidays and birthdays and—

She was there.

Always.

And...she was hot and sexy and gorgeous. And he wanted her.

But she was seeing someone.

So, he stayed away, kept his distance, rolled his eyes when she crowed, snarked back when she led with sarcasm, huffed out laughter when she threatened him...and generally acted the part of the annoying older brother.

Inside?

Inside, he'd cataloged enough fantasies to write a dozen romance novels.

"We can play something else," Kate offered.

He shook his head, smiled at his sister's friend. "Nah. I'm good. My eyes need a break." A nod to the fridge. "I'm gonna grab a beer."

There were offers to join him, but he waved them off, and in the end, he went out onto Cora's back deck alone, plunking into one of the chairs, holding his bottle of beer by the neck, and staring up at the sky.

He'd finished nearly all of it by the time the slider opened.

Footsteps on the deck.

He glanced up, expecting to see his twin, but it wasn't Wyatt clomping out on the wooden slats. It was...Teresa.

She looked beautiful that night.

Jeans, sneakers, a simple T-shirt. Her hair pulled back into a ponytail. No makeup.

No pretense.

Just...Teresa.

And she was the most beautiful woman he'd ever seen.

But she didn't seem to see him sitting in the corner of the deck, and in fairness, he'd purposely taken the area that was mostly in shadows because he'd just needed some time alone.

In the Hutchins family, there wasn't much to be said for alone time.

Normally, he would have said something to announce himself, would have made some snarky comment just to have her snapping back at him. In fact, he'd opened his mouth to do so, but before he could, he saw it.

It.

She wiped her eye.

Then the other.

And fuck...was she crying?

He'd hopped to his feet before he even processed he was moving. "Teresa?"

She jumped, spinning toward him and clamping a hand to her chest. "What the fuck, Jeremy?"

He was hauling ass toward her, fingers coming to her jaw, turning it toward the lights, and yeah, *there.* Her eyes were damp, tears glistening on the ends of her lashes. "What's the matter, T? Who hurt you? I'll—"

She huffed out a laugh, shook her head. "You can't help but be a protective older brother, can you?"

What he felt for Teresa was the furthest thing from brotherly there was.

"This isn't about me, baby." He slid his hand to her nape, holding her in place. "This is about why you're crying."

She rolled her eyes. "I have plenty of annoying older brothers, Jer. I don't need you to join their ranks."

His fingers flexed. "What. Happened?"

A sigh. "Seriously?"

He just held her stare.

She sighed again, but probably because she had experience with annoying older brothers, she gave in—saved them both the trouble by not drawing out the locking of horns. But she didn't do that giving in softly, it was laced with plenty of fire and spice, plenty of *Teresa*. "For fuck's sake," she snapped. "It's nothing, okay? Sam broke up with me. That's all. My ex-boyfriend is an asshole and—"

"Did he hurt you?"

Was that question too intense considering he had no claim over this woman?

Yes.

Did he care?

Nope.

Teresa glanced over his shoulder, but he didn't miss her rolling her eyes again. Nor did he miss the way that roll of her eyes felt in his heart, how it amused him, tempered the edge of his anger, let that haze of fury ease, especially when she explained, "He dumped me. So, it's not like that feels good, but no, he didn't physically touch me in any way that I didn't like." She glanced back at him. "Or yell, or threaten, or get in my face," she added, stymieing his next questions. "Sam just...stepped on my heart, okay? And that sucks." She wrinkled her nose. "Not that *you'd* know that, considering you're so fucking hot girls are throwing themselves at you."

Jer shook his head. "They don't throw—"

Her brows went up. "That bartender in the restaurant?"

"It wasn't like that," he said quickly. "She just wanted some advice on her—"

Now her lips joined the party, tipping up at the edges. "I *know* you're not going to tell me she wanted advice on her golf game now, are you?"

"She just—"

"Needed help with her backswing?" Laughter bubbled up, dancing across her lips, drawing his focus there. Fuck, but she had the most kissable mouth. "Or was it back *seat* that she called it?" A smirk. "Probably because she was desperate to get there with you—"

"T," he warned.

"Or how about the waitress who slipped you her number?"

"She just—"

"Or I know!" She was laughing outright now, barely able to get the words out, and even though it was at his expense, her amusement settled deep inside him. He liked her. A lot. So freaking much that he didn't care she was laughing at him, so long as she was *laughing*. Of course, through that laughter she gave another so-called example. "Remember the jogger who pretended to twist her ankle? Oh! And the—"

"*T.*"

"And—"

"Teresa."

She blinked, stopped laughing, stopped talking about women he couldn't give one fuck about. And how could he? He *loved* Teresa. Had been pathetically in love with her for too fucking long. Everyone knew it.

Except her.

She looked up at him. "What?"

He shifted his hand on her nape, sliding it so that he was cupping her cheek. "You ever wonder why I never took any of them up on their offers?"

Silence.

Long. Long enough for him to hear the crickets, the crinkling of the leaves as the wind blew through the trees.

"What?" she asked again, though this time it was a whisper.

"You," he said instead of repeating *his* question. "You're the reason I never accepted any of them."

Wide, wide eyes. Another whisper. "What?"

"I like you, Teresa," he said, and since he was already *in* this, already laying it out, he just gave her the rest of it, gave her *all* of it—or well, *almost* all of it because he wasn't about declaring his undying love, not when she was looking at him with that much shock in her pretty eyes. "I like you a lot."

She sputtered. "I-I...but *you*—"

"You've been dating someone, baby," he murmured. "And I don't—I'm not the kind of guy who'd get in between or jeopardize your relationship or who—"

Her lips pressed flat, released, plumping up, tempting him. "Who what?"

"I'm not the kind of man who fucks around with someone else's woman," he said baldly.

She sucked in a breath, released it slowly. "But I'm not someone else's woman."

"No."

Not anymore.

Wide hazel eyes on his.

"You're mine."

Her lips parted. Tempting him.

And...he might have ignored it, ignored it like he had for years.

But then her body drifted closer, thighs rubbing against his, breasts brushing his chest, hands coming to his arms.

And...he just had to taste her.

So, he did.

Two

Teresa

What was happening right now?

What was *happening*?

Jeremy was kissing her.

Jeremy.

Who hated her. Or who at the very least thought of her as an irritating little sister.

He was kissing *her.*

And doing it really fucking well. Well enough that it only took a couple of moments for her to shift from shock to *oh fucking...yeah.*

For her hands to shift from clenching onto hard biceps to sliding up to his shoulders...which were hard, too.

And that wasn't the only thing that was hard—

Heh.

Hard.

Jeremy was hard.

He was kissing her and he was *hard* and he—

"Jeremy, do you—*oh holy shit—*"

She tore her lips from his, turning toward the voice, just in time to see Wyatt with his hand clamped over his eyes and trying to find the door handle so that he could go back inside.

Except, his eyes were covered.

So, he was just scrabbling for the handle and making a lot of noise and chaos...and generally being an annoying older-brother type.

She jerked out of Jeremy's hold, wiped her mouth with the back of her hand.

She was strong, she knew that down to the very core of her being.

She could be brash and annoying and more stubborn than was good for her.

But that kiss...it had opened a latch in her mind, in her heart that she'd slapped so many locks on, it shouldn't just be flying open.

And then she saw Jeremy's face.

Need. *Hurt*.

She'd wiped her lips like a little kid scrubbing off a kiss that was full of cooties.

"I—"

His eyes flashed, a bit of his well-known temper shining through.

Which was reason one for why this wasn't going to happen.

She didn't do yelling, even if it was packaged as just caring so much for someone that he lost his cool every once in a while.

Excuses. Bullshit caveman nonsense that she already had enough of in her life. She couldn't deal with any more of it.

Which brought her to reason two.

She didn't *do* someone treating her like she was a piece of porcelain, needing to be packaged in bubble wrap and kept in a box or put up safely on a shelf, lest she break.

She had enough of that in her life.

She couldn't. She wouldn't.

So, she couldn't.

So, she *wouldn't.*

"I'm going!" Wyatt called, bumping fully into the door, loud enough to alert everyone in the house that there was something exciting and dramatic happening on the back deck. "Nothing to see here. I'm going. I'm—"

For fuck's sake.

Enough of this.

She moved across the deck, shoved Wyatt out of the way, leaving him for his twin, and letting herself into the house. Rafe had just entered the hallway, brows pulled together, no doubt having heard the commotion out back.

"Teresa, are you—"

She sidestepped him. "I'm heading out."

"Wait." He grabbed her arm. "What's wrong?"

"Nothing," she lied. "I'm tired—" Tired of men's bullshit. "And going to head out. I'll see you Monday."

"T—"

"Teresa!" Jeremy called.

Her eyes slid closed. She was really tired, really, *really* tired of men and their bullshit. "I'm leaving," she said, locking eyes with Rafe. "I'll see you Monday," she repeated.

He studied her face for a moment then nodded.

And because he was the protective older brother type, too, he stepped around her, blocking Jeremy's progress, just like she knew he would. Jeremy and Rafe were best friends, but friends didn't trump little sisters. And for all intents and purposes, she was Rafe's little sister. "She's going home, Jer."

Jeremy ignored him. "Teresa."

She didn't stop, didn't bother looking back.

Rafe would keep him from coming after her.

So, instead, she just hit the table in the hallway, grabbed her purse, and called her goodbyes.

"No *Catan?*" Cora asked from the kitchen.

"I've got a headache," she called back. "Rain check, yeah?"

Teresa didn't wait for a reply, just slipped out the front door and got in her car.

But when she drove off, her gaze went to the porch.

Jeremy was standing there.

Watching her drive away.

———

Sighing, she sat back in her hammock, staring up at the sky.

Her heart was aching.

Sore.

Her pride was stinging.

Raw.

Her body ached.

Need.

That kiss...

Holy fucking hell, that *kiss*. She should be thinking about her heart, about the ache and how shitty it had felt when Sam had taken her out to dinner and ended things.

He couldn't do it over text like a normal asshole?

Nope. He had to fly home so he could do it in person. He had to be kind and gentle about it, considerate when untangling their lives. Five years they'd been together. Five years, but honestly, she'd known that things had hit their final chapter when he'd moved to the other side of the country six months before.

He'd asked her to go to New York with him.

And she hadn't wanted to.

Her life was here—her parents, her brothers, the Hutchinses, her friends, her job.

Her whole life.

She didn't want to start over.

So, him breaking up with her wasn't a surprise...frankly, it had only been a matter of time.

But...she missed him.

Sighing, she closed her eyes and forced herself to stop and really think.

Did she actually miss Sam? Or did she miss having someone to spend her nights with? To cook dinner together and watch crappy TV with? Did she miss having someone she could con into seeing a romcom, trading it for an action flick at a later date?

Did she miss having *someone?*

Or did she miss having Sam?

Unfortunately, she thought she knew the answer to that.

But she wasn't ready to admit it, definitely wasn't ready to think about what that said about her—spending five years in a relationship with someone and at the end of it, all she could think about was that she didn't miss Sam...

She missed the companionship.

And she'd lied to Jeremy, which was just adding to her asshole-ness.

Stepped on my heart.

Had he?

Or was she just thinking she should be feeling something and because she wasn't—aside from feeling inadequate and insecure because she *wasn't* a mess after a five-year-long relationship had ended.

Sam was great.

But there was something wrong with her.

Had to be.

There had to be something broken in her that made her this way. What normal person wouldn't be distraught? Hell, her own mother had cried more when Teresa had broken the news of Sam moving in the first place.

When she found out that Sam was moving *on*...

Her mom was going to be a mess.

And after she passed along that the relationship was over, dealt with her mom's sadness over that fact, Teresa would be here, in this hammock, wondering what was wrong with her.

Wondering why she didn't feel.

Or didn't feel properly.

Which was the same thing that she'd been wondering on that deck. Same as she'd been feeling when she'd cried, actually cried on Cora's deck (and yes, it still counted as crying, even when it was just a couple of tears, especially since she hadn't cried at anything other than a Hallmark movie or SPCA commercial in freaking *years*).

And it was the same as she'd been feeling when she'd lied about those two tears to Jeremy.

Because she couldn't tell *him* the truth.

He'd look at her like...

Well, like there was something wrong with her.

But now...

He'd kissed her.

And the kiss...

She sighed, opened her eyes again, staring up at the twinkling stars, remembering that kiss, remembering *everything* about that kiss. The softness of his lips, the roughness of his stubble, the sleek dart of his tongue, the strength of his body when he held hers, how big he was, how small *she* was, how safe she'd been, ensconced in his hold.

And...

What that kiss had made her feel.

Which was everything.

THREE

JEREMY

S wear to fuck, but sixty-five percent of his job was emails.

Thirty-three percent was meetings.

And a whopping two percent was actually doing the tasks that were listed in his job description.

And it was six-thirty in the morning, he'd gotten into the office early to clear some of those tasks...and his inbox was already out of control.

He was tempted to empty the entire thing, to pretend that there hadn't been emails in the first place.

He was *tempted* to walk right out of this office and quit this job.

He was tempted to chuck his laptop against the wall, just to teach his inbox a lesson first.

Admittedly, he wasn't in the best mood.

But he hadn't slept well all weekend.

Teresa.

That kiss. Those tears. The *shit* his brothers had given him when they'd found out what he'd done and why she was upset and that it was probably his fault along with the fucker who'd stepped on Teresa's heart.

Big. Brash. Confident. Strong.

Not the woman with the stepped-on heart standing on Cora's deck, surreptitiously wiping her eyes.

Not the woman who'd pulled away from him, who'd left a Game Night (her favorite activity) early.

Because of him.

So yeah, he'd gotten shit, and it had been well-deserved.

And he'd spent the weekend alternating between wet dreams and guilt.

Neither of which was conducive to rest.

Which was why he'd given up trying to sleep and had just gotten up, showered, dressed, and come into work in an attempt to get something productive done.

Something he'd had approximately twenty minutes to do before there was a knock at the door.

It was six-thirty.

It was still dark outside.

He'd thought he was the only one in the office.

And...

"Hey, Jeremy."

Christ.

Not *her.*

Bianca was young, smart, and wanted to fuck him.

Teresa had teased him about pulling a lot of women, and while he didn't do all that poorly in that department, he was far from a Lothario. He couldn't abide bullshit and games, and Bianca was nothing but games.

How he knew this?

Because she hadn't even looked at him until he'd gotten a promotion three months ago.

Now...she looked.

And looked some more.

And genuinely drove him fucking nuts, jumping into his limited time that was free of meetings or trying to tackle his inbox, and making it so that he felt like he had to be a dick to get her to leave him alone.

Not that she seemed to take a hint.

Case in point, he didn't bother looking up from his computer. "Not a good time, Bianca."

Silence.

Though, unfortunately, it wasn't punctuated by her footsteps as she walked away from him and his office.

It was, *unfortunately,* punctuated by a sigh.

A long, disgruntled sigh.

"I was hoping that you could look at this work order."

"Can't," he clipped. "I'm slammed today. You can send it to Stephanie"—his assistant—"and I'm sure she'd be happy to walk you through the process. Again," he added, knowing he was a bit of a bastard for saying that, but wanting to make it clear that there was a firm boundary between them.

Again.

More silence.

Long enough that he risked a glance up, hoping that she'd gone.

Fate wasn't that kind to him.

Bianca was still there, still leaning against his doorframe, in heels, a low-cut shirt that practically begged everyone, man or woman, straight, gay, or in between, to stare. Because she had a gorgeous rack, and pretty much everyone could appreciate beauty.

If only that beauty wasn't attached to her mind and personality.

See? Bastard.

But her tits (and annoying persona) aside, he didn't date people from work, especially not subordinates.

That was a recipe...for making his job even shittier than it already was.

The economic climate meant that it wasn't a great time to look for a new job, so he was sticking it out for now, waiting for things to settle before he made a shift.

But he would be making a shift.

Because his job as it was, the extra responsibilities, the extra headaches and employees he suddenly needed to manage (all without extra pay or benefits) meant that he was unhappy.

So, biding his time, planning ahead, considering where he might want to go.

And putting in a shit-ton of applications, tidying up his resumé, squeezing in as many interviews as possible.

Which weren't many.

He glanced back down.

"Jeremy."

Sweet Christ.

Her voice was closer now, and he looked up to see she'd perched on the edge of his desk, that tight skirt of hers riding up to show the edge of lace stockings.

"I'm not trying to be a jerk, Bianca. But this really isn't a good time."

Fingers grazing over his where they'd paused on his keyboard.

He jerked back. "Bianca," he warned.

"I just want—"

His phone rang, and thank fuck. He didn't give a shit if it was a telemarketer or his grandma, but he was striking up a conversation and keeping in it like it was the most interesting thing he'd ever heard until Bianca finally got a fucking clue and left.

He snatched up the receiver.

"Jer."

His sister.

"Just a second." He covered the receiver, glanced up at her. "I need to take this."

Bianca didn't move for a long moment. In fact, she leaned closer, making it clear that the lace covering those gorgeous tits matched the top of her stockings.

He brought his eyes to hers, deliberately kept them there.

And when she didn't move, he lifted his brows.

Finally, she shifted off his desk, sauntered to his door.

"Sorry about that," he told his sister, pausing again to call, "Close that behind you, will you?"

A toss of shining brown hair, a flash of irritated eyes, but she closed—or more like *slammed*—the door behind her.

"Christ," he muttered.

"Jer?" his sister said again. "You good?"

"Fine," he grumbled. "What's up?"

"I need a favor, big bro."

"Anything."

It wasn't any empty word. He would do anything, literally *anything* for his baby sister. Not just because she was his baby sister, but because he'd promised his father that he would take care of her. His dad was gone. He was the oldest.

So, if his baby sister needed a favor...

She'd get it.

"Ben invited Rafe to a dinner, and I need you to come and round out our numbers."

"Okay."

"Just okay?"

He chuckled, leaned back in his chair. "When have I ever denied you anything, baby sis?"

"Never." She laughed. "Otherwise, what good would it be to be the baby sis with six older brothers?"

"None," he quipped. "Now, please tell me that you're not going to get me into a suit for some meal that is made up of courses the size of quarters and stilted conversations with some boring old investors."

Ben was Ben Bradford, billionaire tech maven and all-around nice guy.

He and Rafe were friends—mostly because Rafe had designed every campus for Ben's business, from the first small complex to the large multi-block buildings the tech company now utilized.

Since Rafe was his best friend and Cora was his sister, he'd go to the dinner, even if it had stupid quarter-sized courses that meant he'd have to hit up In-N-Out afterward, but he'd met Ben before and he was a good guy, so maybe there was hope.

"No clue," Cora said. "All I know is that it's black tie and we need even numbers."

Christ.

It was worse than he'd first thought.

Not just a suit, but a tux.

He groaned. "You'll owe me."

"You just said you'd do anything for me."

"I changed my mind."

A huff. "Some brother you are."

"When is this party?"

"Friday."

He sighed. "The Gold are playing Friday."

"Is this where I remind you that you said you'd do anything for me?" she asked sweetly.

"No," he muttered.

"Good." He could practically see her beatific smile. "Then I'll see you Friday."

"I still say you'll owe—"

She hung up before he could finish the statement.

Which was just as well, considering he didn't mean it anyway.

Four

TERESA

"But I hate dressing up."

"Liar," Rafe teased, tugging at her ponytail. "You don't mind getting dressed up, and I happen to know that you and Cora already bought a new dress and shoes."

"You know what's annoying?" she asked, brushing him off and focusing on the punch list on her clipboard.

"Besides me, my personality, and me again?" Rafe asked lightly.

She sniffed. "Yes."

"Then no," he said. "What's annoying?"

"You." A beat as he huffed out laughter. "And also that you're dating my friend, who then reveals all my secrets."

"I knew all your secrets before," he said, waving a dismissive hand.

She studied the wall, noticed an outlet plate that was cracked, and made a note of it on her ever-growing list. "Liar."

Another tug of her ponytail before his hand came in front of her face to point out a piece of trim that wasn't quite flush with the corner overhead. "*You're* the liar."

Unfortunately, she was.

Teresa was an open book, always had been, always would be —or at least, that was what she'd been careful to present to the world...and she supposed she *was* that in many respects. It was just beneath that outer layer she presented to the world, beneath that outer layer of who she'd thought *she* was, T was learning that she might be someone completely different.

Sam. Her feelings.

Her *lack* of them.

Thirty-one years old, and she wasn't the woman she'd always thought she was.

That was...disorienting.

But she wasn't going to focus on that—or the fact that she was lying, and Rafe knew it.

Instead, she made a note of the trim on her list and moved on.

"So, you'll get all gussied up and come charm the investors?" he pressed.

She sighed. "I can't decide if I'm more disgusted because you want me to get *gussied up* or because you want me to charm the investors."

He pointed out a ding in the floor. "You can't work for me forever."

Teresa made note of it. "But I don't need investors."

"If you want to start your own business, you need capital, and since you won't accept it from Ben or me..." He trailed off.

Probably because they'd had this discussion too many times to count.

"I want to start my own business," she said. "We both know I'd be good at it."

"Which is why Ben and I have both offered you seed capital."

"I don't borrow money from friends."

He snagged the clipboard, scrawled down a couple of items, which normally would have annoyed her because, as project manager, it was her job to keep things organized and neat and tidy. But she was more irritated by him bringing up money again, and that was mostly because she *wanted* to accept it, wanted to get her feet wet beneath a banner with *her* company name on it—not because she didn't like working for Rafe. He was a great boss and a good friend.

But because she wanted to be the one...in charge, who put it on the line, the one who the buck stopped with.

Not get dropped in halfway to the finish line of the marathon and cruise over while the rest of the populace struggled.

Maybe it was stupid.

But she wanted to earn it on her own.

"It's business for Ben," he pointed out.

"He's your friend," she pointed out. "So, it's not like he wouldn't donate if you vouched for me." She lifted her brows. "And I'm guessing, since he offered, that you did vouch for me."

Rafe didn't say anything.

Yet that was answer enough.

Because of course he would support her.

"You know," he said gently. "Your dad would—"

"No."

And maybe she said that too sharply, too intently. Maybe it revealed things beneath that outer layer she showed the world... but it was too visceral a response, too instinctual for her to be able to suppress her real response.

Which was absolutely fucking *not*.

Her father wouldn't give it a second thought. He'd cut her a check before she finished the request.

But that wouldn't be her doing it on her own.

That would be—

Not what she wanted.

"So, if not me," Rafe said a few moments later. "If not Ben or your father or your friends"—he hadn't suggested them, not outright, probably because her reply would have been even more intense than before if he had—"then who?"

She'd been saving for a while.

But if she wanted to do it all on her own, it was going to take her years to get there.

Which was the reason, when Cora had asked her to attend the gathering of rich people, she'd bought that new outfit, the new shoes—well, wanting to look good for potential investors *and* also, maybe a bit because the dress had been killer on the rack and even better on her body, showing off all the curves she and her tacos worked very hard for.

That made her want to grin.

But because it would give Rafe some satisfaction to know that he'd read her right about the dress and the investors—and maybe also, that he *was* right, at least about the investors—she bit back the smile.

"What time on Friday?"

Rafe didn't bother biting back *his* smile.

He let it loose.

It was wide and beautiful and *Rafe*.

And God, *must* he be such an annoying older brother?

She already knew the answer to that when his smile widened, turned full-on grin, when he said, "We'll pick you up at six-thirty."

Ugh.

"Fine," she snapped. "But I'm just saying..."

"Saying what?" he asked when she paused her shit-giving to jot down another couple of items they needed to have their teams come in and finish up or repair before the space was turned over to their tenets...

Who would no doubt find their own items for the punch list.

But that was part of the process.

One of her least favorite and most favorite, all at the same time, all woven together—least because the project was nearly over and they wouldn't be in the space any longer; most because she loved gathering all the small details, loved solving problems and finding creative solutions.

That was her lady jam.

Or just jam, because it was weird, her referring to things as her *lady jam*, especially when they typically involved hammers, nails, and buckets of paint.

But she was weird.

And she was in her jam.

And...she needed to finish her snark because otherwise Rafe would get one up on her, and that couldn't happen.

"I'm just saying," she repeated, "that you're really annoying."

"Yup." A pop on the P. He blew on his knuckles, buffed them on his shoulder. "That's my superpower."

"I'm only going to the party so I can woo all those investors, get some capital, open my own business, and then promptly quit working for you."

He grinned.

"Which means that you're on your own with *all* your punch lists."

That grin faded.

"T—"

And suddenly she was feeling a lot more chipper.

She let her own smile out, jauntily making notes and crossing others off.

"Wait, T—"

She slapped the clipboard against his chest.

"*All* of them."

Wide eyes.

Delight sliding through her. There was nothing she liked

more than being able to gleefully torture the people in her life that she loved. She smiled up at him, said, "And since that's going to be the case in the not-so-distant future—"

"Teresa—"

"I think there's no time like the present to start."

"*Teresa*—"

"Oh," she called as she moved to the stairs. "Don't forget to note that the faucet in the break room is loose so the guys can fix it!"

And then she left him still sputtering behind her as she walked out.

Gleefully.

FIVE

JEREMY

He tugged at his bowtie, hating the tux more than he hated wearing suits at work.

At least at work he could take off his jacket, loosen his tie.

Tonight, he'd be stuck in this straitjacket until dinner was over.

Slamming his car door, he rolled his shoulders and decided that Cora owed him pizza and beer for "evening out the numbers."

He'd probably be seated next to some flighty young millionaire's wife or an old battle-ax destined to slice him to the bone at every opportunity.

Jaded?

Yeah.

But then again, he'd been to enough of these by now to understand his role.

That being that he didn't have one.

Because this wasn't about *him*.

He might as well be a traffic cone or a cardboard cutout.

Which was fine.

He knew his place. He'd get some free food, even if it was dressed up too fancily and the portions were barely a mouthful.

There were worse fates for his Friday night.

Of course, he was trying to avoid thinking about better ones, since that would just make this night longer, more miserable.

Of that, he spoke from experience.

A bleep as he locked his doors, then he strolled into the restaurant and was shown to a private room in the back. Soft music, mood lighting, waiters in all black, and a room filled with people mingling.

He barely saw the other people, though.

Because all he wanted to see, to watch, to stare at was...Teresa.

Holy shit on a stick, that dress was...

He'd never seen her in something like that, something skintight, and he choked on his own spit when she turned to talk with someone, giving her his back, letting him see that her dress was *without* a back, its hem clinging at mid-thigh. Her ass. Her legs. Her—holy fucking shit, her *whole* body, set his on fire.

He simultaneously wanted to toss her over his shoulder, take her to his car, and fuck them both senseless, *and* also wanted to take off his tux jacket, wrap her in it, and make certain that no one else on the planet ever saw that much of her body again.

His.

She was his.

She turned again, perhaps having sensed him staring—which he was, and doing it blatantly—and he saw that the front was a lesson in temptation.

Not because it was showing skin.

It barely showed any.

She was covered in tight black fabric from wrists to throat. Not a single inch of skin was showing in that stretch of her body...and it was still the sexiest dress he'd ever seen. There was something about the material, about the way it clung to every curve, revealing without revealing, tempting by not really showing anything.

And knowing that the back...

Okay, so maybe he was inching toward the wanting to cover her up with his jacket direction.

Her eyes hit his and she froze, suddenly becoming a statue, and he knew the feeling, because he'd been struck with the same sensation in his solar plexus, the same sensation of every cell in his body going still.

Focused.

On Teresa.

"You're staring, bro," Cora said, coming up beside him and lacing their arms together. "You'll never have a chance with her unless you show some chill."

"She's—"

"Beautiful," Cora finished. "But she's also working, so don't fuck with her."

He turned toward his sister. "Working?"

A nod back toward Teresa, who'd turned to an older woman and was chatting animatedly. "She's looking for funding for her project management company."

"But she works for Rafe."

That wasn't a question even though he'd meant it as one.

"Yeah," Cora said, answering it anyway. "And she wants to eventually work for herself."

How did he not know that?

"What does Rafe have to say about that?"

Her brows lifted. "You mean about potentially losing his best employee?" Cora smiled. "He's bitching about it every chance he gets, same as he's been doing since she brought it up to him a couple of months ago."

Jeremy frowned.

"But he invited her here," Cora said. "With all these people who have money, so much that they don't occasionally mind parting with it, especially for someone who's proven they can be successful and a good worker. They've all seen Ben's new building, seen the work she and Rafe did on it. They want to hire her, and they definitely wouldn't mind making a couple of bucks back for every dollar they invest in her." His sister shrugged. "So, I think that says enough about how Rafe feels."

It did.

It would hurt Rafe, and possibly his business, to lose Teresa.

But he was giving her this opportunity anyway.

"He doesn't want to make her partner?" Jeremy asked.

Cora smiled softly. "That would be Rafe's ideal," she said. "But Teresa wants to do something different, and she wants to make it on her own. No money from family or friends." A beat. "Or from someone's very successful friend who would absolutely be willing to invest in a young, female entrepreneur."

Not willing to partner with Rafe. Nor accept some seed money from him.

Or from her parents.

Or from Ben, apparently, either.

Stubborn woman.

"Think she'd let me cut her a check?" he asked quietly.

Cora's gaze shot up and humor bled into her face. "I think you're the last person she would *ever* accept money from."

He suspected the same.

Especially after the kiss on the deck.

"Yeah," he agreed.

"Sam really broke up with her?" Cora asked softly after a moment.

He lifted his brows. "She really didn't talk to you about it?"

"She's...well, you know her. It's less about what's going on with her than what she can do for you. She's really good at being there for everyone else, at being capable and confident." A sigh.

"But really, it just means that no one looks close enough to get a glimpse at what's underneath."

He thought about that for a moment.

He'd always said that with Teresa, what a person saw was what a person got.

She was competitive, smart, beautiful, capable, and...Cora was right.

Jer had never seen her vulnerable. Not once.

Except when she'd wiped those tears away.

"I know that feeling," Cora whispered. "Trying to hold it together *all the time* so that you don't look weak, so that someone doesn't sweep in and try to handle something that you can take care of yourself, even if it's hard and makes you want to cry and is so freaking frustrating that a small, secret part of you wants the help." A breath. "But I know that I don't need it, that I can do it myself, that when I do, it's going to feel so, *so* incredible, and I just need the space to get over the finish line myself."

"Cor," he murmured, squeezing his sister's arm. "I'm sorry."

Because he wasn't good at giving her space.

Hadn't ever been.

And they'd had conflict because of it.

"You've seen it," she murmured back. "And you've understood it, with a little help from Rafe." A gentle smile that told him she didn't harbor any ill feelings for his lack of space-giving. "And, truthfully, Teresa comes from her own brand of overprotective. She warned Rafe I was feeling that way because *she* identified with it, could see my frustration because she'd lived it too."

"Yeah. I can see that." Her parents were heavily involved in her life, along with her two older brothers.

"So, I mean this in a genuine way, and not in an asshole sibling trying to piss you off way," Cora said, still gentle. "We all know you like Teresa. That you've liked her for a while. But Jer" —she turned to him—"if you really *do* like her, if you really do want her...for *her*, not for this little-woman-I-can-take-care-of fantasy I think you might have, then you need to make sure that you understand that part of her. The part of her that craves the ability to make her own decisions, to live her own life, to do things on her own."

"I do."

Cora gave him a look that said *But, do you?*

And her next words confirmed that.

"She's independent, Jer. That's part of her identity. A big part of it, from what I've come to learn about her over the years, and if you try to step on that...if you try to pull what you did with me..."

"Cora—"

"If you try to pull that with her, you not only won't be able to keep her—"

"*Cor—*"

"You won't have ever had her in the first place."

Those words struck hard, hard enough that his throat went tight.

And probably knowing that she'd managed an excellent parting shot, his sister patted his arm then slipped away.

Moved to the man she loved.

To the man who'd given her everything she'd ever needed, everything she'd always wanted.

And what he might not be able to give to the woman he'd loved for three years.

Six

Mrs. Jacobs was fucking hilarious.

She sat on the board of Ben's company and appeared to be a hundred years old if she was sixty, but her mind was sharper than Teresa's, and T was finding herself in mental knots without a way to untangle them.

So basically, she felt like a big ol' dum-dum.

Out of her league.

Out of her class.

Out of—

"Don't let that show, dear."

T blinked and glanced over at the older woman.

"Your insecurity," Mrs. Jacobs said baldly. "It shows on your face, and that's the quickest way to shoot yourself in the foot."

"I—"

"Do you think these men feel insecure?" She gestured at the room, to the suited and powerful men as though they were at a boring art exhibit they'd been forced to attend.

"I—maybe?" Well, they probably did, right? No one could

be 100% self-confident. Not all the time. No one could think they were right every single moment of every single day.

"The answer," Mrs. Jacobs said, leaning closer, her voice dropping to a conspiratorial whisper, "is the dumb ones don't." Her lips quirked up, emphasizing the heavy laugh lines she had at the corners of her mouth. Teresa liked the idea of this woman smiling and laughing so much that her face showed it, showed that happiness. She wanted to be like Mrs. J when she grew up, especially when Mrs. Jacobs declared, "And the smart ones do have doubts and insecurities. They're just better at hiding them."

Teresa grinned, working on some laugh lines of her own. "I—"

Mrs. Jacobs poked her on the arm. "So, I'm telling to you wipe that expression off your face, woman up, and know that regardless of what happens with those jokers, *I'm* writing you a check."

"I—but—" Teresa should have had something smart to say, something businesslike, but instead she was standing there like a gaping fish until she managed to clear her throat. "I couldn't—"

"And that's stupidity *and* insecurity talking."

Well, *that* felt nice.

Which apparently was written on her face because Mrs. Jacobs leaned even closer, until the soft floral scent of her perfume hit Teresa's nose. "Business isn't nice, dear. You'll accept the check for the amount you told me you're hoping to solicit over the next months to a year because your business plan is a good one, and I've learned that it's worth it to go with my gut, especially when it's a small amount of money."

Small being relative, Teresa supposed, considering she'd been expecting it to take a year to raise those funds.

"I—" The word was a croak, but she managed to pause, to clear her throat, to breathe, and then to say calmly, *professionally* even, "Thank you."

An approving smile.

A pat to her arm.

"Now *that's* the spirit. Also," she added, tilting her head to the men again, "feel free to impress these bozos, but know that when I send my check over and we sign an agreement, that I don't like to share. If I'm your investor, I'm it." Another pat—or maybe it was a nudge. Forward.

Toward the group of bozos.

She glanced back over her shoulder, saw that Mrs. Jacobs was smiling encouragingly. "Go get 'em, honey."

Teresa let that settle into her—the confidence a stranger felt for her because she'd been able to carry on a conversation, because she had a good idea, because—

She'd been herself.

Teresa had been *herself.*

And that had been enough.

And...*that* settled on her, settled over her, filled...

No.

Felt.

She *felt.*

Because of a little old lady in a pantsuit, with a bedazzled cane, white curly hair...and a laugh line on either side of her mouth.

Teresa smiled, deep and wide.

So much so that lines were probably forming already.

God, she hoped so.

———

Lines were forming all right.

They just weren't from laughter. Or smiles.

Nope.

Her smile had ended about twenty minutes ago when

everyone had found their seats, and she'd found herself seated next to Jeremy.

Yummy Jeremy, whose hotness was undeniable.

Stubborn Jeremy, who'd made it his life's mission to take care of everyone around him.

Jeremy with the scorching irises that had threatened to melt her on the spot when she'd looked into them after he'd caught sight of her dress.

Heat had blossomed in her belly. Her knees had shaken.

Her breasts had swollen, nipples going sensitive against the material of her bra.

She'd *needed*.

And he'd looked like he'd wanted to toss a blanket over her and bundle her from the room.

But that didn't work for her. She didn't want a man like Jeremy. She didn't want to be a woman taken care of.

He was hot.

He kissed like sin.

But he wasn't for her, and that was the end of it.

"Nice dress," he murmured, lips at her ear, and that heat blossomed again, her nipples going hard, and it was good she was sitting down because her knees had definitely gone shaky.

All because of two words.

And his body nearby. And his scent. And the heat in his eyes, making it clear he thought she was hot as hell in her dress.

Which she knew.

But...it wasn't her usual garb, so the fact that he appreciated it...

She shook that off.

"Nice tux," was her only reply.

And then she picked up her wine glass and drank deeply.

Take the edge off.

Ignore him because her mouth would be full—

His leg brushed hers, that strong powerful thigh shifting

against hers, and this dress did *not* have enough fabric to prevent her from *feeling* all sorts of things she shouldn't be feeling.

Because she was thinking of those strong legs and those legs spreading enough so that she could kneel between them—

And her mouth full in a whole different way.

A hot, rough voice in her ear. "Penny for your thoughts?"

She choked.

His hand went to her back—and it needed to be noted that because of her very sexy and very fabric-limited dress—his hand was on the *bare* skin of her back.

And his palm, his fingers were hot and a little rough and—

She'd decided that those two adjectives were her favorites.

"Easy now, baby," he murmured.

She turned and glared up at him. "I'm not your baby," she hissed. "And get your fucking hand off my back."

Jeremy's brows lifted, but he removed his hand, used it to pick up his glass.

Her gaze slid up, and Mrs. Jacobs nodded approvingly, as if to say, *Don't let him fuck up your plans.*

Teresa wouldn't.

She couldn't.

Even *if* he could fill out a tux.

Now Mrs. Jacobs smiled, as though she could hear that thought, too, and though ESP probably wasn't on the list of Mrs. J's talents, based on their interactions so far, Teresa knew her face showed a lot.

Too much.

Damned open book.

She really needed to work on that.

Mrs. Jacobs lifted her brows, tilted her head toward Jeremy, as though saying, *Why not? He's cute.*

Teresa shook *her* head. *He's trouble.*

Mrs. Jacobs grinned, and T could almost hear her thinking, *Trouble of the best kind.*

Yeah, that wasn't happening.

"You never told me that you wanted to start your own business."

She jerked, so engrossed in her nonverbal conversation with Mrs. Jacobs that she hadn't realized Jeremy had leaned close again.

This time she managed to temper her reaction.

No more shivers on her watch, baby!

Just that affable, open book, sitting atop a closed one.

One that Jer wouldn't be allowed to dig out.

Mrs. Jacobs tilted her head in the other direction, as though she were telling Teresa it was her choice. Which it was. Of course, it was.

Though it being her choice, it would be nice if her body got with the program.

"You just going to ignore me all night?"

She took another sip of wine. "That was my plan."

His fingers brushed along her spine. "Because our kiss got under your skin?"

It was the cocky way he said it.

The utter confidence in his tone.

Like he knew *exactly* where her thoughts had been going, as though he were going to turn on the charm and she was going to fall into his lap.

As though the two of them were going to happen.

A forgone conclusion.

Whether she liked it or not.

Those fingers brushed over her skin again.

Touching her when she'd told him not to.

Her temper frayed.

His fingers brushed again. A third time of ignoring her. A third time ignoring her requests.

She clenched her teeth together, tried to hold tight to the slender thread of calm that remained in her psyche.

A soft laugh, right into the shell of her ear—damp, warm puffs of air against her skin. "It did. Didn't it? Just like me touching you right now..." His thumb dipped lower, tracing the upper curve of her ass. "You like it. You *want* it."

And...*snap.*

SEVEN

JEREMY

He hadn't even seen her hand move.

One moment he was sitting next to her, feeling the soft skin beneath his fingertips, smelling her shampoo, smelling *her*—something tropical and fruity, the same way she always smelled.

And the next, he was sputtering.

Wine dripping down his face.

Teresa's chair scraped as she pushed back from the table, then she strode from the room.

And he...well, *hell*. He'd never had wine thrown in his face. It was a chilled white variety that tasted pretty good when it seeped into his mouth. But it burned like hell where it dripped into his eyes.

It was unpleasant.

A throat cleared.

And he remembered he was at the table, at a table with a bunch of rich people.

Who were now staring at him.

Because someone had just thrown wine in his face.

Embarrassment flooded through him.

That throat cleared again, and he managed to sop up some of the wine on his face. As he glanced up, eyes still stinging, he saw the older woman that Teresa had been talking to so intently earlier was staring at him.

Then she raised her brows.

Tilted her head toward the door.

And he was tossing the napkin on the table, shifting before he fully processed that he was a dumbass for sitting there while Teresa ran off and—

His chair screeched back.

He was in the hall a moment later.

A flash of naked skin, blond hair flying up behind her as she turned the corner.

He went after her, wine still dripping down his face, rubbing the burning liquid from his eyes as he moved, closing the distance between them—

Which wasn't hard, he supposed.

Because she'd stopped.

Was waiting for him, hands on her hips, fury on her face.

"I'm sorry."

The words had been on the tip of his tongue, so he was surprised, surprised enough for his feet to slide to a stop, when *she* gave *him* the apology.

He'd deserved the wine in the face.

He'd been pushing her because...he was an idiot who didn't heed his sister's advice, because sitting there next to her with her ignoring him irked him, because he was feeling all these things, and she...wasn't.

Or that was what she was trying to present to the world, to him.

Because he'd kissed her.

He'd felt that she wasn't immune.

He'd felt that her body, at least, had responded to his.

But he'd still been an asshole in that room.

"No," he said. "*I'm* sorry."

Her hands slipped from her hips, arms falling to her sides, a blip of shock through her face before her chin came up. "Yeah. You should be."

His nostrils flared as he inhaled. "I am."

Her eyes narrowed.

"I'll go and leave you to it."

She laughed, but it wasn't amused. It was jagged. It was sharp and rough. "I can't go back in there."

"Why not?"

Now she lifted her brows. "*Why not?*" Another of those unamused laughs.

He shook his head.

"Now you're either getting off on fucking with me or you're truly dense."

He just lifted his brows back at her.

A sigh. "I just lost my temper and threw a glass of wine in the face of my dinner companion...when I'm trying to impress my other dinner companions in the hopes that they might cut me a check." Those brows slid a bit higher. "Do you think that wine-tossing will equal funding?"

"I think it will with the old lady sitting across from us." He shrugged. "And I think the rest don't matter."

"I think," she said and then stopped, sighing, head dropping forward, her fingers rubbing her temples. "I think that I'm embarrassed." Her hands dropped, head popping up. "I'm sorry," she said again. "That really *was* terrible of me. I-I don't know what came over me."

And fuck, her eyes glimmered with tears.

And he felt like even more of an asshole than he already had before.

Because he was responsible for them.

"This is on me," he said. "I'll fix it."

He'd started to turn back, intent on doing *something*, when she caught his arm, yanked him back to face her. Now her eyes were dry, so dry they were sparking with fury. "Seriously?" she snapped.

"Look," he snapped back. "I apologized. I realize I was trying to goad you and that was an asshole thing to do. Let me fix it. Let me make it right—"

"Stop."

He blinked but stopped.

"This is just it," she said. "This is exactly why we could never ever be together, why I could never date a guy like *you.*"

No lie, that stung.

She saw it, too. He knew it by how her voice softened.

"Look, Jer," she said. "I know you think you feel something for me, but this isn't going to work. I'm not trying to be a dick, but truthfully, I can't do this. Not because you aren't a great guy. You are." She sucked in a breath, released it. "But you're not the great guy for me. We're just...not compatible, okay? And trying to push this, trying to force us into something, some perfect fantasy relationship because you think that you like me—"

"I *do* like you, T," he said quickly.

"You don't know me," she replied. "Not really."

That prickled something in his mind, something he couldn't put his finger on, something—

"Is this about Rafe?" he asked. "You know I'd never get in between you two."

"It's not about Rafe. Well, it is, and it isn't," she said. "It's not a good idea to get between my boss and his best friend, and it's stupid to mix my family—and you and your brothers, Cora, your mom, our friends, we're all family in my book. But it's not that, Jer, and you know it."

"Then what is it?" he asked. "We'd be good together."

"We'd be a mess," she countered. "We don't even want the same things."

"Life is messy, baby. But when you find something good, you have to work for it."

Her eyes flashed. "Except, I don't want *you*."

"T—"

"And *you* don't want *me*. You don't even *know* me."

He moved a little closer. "So, tell me about you, T. Let me in."

A quick, jerky shake of her head, and maybe he was seeing something, maybe he was imagining things, but he could have sworn there was fear on her face.

"Baby," he breathed.

"Here's the thing," she whispered, her gaze coming up, locking with his. "I don't want to, and I don't *have* to."

The words were a sharp, sharp slice.

But worse?

She was right.

"So, stop this, okay? Stop going fucking caveman just because I'm single. Stop trying to fix my life when I don't need it. Stop trying to be more than a friend."

His lungs expanded.

"Because if you continue with *this*"—she waved a hand between them—"this will end up with us not even *as* friends."

She took the napkin he was gripping in his hand, slid it free, and wiped his face.

"No more trying to force this," she whispered when she'd finished.

God, her lips were close.

Her eyes were warm.

Her body was giving all the signs that it wanted his, but her words...well, her words were the opposite. And he had to listen to them.

He released a long breath, forced his hands to remain at his sides. "T."

Her eyes slid away. "Please, Jer. Please, just stop with this now. Let it go. Let *me* go."

He didn't want to.

Fuck, he'd been in love with this woman for three years, and he finally had a shot with her.

But...she didn't want him.

So, he had to let her go.

Jeremy stepped back. "I've got some things to handle at home," he said. "Make my apologies for me?"

A nod.

"T," he said before she went off back down the hall. "I get what you're saying. I do. Just..." He inhaled, released it. "I'm here if things change, yeah?"

Her smile was small and sad. "Yeah," she whispered.

Then she turned and walked away from him.

Eight

TERESA

Miraculously, the dinner hadn't been too awkward when she came back to the table.

Without Jeremy.

With a slightly damp seat, the byproduct of her wine tossing.

But much of the awkwardness was dissipated thanks to Mrs. Jacobs.

She'd regaled the table with tales of her eighty-odd years, and though Teresa had fended off a bit of teasing about her throwing arm, most of the room had let the incident go.

And she'd talked about her business a lot by the end of the night.

So much so that Mrs. J had recommended Teresa consider all offers when they came in—even her own—before T made a decision about who to work with.

It was...quite a swing.

It was...still her friend doing her a favor, she knew, because she was at the dinner in the first place. But she was at peace with that, and at peace with the offers because she knew that her idea had merit, that the offers wouldn't have come if that wasn't true, especially with her being an idiot and losing her temper.

That would have been the perfect out.

But she still had options.

So that kept her in her slightly damp seat through the twelve courses, each barely more than a bite.

But now dinner was over, and Cora and Rafe were heading her way and—

She wanted to escape.

In fact, she was searching for her purse, her coat, so she could escape without talking to them, without having to explain her wine-tossing. She'd feign tiredness, catch a Lyft.

Alas, Cora was faster than she looked.

And Rafe was smarter.

Because he had her purse in his big, beefy hand, her jacket folded over one arm.

Ugh. Beauty and brains.

Pretty *and* preventing her escape.

Life wasn't fair.

She wanted to stomp her foot. She *wanted* to throw more wine. But she hadn't suddenly found herself cast on *Real House-wives.* She was an adult (kind of), so she needed to behave like one (kind of).

So, she waited for Cora and Rafe to approach, thanked the latter when he helped her into her coat, and then took her purse.

"What's the tea?" Cora asked, looping her arm through Teresa's. "What did my brother do to deserve a wine lashing?"

Yeah, she was going to share *that* over her dead body.

"It doesn't matter," she said instead. "Jeremy and I talked it through in the hall. We're good now."

If by *good* she meant that she'd gotten him to agree to leave her alone then, yes, they were good. They were *fantastic.*

If by *good* she felt like a total asshole for the way she'd handled herself and the situation.

She'd thrown a glass of wine in his face. Who did that to a person?

She'd acted completely unhinged.

All because he'd pushed her boundaries—which, admittedly, wasn't right either. But she could have handled it better, preferably without the side of light violence and emotions creating a huge, embarrassing scene.

Cora tugged at Teresa's arm, drawing her gaze up to her friend's. "I'm sorry."

"For what?" Teresa whispered.

"Because my brother is a big, overprotective lug, and he should have listened to me when I told him to play it cool?"

Surprise widened Teresa's eyes. "What?"

"He likes you, hun. Has for years, which I know you're too smart to have missed."

Except, she *had* missed it.

When he'd cupped her jaw on Cora's deck, had lifted her face, his lips drawing close to hers as they formed the words *you're mine*, she'd been shocked.

Riveted in place.

Jeremy tolerated her.

Jeremy was annoyed by her.

That he secretly liked her?

Finding that out had sent a thrill through her belly, had filled her with more excitement and happiness than she'd felt in all those years with Sam.

Then the terror had set in.

Then she'd run, just like she was running now.

Because if she stopped, if she gave in and they made a go of things and he...well, if he treated her like he was bound to treat her—

Breakable. Needing protection and safety.

Not an equal. Not a partner.

If she let him in and he did *that*—

It would *hurt*.

And he was Jeremy. Taking care of people was his personality, in his DNA...it was *him*. She couldn't ask him to change who he was, not for her.

So, anything between them was untenable.

It wouldn't be fair for *either* of them.

Even if he made her feel something that she hadn't in years.

Because it would, inevitably, blow up in their faces.

"I know he likes me," she told Cora as they walked to Rafe's car. "But I can't get involved with someone like Jer. I know he's your brother, and I don't want to be a dick about it, but swear to Christ, we would be bad for each other."

Cora stopped.

Which forced Teresa to stop, to look at her friend.

"Why do you say that?"

"I can't be with someone who wants to control every aspect of my life," she admitted. "Who needs to have his fingers in every piece of the proverbial pie, who wants to take over, who tries to handle my shit for me. I live my life for me, and I work hard, and I *can't* have someone taking that away from me."

Cora's hand came to hers, resting on top of it, squeezing lightly. "I understand, honey. Believe me"—a smile—"I do."

"Yeah," Teresa whispered, knowing that Cora, with six annoying older brothers herself, knew how important it was to do things on her own.

She'd fought for that.

She had it.

Because Rafe understood.

He hadn't taken over. He'd stood by her side.

But Jeremy...hell, Jeremy still tried to drive Cora places, still reminded her to set her alarm and lock her doors and check in the back seat before she got into her car. He offered to talk to an annoying neighbor and take her car in for services and oil changes and...more.

And he did that for Edy—Mrs. Hutchins—herself.

Some women might love that.

Teresa felt smothered by it, and she wasn't even living it.

If she *were* living it?

God, it would be a hundred times worse.

A thousand ropes wrapping tight, slowly squeezing the air out of her.

"But I'll just say this one thing and let it settle, okay?" Cora smoothed a hand over Teresa's arm.

No, that was not okay. Very *not* okay. Because Teresa knew that Cora was going to lay out some knowledge, and it was going to make sense and be logical and thus, it was going to be very difficult to ignore.

But she wasn't a coward.

So, she just lifted her chin and said, "Lay it on me."

Cora smiled gently.

Then she laid it out.

"You and I are the same in a lot of ways. We've fought for our lives, worked our asses off, and don't want someone coming in and taking over."

Teresa nodded.

"That's fair. That's reasonable. Hell, that makes absolutely perfect sense."

Another nod.

"What doesn't, though," Cora said softly. "Is when we forbid ourselves from having something, just because we're afraid of what change it might bring."

Teresa sucked in a breath as that hit hard.

"Whether it's buying a home or taking a new job or investing in your own business." A beat. "Or even, if it's investing in a relationship that might not be what you thought you wanted...but is exactly what you need."

A squeeze of her arm, and then they were joined by Rafe and walking to their car.

While Teresa strode silently beside them and absorbed the blows.

Because it made sense. It was logical.

It was reasonable.

She and Cora were the same in a lot of ways.

The difference was that Cora hadn't watched her mother slowly suffocate in her life, slowly disappear in a reality that had taken every bit of light out of her.

Hadn't watched those ropes tighten a bit more every year.

Hadn't spent her entire life watching her mother die by inches.

Or maybe that had just been Teresa.

NINE

"Y ou're looking particularly grumpy," Wyatt said.

Jer slanted his gaze from his TV to his twin.

He *was* feeling exceptionally grumpy.

But he wasn't going to comment on it.

"Which means you *are* feeling particularly grumpy."

A grunt was his only response.

One, because his day had been shit, after a shitty weekend, after a shitty Friday night—all of which he'd spent beating himself up for being a pushy asshole at every opportunity.

Two, because *this* day, in particular, had been extra shitty.

Bianca had shown up to work early, matching his start, and had refused to leave his office, doing it so intently that he'd escalated from trying to give her a gentle cue to make phone calls and ignoring her to straight up asking her to leave, none of which had worked. Even when he'd asked, she refused to go and he'd seriously been considering grabbing his shit and getting the fuck out, when his admin, Shannon, had shown up.

Shannon had cottoned on to what was happening immediately, and the two of them had been successful in getting Bianca to leave.

But the interaction meant that he'd spent the better part of his morning making a report to HR and not doing any of his work and having to cram his meetings into the remaining part of the day.

He knew they'd pulled Bianca in after him, along with Shannon later that afternoon.

Hopefully, between his complaint and Shannon's support, that would be enough, and Bianca would get a clue.

But seriously, there was one woman in his life who he was in love with, and she didn't want him, wouldn't give him the time of day. Ever. The *ever* part being made quite clear and in a way that couldn't—and wouldn't—be ignored. And there was another woman who, maybe wasn't in love with him but had an unhealthy fixation, and all *he* wanted her to do was leave him alone.

The juxtaposition told him that fate had a fucked-up sense of humor.

The similarities reminded him why he'd walked away in the restaurant, and why he wouldn't push.

He didn't want Teresa to feel this way.

Uncomfortable. Cornered. Frustrated. Prevented from doing what she wanted to do.

So, he'd keep his distance.

He'd move on.

Just not with Bianca.

So yeah, he was grumpy.

Because his shit weekend had been punctuated by a shit Monday.

He wanted an out-of-the-office job. He wanted to be doing something that he actually liked. But he also didn't really know what he wanted to do. His focus had always been on doing something that paid well.

His job ticked those boxes.

But he didn't like it.

Not in the least.

So, double yeah, he was feeling really fucking grumpy.

And his twin pointing it out only added to it.

"I can go," Tiffany, Wyatt's girlfriend, said. "Let you guys talk it out."

She was a twin herself.

She understood Twin Powers.

She was also empathetic and nice, and he liked her for Wyatt. Liked her for his twin a lot.

Both she—*and* her twin—were sweet girls. But they were too soft for Jeremy. He wanted loud and brash and beautiful and strong. He wanted someone who could be his equal, who wouldn't be afraid to go toe-to-toe with him and tell him off if he was being a douche.

"No," he told her. "I'm fine." He slanted a look at his brother. "It's just been a long week."

"But it's only Monday."

"Yeah."

"So that's one day into the week."

For a second, he thought she was serious, thought that she really didn't get what he'd meant, but then he saw the dash of humor in her green eyes and realized she was fucking with him.

Quietly.

Gently.

His lips twitched.

So did hers.

"Yeah," he said.

"Does your long week mean you get to have another beer?"

Now he smiled for real. "Yeah."

She did, too, standing and snagging the empty bottles, disappearing into his kitchen. Wyatt didn't say anything in her absence, and neither did he. Part of that was because the action in the game had kicked up, and part of it was because Jeremy had used his Twin Powers to command his brother to shut the fuck up...and miracle of miracles, it had worked.

A few minutes later, Tiff was back, handing them each a beer, and setting a plate in front of them.

Cheese, crackers, and fruit.

Wyatt glanced at him, lifting his brows and Twin Powers or not, Jer heard the *see what magic my woman weaves?*

She did weave magic—diffusing what would have certainly turned into a fight between him and Wyatt, taking the edge off his shit mood, bringing them beer and food.

Tiffany was great.

There was absolutely no doubt about that.

Just not for him, and neither was her twin sister, Melody.

"Gotta call my dad, baby," Tiffany murmured, leaning close and resting her palm on his brother's chest, brushing her lips over Wyatt's.

Then she'd slipped down the hall, opened the sliding door off the kitchen, and ensconced herself onto his patio.

She'd been over enough to know where everything was.

So had Melody.

But Melody didn't weave magic for him.

He knew that there had been some hope for the twins marrying twins thing amongst his family—mostly so his brothers and Cora could give him and Wyatt shit about the twins marrying twins thing.

He'd settled that hope.

Or so he'd thought.

Because just as he'd began to really get back into the game, tying not to be jealous of his brother and what Tiffany was to him, Wyatt dropped a Melody-sized bomb.

Though it wasn't obvious at first.

"So, Grumpy," Wyatt said. "Would telling you that I have Gold tickets for Thursday's game wipe that scowl off your face?"

No.

Because tickets wouldn't change the fact that Teresa didn't want him.

And tickets wouldn't help Bianca get a fucking clue.

But he wasn't going to complain. He loved watching hockey and he especially loved watching it live.

"Yes," he muttered. "So long as the next thing you tell me is that I'm invited."

Wyatt grinned. "Would I be so cruel as to tell you *I* have tickets, but not have a ticket for *you?*"

He lifted his brows, shot his brother a look.

Yeah, Wyatt would.

He fucking *loved* torturing Jer.

Not that Jer minded pushing Wyatt's buttons right back.

It was brotherly affection.

It was brotherly...torture.

"I have a ticket for you, if you want it," Wyatt said, surprising him.

He didn't delay. "I want it." He hadn't gone to a game in forever.

His brother scooped up a handful of crackers and cheese. "Okay." He stuffed a cracker in his mouth. "It's yours."

Jer grabbed his own cheese and crackers (though he added a dash of fruit along with it), but as he shoved it into his mouth, the way that Wyatt had the ticket was his had Jer's nape prickling. "Who else is coming?" he asked suspiciously once he'd chewed and swallowed, washing the snacks down with a swig of beer.

"Me. Tiff"—a tilt of his head toward the kitchen, toward the patio—"You."

But there was an unspoken *and* in his words.

Jeremy felt that right in his gut.

"And Melody."

He dropped his bottle on the table. "Wyatt."

"It's not a setup," his twin said, leaning forward on the couch. "We have four tickets. Melody wants to hang with her sister. I want to hang with my brother, who conveniently likes hockey a lot."

"Convenient," he said dryly, scooping up the bottle.

"And if you *happen* to hit it off with Melody"—he shot Wyatt a glare, who lifted his hands in a gesture of surrender, bottle clenched between thumb and pointer finger—"then who am I to stand in the way of true love?"

"Christ," he muttered.

He needed seven more beers for this conversation.

Wyatt leaned back, drinking deeply. "So, you gonna come?"

"Where are the tickets?"

"Attacking side, eight rows back."

Great seats.

Fantastic seats.

"Christ," he muttered again.

"You're coming."

A sigh. Curses rattling through his head, barely kept in check on his tongue.

He took another sip of beer.

Fuck.

"Yeah," he grumbled. "I'm going."

Wyatt grinned.

Though, miracle of miracles, he finally shut up and let Jeremy watch the rest of the game in silence.

Ten

TERESA

Teresa pulled into her driveway.

It was Wednesday night.

She and her mom went and got pedicures and manicures every Wednesday.

Well, pedicures once a month and manicures weekly.

A waste of money—for Teresa, especially, since her manicure barely lasted through the following day (thus was the sad fate of a project manager for a construction company). Though maybe when she was a project manager turned successful CEO, whose app was the real estate version of Tinder for businesses (rolling the app out for residential properties was also in the works... along with the rental market), maybe then her manicure would last longer than twenty-four hours.

Maybe *then,* she'd get a manicure every day.

Which would be an egregious waste of money, not to mention time.

She'd be too busy being successful to have daily manicures, thank her very much.

Anyway, she was delaying.

She loved her family, truly she did.

But Christ, she hated Wednesday nights.

The front door opened, her father poking his head out, and she felt the ropes snake around her, felt them begin to wrap tighter as he bounded down the steps. "All good, sweetheart?" he called as she grabbed her purse and pushed open her car door.

"Everything is fine, Dad."

He came close, snagged her purse from her hand, something she didn't bother fighting him on. She'd done it enough over the years and had always lost. That was how he cared for his girls. They were little princesses to be sat atop a pillowed throne. He bent a little, crouching so he could stare deep into her eyes. "There a reason you're sitting in your car instead of coming in?"

"It's been a long week already," she said.

"Do I need to talk to Rafe?" he asked, concern immediately filling his expression. "Is he giving you too much responsibility?"

Did she need him to talk to her boss? Of *fucking* course not.

Further than that, did she want her father to talk to her boss about downsizing her responsibility? Good God, that was even worse.

"No, Dad," she said. "I'm fine. Work is fine. I'm just busy. That's a good thing, right?"

More studying, but after a moment, he smiled, chucked her under the chin. "That's my baby girl, always such a hard worker." He slung his arm around her shoulders, tugged her close to his side. "Just don't overdo it, okay?"

"Yeah, Dad. I won't."

"Your mother cooked for you."

Of course, she had.

"I told her I'd take her out after our manicures," she said on a sigh.

A squeeze of her arm. A kiss to the top of her head. "Better that you save your money, sweetheart. That way you can invest in your business."

"Right," she whispered, thinking about the offers she'd received.

Offers. Yup.

Despite her wine shenanigans, she'd received three offers.

The full ask from Mrs. Jacobs.

Two partials from Ben's associates.

She'd reviewed them, and they were currently with her attorney, but she'd been leaning toward Mrs. Jacobs' offer, even before she'd received the paperwork. After? She was leaning even more heavily. The other two wanted a bigger slice of the pie with less upfront capital, and sure, Mrs. J wanted to get paid, and, obviously, would get a good chunk of the profits.

But not more than Teresa was willing to give away.

So...yeah, unless there was anything sneaky in the legalese, Teresa might have an investor.

She might be ready to start rolling out her app.

Which was why she wanted to be home, troubleshooting with her designer, drawing up plans for how to connect with real estate listing sites and databases.

She wanted to be *working*.

Not walking into her childhood home while not even allowed to carry her own bag, and about to spend the next two hours with her mother...

Who would have much to say on the fact that Teresa was single—she'd broken the news about Sam the previous Wednesday, which had meant that she'd dealt with two hours of teary eyes, disappointed sighs, and a whole plethora of statements that began with, "You should have..."

Her mother who definitely wouldn't be open to Teresa taking on another project—even if that project was her dream.

Because she should be done sowing her wild oats by now

(and yes, for her mother, working outside the home was *wild oats*).

Because she should be settling down and having a wedding that used up every dollar of the fund her mother had been saving in forever.

Because she should be popping out babies left and right.

"My baby!"

Her dad squeezed her again before releasing her and dropping her purse onto the small table her mom kept in the entryway for just that purpose.

"Hi, Mom," she said.

Tight arms around her, a warm, strong Mom Hug, before she released Teresa, before she pulled back, gripping her arms, and staring at her face, declaring, "You're not sleeping enough."

"I'm fine, Mom. Just a busy week at work."

Narrowed eyes, a deep inhale, the exhale releasing her next words. "You work too much."

Here it went.

"You'll never get married if you work too much."

Hey, Mom, she felt like saying. *Funny story, but I don't actually want to get married. Kids are a fifty-fifty, but marriage is a definite no.*

That would be *scandalous.*

"Dad said you cooked?"

Her mom paused, probably weighing whether or not it would be worth continuing to argue with her stubborn daughter. Thankfully, she appeared to decide to table the argument because then she wove her arm through Teresa's, and they went into the kitchen.

Which, admittedly, smelled delicious.

Her mom was a fabulous cook.

God knew she'd had plenty of time to practice at it.

She was also a great baker, a decent floral arranger, and could wrap presents with all the precision of a Hallmark employee.

Did they actually wrap presents there?

Maybe not.

But Teresa digressed.

The point was that her mom excelled at all things home and hearth, and that was fine. What *wasn't* fine? That her mom thought Teresa's entire existence needed to be that, too.

Find a good man.

Settle down.

Have babies.

Just thinking about the checklist her mom had tried to engrain in her over and over through her life practically gave Teresa hives.

She loved her life.

She wanted her mom to love what she was making of it, too.

But that wasn't to be.

So, she dealt with it, spent her requisite time with her family —dinner with her brothers every other week, mani-pedi nights with her mom, Saturday projects with her dad, and meals as her mother arranged.

She loved them, loved the time together.

She just...wished they could see her.

Wished they could love her for who she was, not who they thought she should be.

"Come and sit down, baby," her mom said, already pulling down plates and serving up some delicious smelling pasta. A bowl of salad was on the table, along with a basket of bread, a fruit salad, candles, and flowers. "You're too skinny. You need to eat more."

She *needed* to fit in her jeans.

But her mom had made pasta and homemade bread.

So, Teresa would be eating it (along with a bit of salad and fruit because she liked to pretend to be healthy...and both were tasty, too—they just weren't homemade bread and pasta).

"I can help," she said, moving toward her mom, reaching out a hand out for a plate.

"No, no. Sit. *Sit.*" Her mom scooped up a big serving of pasta, dropped it on the plate. "I'll bring it over."

Her dad, decades of this marriage under his belt, had the memo already, was in his seat at the table.

So, Teresa followed his lead, sinking into the chair opposite him.

Her mom served her dad first—as one did, at least in this household—then she set a plate in front of Teresa before grabbing her own plate.

"Eat. *Eat,*" she ordered as she sank into her own chair.

Teresa picked up her fork, shoveled up a mouthful, started chewing. But even before the delicious sauce was fully processed her taste buds, her mother dropped another slice of bread onto Teresa's plate.

Another *buttered* slice.

"More bread, baby."

Her shoulders inched up, discomfort boiling in her belly, competing with bites of pasta. "Thanks, Mom, but I'm fine—"

A beatific smile.

Another buttered bread hitting her plate.

"You'll never get a real man without curves on that body."

Teresa's shoulders inched up further.

That discomfort boiled over.

But she crammed it down, shoveled pasta and bread and fruit and salad to sit on top of it, felt the ropes *snick* in to keep it in place.

Just like always.

Eleven

Jeremy

"Why didn't you call me sooner?" he asked, peering behind the washing machine, and fiddling with the connection.

Yup.

Definitely dripping water.

Silence greeted him.

"Mom?" he asked again, trying to tighten the connector. It was thoroughly stripped, and water kept dripping, joining the little puddle on the floor, having soaked through the towel that she'd put there.

She reappeared at his side, bending beneath him, and scooping up the wet towel, dumping it into the sink, and replacing it with a new one.

"Because it's the middle of the week, and I have one person living at this house. My washer leaking isn't an emergency situation."

"You need to have a working washer."

A sigh. "Honey, stop."

"Mom. You're out here by yourself, none of us are really close—"

"You're saying thirty minutes—forty tops—isn't close?" she asked dryly, wringing out the towel into the sink basin.

"Well, it's not around the corner," he said, giving up on the fastener and stopping the cycle on the washer so no more water would run through the lines. "I'll have to go to the store and get some parts."

She stepped in front of him, swiping the line with a towel, drying the wall. "I have a plumber coming tomorrow."

"Cancel it," he ordered. "I can fix this."

"Honey."

There was a sharp edge to her tone that set him on edge.

He wiped his hands, leaned back against the doorway of her laundry room. "What's up, Ma?"

"I *have* a plumber coming tomorrow."

"It'll take me twenty minutes to go to the hardware store and back—"

"*Honey.*"

That wasn't just a sharp edge. It was sharp through and through, whipping across his skin and slicing deep. "What's wrong?"

A sigh, her face softening as she crossed to him and cupped his cheeks in both hands. "Nothing, honey. Just go to the hardware store. I'll keep dinner warm." She pressed a kiss to his forehead, dropped her arms, and moved into the hall.

He watched her go and thus, saw the slight shake of her head.

"Hey," he said, moving after her, catching her arm. "What's wrong?"

She tugged free. "It's fine, baby."

Maybe normally he would have taken that at face value, would have gone to the hardware store and taken care of the washer—

Stop trying to fix my life when I don't need it.

Teresa had said to him.

Said it with defeat in her eyes, as though expecting him to not listen, her posture so much like his mom's as she walked away from him...

It made him wonder.

Damn. It made him *wonder.*

He stepped in front of her. "Mom."

She sighed again, her head dropping forward so her chin plunked down against her chest. "Let's just have a nice night, okay?"

Said like she was trying to placate a small child.

"Mom, seriously, what the *fu*—heck?"

Her head came up, eyes locking with his. "You know, sometimes I really wish your father hadn't died."

He frowned.

Didn't they all?

"Or maybe I mean to say if he'd died, I wish he'd done it fast, not long and slow with plenty of time to fill your head with bullshit."

That—

Every muscle in his body went taut as hurt and disbelief rolled through him.

Now he didn't bother censoring the curse words she wasn't a fan of. "What the fuck?"

"It's bullshit, and it's going to mess up your life." A muscle in her cheek ticked when he stared at her, mouth falling open. "No, it already *has* messed you up."

"What—I—"

"He knew he wasn't going to be here. He knew that he was leaving you, me, *us*, and he told you things, made you promise stuff he shouldn't have." Her shoulders lifted then dropped on a breath. "You were a baby. He shouldn't have put that on you."

"I'm the oldest. I—Cora was just a baby. I was old enough—"

"No, sweetie." She gripped his arms. "*You* were a *baby*. You shouldn't have been worrying about taking care of me, about your siblings. You'd lost your dad, too. You should have been allowed to feel that, to grieve." Another sigh. "I should have allowed that."

"I didn't need that," he protested. "I was fine. I *am* fine."

Her eyes were sad, almost unbearably so. "And that's where I failed." A shake of her head. "That's where your dad failed. Where we *both* failed. I relied on you too much, and that wasn't fair—"

"Of course, it was fair, Mom. There was six of us and one of you. We wouldn't have gotten through it without working together." He took her hand. "I didn't mind then, and I don't mind now. I like taking care of you guys. I like being here for you now."

"Do you?"

He opened his mouth to repeat his previous statements, but something in her expression had him pausing, considering.

Did he like being the one to help? To step in and take over? To make sure everything was functioning as it should? To be certain that everyone was taken care of and had everything they needed?

Yeah.

He did.

Of course, he did.

Of course, he liked it.

That was who he was. That was how he showed his love. It had always been that way, would always *be* that way.

"Yeah, Mom. I do."

Silence.

Long, tense silence.

Long, tense silence filled with the growing sensation that he'd just disappointed his mother and had done it in a big way.

"Right, baby." She let her hands slide away, turned toward the kitchen again. "You go to the hardware store. I'll be here."

He felt like there were words she was thinking that she didn't speak out loud.

But he wasn't a fucking mind reader.

He wouldn't ever be.

Not even if the look she'd just shot him was too similar to the one that Teresa had given him in a different hallway, on a different night.

Not even if that look settled like a thorn in his belly, poking him, telling him nonverbally that something wasn't quite right.

That he was missing something.

Big.

Big and heavy and—

His mom stuck her head back out into the hall. "Go to the store, honey. I'm going to cancel the plumber."

Right.

He grabbed his coat from the hook and shrugged into it, listening to the sound of his mother canceling the plumber as she bustled around her kitchen, covering plates and popping them into the oven to stay warm.

Keeping dinner ready for him.

Taking care of him.

So, he would take care of her. Always.

He would take care of all of them. *Always.*

Just like he'd promised his father.

He grabbed his keys, shoved his cell into his back pocket, and slipped out the front door, locking it behind him.

The trip to the store didn't take long.

And it hardly took a minute to repair the water line, to stash the extra connectors he'd bought in case it happened again in his mom's toolbox.

Throwing in the wet towels and starting the wash only took a few more seconds.

They needed to be washed.

Plus, he needed to test the lines, to make sure they weren't leaking.

And if he moved them to the dryer before he went home after eating a delicious meal of meatloaf and mashed potatoes, then that was just because he was thoughtful and cared about her.

And if after he took care of the towels, he ignored the haunted look she gave him as he kissed her cheek and said goodbye...

It was only because he loved her.

Love was care.

Thoughtfulness.

Always.

Without exception.

TWELVE

TERESA

They were eyeing her plate, and she knew the next comment was going to piss her off.

"I'm not that hungry," she snapped, going on the offensive. "I told you that before we came here, if you remember?"

Here being a hamburger place they all loved—her included.

But the serving sizes were huge.

Think half-pound patties and an entire basket of fries. Per person.

Plus, she'd gotten a milkshake because...milkshakes were life.

And did she drink that first and possibly ruin her dinner?

Yes.

But it was Nutella flavored with chunks of cookie dough and a huge mound of whipped cream, slops of Nutella spooned over the top—all of which were melting and threatening to drip down the sides of the glass.

So, she had to take one for humanity and the dishwashers and bus people.

She'd had to save them from a pile of melted ice cream and Nutella.

Just doing her duty here, folks.

But all that duty meant that she'd barely had a quarter of her burger and certainly hadn't made a dent in her fries, aside from those she'd dipped in her shake, like any sane person would do.

"You're off," Anton, her eldest brother said, setting down his burger and doing his best to fix her in place with a look.

"I'm immune to that"—she said, waving a hand at his glare—"so just wipe it away. I'm off because I've had a long week, I'm fighting with a friend, and I saw Mom and Dad on Wednesday."

"Who?" Gabe snapped.

"Who am I fighting with?" she asked, not bothering to pretend she didn't know what he was asking.

A nod.

"None of your business," she told him, ignoring his scowl, the way he glanced at Anton, and silently solicited their older brother for help corralling their younger sister.

Anton—well, she and Anton were in an okay place at the moment.

He was still pushy.

But he'd hit up against her limits a couple of years ago, and she'd pushed back. Since then, she wouldn't say that he necessarily saw her as a capable equal. And yeah, that still stuck in her craw, but she'd long since learned that she couldn't change other people's opinions of her, could only control how she felt, where she found her worth, and who she spent her time with—the last of which Anton understood, because she'd made it fucking clear that would not be *him* after he'd showed up at her work and threatened Rafe about some stupid interaction with an a-hole of a client (not that her big, tough, protective boss had gotten upset, since they both spoke caveman, but thankfully, he had respected her enough to let her handle her own shit—AKA her own family).

Regardless, he'd gotten the message, and he'd backed off then, just as he did now when she shot him a look.

"I'm just saying you're off, T," Anton murmured. "Not that you owe me a verbal accounting of every thought and interaction of your week."

"Says who?" she grumbled.

He stole her spoon, scooped out some of the dredges of her milkshake.

"Hey!" she snapped, reaching for the spoon.

"Says me," he said, not giving it to her, still working on her shake.

Brothers. *Seriously.*

"What did the parentals do?" he asked.

She sighed, picked up a fry. "Nothing. They were their normal selves."

"So, they drove you an inch away from crazy," Anton quipped.

"Yup." She waggled her manicure, which, miracle of miracles, had survived mostly intact up until this point. "But at least Mom and I have nice nails."

Gabe leaned back, crossed his arms. "You know they mean well."

That was...triggering, though she bit back the retort that immediately wanted to escape.

She knew they meant well, but it was also a cop-out, dammit, because she'd told them how it made her feel unheard and incapable, how it smothered, how it made her want to lower and lower contact until she didn't see them hardly at all.

In fact, she'd done that.

During college.

Had gone to one on the other side of the country, stayed there for every holiday, got internships every summer so she didn't come home.

But then her mom had gotten sick.

And…Teresa had moved back.

She loved them.

Loved her family even though they drove her bonkers. She didn't want to miss out on time with them. She just wished…

All the same things she'd been wishing for years.

All the same things that wouldn't happen.

Because they wouldn't change…and neither would she.

Anton set the spoon down on the plate catching the overflow of her milkshake then wrapped his hand around hers, squeezing lightly. "I'll talk to them."

Again.

He'd get them to calm down.

They listened to him.

Kind of.

But then eventually fell right back into the same overbearing shit as had happened Wednesday, and look, maybe she was a whining asshole for complaining about her parents wanting to be too involved in her life, especially when so many other people craved to have parents who loved them, who wanted to be involved.

She was lucky.

But sometimes it was really hard to see that.

"Thanks," she said. "But I can handle them."

Anton studied her for a long moment, but eventually he nodded, picked up the spoon, and went back to her milkshake, the stink.

"You know," Gabe said, always on their parents' side. "We're lucky to have Mom here at all, and you know that it was a close call after Dad's heart attack."

"Yes," she agreed. "That's why I'm here in California."

Gabe's lips pressed together, but he didn't comment.

She held his gaze.

And thankfully, he let the topic drop, then proved exactly why she still had these dinners, why she loved the big lug.

Because unlike her parents, he could take the hint and move on.

"So, if you don't want to talk about your week and why it's put that grumpy, little sister expression on your face"—she narrowed her eyes in his direction—"do you have any update on the app?"

Her body relaxed.

She softened her glare, actually smiled at both of them.

And then she told them about the dinner—sans her wine throwing. She told them about the offers and the contracts she'd been sent and was reviewing—along with her attorney. She told them how she thought it was actually going to happen and she was going to get the funding she needed to get the necessary resources that the app needed to be successful.

"The actual coding is simple," she said. "I finished most of it just by watching YouTube tutorials, and the rest of it, my engineer helped me with. But I wasn't having much luck making the connections to get the actual listings from the various databases. Well, that, and the connections I did make were going to mean parting with more capital than I thought was prudent. But luckily, Rafe and Ben connected me with some people, and one lady in particular, Mrs. Jacobs, has a ton of real estate experience and has made a good offer."

"That's awesome," Anton said, snagging a few more of her fries.

"Yeah," she agreed excitedly. "And then if the rollout goes like planned, hopefully we can secure some advertisers. Eventually, I want to charge a fee to list a property and/or a membership cost or a match charge to expand the avenues of income. But that would be much further down the line. We need users first."

Pride on Anton's face.

Maybe even a glimmer on Gabe's, too.

They talked a few more minutes about her future plans— free memberships for those looking for low-cost rentals, charges for landlords who listed above market price, maybe even connecting homeless shelters and people looking for housing.

It was all big picture.

All hope that someone would want to use it.

But she had faith and she'd worked her ass off and it was so close she could almost picture this all beginning to happen.

So, she was going to hold on to that.

And she did through the rest of dinner, through hearing about Gabe's new job, through hearing about Anton and his girlfriend moving in together.

She held on to it through paying the bill (though Gabe won that round).

She held on to it all the way to her car, through Anton's hug and tug of her ponytail, through Gabe's squeeze.

But it slipped away when Gabe pulled back and ordered, "Don't be so hard on them, yeah?"

Same old shit.

Her sadness was a heavy, heavy cloak dropped onto her shoulders, weighing her down.

She'd relaxed.

She'd thought she and her brother might be making actual progress, but Gabe still saw her as a little kid he could order around.

And when push came to shove...

Nothing had changed.

She swallowed hard, shoved down the hurt, sat in the driver's seat, and said, "Yeah."

Then she closed the door, turned on the ignition, and drove away.

Things didn't change.

She'd forgotten that for a moment.

A sigh.

But she wouldn't forget.

Not ever again.

THIRTEEN

"I've got it," he said, snagging the bag of Gold souvenirs from Melody.

It was full to bursting, the presents for her nieces and nephews putting the plastic bag to its limits.

But she'd insisted on finding something special for each one of her nieces and nephews before she left the store.

It was sweet.

It was Melody.

She'd sent Tiffany and Wyatt off, tried to send him off as well, not wanting him to miss any of the game while she did her shopping.

But he'd stayed, not wanting to leave her alone.

And maybe that made him one of those controlling, alpha-holes that Teresa had been comparing him to.

Maybe he *was* controlling.

He preferred to think that he just cared.

Smothering a groan, knowing he wasn't any closer to an answer that made sense in his head, or one that he could stand to *keep* in his head, he rolled his shoulders.

"I can take that, you know."

He blinked, glanced down at Melody who was smiling up at him. "I'm fine."

The words were terse.

The words wiped that smile off Melody's face. "Okay," she whispered.

Fuck. He was an asshole.

He caught her arm, squeezed it lightly. "I'm sorry," he said gently. "It's been a hell of a week."

"You were rolling your shoulders like they hurt." Another whisper, so quiet he had to lean close to hear her over the din of the arena. "I didn't want you to hurt on my account."

Ass. Hole.

He leaned a little closer, squeezed her arm again. "I'm sorry," he said again. "It's not you. I promise."

A nod.

And he found himself moving closer still, cupping her cheek. "I really am sorry."

She nodded again, face gentling. "It's okay."

It wasn't, but he didn't want to draw this out further, so he just dropped his hand, straightened, and nodded toward the opening that would lead down to their seats. "Should we go watch some hockey?"

Melody smiled and they started walking. "You go ahead. I'm going to grab myself a drink and some snacks. Do you want anything?"

"No," he said, veering toward the food counter. "What do you want?"

"I can get it—"

He pulled out his wallet. "What do you want, Mel?"

"A pretzel, M&Ms, and a Diet Coke."

"Right." He turned to the worker, gave him her order,

brushing her aside when she tried to pull out her card to pay. "I've got it."

She grabbed the pretzel, he pocketed the candy, and picked up the soda, not wanting her to carry the cold drink.

"Good?"

"Yeah," she said, and her smile had taken on an edge he hadn't seen from her before. "Thanks for the...food." A nod to the snacks. "I didn't get a chance to eat dinner."

"Oh, Mel. Why didn't you say something earlier?" He turned back to the counter. "I'll get you something that'll actually fill you up—"

"No. Thanks."

Firm enough that he actually stopped.

Mel firm?

That was...strange.

So was the look in her eyes.

"You okay?"

"Fine."

Now she was the one doing the clipping out, rolling her shoulders as though she were shaking off an annoying buzzing bug.

"Let's go."

She took off for the stairs leading down to their seats, having to pause because the game had begun, and they needed to wait until a whistle to move along the aisle.

"What happened?" he asked.

A sharp breath. "I am capable of deciding when and what I want to eat, you know."

He rocked back slightly on his heels as her words collided with his eardrums—harsh and hard, and definitely not anything like the Mel he'd come to know during his brother's relationship with her sister. "Mel—"

A glare at him, at his hands, full of her drink, her bag. "*And* I can carry my own things."

The whistle blew.

She spun away from him, started marching down the stairs, fury in each step.

Blinking, thoroughly shocked and more than a little confused, he stared after her.

Then he realized he was staring and not moving, so he started descending, moving toward their seats.

"I'm sorry," he said as he caught up with her.

"Yeah, you said that before." Cold words and she didn't turn to face him. "I'm not incapable."

No, she wasn't.

He'd been helping.

He'd *thought* he'd been helping.

But instead, all he'd managed to do was piss off one of the most patient people he knew and make her think that *he* thought she was incapable.

Was that what he'd done to Cora?

To Teresa?

Fuck. Probably.

No. *Definitely.*

He'd done it to his mom, too, and...shit...he'd done it to every woman he'd ever dated.

Before he'd died, Jeremy's dad had told him to watch out for the women in his life, to protect them and care for them.

But his dad hadn't made his mom feel like she was useless, hadn't put that look in her eyes.

And he suddenly understood *exactly* what Teresa had been saying in the hall, finally understood what she was afraid he was going to do to her if she let him in.

Make her small.

Take away her choices.

Fuck. Was he seriously that much of an asshole?

Yeah.

Maybe even more of one because he'd always thought he was a good guy, always thought he was the *best* kind of man.

"I know you're not incapable," he said softly. "I do," he added when her shoulders crept up, body language telling him she didn't believe one word of what he was saying. "I—" A breath, and he just decided to level with her. "Look, someone recently told me that I have a tendency to take over. I didn't take her seriously—"

A snort.

"And now, I realize I should have."

A glance over her shoulder, eyes narrowed at him. "Yeah, you should have."

"Yeah," he agreed. "But I'm a stubborn asshole who likes to think he's right."

"A dumb, stubborn asshole," she muttered, turning around, and walking again.

"I might be dumb," he said as they started to shuffle along the row to their seats, wanting to see her smile, and glad that his self-deprecation managed to, at the very least, curve her lips up on the corner he could see. "But I can learn."

Her brows lifted and she shot him a look. "Really?" she asked dryly.

"Really," he said as they slid into their seats. "And while I can't promise I won't do it again," he admitted, which was probably not the smartest course of action, the smartest thing to say to the pissed-off woman next to him, admitting that he would probably fuck up at some point in the future. But though he might be an idiot, he wasn't a liar, wouldn't start now. "I *can* say I didn't get it before. I can tell you I didn't understand what the big deal was. I was taking care of the people in my life who mean something to me—"

She sat down, her expression having gone gentle. "I get that."

He sat, too. "I didn't get it, didn't understand what she was telling me."

Mel took the drink from his hand, plunked it in the cupholder. "She sounds smart."

"She is."

"She also sounds like the type of person you should be listening to."

Yeah, he should have been listening.

Not just Friday in the hall.

For the last three years.

Regret sliced through him.

Which must have shown on his face because Mel squeezed his hand. "It'll be okay."

He shook his head, staring out at the ice, feeling like an even bigger idiot than he'd first thought. "Nah, Mel," he muttered. "I fucked it. Well and truly fucked it."

"*Jer.*"

He looked back at her.

"You said she's smart."

He nodded. "She is."

A pat to his hand before she broke off a piece of her pretzel and offered it to him.

A piece he would have refused before.

A piece he understood now was a peace offering.

He took it.

Mel smiled.

"She's smart. So, *show* her you can learn, that you can see and understand her perspective, that you're not always a giant pushy pain in the ass, but a *good* guy." She glanced at the ice. "Show her that you can change, and she'll see it."

He inhaled, took a bite of that pretzel.

And smiled for the first time in a week.

Fourteen

"Booyah, mofos!" she declared the following evening, tossing down her last card. "UNO champion once again."

Cora groaned, tossing *her* final card onto the discard. "So freaking close."

"You'll never beat me, muahaha." She pressed her fingers together in a rolling pattern, a la the stereotypical evil genius ready to monologue.

"We will if we ban you from future Game Nights," Heidi, Cora's friend, grumbled, but she shot Teresa a smile that told her she was teasing.

Which Teresa ran with. "That *is* one way to win."

"Outside the box thinking is our specialty," Stef, another friend of Cora's, chimed in.

"Damn right it is," Kate, the final member of the trifecta of Cora's friends, said on a smile. "Because clearly UNO isn't."

That had them all laughing as Teresa shuffled the cards and

dealt the next hand. This time T wasn't the winner, but as always, it was a hard-fought battle until the end.

"All right," Steph said as she dropped her hand onto the table. "I'm UNO-ed out. Can we continue on with the bad reality TV and junk food portion of our night?"

There was a round of agreements, including from Teresa herself.

She'd survived her mother on Wednesday, her brothers yesterday, and though she was normally a social person, the game night scheduled for that evening hadn't been something she wanted to attend.

She'd actually considered blowing it off, staying home, and consuming her body weight in junk food, but then she'd decided that feeling mostly came from wanting to avoid Jeremy.

And she wasn't going to let the weirdness between them stop her from enjoying herself, from enjoying her friends.

She needn't have worried.

He hadn't shown.

Wyatt had, though, and he'd brought his girlfriend, Tiffany, and her twin, Melody.

That latter of whom had let it slip that the four of them had gone to the Gold game together. Twins on a double date.

How cute.

And Melody was beautiful and exactly the type of temperament that Jeremy wanted.

Sweet and soft. Moldable.

Not pushy and loud and with a sharp refusal of anything tying them together.

Just a really lovely person.

Teresa smothered a sigh but got up to get everyone another round of drinks, including Wyatt, Ben—Stef's man—and Rafe, who'd all absconded to the back deck.

Then she settled onto the couch, taking an open seat next to Melody.

(See? No hard feelings on Teresa's part).

That seat had a prime view of the front door, though it left a bit to be desired of the view of the crappy reality TV show they were all addicted to.

All of that meant, of course, that she saw the front door open.

And Jeremy walk in.

His eyes came to hers immediately, and she braced expecting...something. Something that wasn't him sending her a small smile, nodding, and moving toward her.

Breath going taut in her lungs.

Because he was coming close and yeah, she might not want a relationship—or *couldn't* have a relationship—with Jer, but he was still gorgeous and confident and sexy as fuck, and that fact bubbled through her veins...okay, no. That thought, those *facts* arrowed right between her thighs.

She sucked in a breath when he bent.

She'd told him to leave her alone. Demanded space. Set a firm boundary.

She should be pissed he was pushing it, that he was leaning in, bending toward...

Melody.

Kissing *Melody* on the cheek. "Hey, honey," he murmured in a soft voice.

Soft enough that she only heard it because she was sitting right next to Melody.

"Hey," Melody said softly, pressing a kiss to his jaw in return. "You good?"

"Yeah," he said, and maybe it was a little gruff.

Mel heard it, too, Teresa knew because the other woman pressed her palm to Jeremy's cheek. "Get yourself a beer and relax."

"Orders?" he teased, covering her hand with his own.

"You know me." Mel smiled. "Always with the orders."

He chuckled, straightened, and glanced at Teresa. "Hey, T," he murmured.

And then he was gone—or well, he'd gone into the kitchen —and she heard the fridge open, the soft *clink* of glass as he pulled out a bottle of beer, heard the soft *whoosh* of the sliding door, his footsteps as he moved outside to join the guys in the back yard.

And she...was there, eyes glued on the TV, the show playing but she hadn't absorbed as she settled in the fact that Jeremy hadn't pushed.

He hadn't *pushed*.

And she felt...

It didn't matter. He'd done as she'd asked, what she wanted.

She should be happy.

So why did him walking away from her feel like shit?

"Fuck," she whispered, knowing that she was so totally fucked up, so out of line. He was doing as she'd asked, and she was upset?

Fucked up.

"You good?"

She glanced at Melody and forced a smile. "Oh yeah, I'm good. I—" She straightened. "I just remembered something."

Lame.

But Mel was too nice to call Teresa on it.

"Oh," she said, smiling sweetly. "That's...challenging."

As challenging as Teresa's fucked-up brain conjuring up some bullshit? No. But an excuse that was going to allow her to extricate herself from this couch, this house, this situation? Yes.

"Yeah," Teresa agreed, and then excused herself, slipping into the kitchen and eyeing the plate of brownies.

She'd already had more than her fair share of them.

She walked toward the plate anyway, shoving one of the delicious chocolate squares into her mouth, and then another because she needed to medicate her fucked-up brain with cocoa powder and flour and eggs and a dash of salt and oil and...whatever the hell Kate put in these to make them taste good.

Weed?

The way she felt calm immediately settle into her veins made that a possibility, albeit one that was highly unlikely to be true.

Chocolate was medicinal, plain and simple.

That thought had amusement coiling in her belly, her lips turning up into a smile just as the slider opened and Jeremy walked in, his gaze behind him as he said, "No worries. I'll grab you one—"

He cut himself off when he turned forward, saw her hunched over the plate of brownies.

"You good?" he asked.

"Chocolate," she said unnecessarily.

His mouth quirked. "Right." But then he didn't engage further, just moved to the fridge, grabbing a couple of beers, and setting them on the counter.

Meanwhile, she shoved another brownie in her mouth.

The fridge closed while she frantically chewed and swallowed.

But he didn't come near her, didn't say anything. He wasn't giving her the silent treatment, and there was no tension in the room (aside from the tension in her head that had her reaching for still another brownie). In fact, as he used the bottle opener to pop off the metal caps, tossing them in the trash, he asked, "Need a top up?"

"I'm good."

"Okay," he said easily, putting the opener back down in front of the rest of the bottles of alcohol, cups, and various mixers and accouterments.

He snagged the beers, headed for the back door.

She should have shoved another brownie in her mouth.

She didn't.

Which was probably why she said what she said next. "Wait."

Okay, so it wasn't Shakespeare.

But it stopped him from stepping out onto the back porch, had him turning back toward her, lifting his brows in question.

"You and Mel?" she asked.

His expression went blank, and her heart sank. It shouldn't have.

It *shouldn't* have.

But his face was answer enough.

"T," he began.

She picked up another brownie. "I'm happy for you guys. She's perfect for you."

His lips parted, something in his expression that she couldn't discern. But then those lips pressed flat, turned up at the edges, and he nodded. "Thanks, T."

He slid open the door.

And disappeared out into the night.

Leaving her...to her fucked up thoughts.

And her brownies.

FIFTEEN

.

JEREMY

"And why do you think you would be a good fit for our company?"

Why?

He *knew* the fit wouldn't work.

He'd known that from the moment he'd walked into the lobby, checked in at the security desk, and waited for Cheryl, the hiring supervisor, to interview him.

The feel was wrong.

He wouldn't be happy here, not in the long term.

But it would be better than dealing with Bianca, with the meetings and emails and untenable hours.

And even if he didn't get this job, this interview was good practice.

For future interviews.

For future bullshitting.

For current bullshitting.

Which reminded him that Cheryl was staring at him,

patiently waiting for an answer. He needed to get on with the BS-ing.

So, he smiled, he bullshitted.

And he thought he did a decent job at spinning the truth with the lies, giving the softball question an answer that sounded genuine and personalized to the company.

Either way, that was the end of the interview, and he was in his car, heading back to work a short time later—the former felt like he was actually doing something to make his professional life better instead of just being miserable and feeling sorry for himself; the latter felt like shit, mostly because he walked into his office and Bianca was there.

He ground his back teeth together, paused in the doorway, and called, "Shan?"

His admin was coming out of the break room with a mug of coffee. She glanced up when he called her name, but her gaze went right to the window in his office, to Bianca standing inside, and her face filled with thunderclouds.

"Want me to take notes?" she asked as she came close.

"Please, God," he muttered.

A nod, punctuated by her grabbing a pad and pen, and then she preceded him into the office, plunking herself into a chair in front of his desk and clicking her pen. "Okay, I'm ready."

Bianca looked from Shannon to him.

"Go ahead," he encouraged.

And then he and Shannon waited.

For a long time.

"I need some help," Bianca finally said.

He lifted his brows.

"With the Murphy project."

"Tell me about it."

More waiting. A glance toward Shannon as though she expected the other woman to up and disappear.

When she didn't, Bianca huffed out a breath and snapped, "Never mind."

A moment later she was stomping out of his office.

"Trouble," Shan whispered once she'd gone.

"Yeah," he muttered and sighed. "Thanks."

She nodded, clicked her pen again, and grabbed her things. "Anytime."

He went back to his day, but not before he walked down the hall and made another report to HR.

———

She was here.

It was Sunday dinner.

He was trying to play it cool and not be a controlling asshole, but she was carrying a ton of fucking bags and struggling to open the front door.

Literally, every bit of civility demanded he take the bags, that he carry them in for her.

That he, at the very least, open the fucking door.

The last he could do.

That was being polite, not controlling.

But he couldn't lie and say he wasn't spending too much fucking time trying to wind his way through the maze of social situations and how he used to act and react and how he *should* react based on the confrontation with Teresa, that conversation with his mom, and Mel's fury at the Gold game. Even how Bianca was acting and what it made him feel was factoring in.

So...Jeremy was in the unenviable position of being a grown-ass man who'd spent the last decades thinking he knew exactly who the fuck he was and who he should be...

And now was reevaluating everything.

And trying to prove to the women in his life that he had taken note, was reevaluating, wasn't—

A controlling asshole.

So, there was that.

But he *could* open the door when someone's hands were full. Polite. Thoughtful. Not a pushy alpha-hole.

Of course, in the time it took for him to process that, Teresa had already made it up the walk and to the front door. He snagged the handle, pulling it open.

Her eyes went wide, and when his gaze dropped, he didn't miss the fact that her fingers coiled around the bag handles, as though expecting him to snatch them from her hands.

And, yeah, maybe he was a pushy alpha-hole.

Because a couple of weeks ago, he would have taken the bags, wouldn't have heard any of her arguments. Just would have taken them right from her grip and carried them through the house.

Making her bend to his will in the name of politeness, in the name of him caring for the people in his life, his family.

Yeah, that realization didn't feel good.

None of these new understandings over the last couple of weeks had felt good.

"Um..."

He blinked, realized he'd opened the door but hadn't stepped back to let her in the house. "Sorry," he muttered, moving his ass out of the way.

"All good," she said, brushing by him, the bags rustling as she moved.

"Need some help?" he couldn't help but offer.

"I'm fine," she said immediately. Automatically.

"Yeah," he whispered, turning from her, closing the door with a decisive *snick*. "Everyone's in the kitchen," he added, flicking the lock.

She started heading that way then paused, glanced over her shoulder, staring up at him, studying his face. As though searching for some answer that she wouldn't get. Or maybe for an answer she already had, considering the way her brows pulled together, her head tilted to the side.

"Are you feeling okay?"

His entire foundation had been crumbling over the last couple of weeks, shifting everything he'd thought he should be, how he should act. He'd been helping, just being a "good guy." But he'd nearly pushed his sister away, annoyed the shit out of his ever-patient mother *and* Mel.

Show her you can learn, that you can see and understand her perspective, that you're not always a giant pushy pain in the ass, but a good guy. Show her that you can change, and she'll see it.

Mel.

Smart, thoughtful words.

"Yeah," he said, and normally he would have brushed it off, coaxed the bags from her. But instead, he decided to tell the truth. "What you said to me..."

Regret on her face.

Regret that had him moving closer, cupping her jaw. "No, it was the right thing to say. I needed to hear it. I just..." He inhaled and shook his head. "I just didn't quite understand what it was going to make me ponder." His eyes connected with hers. "I'm glad you told me," he said again.

It was just that pretty much everything he was feeling and thinking had changed.

And the woman standing in front of him with her arms laden with bags was responsible for it.

But he didn't tell her that.

Her brows dragged even closer together. "It wasn't all you," she said. "I mean, I don't think we'd be good together because we want different things. But...that explosion." A breath released slowly. "It came more from me." Her voice dropped. "And from my own hang-ups, my own past."

He wanted to dive in, to demand answers.

Show her you can learn, that you can see and understand her perspective.

He bit his tongue.

"I understand," he said softly, though he couldn't ignore the fact that she was carrying the bags, that they looked heavy, that he should be carrying them. "Really, I do."

He bit the inside of his cheek, pushed down the urge to take the bags.

She didn't want that.

More studying. More staring into his eyes as though she could see his soul.

Then, surprisingly, she smiled and lifted one arm.

"These are getting heavy, mind carrying them into the kitchen for me?"

Sixteen

Teresa

Stupid.

She'd fought him about taking care of her.

And now she'd let him carry the bags in, as though they were so heavy she couldn't handle the weight. Probably undoing any progress he might have made.

Stupid.

It was just...he looked so unsure standing there, and a little sad.

And he *hadn't* been pushy.

Not in that moment.

Not last night.

Woo-hoo! He'd acted like a normal human being for two whole nights in a row. Color him changed! Now it was time to throw herself naked on the altar of feminine sacrifice, her thighs falling right open so he could slip between them and fuck her senseless.

Right.

She might be losing it.

Too much socializing this week.

Too much of this man, *any* men.

Too much—

A breath. *Or* she could make this not a big deal and just let the man carry the bags in because he'd offered and they *were* heavy and she was still carrying half of them.

He hadn't commented after he'd slid the bags off her wrist and gripped them, just moved past her and into the kitchen, holding the plastic handles in big, strong hands.

Big, strong hands that had probably been on Melody's body.

Which...was a thought that shouldn't have even entered the atmosphere around her mind, no matter that Mel was nice and good for Jeremy. Plus, she was a twin, and *her* twin was dating Jeremy's twin brother, Wyatt. They had that twin with twin thing that always ended up on the cover of *People* with an adorable photo showcasing the foursome and—

Losing it.

Teresa was *losing it.*

She shook her head, forced her feet into motion, and carried her half of the bags into the kitchen.

"Teresa!" Mrs. Hutchins cried, coming over to her, and pressing a kiss to her cheek. Her hands were covered in some sort of food—maybe cookie dough—and oh, please God, let it be cookie dough.

"Mrs. H!" she cried back, turning her head so she could press her own kiss to the Hutchinses' mom's cheek.

"Edy, honey," she corrected gently—as she always did.

"Right, Mrs. H."

An indulgent smile, a small shake of her head, but then her eyes went to Teresa's arm, full of bags, and to the side. Teresa turned, saw that Jeremy was setting down his load.

"What have you done?" she asked quietly.

Teresa smiled. "Mom was busy baking today. She dropped by a few things. Don't worry," she stage-whispered. "It's not all for you. She packed up plenty for the boys and Cora and Rafe. And I think for Tiffany and Mel, too."

Her mom might have made her entire life about creating a home, taking care of her husband, her kids, but she was also thoughtful.

No one would be left out on her watch.

And definitely, no one's belly would *dare* to leave her presence without being full to bursting.

"That's so sweet," Mrs. H said. "I'll have to have them over for dinner as a thank you."

"My mom would like that." She leaned a little closer and touched the bag at her elbow. "I also have those books that we talked about." A wink. "I'll put them in your bedroom."

Excitement in Mrs. H's eyes. "Oh, from the series we talked about last weekend?"

Teresa nodded. "Yup."

A wide smile. "I know what I'm doing tonight."

"Bath, early bedtime, and staying up into the wee hours reading?"

"Yup!" Another kiss to Teresa's cheek. "I'm gonna finish these up." Her lips curved. "Glad I made your favorite."

Pumpkin chocolate chip.

Booyah, motherfucker!

She did a little fist bump, deposited the rest of her mom's spoils next to the bags Jeremy had left on the counter then dropped the books in Mrs. H's bedroom.

When she came back, the bags were where she'd left them— and yeah, maybe that was a little weird. Normally Jeremy would have unpacked everything, stacked the containers, folded and stored the bags, but he'd brought the bags in and left them, and was...sitting at the old, scarred table shoved into one corner of the kitchen.

By Melody.

Teresa sucked in a breath, released it, slowly.

Right.

Then she moved to the bags and began unpacking.

———

"Thanks for the cookies, Mrs. H," she said, wrapping her arms around Jeremy's mom, and hugging her tight.

"Edy."

"Right," she said lightly.

A tug of her hair. "Thanks for the books."

She leaned back. "Enjoy them."

"Oh, I will." A nod to the container in her hands. "Enjoy *them*."

"I will." She waved, exchanged goodbyes, and then headed down the walkway, moving to her car. She'd had to park a little ways down as parking was always tight and the Hutchinses were a large crew, so she was down around the corner, well out of sight of Mrs. H's house.

Normally, Jeremy or one of the guys would have walked her.

But though Rafe and the rest of the boys had offered, she'd turned them down. It was early yet, and this was a safe neighborhood, and she could walk herself to her car.

Look at her go.

Jeremy hadn't offered, though.

Not after she'd thanked Rafe and refused his escort (and then refused Wyatt and then the rest of the brothers). Her gaze had locked with Jer's for a moment after the exchange with his brothers, but he'd just given her a nod and had let her walk out of his mother's house.

What alternate reality had she stepped in?

Was he really changing because of what she'd said?

She...was a little unnerved.

Mostly because she kept hearing Admiral Ackbar in her head declaring, *It's a trap!*

But he hadn't followed her out, hadn't protested, and as she approached her car—she did a quick scan—he hadn't somehow gotten ahead of her and was waiting in the bushes.

She was alone.

Gloriously alone.

So, why didn't she feel good?

Why was all that glorious *aloneness* sitting heavily on her chest as she got into her car and started up the engine, driving down the quiet, dark road?

She had gotten what she wanted.

Exactly what she wanted.

Right?

SEVENTEEN

JEREMY

"Mom?"

She was standing with her back to him, her hands in the sink, the water running, the dishes being washed with the speed of a woman who'd raised seven (okay, basically eight considering Rafe had practically lived there) kids in a house where there was a constant revolving door of friends coming and going.

No matter how tough things were, there was always food in the fridge and pantry, a batch of cookies in the jar.

"I don't need help, honey," she said.

"I know." He leaned back against the counter next to her, hopping up and sitting on the granite he and Rafe had installed.

She slanted a look in his direction and he immediately hopped back down. Well trained he was. "You know doing the dishes clears my head."

"Pretty much the only time you got the least bit of quiet."

Her gaze drifted to his. "Because we'd all disappear as soon as the sponge came out?"

A grin. "Exactly." She leaned toward him, eyes twinkling. "Spoiler alert, I didn't mind."

He laughed, picking up a towel as she dropped a pan on the drying mat, wiping it down, and stacking it next to him as she continued washing.

But he didn't say anything further, just gave her the quiet as he sat on the counter, drying the pots and pans.

When she'd finished washing up, he put them away as she loaded the dishwasher.

"Are you okay?"

"I'm fine."

A pause. "I wanted to apologize."

He closed the drawer under the sink. "For what?"

She shot him a look.

Right.

The stuff about his dad, and all the shit that had been swirling around his brain for days now.

"It's fine, Mom."

She snagged the towel from him. "It's not," she said softly, surprising him by hopping up on the counter and patting the spot next to her.

He joined her, her familiar scent—flowers, baked goods, *Mom*—surrounding him.

She glanced at him, stated baldly, "I meant what I said. I wish your dad hadn't put those thoughts in your mind."

His brows tugged together.

"I'm *so* glad you're kind and thoughtful and care about the people in your life."

Those were good things. Those were the *right* things.

A shake of her head, as though she read his thoughts. "But I hate that we somehow made it so that your entire identity comes from taking care of others and not thinking about yourself, baby." She sighed. "I mean, I don't think that you've thought about *you* first from the moment your dad died. No," she added. "I think it might even go back as far as from when he got sick and wanted you to watch out for us all."

"This wasn't parentification, Mom," he felt obligated to add. "You guys let me be a kid."

"Did we?" she asked softly. "Did *I?*" Another shake of her head. "I'm not so sure."

"I didn't even know how to do laundry until I was nineteen and you got tired of me bringing my clothes back from school."

Her lips curved. "Yeah." But then she sobered. "But did you ever have a night out where you weren't thinking about your siblings? About me?"

"Mom—"

"In the years since, have you ever fully detached from us, had a weekend partying with your buddies and not spared us a second of worry?"

He paused.

But it didn't take long to know the answer to that.

It was no.

He'd spent the majority of his life worrying about them—about his mom and if she was overwhelmed, about his siblings and making certain they remembered their dad, that they were happy and healthy. He'd helped with homework and college applications. He'd taken them to movies and talked about girl-friend problems.

"Have you even had *one* night of that?" his mom pressed.

"Mom."

"Did you *ever* know what you wanted? Or did we always shadow every decision?" Her hand came to his arm, gripped tight. "Do you even know what you want now? Or is all of it tangled together, knotted so tightly that you can't look into your own mind and make a decision that isn't somehow connected to what *we* need?"

His nostrils flared when he sucked in a breath.

And that was answer enough.

"I was wrong to let you do that," she whispered, eyes glimmering with tears. "*He* was wrong to engrain that in you, but I should have put a stop to it."

He released that breath. "You worked your ass off. We had to come together to make it work."

"Maybe." She rubbed her hands on her jeans and sighed.

His heart was pounding.

Because he was thinking about all of those questions, and he was thinking about the answers.

He didn't know what he wanted—except that he wanted Teresa.

He didn't know if he'd *ever* made a decision for himself.

He hadn't had a weekend where he wasn't worried about his mom or his siblings—fuck, he had six of them. There was always something or someone to worry about.

"That wasn't your job then," she said. "And it isn't your job now."

It was instinct to want to argue, but the conversations with Mel, with Teresa, with his mom before, they were all floating around his brain, telling him to slow down, to think about the answers to those questions that hit hard and fast and deep.

It wasn't his job to take care of everyone in his life.

It *wasn't* his job.

"It's easy, you know," she whispered when he didn't reply. "Easier to spend so much time making your life about everyone else."

"What do you mean?"

"If you spend all of your time worrying about everyone else, you don't have to think and reflect. You don't have to look closely, to consider what you want, to *dream*. And if you don't have time to do any of that, then you get to stay in your safe little box, never putting yourself out there. Never *risking* anything. Spending your life hiding."

He inhaled sharply. "Ah, hell, Mom."

"Sorry, honey. I should have said these things to you long ago." She touched his cheek. "And if it happened today, if I lost your dad and was back being a single mom with seven kids today, I would have done so much differently."

He was still reeling from her words, but he managed to say lightly, "Hindsight."

Her lips pressed flat then tipped up at the edges. "Yeah. And it's a pain in the ass."

His mom so rarely cursed that it shocked a laugh out of him.

"I really am sorry," she whispered.

"I'm okay, Mom," he said. "I swear."

"I know you're okay," she muttered, rubbing her hands on her thighs again. "But I don't want you to just be okay. I want you to be happy. I want you to be with someone you love."

So did he.

But she didn't want him, not as he was.

And that—

"What is it, baby?" She cupped his jaw, turned his head toward her. "What's eating at you?"

Besides the earthquakes continuing to strike his mind, rattling everything and making him think way too much?

He could lie, like he might have before this conversation.

He could pretend he was fine.

He could tell her about Teresa.

No.

He couldn't do any of that, not right then.

But he could take a baby step forward, could let those words sit inside his mind, store them to consider later. And he could do that later, but still be open with her now. He could step outside of his comfortable, safe box and *share*.

So, he told her about work, about Bianca. He should have

probably talked to her about Teresa, about what she'd said, what *Mel* had said, and how those talks had mirrored their conversation from the other day.

But that...was an open wound.

He needed time to heal, to think, to *dream*.

For now, though, he slid back the lid and peeked out.

Eighteen

Teresa

She clicked her pen and tucked it into its spot on her trusty clipboard.

Had one of the guys stolen it last night and returned it surreptitiously with her name bedazzled on the back?

Yup.

Was she rocking the sparkles today anyway?

Also, yup.

Also, she was kind of liking the sparkles. They went with the chipped glittery polish on her fingernails.

She hugged it to her chest, an unconscious action she knew she did regularly because Rafe had pointed it out more than once. So now she was aware she did it but still couldn't stop herself, mostly because she was keeping her list safe. It was all backed up, of course, something she printed out every morning and updated in the evening before she shut down for the night.

But there were her notes from the day that could be lost.

And, frankly, the list was her baby.

If it was damaged or misplaced or stolen by a freak robber

who really, really liked her bedazzled clipboard, then she was going to be frantic.

And sad.

Because...sparkles!

(Also, did she do mental jazz hands as she thought that? Maaaaybe).

Grinning to herself, she looked up at her boss. "What?"

Rafe shrugged. "Did you note the change about the trim?"

"Of course, I did," she said before adding, "As you well know."

He nodded, but the expression on his face didn't clear.

"What?" she asked.

A blink and then his face had returned to normal. "Nothing, kid." He ruffled her hair. "Just gonna miss you and your clipboard when you're gone."

"Because of the sparkles?" she quipped.

"Because you're my right hand," he said. "You know what I need before I need it."

She did.

Part of that was because they'd worked together for a long time, and she knew Rafe like she knew the back of her hand. Part of it was because she was smart and capable and while this job had a lot of moving parts, it wasn't rocket science.

She just needed to make certain that everyone had the things they needed at the right time.

Simple as that.

"You'll find someone else."

He groaned. "I'm not ready."

A pat on his arm. "Don't worry, honey. I'll train them up good for you."

"Them singular or them plural?"

She paused, considered that. "Probably plural."

Another groan, but then his gaze went to the windows. "You going to come to lunch with us?"

Teresa glanced around the space, doing a quick check. The crews were working, and she had to put the new trim order in before going to the next job site.

But she had time for lunch.

Especially when it meant that she could hang out with Cora and the two of them could give Rafe shit.

"Sure. Where are you guys going?" she asked, albeit a little distracted—mostly because she'd just noticed that one of the boxes of flooring that had been delivered was wrong. "I'll drive myself so I can head to the Thompson site," she said as she pulled her pen out and made a note to track down what had happened.

"Luciano's," Rafe said.

"Sweet," she said, hearing the door open as she was finishing her addition.

"I knew you'd feel that way." He grinned down at her just as his cell rang. Frowning, he pulled it out, glanced at the screen. "Aw, fuck. It's fucking Jenkins," he muttered. "Would you mind driving him over, and I'll meet you there? This will take a while."

"Sure," she answered before she fully processed the words.

Mostly because Luciano's had the *best* homemade pasta, and she was mentally licking her lips in preparation of bread and fettuccini alfredo.

Yum.

"Wait, *him?*" she asked, glancing up and seeing Jeremy walking across the space.

"Jer," Rafe was already calling across the room. "Teresa's your ride. Meet you there."

"Wait," she said again, but Rafe was already swiping across the screen, already answering the call.

And Jeremy...

Jeremy was staring at her, *watching* her.

Waiting to see what she would do.

Her fingers clenched on the clipboard; she sucked in a breath through her nose.

Her eyes hit on that box of flooring, the one that didn't fit.

And she sighed.

"Come on then," she said, walking over to him. "I need carbs."

They'd gotten in her car, and she was driving them to the restaurant before he spoke again. "You know that Rafe probably arranged that."

She shot him a look.

"To get us together."

Another look, this time with raised brows.

"Not..." A shake of his head. "Not *together*, but to make peace between us."

"There's not peace between us?"

Now it was his turn to raise *his* brows. "I mean," he said. "You made it pretty clear that I fucked up and did it big."

And then she'd gotten all soft on him and let him carry her bags.

Ugh.

"That's because you did."

"I'm not denying that," he said. "I..." His gaze shifting, going out the window. "You're not the first person to say that," he murmured, then sighed. "You're just the first person who really got through."

She paused, considering that as she made a right turn. "Why?"

He laughed, and it wasn't exactly warm. "Because I want you. Because I'd imagined it, pictured how good things would be between us. But you were right," he said softly. "I don't really know you." A beat. "Or maybe it was just that I didn't know myself."

Teresa waited for him to expand on that, to make sense of the last, but he didn't.

He fell quiet.

"What do you mean?" she pressed after a moment, pulling to a stop at a red light, glancing over at him. A muscle in his jaw flexed, and his gaze continued to be fixed on whatever he was looking at outside the window.

But he didn't answer her.

"Jer?"

He turned toward her. "Did you always know who you were inside?"

Talk about a rapid swerve in conversation...and paid with what he'd said a few moments before...

Well, this was getting to be a lot more complicated than she'd first thought—this wasn't big, broody alpha meets woman and goes caveman.

This was...shadows in his eyes and a hint of hurt and—

This wasn't the Jeremy she knew.

"Jer," she whispered, reaching out a hand, intending to grab his, to soothe some of that hurt, but he didn't move, didn't allow her fingers to wrap around his.

He just nodded slightly. "The light is green."

She pulled back, pressed her foot down on the gas pedal, and she drove.

"No," she whispered after a moment, slanting a glance in his direction. "Hell, half the time, even now, I don't know what's going through my mind."

Silence.

Then, "Really?"

"Yeah," she whispered, "and I think that's why I reacted so poorly to"—one hand off the steering wheel, gesturing between them—"I was reeling."

About what she was feeling and *should* be feeling and what that kiss had done to her soul.

Because with one touch of his lips, he'd made her feel more than Sam had.

Because that undid everything.

Because she had a hole inside her, and she didn't want to fill it with another person, *couldn't* risk doing that and losing what she was. She wanted—no, she *had*—to fill it herself.

"I'm sorry for that," she whispered. "I shouldn't have acted like that."

"I was the one who was out of line. I thought..."

She waited as he trailed off, as he paused again.

"Well, I thought a lot of things." He shot her a smile. "Clearly, I'm wrong."

That was...heavy. That stung her, mostly because she could feel that *he* was hurting, that part of it was her fault. So, searching for a way to lighten the conversation, she said, "Happens to the best of us."

A rough chuckle. "I guess it does."

"So," she asked, continuing along that vein. "You really think Rafe arranged this?"

"Of course, he did."

"Even Rafe doesn't have the power to summon Jenkins's complaining phone calls."

Jeremy glanced over, lifted a brow.

She paused, realized that he could have easily set a call with Jenkins, knowing that Jer was coming for lunch, that she wouldn't turn down Luciano's. "Damn interfering man," she muttered.

Another chuckle, this one less rough. "We do that."

Sighing, she turned into the parking lot. "And you think he wants peace?"

"I know he does." A beat. "It's a pain in the ass for his right hand and his best friend to be at odds."

A curl of mischief (okay, some might say *evil)* trailed through her belly as she put the car in park and turned to him.

"What do you think he would think of that right hand and best friend coming together?"

"For?"

She rubbed her hands together, a burst of fake evil laughter filling the car. "For dastardly deeds, of course."

Amusement in his eyes.

A smile on his face.

Something settled in her.

Then settled further when he brushed his fingers along the back of her hand and grinned. "I'm in."

Nineteen

Jeremy

Our dastardly deeds begin today. Jenkins job site. 5 pm.

It was five after five, and he was late because he'd been waylaid by HR on the way out the door.

They weren't going to take any action against Bianca.

It was...frustrating.

But not unexpected.

She hadn't really *done* anything (their words, not his), and he'd found out that she was the owner's niece.

Nepotism.

How...cliché.

Ultimately, he needed to get the fuck out.

So, once he'd finished with whatever evil act Teresa had in mind for them tonight, he was going full steam ahead with the resumé submissions.

How he would end up with a position that wasn't going to lend him the same unhappiness, he didn't know.

But he had to at least try.

Try to do something better. Try to think about what he wanted, as foreign as that concept was.

A knock on his window had him snapping out of his mind, turning to see that Teresa was standing outside his car.

And fuck.

Her smile.

It was *her* smile, and it was pointed at him, and it wasn't brittle and filled with sharp edges because he'd pushed her so far that she was keeping her distance.

It was *Teresa*.

His heart skipped a beat and then expanded in his chest, pushing against his ribs.

"Come on, hot shot," she called through the glass. "Let's go."

He turned off the engine, popped open the door. "Hey."

Early evening sunshine clung to the edges of her blond hair, to her brows that dragged together into a frown, to the clipboard in her arms that was...sparkling.

"Um..." He pointed at her name, emblazoned in sequins. "Care to explain?"

"Explain what?" She glanced down. "Oh." A roll of her eyes. "The guys decided I needed sparkles."

He grinned. "Because of your sparkling personality?"

"Damn right." Her chin came up, lips twitching. But then she sobered, head tilting to the side. "You good?"

No.

He was a fucking mess.

Work was fucked. His head was *more* fucked. He was reconsidering everything from his personality to how he interacted with his family to what he wanted in the future.

But he didn't want to think about that right then.

He just wanted to be in this moment, wanted to enjoy hanging out with Teresa, even if it was for dastardly deeds.

Hell, who was he kidding?

He was looking forward to being dastardly, to doing the deeds, to hatching whatever plan it was that Teresa had come up with to torture his best friend.

Friends tortured friends?

Well, sometimes.

And that thought had him relaxing enough to close his door, to lock up, to turn to Teresa. "Dastardly deed time?"

"Jer," she said. "You good?"

"No," he admitted. "But I want to forget about that for a while."

She studied him closely, eyes piercing him. Then she nodded. "I can make that happen."

He reached out, tugged lightly on a strand of hair that had escaped her ponytail. "I know you can."

Lips parting, eyes warming.

Their bodies were close.

He could feel the warmth of her, smell her shampoo, see the flecks of gold in her irises.

But she didn't back up, and he felt the heat of her breath on his skin.

Close. So fucking close.

God, he wanted her.

Wanted to spin them, to press her back against the side of his car, to kiss her—*no,* to fuck her with his mouth, to fuck her with his cock.

Her nostrils flared.

The gold in those irises expanded.

Her lips parted, the tip of her pink tongue dipping out, tempting him.

A breath.

Then he managed to summon the strength to step back.

"Dastardly deed time?" he asked lightly.

She went still and, fuck, if her body didn't come a little

closer, tempting him further. But then her lids slid closed, and she released a breath, and—her eyes opened.

Gold tempered.

Tongue safely in her mouth.

"Yes," she said quietly. "Dastardly deed time."

———

"Rafe is going to kill me," he muttered two hours later.

Teresa tore the plastic wrap with her teeth, tucking the roll into its box, and smacking it into his open palm.

He gave her his other hand, helped her up, not that she needed the assistance.

But frankly, he was taking every chance he could to touch her.

Feeding the need inside him.

Not pushing.

And she'd come.

Letting him help her make mischief, letting him touch her.

Letting him assist with her torture of Rafe.

"What are you talking about?" she asked lightly as she hopped to her feet, slipping her hand from his, turning to study their handiwork.

And grinning.

"He's going to love it," she added, studying the toolbox that had been wrapped in the thin, stretchable sheet of plastic, inside of which were his tools...each of which had been neatly covered in that same wrap.

The man wasn't going to be able to so much as open a box or hammer a nail or screw a screw without fighting with the clinging plastic.

"He's going to hate it," Jeremy said.

"He's going to hate it," Teresa agreed.

He fought a smile. "It's going to be great."

Teresa didn't fight it, just let the smile out. "It's going to be great," she agreed again.

Fuck, if laughter didn't bubble up in his throat, if it didn't escape into the space around them. Hell, if he didn't feel so much fucking better after their *dastardly deeds*, even if their fun would be at Rafe's expense.

Though, he supposed he owed his best friend at least *one* dastardly deed considering he still hadn't forgiven Rafe for hijacking his container of Oreos and replacing all the centers with toothpaste.

Toothpaste.

Had that happened in the last ten years? No.

Had it happened in college when they were assholes who got off on stuff like that? Yes.

But...toothpaste!

Plastic wrapping Rafe's tools was only a small payback.

Plus, Oreos had been expensive as fuck for him back then. He'd barely been able to afford the necessities—

No.

He could have afforded more, but he scrimped and lived on a hundred dollars a month (after room and board) because he hadn't wanted to ask his mom for anything else.

Because Wyatt had been in school, too.

Because she had other kids to take care of.

Because it had all been too much for her.

Because...

No.

What had he wanted?

To not be a burden by being the one who was taking.

So, he never took...which meant he'd been the most noble, the most self-sacrificing and virtuous and—

Fingers on his jaw.

"What are you thinking about?" Teresa asked softly.

He pushed that down, focused on the concerned woman in

front of him. "Everything and nothing and too many things at once."

Her eyes gentled, lips turning up. "Well, that's cryptic."

He snorted. "You said some things"—guilt on her face that had him covering her hand, pressing her palm to his cheek, stymieing her apology—"*good* things. But..." A sigh. "They've turned me introspective."

"Which is a good thing?" she asked, disbelief in every syllable.

"Yeah." He smiled again. "Mostly because it distracts me enough to participate in dastardly deeds that are going to piss Rafe off." A beat. "Win-win in my book."

She allowed him the change in subject, flattening her fingers lightly against his jaw before slipping her hand free.

"If you say so."

"I say so."

Her lips twitched, but then she tilted her head to the door, and he listened to her unspoken cue to leave the building, holding the door for her as she followed him, waiting while she set the alarm and locked up, walking her to her car, waving as she drove away.

None of which she protested before he got into his own car and went home to his resumé.

Maybe because he was learning—caring but also taking, *sharing* enough that she wasn't the only one who had to be vulnerable.

In fact, *he* was the weaker one in the moment.

In fact, *he* was the one who was taking.

But for once that didn't make him feel anything but settled.

Didn't make him feel weak or selfish.

And it was all because of Teresa and a couple of tubes of plastic wrap.

Fuck, life was weird sometimes.

TWENTY

TERESA

"It's as good as done, my dear," Mrs. Jacobs said, signing her name with a flourish on the contract. "We'll get these to my attorneys and yours, and then I get to sign a check."

"I thought rich people didn't like to give their money away."

"We don't mind loaning it." A grin. "So long as it comes with a hefty return."

Teresa stacked her copies of the contract and smiled. "I'll do my best."

Mrs. J patted her hand. "I know you will."

They spent the next couple of minutes talking about logistics and setting up a few standing meetings both with Mrs. J and her business manager for regular check-ins and mentoring.

Each was important considering the stakes and the amount of money Teresa was soon going to have in her possession.

She needed to be smart and careful.

She needed to not fuck up this opportunity.

So, she was going to be working her ass off, taking advantage of every meeting offered, and she was going to *do this*.

After she walked Mrs. Jacobs to her car and said goodbye. *After* Game Night.

———

"So that's it," she said softly, drying the pot that Jeremy had been scrubbing. "My life is about to get a hell of a lot busier." She dried the outside, dragging the towel up the gleaming sides, over the handles. "Honestly, I didn't expect it all to happen this fast. I thought that it would take months and I wouldn't still be working on all these projects with Rafe. I *thought* I'd be training my replacement and eventually flitting off into the world of entrepreneurship."

"What do they do in the *world of entrepreneurship?*"

"Eat, drink, ritual sacrifices." A beat before she added dryly. "You know, the usual."

He laughed. "What are you sacrificing?"

"Free time, sanity, and the chance to take it all at Game Night."

"Ah," he said, lips turned up into a smile, "is that why you lost tonight? Your poor little brainy brain is all tired from your *meeting?*"

She swatted him with the towel. "I'll have you know, it's a brain-brain *not* a little brainy brain."

"I stand corrected."

"And it is tired." She rolled her shoulders. "*I'm* tired, but it's not just because of the meeting."

"Too much focus on coming up with new dastardly deeds?"

Now *her* lips turned up. "Yes." A beat. "Plus, my fingers hurt from helping Rafe take off all that plastic wrap."

"Your idea."

A glance over her shoulder to where the rest of their group was still playing games. "Yeah, so?"

He stepped closer, one sudsy hand resting on the counter right next to her hip.

And her heart began thudding.

Her thighs pressed together.

Desire pooled in her belly, gathered in her fingertips, making them shake with need.

"So, I guarantee that Rafe isn't buying your little innocent act," he murmured, mouth close to her throat, making her shiver.

"I know."

Rafe did, too, which was why she'd spent several hours with him unwrapping the plastic that morning, helping while he grumbled (though he *had* laughed outright when he'd first seen it).

"So, why are you in here instead of in there terrorizing the crew?" he asked. "Plotting new shenanigans?"

Another glance over her shoulder, but they were firmly entranced in a new game that Melody had brought called *You've Got Crabs*.

It was fun.

But Teresa hadn't been in the mood.

She really *was* tired, after work, after her meeting, after running around and getting stuff together for tonight. But it was more than that. When Jeremy had slipped into the kitchen and begun doing the dishes, she'd followed him. Not because she was annoyed he was doing the dishes without her asking (pushy alpha male syndrome rearing its ugly head as he helped—again—without getting her permission).

But she hadn't cared about that.

Instead, she'd followed him because of the look in his eyes.

"No," she murmured. "No shenanigan planning."

"Really?" he asked, damp fingers brushing hers.

"Really." Honestly, she had no clue what she was doing in here, with this man.

Except...she didn't feel numb when she was with Jeremy. Instead, it was a cacophony of emotions, of thoughts, of contradictions.

Get closer. Stay away.

Embrace the feelings. Run from what they'll turn her in to.

"What's going through that head of yours?" he whispered.

"Too much," she whispered back.

Warmth in his eyes, his damp finger brushing her cheek. "In what way?"

Yeah, she wasn't touching that one with a ten-foot fucking pole. "Why don't you tell me why you took the first opportunity to get away tonight?" she asked, touching the bristles on his jaw. "What put that haunted look on your face?"

He stilled.

She stilled.

"Was it me?" she asked. "What I said?"

That they wouldn't be good together. That she wouldn't ever be able to like or love a man like him. Words that she now understood came from fear, from not understanding or liking what he'd awakened in her.

Not safe.

Not in her bubble.

"I told you, baby," he said softly, stepping back and going on with the next pot. "What you said was a good thing. It made me think."

"I'm sorry."

His head came up from studying the pot, mouth tipping up. "For making me think?"

She laughed. "For what I said. I—" A shake of her head. "I was feeling vulnerable and upset, and what I said was more about me than you. Not," she added, "not that I can stand the whole alpha-hole bullshit. It's just—"

He waited, scrubbing the pot.

"It's just that I'm not usually such a bitch."

"You were hurt, and I pushed at the wrong time." He set the pot on the counter, and Teresa started drying it.

"No. Okay, yes, I was hurt," she added when he glanced at her in confusion. "And yes, you pushed, and it was the wrong time, especially when I asked you to back off."

Guilt in his eyes.

"But—"

He froze.

She stepped closer, shoved herself between his body and the sink, felt the cool porcelain of the basin on her back, the hot press of him on her front.

But his face.

God, *the way* he looked at her...

It felt natural to rest her hands on his chest, to slide them up until she was cupping both of his cheeks.

"But you're a good man," she whispered. "You're a good man, and *anyone* would be lucky to have you in their life."

He inhaled, but the exhale didn't come, not when he was so still against her.

"*I* would be lucky to have you."

The exhale came then, shuddering out of him, skittering along her lips.

And...she had to capture it.

Capture that breath in her own mouth, feel his lips against hers, his tongue—

"Teresa," he whispered.

"Kiss me," she whispered back.

But she didn't wait for him to reply, for him to move toward her.

She rose on tiptoe, used her hands to drag his head down to hers, and...she kissed him.

No hesitation. No delay.

No awkwardness.

Just her and him and the kiss.

Just her and him and all the things he made her feel.

Just her and him and his tongue sliding into her mouth, his hands on her body, molding her to him.

Just her and him and—

"*Oh!*"

Gasping, she jerked away from Jeremy, leaned to the side... and saw Melody had walked into the kitchen.

Melody, who was perfect for him.

Melody, who'd gone on a date with him.

Melody—

Who turned and hurried from the kitchen.

Twenty-One

"Shit," he muttered, stepping back from the lush temptation of Teresa's body, turning in time to see Melody disappearing down the hall.

"I—"

Teresa bit her lip, shook her head.

Then gave him a light shove. "Go," she ordered softly. "Go talk to her."

He didn't want to leave Teresa, but he hadn't missed the glimmer of hurt on Melody's face. They weren't dating, and she knew about his feelings for Teresa.

But...maybe he'd misjudged something.

Maybe he'd missed—

Fuck.

He ran his thumb over her bottom lip. "I'll be right ba—"

Her fingers around his wrist, gripping tight. "Don't make promises you can't keep."

What the fuck?

"T, baby. It's not like—"

"Go," Teresa ordered, spinning away from him, disappearing into the garage before he could get out another word.

He took a step in her direction, but then he heard footsteps in the hall, heard Mel call her goodbyes, and he moved to head her off.

One fire at a time.

"Hey," he said gently as she shrugged into her coat.

Yeah.

Right there.

That was hurt in her eyes.

Fuck.

He moved toward her, took her arm.

She stepped back, gaze slanting to the kitchen. "I'll...um...see you later."

"Mel—"

But then she was through the front door, and he was heading after her, following her out onto the porch.

"Mel," he said again.

And fuck, there were tears on her lashes.

He could no more turn away from her sadness than he could turn off his attraction to Teresa. Quickly, he closed the distance between them, tugged her into his arms. "Mel, honey, I'm sorry. I thought you knew how I felt about Teresa. I-I...I didn't—I wouldn't have kissed her if I'd known you felt that way about me." Lie. "I wouldn't have kissed her without talking to you first."

That, at least, was the truth.

But he barely had a moment to sit in it because then Mel was spinning in his hold, glancing up at him in surprise.

"I—"

She blinked.

"You—"

He sucked in a breath, waited for her to get a full sentence out.

And when she did, it was fuck's all away from what he'd expected her to say.

"It's—*this*"—she waved a hand at her face, the hurt, the tears, the flush on her cheeks—"it's not for you."

He frowned. "Then who?"

"Asher."

―――――

He'd rocked back on his heels, momentarily stunned into silence.

But by then she'd already pulled away from him, was walking down the driveway to her car.

"Mel," he said, chasing after her. "What do you mean it's about Asher?"

A shrug, her pace increasing. "It doesn't matter."

"Mel," he began again.

"It's fine, okay?" she snapped. "I don't need you to—"

"Did he do something…"

"Something?" Her smile wasn't amused. "Yes, he did *something*." Now the pain came back into her eyes. "He's not interested." A shrug. "It's fine. I'm fine. I don't need rescuing."

"Oh, honey," he said.

"I *don't* need rescuing."

"But you might need a hug considering that it stings like hell when someone doesn't return your feelings."

Her protest had already been forming on her lips, but his words had her freezing. "I—"

Fuck it.

He wrapped his arms around her, tugged her close. "Hugs equal good."

"I—"

He held her tighter, whispered, "Shut up and get in here."

Sniffing quietly, she hugged him back. "Damn you and your *learning*."

Laughter in his chest. He smoothed his hand over her hair. "Old dog, new tricks."

"Exactly," she grumbled, burrowing closer. "Not fair to pull those new tricks on me."

The hug lasted for long enough that she stopped sniffing, that she began to lean less heavily against him. "You're responsible for those new tricks," he murmured. "You helped me get my head on straight."

"I'm glad."

"Which means that I know you can help Asher sort his shit."

A sigh. "Not wanting me isn't shit," she said softly. "It's just..." Another long, slow exhale. "He doesn't want me."

Hell.

She was killing him.

"Mel."

"Uh-uh. No soft in your voice. I just got myself together."

He tugged her ponytail. "I think that you're always together, honey."

Laughter bubbling up in her chest, off her tongue. "It's funny you think that."

"And Asher—"

"Enough about *Asher*." She was fierce. Intense. Beautiful.

"Asher's an idiot."

"That we can agree on."

Sad again. Shit. "Okay, honey. You're going to go home, you're going to have a nice, warm bath, and you're going to forget about my idiot brother."

Now she smiled.

Better.

"And then we're going to have lunch sometime soon. You're going to complain about my brother. Or better yet, you'll tell me about the awesome new guy you're dating."

"Learning," she whispered, touching his jaw.

"Trying," he whispered back.

Another smile, and then he was linking his arm with hers, walking her to her car, and tucking her inside.

A wave and she shut her door.

And as he turned back to the house, he saw his brother standing in the doorway.

And Asher didn't look pleased.

———

The sink was empty by the time he made it back inside, Teresa nowhere in sight.

Asher wasn't either and as he searched the kitchen, poked his head into the garage, he heard Asher's truck start up, heard it take off down the road.

But he was less concerned about his brother (and his brother's idiocy about Mel) and more concerned about Teresa.

That kiss.

Her touch.

Her body.

Now gone, any progress eroded by an interruption—one that she was totally reading wrong, one he hadn't made any better by running off after Mel.

Stupid.

But...he wouldn't be the man he was if he didn't care about the people in his life.

He was learning that, too.

There was just a difference between caring and taking over.

More learning.

Though he would take some learning about where Teresa was right about now.

The house had emptied. He was alone...having hoped that

the aloneness would actually translate into being alone with Teresa.

But she hadn't reappeared.

And he was left wondering if he should stay or go.

He owed her an explanation, he knew that much, but if she was avoiding him, then how the fuck was he supposed to give it to her?

Tear her house apart?

Demand that she show herself and talk to him?

Demanding got him nowhere with her, and if he started busting down doors, then he would get even less than nowhere.

Okay, no busting.

Instead, he'd *open*.

Inhaling and exhaling, he moved to the garage, pulling it wide, and—

He froze.

It was empty.

Her car was gone.

And seriously, her fucking car was *gone*.

A bolt of fury skittered down his spine, sending his pulse racing, anger through his veins.

Gone.

She'd moved close to him. She'd opened up to him.

She'd *kissed* him.

And then she'd just left him, without talking to him, without sorting *anything*.

She'd just *left*.

Suddenly, he wondered why he was trying so hard, why he was fighting, why he was learning, when none of it made any difference.

Not to Teresa.

It would always be like this.

Him trying.

Her pushing him away.

He closed his eyes, sucked in a breath, trying for calm, wishing for it, wanting it to guide him, to help him show her that he was—

It *would always* be like this.

"So, what is the fucking point?" he muttered, closing the door to the garage.

He didn't know.

He *didn't* know.

And that was what prompted him to flick off the kitchen lights, to walk out the front door.

There was *no* point.

But because he was him, because he was the man he was, because he wouldn't be able to sleep otherwise, he used her hide-a-key and locked up.

Maybe no point to his learning.

But he would make sure she was safe anyway.

TWENTY-TWO

TERESA

She walked into the hall, having half-expected Jeremy to be waiting in the shadows.

He wasn't.

Her house was empty.

The counters wiped down, the lights off (minus a couple left on so that she could safely navigate). It was Jer's doing.

She knew it with one look.

But Jeremy wasn't here.

He'd...left.

And that—

Fuck. What the hell did she do with *that?*

He was supposed to stay and fight for her, to leave Melody and declare—

She yanked those thoughts to a fierce and almost painful stop, the mental whiplash intense enough to make her stagger.

She didn't want a man to demand and push, to act like her father and brothers—like *he* knew better, like *he* got to decide what was right for her. She didn't want *anyone*, but herself, her work, her freedom.

So why did the quiet, the solitude and silence she'd bought with that demand for freedom hurt so much?

"You're a fucking mess," she whispered to herself, locking the door to the garage, and making her way through the downstairs of her house, flicking off lights...

Encountering something taped to the light switch that crinkled.

Paper.

A note.

From Jeremy?

Heart pounding in a way that was definitely not numb, definitely not feeling enough—it was feeling too much, and all of it was twisted and tangled and a fucking *mess*.

Her fingers shook when she pulled the note from the wall, and she could barely unfold it.

But after a moment, she managed to open it.

To see the words.

To feel...

A bit empty.

He'd just told her that he'd locked up.

But she felt enough, understood enough. She'd hurt him.

She'd watched him through the kitchen window, holding Melody, touching her, talking to her (and no doubt doing it in that soft Jer Tone), and...Teresa had been jealous.

No right to be.

She didn't have rights over Jeremy, didn't have any claim. She'd made it clear she didn't want one.

But seeing him with Melody in that way.

He was lost. He wasn't hers.

He—

The doorbell rang and for one breathless second, she thought it was Jeremy. That he'd come back and they'd—

What? Talk it out and live happily ever after?

She snorted.

That wasn't real life.

Especially when she heard, "Teresa, open the fucking door!"

Gabe.

What the hell was her brother doing here?

Hurrying, she crumpled the note, shoved it in her pocket, then moved to open the door. "Gabe, what's—"

He pushed past her, almost knocking her back a step as he stormed into the hallway. "What the fuck, T?"

There was way too much happening in her head to discern exactly which *what the fuck* he was referring to.

"What are you talking about?" she asked, closing the door.

"Lock that," he snapped.

She'd already been reaching for the dead bolt, but the snapped-out command had her jerking her hand back. "Why?" she asked sharply. "You won't be staying." She crossed her arms, leaned back against the wood. "It's late and I'm tired. Yell at me for whatever it is you've come to yell at me about"—that numbness began creeping into her toes, snaking up her calves because late-night visits were never about anything else—"and then let me get to bed."

His expression clouded for a moment. "What are you talking about?"

A sigh and she forced her tone to go neutral, made easier because the numbness had crept into her torso now, settled into her belly. "What are you upset about?"

That had his face clearing, him stepping closer, close enough that he could grab her arm and tow her away from the door. She heard the *click* of the lock engaging, the evidence of him not listening to her, of no one in her life *listening*—

Except Jeremy.

He'd listened.

Well, he was gone now, wasn't he?

"You blew Mom off, and she's upset."

That wasn't what she'd expected him to say. How could it be? It was so fucking absurd that she was momentarily stunned silent.

"What are you talking about?"

Gabe narrowed his eyes. "You know she looks forward to weekly manicures, and you canceled."

"I rescheduled to *one* day later because I have a business meeting," she snapped.

"You know she likes her routine."

Their mom did. That was true. But, fuck, sometimes routines had to shift, to change, to allow for people to shift and change and grow.

"You can't be serious right now," she whispered. "You're showing up to my house at nine at night, berating me about changing my mani-pedi day with Mom from Wednesday to Thursday nights?" A beat then when he didn't immediately answer, asking, "Is that seriously why you're here?"

His expression rippled, and she felt something in her respond, the numbness creeping back. "Mom is upset."

She inhaled, released it.

"Why are you really here, Gabe?"

For a second, for one *fucking* second, she thought that she was going to have an honest conversation with her brother.

But then his expression shifted again, settling into mulish lines she knew all too well, and he crossed his arms. "Just because you think this stupid idea of yours for an app is going to be successful, doesn't mean that you should sacrifice your family." The words connected with her torso like bullets—*thud, thud, thud*, in rapid succession, one after another. But even as she was breathing through the pain of his words, he went on, and pain turned to numb. "Mom did *everything* for you. Mom sacrificed her career, her free time, her body, her—"

"I didn't ask her to," Teresa yelled. "I didn't want her to sacrifice anything. I didn't *want* to be born. I didn't *want*—"

"To what?" He threw up his hands. "To be part of our family? To be *stuck* with us? Always too good for family and home and *us*, always wanting more than what we could give you, huh?" He turned away. "Well, I'm so sorry that we're not enough."

The numb settled so heavily over her that she could barely breathe.

"My app isn't stupid," she whispered inanely.

Inanely because it was probably the least important to address of what he'd just spewed at her.

He laughed, bitterly. "That's all that matters to you, isn't it? The life you're building without us. The life you've built with your friends. Replacing us. Replacing us with newer, better models that can cut really big checks."

Her inhale was so sharp that when she glanced down, she expected to be bleeding.

She wasn't.

Of course, she wasn't.

"So," she said softly, the numbness gripping even more fiercely, "Are you jealous of the life I've made—that I'm *making* —for myself? Or do you really hate me so much?"

Now the bitter disappeared. "I, I didn't mean—"

"Is that what you think I am?" The numbness threatened to retreat, but she gripped it tightly to her, a sheet clung to her breasts after meaningless sex, a jacket pulled taut against bracing winds. Because her eyes were stinging, and she needed the numb, needed it to fully submerge her. "You really think that I've been working so hard just for *money*? You really think that my dream is nothing more than what I can con out of people?"

His eyes widened. "Teresa, honey. I lost my temper. I—"

She turned her back on him, reached for the lock on the door, and disengaged it. "You didn't." She sighed. "You know why it's a chore for me to spend time with Mom? With you?" She didn't wait for him to answer, just pressed on, because as much as she was clinging to the numbness...

It hurt.

"Because you look at me like *that.* Like I don't belong. Like I can't ever be one of you." She pulled open the door. "I'm just a burden, an object to take care of. Not a person. Not a woman. Not an adult. Just another obligation."

And she couldn't live with being that.

"Teresa," he whispered. "I shouldn't have said that."

She couldn't look at him. "No," she whispered back, "you shouldn't have."

He reached for her. She saw it out of the corner of her eye and stepped back enough so that his hand didn't make contact. "I'm sorry."

"There's truth in anger." She turned for the kitchen. "Just like there is some truth in me not wanting to be like Mom. I want to make my own way. I want to at least try for what I've dreamed of. But..." She shook her head. "You'll never see me as anything but your sick little sister, will you?"

"We almost lost you."

That was true. She'd almost died—a freak infection that the doctors had barely figured out how to treat in time.

But they had.

She was here. She was alive.

She'd been alive for two decades since.

Been smothered in this cage they'd built, until she escaped, until she *lived.*

She wouldn't go back.

"You *didn't* lose me then," she said then added, truth strengthening her tone. "But I'm..." A sigh. "If it keeps going like this, you will. You will lose me."

He went stiff, like a shock had gone through his body, but then he recovered, and this time she didn't dodge the hand that gripped her arm tightly, anger in his voice. "If you keep pushing everyone away, you will end up alone, T."

"That's the thing, Gabe." She stepped back out of his hold. "I'm *not* alone. You guys just refuse to see it. Refuse to be part of a life that isn't what you think I *should* want."

His lips parted.

She shook her head, exhaustion practically dripping out of every pore. "Go home," she said on a sigh. "Just go home to your perfect life, your expectations I can never live up to. Stop trying to cage me, to turn me into something."

And...

And he did.

He went home.

And then the only sound that filled her ears was the *click* of the lock sliding home.

TWENTY-THREE

JEREMY

Christ. Not again.

He hadn't slept last night, every part of him wanting to go back to Teresa's, to talk to her and explain.

But he'd already tried pushing.

It didn't work.

So, he'd decided to give her some space, and then he was going to explain later.

Because they'd made progress and there could be no more confusion, no more of her misunderstanding whom he wanted.

Her.

Only her.

Always *her.*

Even if he didn't understand what he wanted for life, the man he was if he wasn't caring for everyone else all the time, he understood what his heart was telling him.

He needed Teresa.

She was his.

So, leaving her house hadn't been easy, leaving and not checking up on her, making certain she was okay, had made it back home, was *safe,* had been even more difficult.

But he'd given her the space she needed.

Even if it meant he hadn't slept.

Plus side? He was in early to work. Which meant that he might actually catch up for once. Or maybe he could stay buried as always and take an extra-long lunch today. Just for shits and giggles and for all the times he'd had to skip eating, working through for the corporate machine he was getting really fucking tired of being part of.

But any of the pluses of him coming in early and that hopefully long lunch had been dashed the moment he'd walked through his office door.

Bianca was there.

"Jeremy," she crooned, crossing over to him.

"You're beautiful," he said, trying to appeal to logic. There had to be some of that in there somewhere, right?

Her smile was unhinged. "Thanks, baby."

"So beautiful," he pressed on, "that you don't want someone who doesn't want you back, right?"

A hint of anger in her eyes, her nails digging into his chest. "Of course not," she snapped.

"So..."

Those nails dug in a little deeper.

And he gave up on logic.

Mostly because she was lifting up on tiptoe, her lipstick-painted lips coming close to his.

He shoved her back and kept shoving her until she was out of his office.

Then he detached the talons, slammed the door, and flipped the lock.

He looked at the pile of papers on his desk. He looked at the clock, at the hour he'd come in just so he could catch up, so that he could take lunch, even maybe a rare, long one. He looked out the window at the woman who thought she could push him into something, just because she was related to the boss. He thought of HR and all they hadn't done to support him. He thought of his boss and his promises to look out for Jeremy at promotion time. And then he thought of the promotion that *had* come, the additional responsibilities and a fancy title, but no additional money to go along with it.

That would probably would *never* come.

And...Christ.

He thought about what he wanted.

An answer he still didn't have.

But what he *did* know?

That *this* wasn't it.

He tugged on the pull for the blinds, let them drop over the glass between them.

Then he went to his desk.

And he drafted his resignation email.

A moment after he hit send, Jeremy walked out of that building, and knew *knew* he wouldn't ever go back.

———

"Damn," he said, taking a long sip of the coffee. "Honestly, I didn't understand what all the hype was about."

Melody grinned. "That's because you hadn't had it."

"True enough." He nodded at the plate full of pastries in front of them. "Please tell me that these live up to the hype, too?"

A chuckle. "Why don't you try them yourself and find out?"

He picked up a homemade donut, took a big bite.

"Fuck," he said through the mouthful. "You're going to be responsible for making me fat."

She started laughing, picking up her choice—a chocolate croissant.

She was just taking a bite when the front door opened, and he instinctively glanced up at the sound of the little bell tinkling.

And then froze, a huge bite of donut in his mouth, clumping together, gluing his teeth together, nearly making him choke when he inhaled rapidly.

He coughed, and Mel looked up. "Oh God, are you okay?"

She got up out of her chair, patted his back. "Do you want me to get you a glass of water?"

"No." He coughed again. "I'm good," he croaked.

"I know the baked goods are yummy," she murmured, "but I feel it must be said that I didn't advise you to inhale them."

He managed to get the coughing under control, narrowed his eyes at her.

Her eyes twinkled as she lifted her hands, palms up. "Just saying."

Amusement in his belly, until he looked up, saw that Teresa had frozen near the door, and the look on her face—

Fuck.

"What is it?" Mel asked, reaching for him again—then freezing. "Crap," she whispered. "Go to her."

Another woman telling him to go.

Christ, this was becoming a habit.

He dropped his donut to the plate, hopped to his feet, and moved to Teresa. She was putting in her order. "T," he murmured.

She glanced up at him, glanced away. "Jeremy."

Fuck. Her tone was—

"That'll be $3.83," the cashier said.

"No pastries?" he asked.

Her glance up at him was colder. "No."

So, he did the only thing he could. He pulled out his wallet and gave the cashier a five. "Keep the change," he told the woman behind the counter before grabbing Teresa's coffee and walking away.

Doing the only thing he could.

Pissing her off.

Breaking through the cold.

Forcing her to acknowledge him.

Maybe he would have thought that was completely the wrong thing to do with everything he'd learned about this woman so far, everything he'd learned about himself. But the cold in her wasn't...*her*. Wasn't annoyance that he'd pushed.

It was...hurt.

Over Mel?

He glanced back over his shoulder at Teresa, studied her.

Not Mel. Or not Mel entirely.

It was...something else.

"Baby," he began.

She turned from him. "Keep the coffee." Frost in her eyes. "Since you paid for it."

Tart.

Just a bit of sass that encouraged him to say, "Melody and I are just friends."

A look—a dash of fire. "Right." But she didn't say anything else, just left the coffee in his hand and turned for the door.

He followed her out. "I quit my job today."

Her pace skittered. "I—that's good," she whispered. "I know you were unhappy." She started to turn away again.

"Also, Mel and I aren't dating. Never have. Never will."

"It's okay," she said softly, backing away from him. "She's pretty and nice and—"

"Has the hots for Asher."

She stopped. "What?"

"Who apparently doesn't return her feelings."

Her shoulders rose and fell on a breath, but she didn't speak.

"Since I know something of that," he said, doing the

speaking for them both. "We got to talking. This, of course, being after she put my ass in its place." He shoved her coffee in her hands. "After someone else did, helping me think through and making me realize that I *was* an ass."

A glimmer of warmth in her eyes. "I knew I liked her."

He stepped closer, cupped her cheek. "I know I like you," he whispered. "No one else. Just you."

Twenty-Four

"*I know I like you. No one else. Just you.*"

And hell, if the numbness didn't fade away, didn't immediately have her eyes burning.

"Jer," she whispered.

His fingers on her cheeks flexed. "What is it?" he asked, the question as gentle as those fingers held her face. "What's happened?"

"I—"

The tinkle of the bell.

Mel's soft voice. "I'm sorry to interrupt."

He glanced over as though annoyed. At least until he saw the to-go cup and bag in her hand.

"Why don't you two take these and walk?" Mel asked gently as she passed over the items, nodded to the right. "There's a park around the corner." A beat. "Where you can talk." More command and less gentle.

Without waiting for an answer, she turned on her heel and walked the other direction, and amusement bubbled up in Teresa's chest.

"Matchmaking," she whispered lightly.

A sigh. A shake of his head. "Yeah."

And now she felt like a bit of an idiot.

"Clearly, I misjudged that situation."

He touched her cheek again. "Yeah."

"I—" She bit her lip, a small part of her wanting to run, to lock things down, to cling to numb. But...she hadn't slept, and Jeremy was touching her, and—

She felt.

So instead, she asked, "D-do you *want* to walk?"

His arm came around her shoulders, and she didn't resist him tugging her near.

"What's happened?" he asked again.

She didn't want to talk about it. Well, she did and she didn't and hell, she had no fucking clue what was going on in her mind. Which was why she asked, "Why did you quit?"

"Bianca."

"It's early in the day for her to have struck, isn't it?"

He snorted. "That's what I thought." He tugged her to the right. "But she's not the only reason I quit. I just...fuck."

"What?" she pressed gently when he didn't go on.

"My Mom asked me not too long ago."

"Asked you what?"

A sigh. "Asked if I knew what I wanted. If I'd ever stopped and actually asked myself what I wanted."

"What was your answer?"

He shot her a look that told her enough.

He hadn't stopped and thought about his own wants.

"She pointed out that perhaps I'd been too focused on smothering everyone else in the name of taking care of them, and since another woman had mentioned something like that before." The ghost of a smile. "And since another reamed me about the same thing just a couple of days later…I've been thinking."

"Who?" she couldn't stop herself from asking.

"Mel."

Her brows shot up. "*Mel?*"

He grinned. "Yeah, surprised the shit out of me, too." He sobered. "But it did get me thinking."

She felt as though she should be holding her breath. "About what?"

"About what I wanted and what I was doing and how I cared for the people in my life."

He led them to a bench, and she sank down beside him, snagging the bag from his grip. Oh, thank fuck, Mel had given them chocolate croissants.

Her favorite.

Yum.

She pulled one out, took a big bite, and asked, "And what did you decide?"

"That my mom was right," he said, plunking the bag onto the bench next to him. "And you were right. And that Mel was right."

Suddenly, the croissant wasn't very tasty. She set it back in the bag, took his hand. "About what specifically?"

"I'm a pushy alpha-hole," he said, smiling at her. But it wasn't *Jer's* smile. It was fake and sad, and she hated it. "And also, that I'd spent so much time thinking about what everyone else needed and how to get it for them that I didn't stop to consider what I wanted." His eyes hit hers. "Except for you. *You* I considered a lot—how much I want you, your body, your brain." Fingers on her cheek. "Your face to soften when you look at me."

She drew in a breath, and it was far from steady. "I don't want you to change who you are for me."

"I'm not."

She gave him a look. "Really?"

"I'm not," he said again. "Did you all get me thinking? Of course, you did. Did it sting? Fuck, yeah. But...I needed it. I was stuck and—" A breath. "I may not fully know the man I am without all of that alpha-hole-ness, but I *do* know what I don't want to be. And that's more than I had before. *Much* more."

The fact that he could tell her this, show his vulnerable underbelly, *share—*

"I'm glad, Jer. Really glad."

He shrugged. "So, I'm a work in progress." Now he smiled at her for real. "Want to get in on the ground floor of a really great remodel?"

Laughter on her tongue, and fuck it, after last night, she let it out.

Let herself rest her head on his shoulder.

"Yeah," she said, making a silent promise that she was going to help him sort out his head, make sure he figured out exactly what he wanted, and then do her best to give it to him. "I want in."

Because the man was strong and he was pretty fucking wonderful, and she thought, fucking hell, she thought that she might be falling for him.

As that radiated through her, she paused, waited for fear to erupt.

But it didn't.

Instead, the thought seemed to have gripped tight to the numb, digging its claws in, drawing it into her body, discarding it.

Leaving her open and vulnerable.

And it gave her strength.

To share.

"Gabe came by last night after everyone left." After he'd left.

A line of stiffness entered his body. "And how did he hurt you?"

A careful question, one that spoke to how very well he actually knew her, and she knew she had a choice. She could cling to the numb, could try to wrap it around herself again, or...she could find some courage.

So...

Teresa sucked in a breath, released it slowly.

And she told him. *Everything.*

About being sick as a kid and how it had left her in a velvet-lined cage, how she'd felt smothered at every turn, and it had been increasingly more and more difficult to do her own thing, especially after they'd nearly lost her mother. Then she couldn't push without feeling guilty, without putting that hurt look on her mother's face, who had nothing but her family in her life. She told him how her brothers and parents kept pushing Teresa down that same path. How she should find a man to keep her safe. Have babies. Live her life small so that she would always be protected.

"I love them," she said. "I really do. But I can't," she whispered. "I can't be in that cage, not any longer."

"I know," he told her, running his fingers through her hair, and finally, finally she had the sense that there was someone on this planet who *did* get her, who understood.

Because he'd looked unto himself without artifice.

Because...

He was different.

"And what's worse is that I thought he'd finally understood. Anton did. He said he was proud of me, and he *was* excited I'd gotten an investor. But Gabe, Gabe said—"

She pressed her lips together.

Jeremy's hand stilled. "Said what?"

"He said my idea was stupid and my parents sacrificed everything for me and that I was ungrateful and that I was hurting my mother because I'd changed the date of our mani-pedi night, but that wasn't all. Then he—" She broke off. "It doesn't matter."

"It does." Jer sat up. "It *does* matter."

Maybe it did. Maybe she needed him to know, to pass judgment, too.

"He said I was nothing but a con woman who only cared about money and didn't care who I stomped on to get what I wanted."

TWENTY-FIVE

JEREMY

It was lucky that he'd already sat up, already removed his hands from her.

Otherwise, he might have dumped her from his lap when he lurched to his feet. "He fucking *what?*"

Yeah, it was a bellow.

Luckily, there was no one around.

"He said you—" Jer clenched his teeth, grinding them together. A breath. Two. *Three.* Christ, none of them helped.

"Jeremy."

Another breath. Another two. Three. *Four.*

Only then did he manage to make himself sit down.

"Honey," she whispered, covering his hand. "I'm okay."

"No"—he leaned in, brushed lightly beneath each eye—"he put those shadows in here. He shit on your dream, the one you worked your ass off for."

"Jer."

"And parents sacrifice for their kids; that's what they do!" He fisted a hand, pounded it against his thigh. "They're not supposed to hold it over their kids' heads."

"No," she said softly. "They're not."

"And your app is a great idea. You know it is, otherwise all those investors wouldn't have wanted to get a piece of it, a piece of you." He touched her cheek. "Plus, you've been working on getting it off the ground all while you've been managing those projects with Rafe. He's told me more than once that you're most of the reason he's been successful."

She inhaled sharply, her pulse pounding fast in her throat. "Rafe said that?"

"Yeah, baby."

"I—it's not that I didn't know he appreciated me. But I just…"

"It means more that he told his best friend."

"Yeah," she whispered.

The warmth in his belly, in his heart.

He cupped her cheek fully, lifting her face, staring into her eyes, trying to make certain she knew the truth of every single word he was speaking.

He believed all of them.

He believed in her.

"And if they can't understand how much value you bring, honey, then that's their problem," he said, brushing his thumb lightly over her skin. "Because I do. Rafe and Cora and everyone else does, too."

She inhaled. "Jer."

"You know it's true."

An exhale, her palm covering his hand. "I like you," she whispered.

That warmth grew. "I know," he whispered back.

A huff of air, a flashing in her pretty hazel eyes, the gold growing. "Annoying."

"That, too."

"Cocky."

He lifted a brow. "You sure this is the path you want the conversation to go along?"

Now laughter joined the party, and she leaned in, brushed her lips against his. "You sure you still want this messed-up woman whose own family doubts her?"

Sad hadn't been invited to the get-together.

Unfortunately, it had decided to crash in anyway.

Bastard.

"You sure you want to let in a messed-up man who doesn't even know his own heart or head?" he countered, just to see her smile.

A breath before she captured his hand, brought it to rest on her chest, just above where her heart beat beneath her ribs. "I'm sure."

Then she smiled.

"Good," he whispered. "Because as much as I want to say I'd keep my distance"—he ran his thumb over her bottom lip—"I don't think I can."

Soft.

Fingers twining with his.

Curvy and soft.

Body pressing to his.

Warm and gentle and *soft*.

Heart beating against palm.

"Neither can I," she whispered.

Relief, heady and heavy, coiled through him, seizing his lungs, making it nearly impossible for him to suck in a breath.

But then he did.

He breathed. He sat in this moment. He let himself just be there with Teresa. Without worrying. Without trying to fix everything.

Just with her.

Just sharing breath and body heat and skin-to-skin contact.
And...it was perfect.

————

Eventually, they pulled apart and ate the pastries Mel had given them, drank the now lukewarm coffee.

They talked, not about heavy shit.

They talked about boardgames and TV shows.

They talked about nothing important.

And it was fucking wonderful—all that he'd hoped for.

But then her phone chimed, and he remembered it was a weekday, that she had to go to work.

He might be going on four whole hours of footloose and fancy-free, but she had responsibilities.

So, they packed up their trash and he walked her to her car, and it spoke of how much progress they'd made, how much distance they'd covered that she didn't protest, that she let him hold her hand.

That she let him press her against her car, run his hand along her side.

That she let him brush his lips over hers.

But eventually, he had to lift his head, had to let her go.

But, good God, he didn't want to.

Which was probably why he asked, "You free for lunch?"

A flash of straight, white teeth. Humor in her bright, hazel eyes. "Is this what it's going to be like to date an unemployed man?"

"Yup," he said, kissing the tip of her nose.

Laughter that she let him taste on his tongue.

Then she pulled back.

And she smiled at him. "I can go for lunch." Her fingers drifted across his jaw and then she turned, tugged open her door.

Legs in her car, fingers brushing his as she reached for her belt.

He pulled it over her, snapped it in place, took advantage of the fact that they were close, and kissed her again.

This time it wasn't short, wasn't just a taste.

It was a clash of teeth and lips and tongue. It was a dangerous kiss for a parking lot, for somewhere he couldn't strip her naked and fuck her in every way he'd dreamed of.

Her cell went again, and he pulled back, bumping into the steering wheel, making the horn blow, the noise finally snapping him out of the haze.

"Dangerous woman."

Her fingers on his jaw. "Dangerous *man*." A beat. "I really have to go."

He leaned back, crouching in the opening of her door. "I know."

"Jeremy?"

He'd begun to straighten.

Her voice stopped him. "Yeah, baby?"

"What do you want to do?"

"You," he answered without hesitation.

Lips twitching, she touched her jaw. "I meant, what do you want to do for work?"

That had him freezing, had that knot in his belly coming back.

But he still answered her truthfully. "Fuck if I know."

Soft eyes and fingers and heart.

"Honey," she whispered, sympathy in the endearment.

He felt that sympathy deep in his gut. "I know."

"You'll figure it out."

"I know," he murmured. "But maybe—"

Her breath seemed to catch in her lungs as she waited.

"Maybe I'll figure it out sooner if…" he trailed off, wanting to ask, quite desperate for it, actually, but the words had clumped up in his throat, making it nearly impossible to get them out.

"If?" she prompted.

"If you help me."

And then he got to see the most wonderful thing.

He got to see her smile.

Twenty-Six

Teresa

"Okay," she said the next evening. "I have a plan."

He grinned at her, having opened the door wide, even though she hadn't even made it all the way up to his porch.

"Yeah?" he asked, snagging the bag of takeout from her.

Something she didn't protest.

Because he understood that he didn't need to take over everything. Because he made it clear that he knew she was capable of taking care of her own shit.

Because he'd bit back his alpha-holeness and let her buy him dinner.

She grinned.

She'd underestimated him, and he'd shown her that he was so much more than she could ever hope for.

He'd asked her for help.

He'd been vulnerable.

He'd *talked* to her, didn't just jump in and try to solve all of her problems.

Yup.

Falling.

Sliding down a slippery slope.

And...

Not caring. No worrying. Not trying to stop herself.

Not any longer anyway.

Because she was *feeling*.

Feeling so much that she was bursting.

"What's the plan, anyway?" he asked, stepping back as she strode into his house, moving down the hall and into his kitchen.

She needed a flat surface and plenty of space to spread out—

Which sounded...

Not the best.

Okay, well, it sounded really good actually. Her and Jeremy and a flat surface with plenty of space to spread out. If the man fucked as well as he kissed...

A breath.

Not here for that.

He'd asked for help, and she was going to come through, and if she got a few orgasms along the way...

She'd just consider that a bonus.

Grinning, she pulled out her laptop and folders. Organized them according to her checklist.

Lists. Folders. Papers.

Being organized and prepared and making sure everything was where it should be, that everyone had what they needed.

Her superpower.

Jer was unpacking the food, and she knew there was a perk to dating an alpha-hole (not a fair descriptor, she knew now). But the point was that he paid attention; he knew her. Which meant that he knew exactly which of the Chinese food dishes and how much to put on her plate. He knew that she wanted a beer to go along with it.

He knew that she wanted chopsticks for all the food, but a spoon for the fried rice so she could scrape every last bite.

Slipping down that slope even further.

"Here you go, baby," he murmured, kissing the top of her head as he slid the plate next to her and put her beer on a coaster.

"Thanks."

A brush of his knuckles along her throat.

"Anytime." And then he was sitting across from her, his own plate in front of him, his own beer on his coaster.

She felt a bolt of guilt from not knowing what his choices would be.

From not paying attention when he clearly had.

From being too scared of feeling anything to try.

So, she did the only thing she could.

She took note of those choices now, filed them away. He had her organized and prepared mind at a disadvantage, knowing what she liked, probably knowing everything about her from her favorite color to her favorite cocktail.

She couldn't let that stand.

Reconnaissance, asking the right questions, making the correct mental notes—

Those were going to be her friends.

Jeremy wasn't the only one who could be detail-oriented.

That was her superpower.

A tug of her ponytail. "What has put that fierce look on your face, honey?"

"I'm going to figure out every single thing that you like, and I'm going to give it to you."

Was that spoken as fiercely as what her expression probably looked like? Maaaybe. But was it worth it because of what *his* face looked like when he heard her words?

Yes.

Definitely.

"Baby," he whispered.

"Eat your food," she ordered, emotions in her belly, filling her. No numbness. No fear.

Just...Jeremy.

———

"All right," she said once they'd finished their first helping. "Time to get down to business."

He set his fork down, took a swig of beer, and then leaned back in his chair.

"All right then," he told her. "Lay it on me."

"First." She set a list she'd compiled in front of him. "Tell me if you've done any of these and liked or disliked them."

He took the list, studied it for long moments.

Then looked up at her, pointed to a few. "These three. Hated the first. Meh about the second and third."

"Any interest in the rest?"

More studying, then, "No, baby. Not really."

"Okay then," she said, clapping her hands together and getting down to business. "Then there's nothing to be done about it."

His brows drew together. "Um, about what?"

She clicked her pen, grinned up at him. "It's quiz time, baby."

———

"Would you rather be a wildlife expert or a public relations expert?"

"How are those the choices?"

She shrugged. "Are you arguing with the Princeton Review?"

"I'm arguing with something that is patently stupid."

"You must choose," she demanded, channeling her inner Gandalf *You shall not pass!*

"Uhh...wildlife expert."

"Huh. *Really?*"

"What?" he asked. "Is that bad?"

She widened her eyes, just to fuck with him.

"Teresa," he warned.

She clicked the selection, brought up the next question. "Okay, a TV anchor or a company controller?"

"What's a controller?"

"Don't ask me," she said.

"Um, controller," he replied.

"I thought you didn't know what that was."

"I don't."

"I see why you're confused about the prospects of your career."

He snorted. "Keep up with the sass, and I'm coming over there."

She waggled her brows. "You promise?"

His chair slid back, and he started to get up.

"Wait!" He shot her a look. "We have more questions."

"Is this where I say I don't care about the questions?"

"Jeremy Hutchins, we are being serious here!" she snapped, but she was smothering a smile. Because he was relaxed and across from her, and she was making him laugh. "We are trying to determine your future."

His foot brushed hers. "Ask your questions, baby."

"Bookkeeper or electrician?"

"Electrician."

"Accountant or history professor?"

"Accountant."

"Writer or elected official?"

"Writer."

That had her pausing. "Really?

He shrugged.

"What story would you tell?"

"One of a pushy feminine-hole who is determined to solve all my problems."

Now she didn't bother smothering her smile, she let it loose, along with her laughter.

"That sounds—" He broke off and then he was laughing. "I'm sorry, that sounds disgusting."

It did.

Really, it did.

She grinned.

"Though," he murmured, shifting so he snagged her foot with his, bringing hers into his lap, slipped off her shoe and started rubbing the sole. "I wouldn't be opposed to being *in* any of those feminine holes."

A narrow-eyed glare, but truthfully, she was having a hard time focusing with his hands on her. "Audit manager or safety manager?"

"Safety."

"Right," she said, plugging it in as he tugged.

She gasped, ass sliding forward a few inches in her chair, moving her so that her foot was firmly in his lap, and hell if it didn't brush against the hard length of his erection. That was...*wow*. But then his hands were drifting higher, warm through the thin fabric of her leggings, pausing at the back of her knee before moving higher, making patterns on the inside of her thigh.

She shivered, and hell if her legs didn't spread a little wider, giving him more access.

"Baby?" he asked.

His hands were still moving, body leaning forward so that they could slide farther up.

They brushed the damp fabric in between—

Her breath hissed out.

"Teresa?" he asked.

"Mmm?"

"Do we really care about these answers?"

No. No, she didn't. Not at all.

But...she was supposed to be looking out for him.

"There's only two more questions."

"Give it to me."

"That's my line," she whispered.

A flash of white. "Ask me the two questions, baby."

She did. For the life of her she couldn't remember what they were, but she'd dutifully recorded his answers, and hit submit, and—

The results came up.

Twenty-Seven

Jeremy

He glanced at the screen.

Then he glanced at her.

Then he glanced back at the screen.

Then he glanced back at her.

"I—" She broke off.

His eyes went back to the screen.

And then he grinned, laughter bubbling up, escaping, and joining with hers.

"A children's party artist."

She bit her lip.

"What does that even mean?"

Her mouth turned up. "It means..." She giggled. "Oh my God, it means that you need to learn how to tie balloon animals." A beat. "And clowns. You need a clown suit."

"I know how to tie balloon animals."

Her foot jerked in his lap. "No, you don't."

"No, I don't," he admitted.

Then her foot was bouncing in time to his laughter, and his hand was between her legs and...

Fuck it.

He dropped her foot to the floor, pushed back his chair, and tugged her out of hers. She landed on his lap with an "Oof!"

"Teresa?"

"Yeah?" she whispered, her hands coming to his shoulders.

"Can we stop with the tests?"

Petting him. Gently.

Then firmly.

Hands drifting down to dip beneath his shirt then back up, dragging along his skin. "Yeah," she whispered. "We can stop with the tests."

"Thank fuck."

He lurched to his feet, taking her with him, spinning and dropping her onto the counter.

"Wh—"

One jerk had her shirt over her head.

"Fuck," he whispered, stilling, staring at her.

"What?"

"You are so fucking beautiful."

Gold sparks in her hazel eyes. "Jeremy."

"Shh now," he said. "I'm trying to look at my woman."

An arched brow...an arch smile. "*Your* woman?" she asked *archly*.

Fuck, she was cute.

"Yeah," he whispered. "Mine." Fingers drifting along her collarbones, down between her breasts.

"Are you mine, too?"

No hesitation. "Yes."

She grinned. "So, if you're mine, does that mean I can have my wicked way with you?"

"I thought that was what I was trying to do to you?"

"No," she whispered, even as he dragged his fingers along the curve of her belly, over one hip bone and the other. Her breath caught. "You're being decidedly too slow and careful."

"Slow?" He chuckled.

"Yu—*yup*." More breath catching, and maybe it just happened to coincide with more of his fingers tracing over her skin, up her ribs, beneath the band of her bra.

Around to her back.

A flick had the bra open—

And thank fucking *God*.

Her breasts. Holy hell, her *breasts*.

He bent, sucked one of her nipples into his mouth, gathering her closer to him when she gasped, back arching, fingers digging into his hair, holding him to her.

"That's—oh, Jer. Honey, just like that." Fingertips digging into his scalp, pressing her breast into his mouth.

Rolling the bud over his tongue, gripping the flesh of her breast, molding it in his hands.

Already, his cock was throbbing.

He'd been hard from the moment she'd brushed up against him in the hall, had been aching since he'd sat down across from her.

He'd wanted her for three years.

He'd needed her...well, maybe, he'd needed her forever.

But he needed to feast on her breasts, he needed to spend an eternity kissing them, stroking them, memorizing every freckle and sensitive spot.

She didn't want that—or maybe it was just that her patience had run out.

Maybe his had run out, too.

All he knew was that the next moment, she was on her feet, and her breast was sliding from his mouth, and his shirt was over his head.

Her fingers went to the button of his pants.

One flick had them open.

One drag had the zipper down.

One—

"Oh, fuck," he growled when her hand wrapped around his cock, stroking him inside his underwear.

Her lips sliding over his nipple, teeth dragging along the sensitive bud.

He growled again, but then he got his shit together.

His woman was touching him, was driving him crazy. He needed to do the same, needed to make her melt, make her weep, make her shatter into a million pieces so that he could catch them all, so that he could keep them safe.

His hands went to her waist, pushing down the waistband of her leggings.

"Jer—"

He dropped to his knees, dragging her underwear down as he went, pressing a kiss to the small thatch of curls at the apex of her thighs.

A soft sigh.

"Yes?" he asked, hands coming up the insides of her thighs, pressing them apart.

"Lick me," she ordered.

Fuck, yes, he wanted to do that.

A flick of his tongue, tasting, teasing, before he gripped one leg, dragged it up and over his shoulder. She staggered, but only for a moment. Then she was catching herself on the edge of the counter, arching against him, pressing her pussy and all those wet folds to his face.

He used the flat of his tongue, dragging it through her, circling the bundle of nerves, sucking hard when he found the spot that made her shudder and call out his name.

But then her fingers were in his hair, dragging him up. "More," she whispered.

"I'm trying to do that, baby," he murmured, fingers dipping into her heat, slick with her need.

"No," she whispered, shoving his pants down. "I want *more.*"

Then her hand was around his cock.

"More," she whispered again, pushing against him, using the leverage to prop herself on the edge of the counter.

Naked breasts gleaming from his mouth. Lips swollen and red from his kiss.

She slid back and lifted one foot, placing it on the counter's rounded edge.

Lifted the other.

Naked pussy, slick folds on full display.

From her need, from his mouth.

For *him.*

"More," he agreed, stepping toward her.

Wanting to be inside her, needing it. Butt not yet anyway.

But when he went to drop down again, to lick and kiss all that damp heat, she caught him again, drew him against her.

Maybe he could have fought her hold.

Maybe he could have knocked her hand away, loosened her grip.

But her eyes were molten, her need evident. Her body was open, on display for him.

For *him.*

And then she was already guiding his cock toward her, and the tip was stroking through her hot, wet folds.

An arch of her back, a twitch of her hips.

And he was inside.

She clamped down hard enough for him to see stars, and she was slick enough that his orgasm was dangerously close with just one stroke.

There was no time for coaxing her pleasure from her.

No time to go slow and soft.

He needed to get her over the edge, and he needed to do it quickly.

Otherwise, their first time was going to be...

"Jeremy?"

He glanced down at her, eyes gone hazy, thoughts slow, mind focused on one thing only.

"Yeah, baby," he managed.

"You need to move." Fingernails digging into his waist, sharp bites of pain that focused him.

He blinked, realized he'd stopped. "Yeah, baby?"

A growl. A nip on his jaw.

One that undid the modicum of control he'd managed to grab.

One that had him *moving*.

One—

She clenched around him.

That had his mind shutting off, his body focused only on pleasure—on hers, on his, on *theirs*. Hard, deep strokes. Long, drugging kisses. Hands caressing the spots that had her writhing against him, had her breaths going jagged, her hips bucking against him, her—

Head falling back as she cried out his name, her pussy convulsing.

Tightening, relaxing. Tightening, relaxing.

Tightening—

He fell over the edge.

Plummeted straight for the earth, the impact shattering him into a million pieces.

And it was Teresa who caught each and every one of them.

Teresa who pieced him back together.

It was fucking *glorious*.

Twenty-Eight

She was bursting with feelings.

They were pulsing through her so intensely that she felt like she was a raw nerve, exposed, aching—

Jeremy's arms tightened around her, and the surge subsided.

Letting her breathe.

Letting her think.

She wasn't numb.

Nope.

She certainly wasn't numb.

She was—

Okay, so she was freaking out a little bit. The sex had been... fucking incredible. But it was what had come before that.

Sitting across a table from him, eating takeout, joking around, even as he played along with her entire plan, letting her help him.

And then helping her have an orgasm that nearly broke her in two.

And it was their lunch the day before.

The coffee and talking in the morning.

It was layers and layers of feelings, and she didn't know if she should be holding her breath, expecting the numb to creep in around her again, or if she should be reaching into the recesses of her mind trying to get it back.

Because this was...

"Baby?"

She blinked. "Yeah?" she asked carefully.

"Want to share why you're thinking so hard that smoke is practically coming out of your ears?"

No. She didn't want to share.

She wanted to keep the argument with herself buried deep.

She didn't want to show Jeremy the broken pieces of her. He might hear it and look at her like she was fucked up, like she was broken, like she was *wrong*.

In fact, she wanted to toss the covers back, to get dressed.

To go home and—

What?

Be alone? Cling to not feeling anything, to sit in the broken pieces of herself?

To be miserable again?

To miss out on takeout and stupid quiz questions, stolen kisses in the kitchen on Game Nights, coffee and croissants and—

Did she want to miss out on Jeremy?

No.

But was she ready to blurt it all out, to see his face change when he heard?

What if he acted like Gabe? Her brother was supposed to love her unconditionally, was supposed to be proud of her and—

He'd hurt her.

What if she shared and Jeremy hurt her, too?

That would—

Well, she thought that Jeremy had the capacity to wound her more deeply than any other person.

"It's okay, baby," he murmured, rubbing his hand up and down her back. "There'll be time."

A bolt of annoyance.

Not at him.

God, he was *Jeremy*. He loved his sister, his brothers, his mother, his friends. He loved...*her*.

The thought wrapped around her middle, pulled tight, lashing her in place, forcing her to see, to accept, to understand that he'd shown her nothing but the fact that he loved *her*.

Had loved her for years.

She'd been an idiot to miss it.

She'd been too *numb* to acknowledge it.

But she wasn't numb now. And she was looking at a man who had listened to her, had validated her feelings, had pulled back when she asked...and then he'd taken it a step further by looking into himself, by reflecting on what he was doing and how he was living and what he wanted the future to look like.

All of which had led him here.

With her.

And...how could she go back to being numb?

How could she retreat in the face of such courage?

How could she *not* love this man back?

Spoiler alert.

She couldn't.

That love and affection for him was buried deep, sewn tight, and it wouldn't be dug out, wouldn't be cut loose.

She loved Jeremy Hutchins.

She wasn't a coward, wouldn't run from him.

So, she did what any self-respecting woman would do.

Teresa shifted in the circle of his arms, and—

She *gave*.

————

His arms had tightened slightly around her when she mentioned Sam, probably thinking about her trampled heart—since that was how she'd phrased it when he'd asked her all those weeks ago.

But now she admitted what really bothered her.

"I thought there was something wrong with me," she whispered. "I'd been with him long enough to feel something, that I should have felt something—"

A hand on her back, slowly stroking, soothing. "But you didn't."

"No," she whispered. "I didn't. I should have. I know I should have—" She clamped her teeth together.

"Why do you think you didn't?"

She blinked. "What?"

He shifted them so they were face to face, rather than her hiding her gaze by pressing it into the curve of his shoulder, the spot that seemed perfectly crafted, perfectly formed for her and her alone.

But now she was on her side, facing him, and there was nowhere else to look but into his warm brown eyes.

"Why do you think you didn't feel anything?"

"I loved him," she said. "I think I did, anyway." Though, looking back, it wasn't anything like what she felt for Jeremy, not even close.

But that wasn't *why* she hadn't felt.

Why she hadn't *let* herself feel.

"Sam must have known," she whispered.

A hand on her cheek, brushing back the hair tickling her skin. "Known what?"

"That I didn't love him." A breath. "That I wouldn't *let* myself love him." Another. "Not like I love you."

His nostrils flared on a breath so sharp that it practically sliced through her eardrums.

"What?"

"I was too scared, and he...he wasn't like you. He was a good man," she felt obligated to add. "But there was no way that he could awaken the things inside me, not like you do." She shook her head, hair dragging over the pillowcase. "He...he couldn't get through the numbness I had pulled around me. I wouldn't let him."

Jeremy was very still, so still that she thought he might not actually be breathing.

"But you—" She shook her head again. "You saw me, and you're so fucking smart and strong and *thoughtful*. And I'm not just an obligation. You like me— You *love* me."

He nodded, fingers trailing over her arm. "I do."

"I think I always knew, even though I pretended I didn't. It was easier to act like you didn't, and because you got all sorts of female attention it was easier to pretend that you weren't interested in anything but the superficial, and when you proved that wasn't the case, that you saw too much...well, it was easier to push you away. Too controlling. Too much of an alpha-hole. Too...*everything.*"

"I was too controlling," he said with a rough laugh. "And talk about someone seeing too much..." He chucked her under the chin. "You pinned me in one, baby. I needed someone to pull my head out of my ass."

She smiled. "I had a little help from Mel and your mom."

"Yeah," he said. "But you started it."

She had.

And she was starting down the same path in her own head, her own heart.

No more living scared.

No more numb.

"And I *do* love you," he said so fucking gently that her eyes stung. "I've loved you from the moment I first saw you cackling over winning *Spoons* and definitely after you kicked my ass in *Catan.*" His fingers danced across her jaw. "You were alive and bright and...*fuck* if you didn't take my breath away." His face clouded. "I hate that you were hurting and that I didn't do anything about it."

She touched his cheek, the bristles of his beard teasing her skin. "I wasn't ready."

A sigh. "I hate that, too."

She grinned. "Your alpha-hole is showing."

"Maybe." A shrug. "Okay, yeah, it is."

Laughter in her belly. Love in her heart. Joy in her mind. Truth in her soul.

"I know it's important for you to take care of the people you love."

A nod. "Yeah, it is. Though I'm working on making sure that is no longer smothering."

God. She *loved* him. "I know, honey," she whispered. "I was just going to say that I'll make sure I find a way to let you do that."

He frowned, started to shake his head. "No, baby. I won't do that to you. I won't hurt you that way."

"That's just it," she said, snagging his hand and bringing it to her mouth. "I'm starting to understand. See? *I'm* learning, too." She smiled, kissed his palm. "You need to take care of the people you love. I get that. But you also need to make sure it's not the only thing you are. I get that, too, and that's one of the ways *I'll* take care of you."

Understanding in his eyes.

"But I also know now that I need to let people in. That I can't live in numb and be happy. Hell, I couldn't do it and just be content. Not now that I know what it feels like to live with all these pesky"—she thumped a fist to her chest, above the spot where her heart was beating a mile a minute, and grinned at him

—"*feelings.* So..." A breath. "That's one of the ways you'll take care of me." She smiled at him. "And I'm sure you'll find other ways."

To care and not smother. To not let her use a shield of numb to bury her emotions.

Just like she was going to make sure he never retreated behind his care, that he never again lived his life solely for other people and not for himself.

"I can do that," he murmured.

She knew he could.

Because he wasn't her father.

And she wasn't her mother.

They could have something else. Something *more.*

And there would be no more hiding. No more fear.

Just love and life and *feelings.*

And after everything else that had happened, that sounded pretty fucking perfect.

Twenty-Nine

JEREMY

He was sleeping in.

He hadn't done that before.

Not since his dad had died.

It was always get up, get moving, make sure his siblings were awake and ready for school. Then it was up and moving, making sure he didn't miss a single class his mom was paying for.

Then it was up and moving, making enough money to buy his mom a new place, making sure she had what she needed after she'd worked so hard for so many years.

So no, there hadn't been any lazy mornings.

But today he was jobless and had kept his woman—a woman who *loved* him (and further that, who'd actually *admitted* that she loved him, which was an even bigger feat in his book)—up into the wee hours of the morning.

So, he was having a lazy morning.

They both had, but about thirty minutes ago, her phone had chimed, and she'd gotten up, showered, and left.

A shower she hadn't let him join in on, because she only had thirty minutes to clean up, dress, and get to the job site.

He'd retrieved her clothes.

She'd put the leggings back on—without underwear (which hadn't much helped his control in not joining her in the shower) —and borrowed one of his T-shirts.

He needed to fuck her in that and nothing else.

He needed to fuck her a lot of ways—all of which he'd carefully made note of in his mind. Three years obsessed with her meant that he had lots of time to plan.

But...they had time.

And he thought that perhaps it was one of the few times he'd actually thought that.

Not rushing to the future and thinking about all the possibilities, about how everything might go wrong and planning all the things he should be prepared to do in every eventuality.

Instead, he was lying in bed, having just watched his woman walk out the door in his shirt. He was jobless. Maybe a bit aimless.

But not unhappy.

Which, he thought, was a bigger commentary on everything to date that had changed in his life thus far than anything else.

Grinning, he reached for the TV remote, intent on adding watching trashy morning TV on an aimless, jobless morning.

His cell rang.

He glared at it, annoyed, but set the remote down and reached for it, glancing at the screen to see the number.

Was he screening his calls?

Yes. Definitely.

But it wasn't one of the lines from his old job. This was a number that was sort of familiar, which was what had him swiping his finger over the screen and putting it up to his ear.

"Hello, this is Jeremy."

"Jeremy? This is Cheryl from Robotech. I wanted to reach

out to you and tell you that I'm pleased we can offer you a position."

She began listing off salary terms and compensation packages and, frankly, his eyes glazed over just a little bit.

It was a lot of money.

The terms were good.

He'd heard from more than one person that their experience working for Robotech was excellent.

But...none of it lit a fire under his ass.

None of what Cheryl was saying excited him.

Not in the least.

He bit back a sigh as she went on for the next couple of minutes, detailing next steps, and finishing with, "I'll courier over the paperwork and written offer along with our welcome packet and a few other items. You can look it over and get back to me."

Said with the confidence of a woman expecting a yes.

Along with sending a written offer *and* a welcome packet.

He almost laughed.

Clearly, not many people turned down a position there.

Too bad he was far from excited about it.

"Thanks, Cheryl," he said, and they talked for another minute or two as she went over a few final details—when to expect the delivery, confirming his address, when the next orientation was.

Then they'd hung up.

He shook his head, tossed his cell on his nightstand.

Sighed.

Thought about what he'd felt during the interview.

Really thought.

Was his ambivalence from the unhappiness of his old position or was it because he really didn't want to work there?

Could he afford *not* to take the offer?

That was the only question he could answer with absolute certainty.

He had savings.

He had time to get his head straight.

Had time to think about the offer, about the job, about the future—

Maybe it wouldn't be at Robotech. Maybe it would.

He snagged the remote again, found the crappiest morning TV he could put on, and fell right into it.

The only thing he knew for certain?

Today wouldn't be the day he made that decision.

Oh, and he wasn't going to end up as a children's party entertainer.

His fingers weren't made for crafting balloon animals.

———

The courier had delivered the packet, and though he'd signed for it, Jeremy had left it unopened on the counter while searching for sustenance.

His fridge...

Was bordering on the edge of pathetic, but there *was* leftover Chinese, and anyway, he was going to Wyatt's house that night for Game Night. There would be plenty of food, Tiffany would make sure of it—and if not, he'd take his woman out for dinner once they were done.

Grocery shopping could wait.

After grabbing the hot container out of the microwave, he moved to his deck, sitting on a chair that got infrequent use.

Mostly from other people.

He was too busy to sit out here, except on the odd night.

But he liked the space, and he liked that he'd built the deck himself. Well, Rafe had helped and his brothers, too, but he'd picked out the design, the materials, organized the delivery. He'd shopped for the furniture.

He'd been a bit like Teresa, he supposed.

A tiny project manager.

And truthfully, that was the part of his previous job he'd enjoyed—coordinating tasks, making sure the right people were assigned, that they had what they needed.

A puzzle every day.

Something he *liked*.

Now that was progress.

Grinning, he went to text Teresa about that particular discovery and was mentally turning over in his head how to make puzzles sound sexy, when his cell rang in his hand.

Frowning, he glanced at the screen.

Asher.

That was convenient, since he wanted to rip his younger brother a new asshole for hurting Mel the way he had.

He swiped, put it up to his ear.

"Hey, fuckhead, you need—"

But then Asher was talking—

And...

Insults faded; worry intruded.

He pushed them aside and focused on what he did best.

Taking care of the people he loved.

His lazy TV day was over, as was sitting on his deck staring out at nothing while crafting sexy text messages to his woman.

His brother needed him.

"Right," he said when Asher took a breath. "I'll be right there."

THIRTY

"What do you think we should do?" he whispered.

Asher was inside, sporting a black eye.

But apparently, that wasn't nearly as bad as what he'd given to the man Melody was dating—no, correction—the man Mel *had* gone on *one* date with.

The man who'd assaulted her.

And Mel...well, Melody was bruised and bloodied and needed crutches and had five stitches in her cheek.

"The hospital called the police," Jeremy said, shifting so that he could slip an arm around her waist, and this was a time when she didn't know if she was the one comforting and caring for him or if it was the other way around.

And it was a time she realized she didn't care.

They were there for each other.

That was enough.

Because she couldn't focus on herself, on her relationship. She was focused on Mel...fucking hell.

Poor Mel.

Who had woken up not knowing where she was, her head fuzzy from the spiked drinks, her body battered and bleeding, and she'd called Asher.

Jeremy's brother had found her then proceeded to beat to the shit out of the man who'd hurt Mel (deservedly) and gotten Mel out of there.

But by that point, Mel hadn't been thinking straight, at least according to Asher.

She screamed and fought him when he'd tried to get her to go to the hospital.

Screamed and fought so much that he'd relented, had brought her to Wyatt and Tiffany's place instead, where she hadn't listened to her twin, hadn't listened to Asher, hadn't listened to Wyatt.

And that was where Teresa's man had come in.

He'd driven here, had bundled her up in his car, and brought her to the hospital.

No coaxing. No trying to convince.

Just taking her in.

And thank God he had.

She needed the injuries to be documented, the police to come, the crime to be reported, and she needed treatment, care, and support for what came after.

She needed closure.

She needed *them*.

"I—" Teresa squeezed his hand, not sure how to answer him about next steps. "What does she want now?"

He shook his head, face creased with worry. "She wants to have a Game Night."

One Teresa had just spent the last thirty minutes canceling, telling everyone the bare details, not wanting to hide what happened—because Mel had nothing to be ashamed of—but also not willing to give too many.

It was her body, her truth, *hers*.

So much had been ripped from her already.

How could Teresa add to it?

But...

She couldn't be meant to think she was alone.

"Then she's going to have a Game Night," Teresa said.

His face clouded with concern. "She's not up—"

"She needs normal, sweetie," she whispered. "She needs us."

That concern was replaced with determination.

"Then she's going to have it."

"Booyah, mofos!" she yelled. "And in case, you're keeping track" —she lightly bumped Mel's arm with her own—"That's my fourth win of the evening." She buffed her knuckles on her shoulder.

"God, woman," Jeremy muttered, tossing his cards on the table. "Give the rest of us a chance."

"*Never,*" she hissed.

Mel didn't reply.

But she did smile.

It was small, but it was something.

And while it felt weird to be ignoring the giant elephant in the room, and there had been a few moments of awkward, the night had been normal.

For the most part.

Mel was quieter than normal, for obvious reasons, and she'd flinched a few times when someone had brushed by her.

But that was getting better as the night went on.

She scooted her chair close to Jeremy's, and Teresa had boxed her in on the other side, keeping her sandwiched and safe.

The games were easy ones, without a ton of strategy planning. No stress, just fast-paced fun where she wouldn't have to think. And Teresa knew her role—she'd been her usual, loud, competitive, feisty self.

Asher...well, he wasn't himself, even discounting the black eye.

He was brooding, his black mood almost palpable anytime that Mel wasn't in the vicinity. But when Mel *did* come in, he was gentler than Teresa had seen any time in the three years she'd known him.

But Teresa was sensing that this Game Night needed to end early.

Part of it was the fine tremor that had begun to travel through Mel's body—fatigue or memories or something blacker.

The rest was that Mel had wanted a glimpse of normal, and they'd given it to her.

Now they needed to give her space.

She glanced at Jeremy as Tiffany shuffled the cards—and while Mel's twin was trying to put up a good front, Teresa saw that she was reaching her limit, too.

"Reality TV time?" he asked softly.

"Yeah," she said.

Though she would make certain the women and men peeled off quietly and quickly.

This was no late-night binge fest where they ended up sloshed and poured into their designated drivers' cars.

Nope.

This was...

Get Mel settled in front of the TV and slip out quietly.

Her gaze slanted to the side and connected with Cora's, and all at once, everyone was in their normal bustle, gathering snacks and drinks, TV remotes and blankets and pillows.

The men—except for Asher—disappeared, and the women gathered around Mel.

Another hour, Teresa thought—they could get their friend one more hour of forgetting, of numbness, of peace.

Then they needed to back off.

She hadn't counted on Asher, though.

Or, she hadn't counted on Mel's response to Asher leaving.

The girls had slipped away, cleaning quickly and quietly, before gathering up their partners and heading out. The other Hutchins brothers had gone as well.

But when Asher had pulled on his jacket...

Mel had panicked.

"No, no, no!" she screamed, jolting to her feet, the fear in her words jolting through Teresa, slicing deep. "Please," Mel said and took a step forward, putting weight on the ankle she'd sprained and shouldn't be walking on. Wincing, her voice quieting, but the fear in those words no less painful to the casual observer. "Please, don't go."

Teresa slid a careful arm around her waist, taking some of her weight. "It's okay," she whispered. "Breathe, honey, and just tell us what you need."

"Asher," she whispered. "I need Asher."

The air went taut.

"He can't go," Mel said. "If he goes—" She broke off, practically vibrating in Teresa's hold.

Teresa glanced up at Jeremy, at Asher, who'd both frozen in the hall.

Mel's knees buckled.

Teresa went down with her, still holding her tight. "It's okay. It's—"

Then Asher was there, crouching down in front of them, reaching for Mel's hands. "Breathe, sweetheart."

A shuddering breath.

"Good."

Another.

"Good, sweetheart," Asher said gently. "Now, you're coming home with me."

Mel stilled, and it was as though she were holding her breath.

"Ash," Jeremy began, worry on his face.

Asher tugged her from Teresa's hold, gathered her against his chest, and then stood with her in his arms. "She's coming home with me until she feels ready to be on her own."

No argument brokered.

And none given, not by anyone in the room.

They all knew something of the Hutchins brand of protectiveness.

Mel had asked for it.

Needed it.

Asher would give it.

Needed to give it.

And the rest...the rest of it would fall into place.

THIRTY-ONE

JEREMY

"You okay?" he asked softly as they drove.

"Not really. You?"

His fingers found hers, linked them together. "Not really."

"I just..." She trailed off, staring out into the night through the car window. Eventually, she shook her head. "I just...poor *Mel.*"

His rage was a palpable, dangerous thing.

He wanted to go after the man, to beat him all over again, to do worse than what Asher had done. God knew the fucker deserved it, deserved the pain, deserved permanent reminders of what happened to a man when he hurt a woman.

But the man had already been picked up by the police, was being held.

It wouldn't do anyone any good right then.

Besides, Mel needed them more than she needed their anger.

So, he was tempering it. For now.

"Every time I close my eyes, I'm going to remember what she

looked like..." A breath, more rage sliding through him. "When they took her back—" He shook his head, sharply. "Fuck, I'm not sure that Asher will be able to forgive himself."

"He didn't do anything."

Jeremy's fingers clenched on the steering wheel. "Yeah," he whispered, "and I think that's going to be the hardest for him to overcome." He slanted a gaze her way. "It's not that Ash doesn't like Mel—not that he *didn't* like her before. He..."

Fuck, the way he'd been when they'd taken Mel into a room without them, without *him*—

How he'd been tonight...

It wasn't a man who didn't care.

It was a man who cared too fucking much.

"He made it clear he didn't want her," Teresa muttered.

"Well, let's just say that I know a little something of being the *unwanted* one."

She turned to him, and her lips twitched. "Fine, be logical."

"One of us has to."

A swat, then, "I think she'll be okay with him."

"Asher will watch out for her."

"Yeah, he—what the hell?"

He'd just pulled into her driveway...right next to a car that—

"Gabe," she whispered as he slid to a stop, put his car in park.

The brother who'd—

Admittedly, his temper was spiking, mostly because he remembered *exactly* what the fucker had said to his woman. He pushed open his door.

"Jeremy!"

But he was already rounding the hood of his car, barreling up the walk, grabbing the other man by his collar. "You are a fucking *asshole*," he snapped.

Teresa's brother bristled immediately—which was *fair*, considering they'd met each other maybe one time before, and

Jer was putting hands on him and calling him an asshole. But then Gabe's gaze went over Jeremy's shoulder.

Footsteps coming up the path.

Echoing as Teresa came closer.

"Jer," she said softly.

Carefully.

As though he were one second away from losing his shit.

Which...also *fair.*

But before he could reply or even release Gabe, her brother dropped his hands to his sides. "I am," he muttered. "I am a fucking asshole."

Surprised, Jer rocked back on his heels. "What?"

Gabe ignored him. "Teresa, honey, I'm sorry," he said gently. "I'm so sorry about what I said."

A hand on Jeremy's back, gently stroking down his spine. "Can you let my brother go, honey?"

He didn't want to.

He *wanted* to throttle Gabe, to squeeze the breath from his lungs so that he could never speak to Teresa like he had, not ever again.

But...

He trusted Teresa to know what she needed.

Dropping his hands, he stepped back, took a breath, and focused. Not on his own ego, on what *he* needed to give. But on what his woman would need.

Which was *not* him beating her brother to a pulp, unfortunately.

Space to talk to her brother, whose face made it clear that he wasn't here to stir up more trouble. Nope, there was apology in every inch of the fucker.

Sigh.

Turning, he cupped her cheek.

Then he took her purse, reached inside, and pulled out her

keys. A moment later, the door was unlocked, and he was leading them inside.

Space to talk.

But a warm and safe space, he thought, closing the door, and flicking the lock.

Where he would be just down the hall so he could listen in case she needed him.

Care, but not smothering.

Giving what he needed to give, but also giving what would support her.

Fuck, he was positively reformed now.

A thought which made him want to smile, though he smothered the urge and continued glowering at her brother, just for good measure, as he started to walk past them. Kitchen. Beer. Ice cream. He had the feeling they were both going to need it.

Before he made it all the way though, Teresa leaned close and brushed her lips over his cheek. "I love you," she whispered.

The words settled in his heart.

He slid a hand down her back. "Love you, too, baby."

Then he moved on, though not before he saw Teresa turn to her brother and cross her arms across her chest.

Into the kitchen, beer out of the fridge.

But listening to every word.

"Why are you here?" No wiggle room in her tone.

Good.

A long silence then, "I'm so sorry, T. I...shouldn't have said what I did. It was way out of line and—" His voice cut off. "I didn't mean it. I was...*fuck*, I never stopped to think about what you might want. I just assumed that..."

"I was a typical useless female?"

"What? *No.*"

"Then what?"

"Then, fuck, T, I—" The volume of his voice dropped then raised. "I'm jealous, okay?"

That nearly made Jeremy drop his beer, and he leaned back against the countertop in the kitchen, surprised the kid had admitted it, but glad for Teresa that he had.

"You're doing *exactly* what you want," Gabe said, "and you're not scared to go out and try something new and—"

He was getting louder, and Jer had run out of patience.

He moved back down the hall, slipped into her family room.

The siblings were facing off, just a couple of feet apart, and he moved close to Teresa, drew her back against him. A glance up revealed she wasn't upset, that her lips were actually turning up at the edges.

"Reached your limit?"

He brushed his lips over hers. "Yeah." He glanced up. "Just because your sister is a badass, doesn't mean that you can use her like a punching bag."

Teresa's hand found his, squeezed lightly.

"I *know* I'm an asshole," Gabe snapped. "But I'm trying to apologize."

"You said sorry. She accepts—" He glanced down, and Teresa nodded, a bemused smile on her lips. "But it's late, and we've had a hell of a day. You want to rehash this? Do it another day."

"You let him speak for you?"

"Sometimes." Teresa's smile grew. "Because most of the time, he lets me speak for myself."

Gabe inhaled sharply.

"Listen to your sister," he said. "She's the smartest person I know, and she's taught me that the only way to stop being an asshole is to stop thinking about what you don't have, start thinking about what you want, and then going out and *getting* it."

Now Gabe exhaled.

And he did it with a bemused smile on his lips.

"You believe that, T?" he asked.

"With every cell in my body."

"Damn," Gabe whispered.

"What?" she whispered back.

"I'm supposed to be the smarter older brother."

"Bow to my excellence," she teased, but then she broke off on a yawn. "It's—"

"Bedtime," Jer said, hauling her back against his chest.

Her eyes on his. Her hand on his jaw.

"Yeah," she said softly. "Bedtime."

THIRTY-TWO

TERESA

She'd arranged to meet Gabe in a couple of days to finish talking out what they'd started the night before.

But today—tonight—

It was mani-pedi night.

Needless to say, she was not thrilled.

She wanted to check on Mel.

She wanted to *see* Mel.

But Jeremy had texted her that morning and she'd replied and...she'd asked for space. That, along with Asher's reassurance that she was doing okay, meant that Teresa had backed off.

For today.

Tomorrow would be another story.

And she'd better watch out, otherwise she was going to end up pulling an overprotective alpha-hole.

That thought, at least, had her smiling, relaxing enough that she wasn't scowling as she walked up the porch steps and unlocked the front door.

She was...disquieted, though, and upset, not just because of Mel.

But...Gabe had said he was jealous.

Of her.

That was...

Confusing and disquieting and made her wonder if she was missing something else. If she hadn't seen *that* clearly, hadn't understood where his anger was coming from...what else had she missed?

Not that it excused his behavior.

He'd been way out of line.

But he'd apologized and she thought it was genuine, and as Jeremy had pointed out just before they'd gone to sleep last night, time would tell if he'd truly learned.

She had faith her brother had.

And she hoped she had, too.

Now, though, she had to survive mani-pedis, something she was feeling way too introspective for.

"Honey?"

"Just me, Mom."

"Come into the kitchen and get something to eat."

"I'm not hungry," she said as she strode into the room, "but thank you. I made our appointment at the new place you wanted to try this week. We should head out soon so we're not late."

Her mom was stirring something on the stove, but she turned her face up and Teresa pressed a kiss to her cheek. "Tell me everything, baby."

"How long is that going to take to finish up?" she asked. "We have our appointment."

"Your father needs dinner before we go."

Okay, this was the stuff she knew she hadn't missed or misinterpreted. This was the stuff that drove her crazy. Her mom had been ill, had been nearly dead, but she lived...and she'd stepped right back into the cage, willingly.

Her father could cook one damned meal, or hell, he could get takeout the one night a week her mother, his wife went out for a fucking hour.

"You don't need to look like that," her mom said, stirring the meat, "it'll only take a few minutes."

"I know."

But fuck if it wasn't annoying anyway.

"Why do you do it?" she whispered. "Why do you wait on him? He never washes a dish, never folds a load of laundry. I don't think he's ever cooked for you, not even when you were sick and—"

The spoon clinked along the edge of the pot. "Don't," her mother murmured. "Just...don't do this today."

"Why not?" Teresa snapped. "God, if not today, then when? You never change. *None* of you do."

Which wasn't a fair assessment, not at all. Not after what Gabe had shown her the night before, not after Anton's support.

Her brothers might be shifting perspective.

But her parents weren't. Her mother wasn't.

Case in point, her pulling the pot off the stove, plating up food for her father. Then she turned to Teresa. "I'm happy in my life."

"Happy in this house? Cooking all the time? Never going out? Never living a life that's not taking care of someone?" Her mother put her pot in the sink but didn't look at Teresa, just moved to the fridge, grabbed a beer.

Teresa stepped in front of her. "Don't you want *more?*" she asked. "Don't you want something for yourself?"

Her mother sidestepped her, put the beer on the table.

"Mom."

She turned, headed for the silverware drawer.

"*Mom.*"

Opened it, pulled out a fork and knife.

"*Mom!*"

"What, Teresa?" she snapped, and it was a tone she'd never heard from her mother before. Warm and soft, not sharp and cutting. "What the heck do you want me to say? I love you and my family. I love my life."

"It's like you're brainwashed." She tossed up her hands. "You don't *do* anything. You don't go anywhere or see anyone or, hell, Mom. I swear to God, you spend more time ironing Dad's underwear than doing something for yourself."

Her mom went still.

Very still.

"You could be so much more. You could live your dream. You could—"

Her mother carefully turned and put the fork and knife on the table. "You talk a lot of dreams, my darling." Her voice was quiet, but steady. *Too* steady. "It's just too bad that the only dreams you recognize are your own."

That struck hard and—

Her mom walked out of the room.

True.

Fuck.

Fuck.

"Mom, wait," she said, running after her. "I-I—"

"Let's pick this up next week," her mother said. "I'm tired."

She was an ass.

Even a bigger one than her brother.

Had she truly not learned *anything* from all that she had been through with Jeremy, all they had both learned? Had she really not reflected on how shitty it felt for her brother to discount her choices?

And she'd just done the same damned thing.

To her mother.

Fuck. *Fuck.*

She caught her arm. "Mom. Wait. I'm sorry."

A smile, gentle, typical of her mom. "It's fine, honey." A pat to her shoulder. "I'll see you next week."

"No," Teresa whispered. "Don't do that. I hurt you. I'm sorry." She caught her mom's hand. "I didn't mean to discount your choices."

"I know," her mother said. "It's just that our choices are very far apart."

That.

It was that exactly.

And she was an asshole to think that her decisions, her dreams were better, especially when she was nursing her own hurt about her choices not being respected by her family.

She'd done the same damned thing to her mom.

"I may not flare hot like you, like your dad, your brothers," her mom said on a slow, deep breath, the hurt still in her eyes. "But there is strength in being soft. There is strength in giving, in *caring* for the ones you love."

Teresa dropped her arm. "I know."

God, she knew.

That was Jeremy.

That was her mother.

"Honey, I know you think that I lost myself," her mom whispered. "But having a family, having people to love was *my* biggest dream."

She reached over, grabbed Teresa's hand, fingers tightening almost painfully.

"That's not your dream." A breath. "I see that now."

Teresa held her breath.

Her mom stroked a hand down her cheek. "I've been so blind."

That breath slid out on a shaky exhale. "Mom—"

"And God—" Her mom's voice broke. "I'm so sorry it took

me so long to understand that." Her eyes glinting with tears. "That wasn't fair to you. I was blinded by thinking I'd lost you, lost all of you. It was easier, safer for me to push you on my path because I understood it. But..." She cupped Teresa's cheeks. "That's not you."

"No," Teresa whispered.

"You need to forge your own path."

"I do." A breath as she covered her mom's hands. "But I was a jerk to not recognize that your path is your own. Just because it's not for me..." She shook her head. "I'm sorry. Really—"

"My baby," she whispered. "So strong and smart."

"Not smart enough to see you for—"

"Stop."

Another sharp word from her mom who wasn't sharp.

But clearly, she had depths that Teresa didn't understand.

And that was something else for her to learn, to internalize, to understand.

"I want you to go out there, baby," her mom ordered. "I want you to build your company. To do it big and bright and make it *you*, and know that I'm here for you, that I'm cheering for you." She kissed Teresa's forehead. "That I *know* you'll be successful because you're finding *your* path, not mine. Now," she whispered, back to that soft, warm mom. "Your dad's dinner is on the table, so now we're getting our nails done."

"Okay," she whispered.

So, she and her mom got their nails done.

And for once, they didn't talk about marriage. They talked about her company and the next steps. They talked about her dreams for the future. They talked about choosing precisely the right shade of red for their nails.

And for the first time in a long time, Teresa had a night with her mom that didn't leave her shredded.

And then when she mentioned Jeremy, she got to see the joy on her mother's face.

"Happy for you, my baby," she whispered when they hugged on the doorstep. "Living *all* your dreams."

She brushed her mom's hair away, stepped back. "Because you showed me how."

And finally, she understood that for the truth it was.

Thirty-Three

JEREMY

He closed his laptop and turned toward his woman.

She was on her phone outside on his back deck, pacing back and forth, her cell pinned between shoulder and ear, hands gesticulating widely.

A delivery had been fucked up, dropped at the wrong job site, and she was making her disapproval well known.

"Ugh," she snapped, stomping back into the house. "I swear to God that I confirmed the location with them *twice* before they submitted the delivery date."

He was sure she had.

He'd seen the master spreadsheet she worked with.

It planned for every eventuality.

"So, when can they move it over?"

Another sigh. "They're short on delivery drivers, so they say that it can't happen until next week. Ugh!" She dropped her cell on the table. "Sometimes these people make me want to tear my hair out."

He tugged her close, drawing her down into his lap. "I know," he said. "But you'll sort it out."

"I always do," she grumbled.

Something occurred to him. "Can they squeeze another delivery into the next couple of days, if it's only dropping a couple of pallets instead of having to repack and load everything?"

"What are you thinking?"

"If they can make another delivery then your problem is solved. The other materials can sit at the other site until they can pick it up next week."

She smiled. "And since it was their fuck up, we won't pay for the second delivery, which means they'll be motivated to pick it up, too. Oh..." She kissed his jaw. "That's *good*, baby." She hopped off his lap, scooped up her phone. "I'm going to call them back right now." She stopped, turned back. "Maybe you should do *my* job, honey."

Then she was out the door.

And he was thinking...

Maybe he wanted to do it, too.

Mel was quiet and sad.

But she was also strong.

"I'm okay," she whispered, staring out at the scene in front of them.

They'd met up for coffee and pastries, but the woman sitting across from him wasn't the same from a few weeks before.

His life had been going great.

And Mel was fighting demons.

"I know, honey," he said gently.

She'd left Asher's house, had gone home, but Asher was

worried, mostly because she hadn't slept a full night in the time she'd stayed there.

And it didn't appear as though her sleeping habits had improved.

Dark circles under her eyes, creases on either side of her mouth.

Poor thing was exhausted.

"I'm seeing someone."

His brows shot up.

"A therapist," she clarified.

"That's good, honey," he said, reaching across the table and squeezing her hand. She didn't flinch, thank God, but the limp way she held his hand told him she wasn't anywhere near okay.

Her phone chimed, and she glanced down at it, pulling free of his grip. "That's work," she whispered. "I should probably head back in."

He didn't argue, just grabbed a bag for the croissant she didn't eat and then walked her to her car.

He hugged her goodbye.

When she pulled back, she stared up into his eyes, a glimpse of that old Mel for a second. "You're happy?"

"Yeah."

Her hand on his cheek. "Good." Then she smiled mischievously as she snagged the bag from his grip. "Mine."

"Yours," he agreed.

"I'm gonna go," she whispered.

He nodded, stepped back, but he didn't miss the old Mel slipping away.

Didn't miss the shadows creeping in.

Didn't miss that after she'd driven away, he'd looked up and saw Asher standing across the parking lot, agony on his face.

———

"Go," he told her, nudging her out the door. "I'll handle the crew. You go meet with Mrs. J and all her minions."

A nod, and hell if she wasn't sexy as fuck walking away from him in that tight business suit.

But then she stopped, spun on her heels, clicking back over to him.

He had her spreadsheets on his laptop.

He had her bedazzled clipboard and her to-do list.

He had her instructions on how to handle both of those.

"You'll call me if you have any issues?"

"Nope," he said, snagging her by the waist and drawing her close when she started protesting. "I'll handle it, baby. I promise. And then when you're done, we'll compare notes, and you'll tell me all the things I can improve on."

A grin. "I love you."

He kissed her.

Because those words.

"You're meeting up with your mom after Mrs. J?"

She nodded. "Yeah, so I won't be back here to yell at you until late."

"I'll make sure to take a nap so that I can stay up late."

"Pain in the ass."

He nuzzled her throat. "Damn, right." A nip to her jaw so that he didn't mess up her lipstick. "Go get 'em, baby."

A squeeze of her arms before she was out of his lap and clicking away from him...and he was enjoying that view, all over again.

Gorgeous ass.

Gorgeous heart.

His.

He smiled, packed up his shit, and then he headed out to the job site.

———

Hours later, he'd had a glimpse of the hard shit that came with Teresa's job.

And frankly, he was exhausted.

Definitely exhausted, but also...fulfilled in a way that he never would have expected.

He liked what she was doing.

The challenge. The puzzle. The people.

Working with Rafe.

He wondered...if by helping Teresa out the last few weeks, if he'd stumbled onto something he wanted to do.

He'd talked to Rafe about it—if he thought that Jeremy might be a good fit when Teresa eventually left, and Rafe had been on board.

With how busy Teresa had been, that time might come sooner rather than later.

But he wanted to talk to her first, to get her thoughts.

He didn't want to step on something she wasn't comfortable with, to cross a boundary that would make her uncomfortable. Work was less important than her, than their relationship.

But...

He was excited.

He felt like there was a whole new realm of possibilities in front of him.

He wanted her to be excited for him.

He hoped she would be.

He hoped she wouldn't think that he was trying to take her spot or push her out or—

"Jesus, man," he muttered, tossing back the blankets, and getting out of bed.

He just needed to breathe and focus and *talk* to her.

That was the way they handled their shit. Not with fear and worrying and getting himself into a tizzy.

So, he grabbed a beer, parked himself in front of the TV, and waited for her to come home.

And waited.

And waited some more.

Finally, when it was definitely way too late for mani-pedis and dinner and maybe post-dinner drinks with her mom, he called her.

It went straight to voicemail.

Had her battery died?

Had—

Lights in his driveway.

Relief oozing out of his every pore.

He plunked the beer on his coffee table, hopped to his feet, and moved to the door, opening it even as she was just climbing out of her car.

"Hey, baby," he began.

"Stop."

One harsh word.

And with it, everything changed.

THIRTY-FOUR

TERESA

She'd made it to the porch.

Was struggling for calm.

But she didn't think she managed it, not when she bit out, "When were you going to tell me?"

For a second, she felt guilty.

Maybe she should slow down, take a beat, and—

But then his face changed.

He was hiding something.

And that momentary thought of slowing down and taking a beat and starting from the beginning disappeared.

"You weren't, were you?"

"Teresa, baby," he said, rubbing a hand across his forehead. "Come into the house and let's talk about what's bothering you?"

"You weren't," she said again.

Some emotion—guilt? excitement? worry?—sliding across his face. "Of course, I was going to tell you. I just..."

"You just...?" She waved a hand, wanting him to go on.

"Let's go in the house." He stepped closer.

She stepped back.

"It's getting late." He shifted toward her. "Come inside, let's talk about—"

"The fact that you're lying to me?"

"Okay—" He took her arm, tugged just hard enough to piss her off. She wasn't a fucking dog to be led around, and his next words sent her anger even higher. "Just calm down, think, and *stop* for a second."

Calm. Down.

Think.

Stop.

"Fuck you," she hissed.

He reeled back, hand falling from her arm. "Teresa," he said softly.

Disapprovingly.

And yeah, so maybe the next thing she did was very dramatic, but her anger had been ratcheted higher and higher and so...

She just snapped.

She reached into her purse and tossed the papers on the porch.

They scattered everywhere.

"What the fuck, baby?" he whispered.

"You lied to me. You said you wanted to change. That you wanted something different, and there it is"—she jabbed a hand in the direction of the papers—"the fucking evidence that you're going to do the same old shit all over again."

He pushed one of the papers to the side, bent and picked it up. "This? Seriously?"

Her temper frayed. "You promised me that you were going to find something that you loved doing and you've been hiding this from me this whole time. The offer was a month ago, the start date is next week! When were you going to tell me?"

"You think I would keep a job away from you?" he asked. "Seriously?"

The evidence was right in front of him.

So, she just pointed to the papers. "The proof is right there."

"Papers," he said. "Papers I'd shoved in a corner of my kitchen, that I hadn't taken action on because I *wasn't* going to take action on them. I interviewed before I quit. I knew I wasn't going to take the job—"

"Then why is there a fucking *welcome* packet in there, and why are there dates for you to come in for orientation?"

"Because no one is stupid enough to turn down a job at Robotech!" he snapped. "Except me, apparently." He kicked his foot through the papers, knocking them to the side. "I knew I wasn't going to take the job, so I didn't bother doing anything with them, especially because everything happened with Mel, and I quit *my* job, and we were sorting our shit out, and I was trying to figure out what the fuck it was that I wanted to do for the rest of my life—"

He broke off.

And it was a good thing.

Because her belly had begun churning.

That instinct that had told her to pause, to stop and think—the one that she'd ignored? Well...she was realizing now that she should have paid attention.

Should have taken that moment.

But she'd come home early to surprise him.

And he hadn't been there.

And the papers had been there, right on his counter.

Taunting her.

Telling her that everything they were working toward was going to unravel. He wasn't learning. It was all bullshit, all a farce.

All something she'd misunderstood.

Just like she'd misunderstood her mom.

She'd seen those papers…and the doubts had come back, the numbness had crept in, clawing up her legs, squeezing tightly around her lungs.

She'd taken the folder. She'd left.

She'd gone back to her place and read every bit of the folder.

Of course, he'd take it. The pay was…incredible. The benefits package…even more so.

And he was going to be unhappy.

And then…eventually…he was going to be unhappy with her.

"I'm sorry," she whispered. "I-I misread this."

Silence.

Then his lungs rising and falling on a breath. "Yeah," he said, bending to pick up the papers, stacking them, shoving them back into the manila envelope. "You did."

"Honey," she whispered, reaching for him.

He leaned back. "Just…not right now, Teresa."

He stood, papers in his hand as he stepped down off the porch, moving around the side of the house.

She heard the trash can lid open and slam closed, and he came back empty-handed and—

Fuck, he wouldn't look at her.

"I think you should go home."

The words…they slid through space, slammed into her heart. "What?"

"I…I think we need a little space. Just for tonight."

"I—*no*, Jeremy," she scrambled after him, but he was already moving to the door. "You promised to take care of me. Let's just take a second and—"

He stepped over the threshold, and fuck, but his eyes were sad. "I also promised to take care of *me*, baby."

That was maybe the *one* thing he could say that would get her to stop.

The only thing.

He took another step back, and the hurt on his face practically eviscerated her.

But then he murmured, "Tomorrow."

She sucked in a breath, trying to summon the right thing.

The door closed in her face.

"Fuck," she whispered.

———

The next morning her phone rang.

She scrambled to grab it.

She hadn't slept, not at all, the entire night.

Every part of her told her to push, to press, to force the issue.

But how could she when she'd asked him to give her space and he'd listened? He'd respected her and...

It wasn't Jeremy calling.

It was Rafe.

Never had she been more disappointed that her boss was calling.

"Hey," she said, wanting to deal with whatever it was as quickly as possible. Because she needed to keep the line clear, needed to talk to Jeremy.

"I just wanted to see if Jeremy was coming in with you today?"

She frowned. "What?"

A beat of silence. "D-do you have a problem with him learning the ropes now? I know you're not going to leave for a bit, but you *are* going to leave, and it's probably going to be sooner rather than later." He waited another beat, probably waiting for her to respond, but she was struggling to put the pieces together in her mind. "I think it would be good for him to walk through some projects."

"What are you talking about?"

Okay, it was less her putting the pieces together and more her scrambling to keep up.

More quiet.

Then...

"You're mad he wants to replace you?"

Wait.

What?

"I think he'd be a good fit, and he's a natural. I wouldn't replace you, you know that, but..."

He kept talking, but honestly, she wasn't hearing him.

Because...

"T? You there?"

Jeremy wanted to replace her?

Wanted to work with Rafe?

That would be fucking *perfect*.

He *was* a natural. And if he liked it, if it all worked out, he'd get the perk of being able to work with his best friend.

"T?"

"Rafe," she whispered. "I fucked up."

THIRTY-FIVE

JEREMY

Okay, so he was feeling more than a little broody.

He knew that he should just pick up his phone and call Teresa.

Talk and hash things out.

But...truthfully, he was more than a little hurt.

She'd flown off the handle; she'd told him to fuck off.

She'd...thought he would lie to her.

He'd opened up to her more than he'd opened up to anyone and...

Hell, he wanted to sit and be mad and be hurt and—

"Christ," he muttered, plunking his coffee mug down on the table and scrubbing his hands over his face.

His phone was right there.

Right *there.*

But...was it what he wanted?

Was *Teresa* what he wanted?

Fuck, what if he was being an idiot? What if he was so

focused on what he shouldn't be, that he wasn't thinking clearly about what he wanted?

What if he woke up one morning and realized it wasn't Teresa?

The thought ricocheted through him like a bullet, zigzagging through his heart, his lungs, his stomach.

And so did the answer.

No.

The only thing he was certain of was that Teresa was it for him.

Which meant he needed to get off his ass, stop being hurt, and do something about it.

Right.

He stood, reached for his coffee mug, turned for the house, and—

Froze.

Because Teresa was there.

She looked...horrible. Dark circles under her eyes, hair a mess, expression...frazzled.

"Baby?"

Her face crumpled.

"Shit, Teresa. What's the matter?"

"I—" She'd been moving toward him, but his query stopped her in her tracks. "What's the matter? What's the *matter?*"

Okay, so that probably had been a stupid question.

"Come here," he whispered, opening his arms.

She shook her head. "I'm so stupid and messed up."

"You're not stupid, baby."

"I am!" she wailed as tears began gathering at the corners of her eyes. "I-I thought you were backtracking, and I thought that you were keeping things from me and—"

"It's okay," he said. "You're here now. We'll figure it out."

"It's *not* okay." She came toward him again but stopped

before she got within arm's reach. "I'm..." A breath. "It's not just that I thought you lied to me, which was stupid because we've been more open with each other than anyone in my life. Ever."

He was glad to hear she felt the same.

That was why her doubt and words had sliced him to the quick.

"Look, honey, I'm not going to say that last night didn't hurt. It did. Of course, it did. But we're going to have misunderstandings. We're going to need space."

"I accused you of backtracking, and *I'm* the one who was sliding in reverse, who was wrapped up in the past and not thinking straight."

He couldn't stand the space between them, so he closed it, took her in his arms. "Why, baby? What did you think I was going to do?"

A breath, her body trembling in his arms.

But she gave him the truth. "I thought if you went back to that type of job, that type of *life*...I thought...*No.* I knew that you would eventually be unhappy with your work, and if you went back to being unhappy with work, that would translate to the rest of your life and—"

She broke off, swallowing hard, gaze darting away from his.

His throat was tight, voice barely a rasp, but he managed to ask, "And?" when she didn't go on.

Her eyes connected with his but only for a heartbeat before they slid away again. "I knew, I *knew* that it wouldn't take long for you to be unhappy with me." Her chest rose and fell on a breath. "I knew that, eventually, you wouldn't want me anymore either."

So that was what had been going through her head.

Christ.

He'd been hurt and insecure and doubting, and she'd been...

Hurt. Insecure.

Doubting.

Not a surprise considering all the ground they'd covered.

He held her closer. "We covered a lot of ground these last couple of weeks. Of course, we're bound to have a couple of small freak-outs."

"You're calling last night small?" she asked, mouth dropping open.

"Considering we're here the following morning with our arms around each other?" he asked, cupping the side of her throat. "Then yeah, honey, I say that last night is small. You're here. I'm here. We love each other." He brushed his thumb over her pulse. "We're going to fuck up. We're going to get mad and stay stupid shit, of course we are. But," he added, shifting closer, drawing her more tightly against him, "the important thing is that we come back together, that we figure it the fuck out, that we move forward because we've learned from those fuck ups."

She dropped her forehead onto his chest. "How do you make it sound so easy?"

He leaned back enough to crouch, to meet her gaze. "Because loving you is the easiest thing that I have ever done."

Now the tears were back, but he knew they were for a completely different reason even before she buried her face in his chest again, the dampness gathering on his shirt. "Dammit, honey," she whispered. "That isn't fair."

He couldn't stand her tears, happy, sad, or in between.

So, he tried to lighten her heart, her mind.

"Because I want to steal your job?"

Her head popped up and even though there were tears on her cheeks, dripping down beyond the corners of her mouth, her smile was still the most beautiful thing he'd ever seen.

"I think it's perfect," she whispered.

"Me stealing it?"

A hand on his cheek, lightly dragging through his beard. "I think it's perfect," she said again. "You'll be great at it." She fixed him with a look. "But I swear to God, Jeremy, if you are even the least bit unhappy, I'm going to make you quit and find something else. I don't care if Rafe is your best friend or not."

He covered her hand, pressed it into his skin, soaked in the warmth. "There are unhappy parts to every job," he pointed out.

"Not for you," she whispered. "You deserve to be happy every moment of every day."

God, he loved her.

"No one has ever loved me like you have."

She sucked in a breath, released it slowly. "I'm just returning the gift that was given me."

And in that moment, he knew, *knew* that with Teresa in his life there wouldn't ever be a time when he was unhappy.

Things might get hard, they would no doubt fight at regular intervals, life would throw them plenty of curveballs, some they'd hit, others would count as strikes.

But through it all, with this woman at his side, he could never be unhappy.

He wouldn't ever dare to.

Because she wouldn't let him.

And that was just fine by him.

Because he knew he had a stubborn streak, too.

And he'd use it to make sure she smiled like that every single day for the rest of their lives.

That was love.

That was learning.

That was perfect.

EPILOGUE

JEREMY, THREE MONTHS LATER

That was it.

The final item checked off the to-do list.

Rafe grinned and clapped him on the back. "Nice work, bud," he said, holding up the keys. "One of the smoothest yet."

"Liar," he laughed, pulling back, and punching Rafe on the shoulder. "But I'll get better at it."

This was his first solo management project.

The first time he'd run one without Teresa partnering with him, double-checking his steps, acting as his sounding board, (and yes, occasionally helping to guide him back in the right direction).

It hadn't been completely smooth, not by a longshot.

But he'd managed to get his shit together.

He'd managed to keep the project mostly on time, and—

He'd finished it.

And...

Hell, he'd be happy if he never saw this building and its troublesome foundation, plumbing, and electrical again.

"Yeah," Rafe said, nodding to the front door. "You will."

Jeremy took the hint and moved that way, flicking off lights as they went.

Then stepped out into the cool evening air as Rafe locked up behind him.

"First project," he said, tossing the keys to Jeremy, "means that you get to do the honor of handing over the keys."

That felt...permanent and final and *complete.*

And that felt exciting, too.

Because he would be looking toward the next project.

Grinning, he snagged the set from his friend, pocketed it.

"Want to get a beer?" he asked.

Rafe shook his head. "Sorry, can't, Cora is expecting me."

He clasped his friend's hand. "No worries. Next time."

They exchanged their goodbyes, and he watched his friend drive away.

Then took a few minutes to sit in his car in front of that building and go over the project in its entirety.

What could be better. What had worked.

The parts he'd hated. Those he'd enjoyed.

What he was looking forward to on the next one.

Satisfied, he nodded to himself, turned on his car, and drove home to shower in absolutely no hurry.

Teresa had a late business meeting, so he'd promised to go to her place. But he needed fresh clothes, and he was running low on his preferred brand of coffee (which had become her preferred brand as well). He wanted to get the extra bag from his house, grab some clothes so he could avoid laundry for another couple of days, and then sneak a few cookies from the secret stash Teresa's mom had smuggled him.

Mostly because his brothers were fucking mooches, who kept eating his share of the batches Teresa's mom been baking.

Teresa's mom had been baking with his mother...and *Teresa*. Yup.

The threesome had gotten in the habit of baking together. Which was win-win for everyone.

Teresa got time with her mom, *his* mom was happy to spend time with them both (and "have some help feeding my boys"), and the boys in question didn't mind being fed, not when it meant the result was their kitchens were stocked with chocolate chip cookies that were good enough to marry (if he hadn't been planning on making Teresa his wife, that was).

The difficulty came when everyone had gobbled down their tasty treats and then tried to steal *his* cookies.

It didn't matter that his share was the largest.

He got the biggest portion because he was the oldest, and maybe because Teresa loved him best.

Plus, he had to keep his strength up.

His woman had an even longer to-do list in the bedroom than she'd kept on her projects.

And he was the lucky recipient of her attention to detail.

Grinning, he pulled into the driveway, and then paused, blinking, momentarily confused why her car was there.

Why the lights were on.

Why...there were shadows moving around inside his house.

Had he forgotten some family event?

It was entirely possible considering the number of siblings and partners and friends in his life that he'd missed some calendar invite and ended up with a full house.

His siblings had keys and could have easily let themselves in.

Aw hell, his cookie stash was probably decimated.

Sighing, he turned off the ignition, got out, and moved up the front walkway, heading for the front door...

Which opened and...

"Congratulations!"

He was right. The room was full.

But he hadn't missed an invitation.

Because...this was for him.

"Late meeting?" he asked as Teresa slid close and kissed him.

She shrugged.

"How'd you know I'd come here first?"

"Why do you think I made that extra pot of your coffee this morning?" A shrug, her expression a combination of No Big Deal and smug. "I know you, honey."

Yeah, she did.

And fuck, he loved her for it.

"I knew you wouldn't leave me without my morning cup." She leaned closer, kissed the hinge of his jaw. "Plus, I knew that you'd try to sneak some cookies." Another kiss. "So, I made a few more batches tonight. Yours are safe."

"Fuck, I love you."

"Yeah, yeah." She patted his arm. "Save the sappy stuff for when we're checking items off on my list later tonight." A wink that had his cock twitching before her fingers wrapped around his and she drew him forward, over the threshold and toward the throng of his siblings. "It's junk food and family time."

"In that order?"

A squeeze of his hand. A smile tossed over her shoulder. "In any order you want, honey."

He drew her back against him. "Baby?" he asked into her ear. "Yeah?"

"There was one more thing I was going to pick up here tonight."

Her brows drew together. "What?" she asked softly. "What did you need?"

He shifted them toward the closet, opened it, and pulled out the small box he'd hidden inside.

"You," he murmured, spinning her toward him so that she could see the contents when he creaked open the lid. "Forever."

Her body stilled as she eyed the ring.

"So, now it's your turn," he said, still softly. "Now, I want you to tell me what you want."

Her hands on his, gripping the box.

Her body melting, her eyes gentle, her heart...*his.*

"You," she whispered. "I want you. Forever."

———

MELODY

She watched Jeremy slip the ring on Teresa's finger and couldn't have been happier for either of them.

They deserved it.

They deserved each other.

They deserved a life that would lead them to happiness.

But she couldn't lie and deny that it hurt, seeing them in their blissfulness.

Mel couldn't begrudge them, *wouldn't.*

It was just that she...

Well, she had spent the last months putting on a damned good front.

She was in therapy. Look at her go, trying to get better!

She went to Game Nights and Girls' Nights and Reality TV Binge Day and work events that needed a twinly escort and Sunday Dinners and days like this—celebrating big milestones that people deserved to be celebrated.

It was easy to stay unobserved—though less so than the previous years because everyone had seemed to take it upon themselves to look out for her after she'd been raped.

She'd. Been. Raped.

Drugged. Beaten. Violated.

Raped.

And...

She was still here, still in therapy, still in the support groups.

And she still felt dirty, used.

Violated.

It had only been three months, the therapist had told her. Give it time.

But how long was she supposed to feel like this?

He got a few moments of pleasure...

And she'd gotten this.

Aching, throbbing, open wound in her belly that never fucking closed, never got clean, never—

"Mel."

She blinked.

Realized that Teresa and Jeremy were now kissing like the newly engaged couple they were, realized she was staring but not really seeing.

Realized that it was Asher who was standing behind her and talking to her in that careful tone that did nothing to help and everything to piss her off.

So careful.

So tentative.

Everyone had tried really hard to treat her like normal.

Everyone except for Asher.

Who looked at her with guilt in his eyes and regret in his bearing and pity on his face.

It made her feel sick.

"Are you sleeping?" he asked, still gentle.

Fuck no, she wasn't sleeping.

She hadn't slept without nightmares, not since that night.

But she wasn't going there. "Of course," she said, turning from the kissing couple, but not turning enough to have to fully face him—to face the man who'd seen her broken and bloody and *raped*, to face the man who'd held her through her nightmares for weeks on fucking end.

Until she'd finally gotten a clear look at *his* face and realized what she'd been doing to him.

Destroying him slowly from the inside out.

His guilt eating at his veins, his regret gnawing at his bones, his pity straining his muscles until they'd reached their breaking point.

"I'm fine," she said, still not meeting his eyes but glancing at his bottom lashes.

Close enough.

Close enough that no one saw the difference.

Because most people didn't actually look each other in the eye, they just connected for quick glances before looking away.

The bottom lashes were close enough, she'd realized.

Especially, when paired with her normal, pre-rape quiet demeanor.

People didn't look too close.

But Asher did.

He looked uncomfortably close.

His rough fingers drew along the edge of her jaw, tilting her head up, and after the assault, she didn't allow herself to shy away—it would be too easy to never allow touch again. But with Asher it was different.

She had to hold herself away, lest she allow her body to crave his touch.

To crave *him.*

He didn't want her.

He'd made that crystal clear before she'd been raped, and after, well, she didn't want someone who only saw her as a victim, as a belonging to protect, a broken object to try to piece back together.

Who only wanted her because something had happened to her.

Not because of who she truly was inside.

But because she didn't pull away that night, he held her close, capturing her eyes, holding her gaze, studying her like he could see every thought inside her head.

And then his hand was sliding over her cheek, along her throat, down her arm.

His fingers were wrapping around her wrist, and then weaving through her own.

Warm.

He was warm and strong and...

The bolt of feeling through her belly was a sick mix of pleasure and poison.

Enough jarring juxtaposition that she didn't fight him when he led her onto the front porch, when he closed the door behind them, when he drew her down to sit on the top step beside him.

"You're not sleeping," he murmured, his free hand lifting, his thumb brushing lightly beneath each eye.

More touch.

More pleasure and poison.

"Don't," she whispered, drawing back.

He didn't fight her, just immediately let her go, let her retreat.

But he didn't step away, didn't leave her alone and go into the house.

And they sat there, in silence, in pain.

"What can I do?" he whispered, after long moments.

Nothing.

There was absolutely nothing he could do.

This was her burden to carry, to shoulder, to dispose of...maybe.

Or maybe it would always be with her.

"I wish I'd never called you."

He went stiff, as though there were an electrical current running through his veins. "Why?" he asked, agony in every word. "Why would you say that?"

"You saw me like that," she murmured. "You saw me, and now we're connected and..."

"What?"

"And you didn't want me before, didn't want me then, and you're only hanging around now because I called you that night, and you think it-it's some fucking moral obligation to help me." Her voice grew stronger the longer she spoke. "But you don't really want me. Not *me*, not this broken fucking woman that I've become. I'm not some used-up puzzle you have to help piece back together. I'm fine on my own."

Charged silence greeted her words.

"I don't see you that way."

"Liar," she hissed, spinning toward him, the anger, oh God, the rage, it boiled beneath her skin, desperate to be released.

He stilled again and for a long moment, just stared at her.

Then his hand cupped her jaw, the warm fingers making her gasp in surprise.

She'd slipped back into cold, into that frigid apartment and the memories that froze every cell in her body.

But Ash was hot, warm embers coating her skin, threatening to alight.

"Good," he said approvingly. "It's good to see you with some fight."

His hand fell away and then he stood, moved toward the house.

She tore her gaze away, forced her breaths to even out.

"But Mel?"

She jerked, refused to look back at him.

"The only thing I ever *did* lie to you about?"

Phrased as a question.

But one he didn't wait for her to answer.

"That I didn't want you."

―――――

Thank you for reading! I hope you loved Jeremy and Teresa as they navigated freedom and finding themselves and the urges of all those over-protective brothers! The next book in the Billionaire's Club world is BAD ROMANCE, book two in the Billionaire's Club: Bad Brothers series. She'd been broken...he was determined to help her put the pieces back together...find out what happens between Mel and Asher in Bad Romance.

CLICK HERE TO READ BAD ROMANCE>

And if you enjoyed BAD REBOUND, you'll love the small town of Stoneybrooke, its swoony heroes, and the klutzy, lovable heroines who steal their hearts. The first book in the series, TRAIN WRECK, is free to download!

"I laughed out loud all the way through the book, except perhaps during the sexy scenes. I'm not telling you what I did during those." —Amazon reviewer

The more she falls for Stefan, the more she risks her career... Don't miss the Gold Hockey series. It begins with the over 400 five-star-reviewed BLOCKED!

"Off-the-charts hot, smexy scenes with one of the best book boyfriends I have come across!" —Amazon reviewer

DOWNLOAD BLOCKED FOR FREE >

I so appreciate your help in spreading the word about my books, including sharing with friends! Please leave a review on your favorite book site!

You can also join my Facebook group, the Fabinators, for exclusive giveaways and sneak peeks of future books.

SIGN UP FOR ELISE FABER'S NEWSLETTER HERE:
https://www.elisefaber.com/newsletter

———

Hate missing Elise's new releases? Love contests, exclusive excerpts and giveaways?

Then signup for Elise's newsletter here!

www.elisefaber.com/newsletter

———

BILLIONAIRE'S CLUB

Bad Night Stand

Bad Breakup

Bad Husband

Bad Hookup

Bad Divorce

Bad Fiancé

Bad Boyfriend

Bad Blind Date

Bad Wedding

Bad Engagement

Bad Bridesmaid

Bad Swipe

Bad Girlfriend

Bad Best Friend

Bad Rebound

Bad Romance

Also by Elise Faber

Benched

Breakaway

Breakout

Checked

Coasting

Centered

Charging

Caged

Crashed

A Gold Christmas

Cycled

Caught

Cap

Covered

Breakers Hockey (all stand alone)

Broken

Boldly

Breathless

Ballsy

Bewitched

Rush Hockey Trilogy

Big Puck Energy

Filthy Puckboy

So Pucking Over It

Love, Action, Camera (all stand alone)

Dotted Line

Action Shot

Close-Up

End Scene

Meet Cute

Love After Midnight (all stand alone)

Rum And Notes

Virgin Daiquiri

On The Rocks

Sex On The Seats

Life Sucks Series (all stand alone)

Train Wreck

Hot Mess

Dumpster Fire

Clusterf*@k

FUBAR

Roosevelt Ranch Series (all stand alone, series complete)

Disaster at Roosevelt Ranch

Heartbreak at Roosevelt Ranch

Collision at Roosevelt Ranch

Regret at Roosevelt Ranch

Desire at Roosevelt Ranch

Phoenix Series (read in order)

Phoenix Rising

Dark Phoenix

Phoenix Freed

About the Author

USA Today bestselling author, Elise Faber, loves chocolate, Star Wars, Harry Potter, and hockey (the order depending on the day and how well her team -- the Sharks! -- are playing). She and her husband also play as much hockey as they can squeeze into their schedules, so much so that their typical date night is spent on the ice. Elise changes her hair color more often than some people change their socks, loves sparkly things, and is the mom to two exuberant boys. She lives in Northern California. Connect with her in her Facebook group, the Fabinators or find more information about her books at www.elisefaber.com.

f facebook.com/elisefaberauthor

a amazon.com/author/elisefaber

BB bookbub.com/profile/elise-faber

O instagram.com/elisefaber

g goodreads.com/elisefaber

P pinterest.com/elisefaberwrite